The
Lost Garden

HALEY ROWE

ASA PUBLISHING CORPORATION

ASA Publishing Corporation
1285 N. Telegraph Rd., PMB #351, Monroe, Michigan 48162
An Accredited Publishing House with the BBB
www.asapublishingcorporation.com

Copyrights©2025, Haley Rowe, All Rights Reserved
Book Title: The Lost Garden
Date Published: 06.04.2025
Book ID: ASAPCID2380947
Edition: 1 *Trade Paperback*
ISBN: 978-1-960104-76-2
Library of Congress Cataloging-in-Publication Data

This book was published in the United States of America.
Great State of Michigan

Prelude

The world was once a place of harmony, sustained by the Garden—a sanctuary of life and magic whose roots stretched deep into the earth, connecting everything. The Garden was the heart of the world, a source of balance and beauty, but its power attracted the greed of the Technomancers. These masters of technology sought to harness the Garden's magic, building machines to siphon its energy and bend it to their will. Their actions unraveled the fabric of the world, dimming the Garden's glow and withering its roots. The land grew cold and harsh, and the Garden became a dying relic, hidden and forgotten.

Yet, the Garden whispered to those who carried its magic in their veins, choosing individuals to protect it and restore the balance. Among them was Kaela, a girl who never asked for this burden but was chosen by the Garden to fight for its survival. As the Technomancers tightened their grip and the rebellion flickered in the shadows, Kaela embarked on a journey to uncover the truth about her connection to the Garden, the power she held, and the sacrifices required to save it . . . *The Lost Garden.*

The

Lost Garden

HALEY ROWE

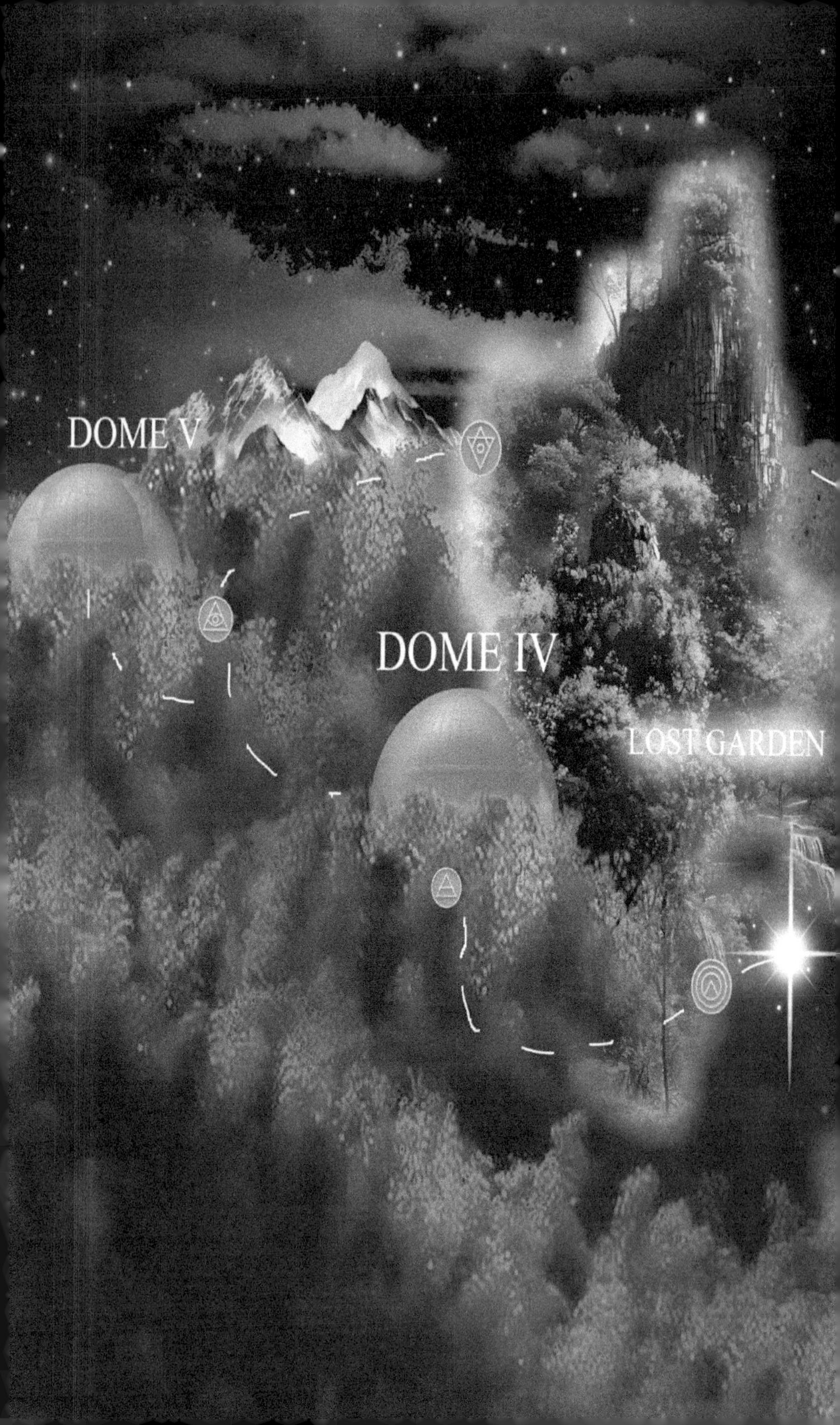
DOME V
DOME IV
LOST GARDEN

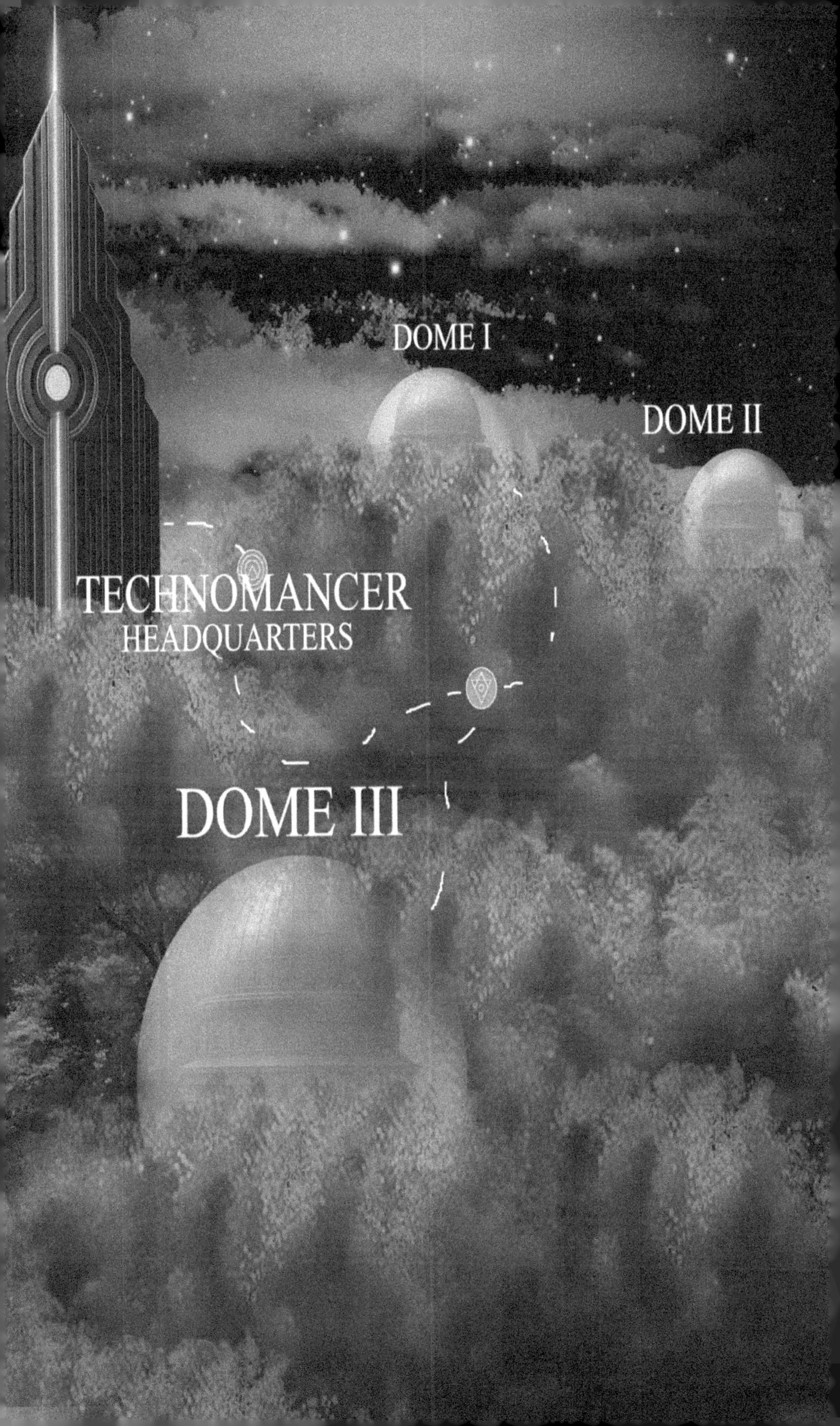
DOME I
DOME II
TECHNOMANCER
HEADQUARTERS
DOME III

Chapter 1

The fire danced delicately in the den, its mesmerizing play of warm light and shadow flickering against the stone walls of the cottage. The heat from the flames warmed the den, providing a delightful contrast to the cold, barren world outside. The aroma of burning wood mixed with the wafting earthy scent of dried herbs, their leaves still hanging from the ceiling, wavering slightly with the waft of air that slipped through the slight fractures in the walls. The den was the heart of the cottage, a place where Kaela could forget, if only for a second, the cold and sickeningly sterile reality BEYOND the dome. Here, in the warmth of this small stone sanctuary, time seemed to slow.

Kaela sat at the aged wooden table, her elbows propped up as she gawked at the tattered photographs sprinkled across the surface. Each picture was a piece of history, her father during his best days, radiant in front of the cottage, laughing with her lively mother, their faces shining with the belief of a distorted future. There was a time when their lives had been full of hope, when the world inside Dome 5 felt safe, secure. But that was before her mother fell sick and her father vanished, before the questions started piling up like the snowdrifts outside.

The cottage had always been a part of Kaela's family, its walls filled to the rafters with memories of generations that had lived and loved here. For as long as she could remember, this had been her home, a refuge from the world inside the sterile dome. Inside the cottage, it was warm. It was familiar. Outside, the dome was a different story.

Beyond the safety of Dome 5, the wasteland stretched out in every direction. An inhospitable landscape of frozen earth and toxic winds. The dome itself, a massive, transparent barrier, was all that separated the fragile remnants of life from the extreme chaos outside. From within, Dome 5 seemed vast and as though it were the only option for safety. But Kaela knew better than to let the dome's illusion of protection pacify her into complacency. The winds howled outside, battering the dome with relentless force, reminding her that the world beyond was taught from birth as a constant threat.

Her eyes wandered to her aunt, Eila, sitting in her favorite armchair by the window. The once-eager woman who had been bound by conscience to raise Kaela after her mother's passing and her father's disappearance now seemed to shrink in on herself, ashen-faced, succumbing to the illness. Eila had always been a rock in Kaela's life, a steady presence that had offered wisdom, guidance and love. But over the past few months, the illness had taken hold of her in ways Kaela couldn't understand, leaving her weaker and more distant with each passing day. The sickness had drained the color from Eila's cheeks, leaving her with a tired, vacant expression. Kaela did everything she could to care for her, to keep the cottage running, but the silence between them had only grown since her father's disappearance. It was as if the space between them had widened, filled with unspoken words and unresolved grief.

Kaela's attention shifted back to the mound of books and papers in front of her. Her father's study had always been a place of mystery and fascination for her. As a child, she'd been drawn to the cluttered shelves and the dusty opus that filled the room, each one brimming with knowledge and secrets. But now, as she sifted through his things, the weight of those secrets pressed down on her. She had hoped that by organizing his work, by uncovering some small clue, she might finally understand what had happened to him. But each day that passed without finding answers or anything pointing in the right direction only deepened the void in her chest. Why had he left without a word? Why hadn't he come back? What had he been searching for? The questions raced in her mind like a relentless storm, each one feeding the other, leaving her feeling more hopeless with each passing day.

The world outside the dome was a constant reminder of the fragility of life, of how easily it could be shattered in a matter of moments. Dome 5 was a haven, but it was also a cage, and Kaela could feel the walls closing in around her. The fire crackled again, its warmth a transient relief against the cold, guttural reality that she was hopelessly trying to accept, although her mind always went back to wondering what could be beyond the dome. Whatever her father had been searching for, whatever had drawn him away from her, it was clear now that she would have to find it somehow. There was no turning back.

She quickly stood, calmly pushing her chair back to not draw attention, and walked across the room to the narrow wooden door leading into her father's study. The door creaked ajar, revealing the familiar clutter of papers, bookshelves crammed with tons of old texts, and the saddeningly faint scent of tobacco that lingered in the air. She had been here many times after her father had disappeared, but each time it felt like stepping into a room filled with ghosts.

Kaela ran her fingers over the old oak desk, the wood smooth beneath her touch. She had never really explored the contents of her father's study before. There had never been time to think straight until now. But now with her father gone, with no one else to care for her but Eila, who has mysteriously fallen ill as her mother had, she felt the pull to understand what he had left behind and why.

Her eyes suddenly landed on a drawer, slightly ajar. She pulled it open, and a small leather-bound notebook caught her attention. It was covered in a layer of dust, its pages yellowed with age and smelling of something only described in historic texts of old-fashioned libraries. She flipped it open, scanning the handwritten notes inside, but the majority of it was indecipherable. She felt sick to her stomach. Nothing made sense.

As Kaela rummaged through the mess of papers on her father's desk, her eyes scanned over the repeating scribbles and hastily scrawled notes, hoping to make sense of them. The old wood floor creaked beneath her as she leaned in closer, sweeping aside faded journals and yellowing pages in search of something, anything that might shed light on her father's disappearance. The scent of dust and ink filled the air, mingling with the faint smoke from the fire in the hearth. Then, something unusual caught her eye.

At the far corner of the desk, tucked beneath the scattered papers, there was a subtle shift in the pattern of the wood. A faint outline, a shape that was distinct from the usual clutter, caught her attention. It was thicker than the other extensive pile of notes, and it didn't belong. Her breath caught as she reached out, fingers hovering over the hidden object. The moment her hand brushed against it, a tingle ran through her, an inexplicable feeling that urged her to investigate further.

With a mixture of curiosity and hesitation, Kaela carefully slid her fingers beneath the pile, her heart beating faster as she unearthed the mysterious item. What she pulled free was a flat tablet-like object, its surface like glass and its edges glowed faintly. She turned it over in her hands, noting the transparency of it, wondering of the significance of this piece of glass. The object was seemingly blank but at the same time, she felt a connection, as if she knew it was more than just glass. The air in the room seemed to grow heavier as Kaela's curiosity overtook her caution. She searched the tablet for anything that could point to what it was. As she looked closer, the tablet started to twinge with light slowly coming to life and a strange weight settled in her chest, a sensation she couldn't explain.

It was a map, but not one she had ever seen before. It stretched across more than just the land inside the dome, as if it had been drawn to represent something far beyond the walls that confined her world. Her eyes darted over the intricate details. Forests that seemed to stretch endlessly into the distance, mountains rising sharply in jagged peaks, and at the center, a vast, sprawling garden. It wasn't just any garden, it was something otherworldly, its beauty captured in delicate lines that hinted at something alive, something breathing. The map seemed to pulse with a hidden energy, as if it held the key to something far more important than mere geography.

But it wasn't just the garden that captured her attention. The map was dotted with symbols she didn't understand, strange markings scattered across the landscape, as though the land itself held secrets waiting to be unlocked. Lines wound their way across the glass, leading to various locations, some marked with a red circle, others with a strange cross or an arrow. Her eyes lingered on the red marks, her pulse quickening. There was something urgent about those marks, something that seemed to call out to her.

She traced the lines with her finger, her skin brushing against the cold glass, feeling the faint tingle of the technology. As her finger glided over the map, a sudden, unsettling sense of recognition gripped her chest. She couldn't place it, but the map felt . . . familiar. As if she had seen it before in some forgotten dream or distant memory. Her heart thumped in her chest, and an unfamiliar twitch ran down her spine. This wasn't just a map of a place. It felt like a map to somewhere important. A map meant for someone to find. Someone like her.

The sound of footsteps coming from behind startled her, the slick tablet slipping from her hands. She quickly scrambled to grab it, her breath coming in short, panicked bursts. She didn't want to be caught, not now, not with something so brilliant and mysterious in her hands. Her pulse raced as she scrambled to hide the map, the glowing, slick glass swirling in her mind as she hid the tablet in the drawer of her father's desk, her heart pounding in her ears. She could feel the weight of the discovery pressing down on her, a secret too big to ignore.

The footsteps grew closer, and she knew that whatever this map was, whatever it meant, it had just become the key to unlocking everything she had been searching for.

"Kaela?" Milo's voice rang out from the doorway, carrying that relieving tone of curiosity and playfulness. "What are you doing in here?"

Kaela stiffened, her heart skipping a beat as she jerked her head toward the door. She moved in front of the drawer in the desk in a not-so-sly manner as if she could hide the mystery away from him. But there was no denying the unmistakable curiosity that had already sparked in his eyes. Milo stood there, his lanky frame filling the doorway, a grin tugging at the corners of his lips. His bright blue eyes gleamed with the kind of inquisitive energy that made him both endearing and a little maddening. He had always been this way, unfailingly curious, always in search of the next puzzle to solve, the next mystery to unravel. And it was this quality that had made him her closest friend, her confidant, for as long as she could remember.

Kaela didn't respond immediately. She was still trying to catch her breath, her heart pounding in her chest. The map started lightly vibrating for only Kaela to feel, as if it was aware of the impending shift it might cause in their world. She had never expected to find anything like this. Her father's secret map, a key to something so much bigger than her, than Dome 5. And now, she was on the verge of sharing it with Milo, of letting him in on something she wasn't even sure she fully understood.

"I . . ." Kaela swallowed hard, her voice barely a whisper. "I found something." She started to take the map out of the drawer, this time more carefully, as though handling a fragile piece of history. She held it out to him, her hands slightly trembling.

Milo's gaze flickered from her face to the tablet in her hands, his smile fading into something more cautious, more intrigued. He took a step forward, his expression shifting as he processed what he was seeing. "What is that?" His voice was soft, but there was an edge of uncertainty beneath the curiosity.

Kaela frowned, her eyes tracing the strange lines and symbols on the map. It felt like a puzzle, an intricate, impenetrable puzzle. She studied it, almost willing it to reveal its secrets. But it only deepened the enigma. "I don't know," she admitted, her voice thick with frustration. "It was hidden in my dad's study, tucked in a drawer. I've never seen anything like this before. I don't even know where this place is." Her finger lingered over the foreign symbols, tracing one of the red circles that seemed to mark something important. "Look at these markings," she said, her voice laced with hesitancy. "None of it makes sense. None of it."

Milo leaned in, his brow furrowed with attentiveness. His eyes scanned the map, his usual playfulness replaced with a brooding focus. "This doesn't look like any place inside Dome 5," he muttered, almost to himself. "Where do you think it is?"

"I don't know," Kaela said, slowly shaking her head. "But . . ." She trailed off, a shiver running down her spine. The feeling of something important, something other, was growing stronger. "It feels important. Like it's something my father was trying to find. Why he disappeared."

Milo stood silently for a moment, considering her words. He averted his eyes from the map to her, and for the first time, Kaela saw a flicker of something darker in his eyes. Concern, maybe, or suspicion. "You think he was looking for this? This Garden thing?" He gestured vaguely at the map, his voice softer, more serious.

Kaela had a feeling of pressure in her chest at the mention of the Garden. Her father had whispered about it sometimes, his voice always low and full of a kind of admiration that Kaela could never quite understand. He had always spoken of it as though it were a dream, an unreachable ideal. But now, as she looked at the map, at the symbols and the red ink that seemed to beckon her forward, she wasn't so sure it was just a dream.

"I don't know," she said, her voice barely a whisper. "But I think he was searching for it. I think he was looking for something. Maybe this map . . . maybe this is the key."

Milo's eyes lingered on her face for a long moment, his usual easy-going demeanor replaced by something more guarded. "You think this is connected to your dad's disappearance?" His words were careful, but his concern was unmistakable.

Kaela nodded slowly, her fingers clenching the map as if it could protect her from the relentless questions swirling in her mind. "Maybe. It doesn't make sense right now, but . . . maybe this is what he was looking for. Maybe this is why he's gone."

Milo took a sharp breath, eyeing the map, then Kaela. He looked at her for a long moment, as if weighing his next words carefully. "If your dad was looking for this," he said, his voice quieter now, "I'm guessing he wasn't the only one who knew about it. If there's a Garden, or whatever this is, it could be dangerous."

Kaela felt queasy after that statement . . . Dangerous. The idea that this map, this thing she had just discovered, could lead to danger made her insides twist with unease. Was this the reason her father had disappeared? Had he been too close to whatever secret this map held?

Milo reached out, his fingers grazing lightly against the edge of the map. His touch was careful, as if he too recognized the dragging pull of the moment. "Let me try something," he said, his voice taking on that familiar spark of excitement she had always known. The gleam in his eyes was back, his curiosity now fully piqued. "I've been tinkering with a few new inventions lately. Maybe I can figure out how to activate it."

Kaela blinked, her heart skipping a beat. "Activate it? What do you mean?"

Milo grinned, the same mischievous grin she had seen a

thousand times before, the one that always made her wonder what crazy idea was brewing in his head. "Well, if this map is as advanced as it looks, there might be some kind of mechanism, or hidden button, or, who knows? It could be more than just a glass tablet. Maybe it's got a way to show us more than it currently is."

Kaela's eyes lingered on him, unsure of what to make of his sudden confidence. Milo was always full of wild ideas, always eager to inspect things and see how they worked. Could he really figure out how to unlock the secrets hidden within the map? Could he help her uncover what her father had left behind?

"Okay," she said slowly, her voice a mix of hesitation and trust. "Go ahead."

Milo's grin widened more than she had seen in a very long time, and Kaela felt a surge of warmth and security at the thought of facing this unknown with him. She had always known that, no matter what happened, Milo would be by her side through every mystery, every discovery. Even if it meant diving headfirst into a world she didn't understand.

"Alright," he said, his hands fidgeting with the excitement of a child on the brink of a grand adventure. "Let's see what this thing's hiding."

Milo beamed, carefully yet excitedly, pulling out a small tool from his bag, a delicate metal instrument that he had crafted himself for such occasions. He began to inspect the flickering edges of the map, gently prodding at the corners, tracing the symbols with the tool, his brow furrowed in concentration. Kaela observed him, her heart racing with anticipation. Whatever this map led to, whatever her father had been searching for, it was the first real lead she had ever had. And with Milo's help, maybe, just maybe, they could uncover the secrets that had been concealed for so long. The room fell into a dead calm as Milo worked, the tension hovering in the air. Then, with a soft beep, the map came to life in Kaela's hands, revealing a holographic screen protruding from the tablet. Her breath caught in her throat.

"Looks like we've got ourselves a puzzle," Milo smirked, his voice filled with excitement.

Kaela stood frozen, her eyes anchored on the pulsing holograph before her. The room seemed to hum with quiet energy, the air heavy with uncertainty and eagerness. Her fingers still glued to the map, the glass becoming slick beneath her touch as she absorbed the weight of what she had just uncovered. The faint smell of the charred fire in the next room and the tobacco from the study filled her senses, but it was the significance of the map, its markings, its strange symbols, that filled her mind, pushing aside all other thoughts. The Garden. The words resonated in her mind, distant but sharp. It was something her father had spoken in hushed tones, a word that had always seemed like an enigma, an unreachable dream. But now, standing here with the map in her hands, it felt more like a calling. A secret her father had been chasing, a path he had been desperately trying to uncover. And yet, that same path had led him into the shadows of disappearance, leaving her with more questions unanswered.

Kaela's heartbeat picked up pace as she etched the lines on the map over and over, her finger following the red circles, the symbols she couldn't decipher. The Garden wasn't just some outlying fantasy. It was real. Or at least, her father had claimed it was. The undisguised evidence he had left behind, hidden by stacks of forgotten papers, tucked away in the drawer of his old wooden desk, were leading her somewhere. Somewhere that held many of the answers she had been desperate for, even before she fully understood the questions. But what was she really looking for? The more she thought about it, the more the weight of her father's search seemed to settle on her shoulders. He had been searching for something, something beyond the dome, beyond the life she had always known. But what if the truth was more dangerous than she was ready for? What if she was unraveling secrets bigger than. her father's disappearance? She couldn't turn back now. Not after the copious amounts of information she and Milo had just discovered.

The realization hit her like a ton of bricks. She had already stepped into the unknown, already opened the door to a mystery that had been tucked away for too long. And now, the Garden was no longer just a vague concept in her father's journals. It was a destination, a place she had to find, whether she was ready or not. Her fingers gripped onto the map, a strange mixture of excitement and fear flooding her veins. The journey ahead would be anything but simple. But the thought of finally understanding what had happened to her father, of uncovering the secrets he had been so seemingly determined to keep, filled her with a sense of purpose.

The possibilities stretched out before her like a winding path, uncertain and full of potential. But with each step, the truth was drawing closer. Kaela knew she couldn't walk this road alone. There were others who would help her. Milo, her best friend, always by her side, his inventions and curiosity a constant source of support. Together, they might be able to uncover the secrets of the Garden. Together, they might be able to unlock the mystery of her father's disappearance. But Kaela knew one thing for sure: nothing would be the same again.

Chapter 2

The warm morning light spilled into the cottage through the small, rounded windows, casting long, soft shadows that danced across the stone floor like flames. The air, still cool from the night, held the faint, earthy scent of the forest beyond the dome, fresh, untouched by the harsh confines of the sheltered world inside. Kaela sat at the kitchen table, her elbows resting on the worn surface, a cup of tea left forgotten and cooling in front of her. She stared out the window, her gaze distant, her thoughts tangled in a thousand directions. Her father's disappearance weighed on her like an endless storm, its implications now heavy in her chest. The map she had found the night before haunted her, its cryptic markings like a puzzle she couldn't quite solve. Something was out there, hidden, just beyond her reach, and yet, there was something else, something strange and inexplicable, growing inside her.

For the past few days, it had been subtle. She hadn't known what to make of it, an odd flicker of warmth pulsing through her palms when she touched the plants in the backyard garden, a magnetic pull when she walked through the overgrown patch of greenery near the cottage. But today, as she stood by the window, the sensation was different. More urgent. More alive. Her eyes drifted to the small potted plant on the windowsill. It was a humble thing, its leaves a dull green, its once-vibrant edges now tinged with brown. Nothing remarkable about it. just a simple houseplant. But as Kaela observed the greenery, her heart fluttered, her pulse quickening. The leaves, which had been drooping under the weight of the cold air, seemed to shift, to stir in response to her presence. It was as if they could feel her, could sense her.

The leaves straightened, curling toward her, reaching toward her in slow, deliberate movements. The plant seemingly stretched to her, its tips unfurling like a hand reaching out from the depths of the earth. It was a delicate, slow motion, as if the plant was breathing, drawing energy from the air around it, or from her. The sensation sent a chill down her spine, as though something magical and alive was stirring just beneath the surface of the world she knew, but that was impossible. right? Her breath caught in her throat. Was this real? She blinked, her fingers twitching toward the plant instinctively, but the moment she looked away, the leaves dropped once more, returning to their lifeless, drooping state. She reached out, her fingers trembling, but the plant remained still, as if nothing had happened at all.

Had she imagined it? The thought weighed on her mind, but the feeling of the unique energy still hummed in the air around her, an invisible force pressing in from all sides. Her heart beats faster, her breath shallow, and she could feel the room eerily quiet, as though holding its breath along with her. The fire in the hearth cracked loudly, the sound unnervingly sharp in the sudden silence. The warmth from the flames seemed to shift in the air, thickening with an unfamiliar intensity, as though the fire itself was responding to the strange energy that filled the room. The walls of the cottage seemed to close in on her, the stone cooled against her skin, but the air, this strange, charged air, clung to her, thick and alive. She felt as though the room itself was watching her, listening. The plants. The fire. Everything.

Her fingers trembling on the edge of the table, the wood cool beneath her touch, and as she did, the faintest tremor ran through the room, an invisible wave, like the quiet ripple of a

stone dropped into still water. The plants on the windowsill, her small houseplant, and the ones in the garden outside, seemed to quiver, their leaves trembling in sync with her own unease. A chill travelled up her spine, and she stepped back, the pulse of energy fading, leaving only a strange, lingering echo behind. What was happening to her? She could feel it, deep within her, something was awakening, something she couldn't explain. The cottage door creaked open, the familiar sound of her aunt's footsteps breaking the stillness. Eila stepped into the room, her questioning eyes scanning the space with a practiced calm. Kaela quickly looked away from the plant, trying to shake the odd feeling that had settled over her.

"Kaela," Eila's voice was soft, the weight of illness lingering in the break in her words. "What are you doing, child? You look . . . pale."

Kaela's heart was still thudding, her hands trembling slightly as she ran them through her hair. She tried to smile, but it felt hollow. "Nothing, Aunt Eila. Just . . . thinking."

Eila gave her a long, curious look, her gaze lingering on the windowsill, where the plant sat, still and lifeless. "You've been working too hard, haven't you?" she said, her tone gentle but firm. "You need rest. We both do."

Kaela nodded absently, but her mind was elsewhere. There was something more, something Eila wasn't telling her. Her father's disappearance. The strange sensations that had been building inside her. And now this. The plants, the air, the energy she could feel but not yet understand. She didn't have time to explain, not yet. But the question that had been gnawing at her since the map had appeared, since these strange events had begun to unfold, echoed louder in her mind now: What was happening to her?

Later that evening, Kaela wanted to make sure what had happened earlier wasn't just her imagination. As she sat in the large chair, Kaela's fingers nervously hovered over the plant, her breath shallow, as though the very air had quickly thickened with unease. She could feel a strange energy in the room once again, a subtle pulse that made the hair on her arms stand on end. With a hesitant breath, she brushed her fingers against the leaves again, and, to her shock, they responded. The drooping fronds lifted, unfurling as if reaching toward her. They were vibrant, unnaturally so, and the green deepened with each passing second, as if the plant itself were alive in a way that wasn't possible. It was magic.

But it wasn't just the plant. There was something else in the air. It hummed, a faint vibration that Kaela could feel in the very marrow of her bones. She closed her eyes for a moment, letting the sensation wash over her. The energy was both foreign and familiar. A tugging pull deep within her that she had no explanation for.

A voice cut through the tension, soft but insistent. "Kaela?" Eilas voice cutting through the tension of the moment

Kaela was startled, jerking back from the plant as though she had been caught doing something forbidden. Her heart was thudding in her chest, and her breath caught a lump in her throat. Eila stood in the doorway, her presence calm but weary, the weight of exhaustion hanging heavily in her eyes. The barely older woman's slow, measured steps echoed faintly as she approached, her gaze narrowing as it settled on Kaela. Kaela quickly glanced toward the plant. The leaves had already started to droop again, their vibrant green fading to the dullness they had carried before. Had it really happened? She can't be going crazy?

Her mind raced, but her voice trembled as she spoke. "Aunt Eila, did you see that? The plant—"

Eila's eyes lingered on her for a moment longer than necessary, a deep, knowing look passing between them. Her gaze softened, but there was something in the way she held herself, a calculated, unreadable quality, a mask that Kaela had come to recognize over the years. She was hiding something. Eila sighed, the sound thick with the weariness of someone who had carried far too many burdens. Her shoulders slumped as she slowly made her way to the table, sitting across from Kaela. There was a flicker of something in her eyes, a flash of old memories that Kaela couldn't place. It was as if Eila knew exactly what was happening, even if she wasn't ready to say it aloud.

"Kaela," Eila said gently, her voice soft but carrying a firmness that Kaela couldn't ignore. "You're working yourself too hard. The house, the papers, your father's disappearance . . . It's a lot to carry on your own. Not that I can be of much help" she gestures to her ever dying body.

Kaela felt a pang of frustration at her aunt's words. She knew the weight of her father's disappearance better than anyone, and the constant ache of unanswered questions was driving her mad. She had been searching for answers for months, but every time she felt close, it slipped through her fingers like smoke. But she also felt empathy for her aunt. It was her brother in law after all, she loved that man just as much as she did, especially after Caroline, Kaela's mother, and her sister, died.

"I'm not imagining it, Aunt Eila," Kaela whispered, her voice shaking now with more than just uncertainty. "The plant—it moved. It—" Her words faltered as she tried to make sense of what had just happened. How could she explain the feeling, the connection she had felt? The plant's response, the hum in the air. It was like nothing she had ever experienced before.

Eila's face softened with a sigh, but there was a strange tightness around her mouth. Her eyes flickered to the plant for a moment, but there was no recognition there, no sign that she had seen anything unusual. She shook her head slowly, her movements deliberate.

"You're tired, Kaela," she reassured her, her voice carrying the weight of a lifetime of hidden truths. "It's not uncommon for stress to make you see things that aren't there. Why don't you take a break? You need to rest. You've been pushing yourself too hard, and it's starting to affect you."

Kaela felt a sudden, sharp pang of frustration, but she couldn't explain it. It wasn't just the plant. It wasn't just the strange energy in the room. There was something else. Something about Eila's tone, her insistence on brushing it off. Something in the way her aunt spoke, the way she avoided meeting her eyes. It was as if Eila was hiding something, and Kaela could feel it like a weight pressing down on her chest.

"I'm not imagining it," Kaela repeated, more forcefully this time. "There's something happening. I don't know what it is, but it's real. I can feel it."

Eila's gaze softened, but the weariness in her eyes deepened, and Kaela could see the battle behind them. It was as if her aunt was deciding whether to say something, whether to share what she knew. For a moment, Kaela thought Eila might speak. That she might tell her everything she knew about her father's disappearance, the garden, the map. But then the moment passed, and the older woman looked away, her expression becoming unreadable again.

"You're right. You're not seeing things, Kaela," Eila said softly, almost too gently. "But you're not ready to understand it yet. It's too much . . . too soon. Your father . . . he was searching for something. I don't know all the details, but I know he was involved in things he never told you about. And I don't want you to get caught up in it before you're ready."

Kaela's heart skipped a beat. Her father had been involved in something? She had always known there was more to his disappearance than he had let on, but this . . . This was a revelation she hadn't been prepared for. She wanted to ask more, to press her aunt for the answers she had been longing for, but Eila's eyes hardened, and the moment of vulnerability passed.

"You need to rest, Kaela," Eila repeated, her voice quiet, final. "Take a break. It will all make sense in time. But for now, just . . . take care of yourself."

Kaela opened her mouth to argue, but the words caught in her throat. Her aunt's quiet authority, her soft insistence, made it impossible to press any further. Eila was hiding something, Kaela was sure of it. But she couldn't force her to dish out the details. Not yet.

Instead, she nodded slowly, her mind whirling with unanswered questions, and watched as Eila slowly turned and walked away. But as she left the room, Kaela's eyes lingered on her aunt's back, the weight of unspoken words heavy in the air between them. Something had changed, and Kaela knew that whatever secret Eila was keeping, it was bound up with her father's disappearance, and with the strange power beginning to awaken inside her.

Kaela's stomach churned, the all too familiar sense of helplessness creeping back in, tightening its grip around her chest. Eila was right about one thing, the stress had been eating at her for months. Since the moment her father had vanished, leaving behind only pieces of a life she no longer felt connected to, the weight of never-ending unanswered questions had hung over her like a storm cloud. But this . . . this felt different. It wasn't just the endless, gnawing ache of questions about her father. No, something else was stirring within her, something new, something raw. The unease that had plagued her since that night in the garden had shifted into something deeper, more unsettling. It felt as though a part of her, some dormant piece, had finally awakened, reaching out toward the world around her in a way she couldn't yet understand.

Her fingers still tingled in memory of the plant's movement, its subtle, almost impalpable shift in answer to her presence. It was as though the earth itself had acknowledged her, recognized her in a way that was both foreign and instinctive. She couldn't grasp it, but she couldn't deny it either. The connection was there, powerful and undeniable. She shook her head, trying to push the thought away. Now wasn't the time to linger on the thought. She had enough to handle without adding this to the pile of mysteries already weighing on her. Her father's disappearance. The cryptic map. Eila's illness. All of the unanswered questions about everything that had been kept from her knowledge. Kaela had spent so many sleepless nights trying to piece together the puzzle, but every time she thought she was getting closer, the pieces seemed to slip through her fingers.

Before she could persist with her spiraling thoughts, the door slammed open, and Milo's voice filled the room, bright and brimming with his usual, infectious energy. "Kaela!" he called, a note of triumph lacing his words. "I think I've got it! The new invention, I've got it working!"

Kaela turned toward him, the heavy weight in her chest lifting just a little at the sight of her best friend. Milo had always been a burst of light in her otherwise murky world. His messy dark blonde hair, perpetually tousled from hours of tinkering, framed his face in that scruffy, endearing way that always made Kaela smile. But it wasn't just his appearance; Milo's willful optimism was like a bandage for her soul. No matter how bad things got, he always believed that everything would somehow work out in the end. His bright grin, wide and infectious, seemed to push the storm clouds back, if only for a moment.

Kaela couldn't help but smile, though the weight of her own thoughts still pressed against her. "Is it going to explode this time?" she teased, her voice a little shakier than she intended.

Milo's grin only widened, unfazed by her sarcasm. "Not this time, I promise," he said with a wink. "It's a new prototype, a device that could help us track the energy sources around the dome. You know, figure out how to keep the power grids stable and all that."

Kaela chuckled softly, despite herself. "You and your inventions. You never stop, do you?"

Milo shrugged, practically overflowing with energy. "Hey, if I can fix the power grid, maybe we won't have to rely on the dome's generators so much. Plus, I've been thinking, there might be something bigger going on here, something that could help with . . . well, everything."

Her curiosity piqued, Kaela raised an eyebrow. "What do you mean?"

Milo leaned in, his voice dropping to a conspiratorial whisper. "You know that map you found in your dad's study?"

Kaela's breathe caught in her throat. The mention of the map sent a sharp, almost physical pain through her chest. It was always there, lingering just beneath the surface, the constant reminder of her father's mysterious disappearance and the fragments of his life she'd inherited without explanation.

"What about it?" she asked, her voice quieter than she meant.

Milo's eyes gleamed with excitement, the kind of intensity Kaela had come to recognize as his 'obsessed-with-a-new-project' look. "I've been doing some research. If your dad was onto something with that map, if it's pointing to something outside the dome, I think I can help. I've got a few ideas that could help us track down whatever he was looking for."

Kaela's stomach dropped for a moment. The idea of uncovering the truth about her father, of finally understanding what had driven him to leave, and hopefully finding him alive, was enough to push aside the strange, unsettling feeling that had been clawing at her all morning. She needed to know. She had to know.

But before she could respond, the soft sound of footsteps echoed from the hallway. Eila's voice, as tired as always, drifted in from the doorway. "Kaela, Milo . . . I think it's time you both take a break. The day's just begun, and you've already worked yourselves into the ground."

Kaela nodded absently, though her mind was elsewhere. The connection she had felt earlier, the way the plant had responded to her, still lingered in the back of her mind, like a whisper she couldn't quite understand. Was it possible that whatever her father had been searching for, whatever secret he had uncovered, was tied to what was happening to her?

Milo's voice cut through her thoughts, light and playful. "Hey, if you're not too busy being all mysterious and secretive, you should come see my invention in action."

Kaela smiled unconvincingly, the corners of her lips turning upward, though the weight of everything she had to uncover still pressed heavily on her. "Maybe later, Milo. I've got something else I need to figure out first."

Milo gave her a knowing look, but he didn't press her. He simply nodded, as if he understood the storm of thoughts racing through her mind. And for a moment, Kaela was grateful for the distraction he provided, even if only for a little while. She needed to focus, to push through the haze of confusion and find the answers she had been searching for. Something was awakening within her, something she couldn't ignore. The pieces of her father's puzzle, and the strange connection to the world around her, were starting to come together. She just had to figure out how to put it all in place.

Milo raised an eyebrow, his curiosity piqued by the unspoken tension hanging in the air. But Kaela didn't have the energy to explain, not yet, at least. She could feel the weight of his gaze on her, the unasked questions lingering between them like an open door. But she couldn't answer him. Not now. There was too much swirling in her mind, too many fragments of a puzzle that were still out of reach. She needed answers, answers that felt just beyond her grasp, like a transient dream slipping away the moment she tried to grab it.

Whatever was happening to her, whatever strange and unsettling power was beginning to stir within her, was now a part of the equation. The plants that responded to her touch. The strange pulse she felt in the air when her emotions shifted. It was as if the world around her had begun to hum with energy, alive and vibrating with a force she couldn't explain. She didn't understand it yet, but she could feel it deep inside her, as if it were a part of her soul awakening after a long, forgotten slumber.

Her mind returned to the Garden, that place her father had searched for so desperately, the place that had entranced him. The mysterious map she had found in his study. The symbols and markings that promised answers. Her father had been drawn to something, something hidden beyond the dome, beyond the walls that had contained their world for as long as Kaela was alive. He had left everything behind in pursuit of it, and now, she was following in his footsteps.

But this new connection to something greater felt like the key to unlocking it all. It was as though the universe itself was whispering to her, guiding her toward a truth that could change everything. It wasn't just about her father's disappearance anymore. It wasn't just about the Garden. There was something more, a deeper, older magic at play, and Kaela could feel it growing stronger within her with every passing day.

She stood at the precipice of something monumental, something that could unravel the very fabric of her reality. And though the uncertainty gnawed at her, she wasn't afraid. She was determined. She wasn't about to stop now, not when she was so close to uncovering the truth. Whatever this was, whatever powers were awakening within her, she would face it full-frontal. The journey she was about to embark on would reveal secrets she could never have imagined, and she wasn't going to let fear or doubt stand in her way. With a deep breath, Kaela straightened her shoulders, a sense of resolve settling over her like a mantle. The answers were out there, waiting to be found. And no matter what it took, she would uncover them.

Chapter 3

Kaela's fingers grazed over the clutter on her father's desk, the undertones of the room pressing in on her. It was as if the space itself held its breath, watching her, waiting for her to uncover something hidden beneath the layers of clues. The desk, with its worn wood and the smell of old paper, had once been a place of mystery and studies for her father. Now, it was a tomb of unanswered questions. The disarray of papers scattered across the surface made her feel even more disconnected. Her father had always been meticulous with his work, and yet this . . . this mess felt like a reflection of the chaos she now felt in her life. The absence of his presence, the unresolved questions about his disappearance, and the map she had found the night before all weighed on her mind, refusing to let her rest.

She flipped through another pile of papers, her frustration

growing. There was nothing of significance. Just old contracts, research notes, and financial reports, all mundane details that didn't hold the answers she needed. Her hands trembled slightly, a feeling she couldn't shake, like something was about to reveal itself. Milo, ever the optimist, had joined her in the search. He was perched on the edge of the desk, his legs dangling and his fingers drumming an erratic beat against the wood. He was quiet now, sensing the gravity of the situation, but his presence was a comfort, his usual energy providing a slight distraction from the tension of the situation.

Kaela let out a long, frustrated sigh as she pushed yet another stack of papers aside, her fingers trailing across the worn, yellowed edges of the documents. She could feel the weight of each paper pressing down on her chest, a suffocating reminder of all the unanswered questions. Her father's disappearance still felt like a jagged wound, one that never quite healed. Every page she turned over seemed to lead to another dead end, another layer of mystery with no way to unravel it. How could he have left so much . . . and still hidden everything?

The thought circled in her mind, the same hopeless question she had been asking herself for months. There had to be something here, something that could explain why her father had vanished, why he had hidden his work, his research, his life away from her. She flipped through another stack, each paper more cryptic than the last, each word more foreign. The more she searched, the more she felt like she was drifting further away from the truth.

"Kaela, he probably didn't want anyone finding it," Milo suggested, his voice low but thoughtful, breaking the heavy silence. His words hung in the air between them, like a flickering light in the dark. "Maybe he knew you'd be the only one to figure it out."

Kaela paused, her fingers stilling on the edge of a thick folder. She looked over at him, his face thoughtful as he leaned against the desk, watching her. His eyes were steady, and for a moment, she wondered if he could see the cracks in her shield. She couldn't tell him how badly she wanted to believe that, how badly she wanted to think her father had left some kind of clue just for her, as if he had known she'd be the one to pick up the pieces. But deep down, Kaela wasn't sure she was the one meant to solve it. She had never been the clever one, the intuitive one. That had always been her father. She had always been the daughter left behind, struggling to piece together a life without him.

She let out a small, wry smile, one that didn't quite reach her eyes. "What, you think he knew I'd be the one to stumble upon his hidden secrets?" Her voice was a mixture of bitterness and disbelief.

Milo's lips curled into a lopsided grin, the kind that always made her feel like maybe, just maybe, things weren't so bleak. He shrugged casually, though there was a seriousness in his eyes, a glimmer of something Kaela couldn't quite place. "Maybe not stumble," he said, his tone light, but with an edge of sincerity. "But you've always been good at digging around. Besides, it's not like you're the only one looking for answers."

The weight of his words lingered in the air. She looked at him, studying his face, his messy dark blond hair, and the way his eyes flickered with the kind of curiosity she hadn't realized she missed until now. Milo had always been the one who saw possibilities where others saw dead ends, who believed that there was always more to a story than what appeared on the surface. He never accepted things as they were. He always wanted to know why, how, and what came next.

Kaela tucked in her lips, her gaze dropping back to the papers, but her mind was far from the task at hand. "I don't know, Milo. It feels like I'm just chasing ghosts. Like he left all this . . . on purpose, but then never gave me any clues to understanding it."

Milo stepped closer, his voice dropping to something softer, more comforting. "Maybe it's not about understanding everything all at once. Maybe it's about piecing things together, one bit at a time. You've always been the one to notice the details, Kaela. The things no one else does."

She shook her head, her frustration bubbling up once more. "I don't even know where to start. It's like there's a puzzle in front of me, but half the pieces are missing. And every time I think I'm getting close to an answer, the pieces get mixed up again."

Milo reached out, placing a hand on her shoulder, his touch

warm and grounding. "You don't have to do it alone. Whatever this is, whatever your dad was hiding, I'm with you. We'll figure it out together. One piece at a time."

For a moment, Kaela just stared at him, the softness in his eyes making her feel like she wasn't so alone in this after all. She hadn't realized how much she needed someone to say that, to remind her that she wasn't entirely on her own in the search for the truth.

"I don't know if I can do this," she whispered, her voice raw with exhaustion. "What if I never find out what happened to him?"

Milo's grip tightened just slightly, offering silent reassurance. "Then we keep looking. Because the truth is out there, Kaela. It has to be."

Her heart softened at his words, and for the first time in days, she felt a flicker of hope stir deep inside her. Maybe, just maybe, she wasn't meant to figure it out alone. Maybe the answers weren't buried so deeply after all. With Milo by her side, maybe there was a way to find the pieces and finally put the puzzle together.

She nodded slowly, determination returning to her eyes. "Alright, then. Let's keep looking."

Kaela turned back to the desk, her mind racing. She had never considered that her father might have intended for her to find something. But what if he had? What if all the research, the strange disappearance, the secretive behavior had been leading to something she was meant to uncover? As her mind was racing, she started to search the bookshelves behind her, when her fingers brushed against something cold and metallic. She paused, then lifted the small, cylindrical object from behind a stack of old books. It was sleek, with a faint, almost imperceptible glow pulsing beneath its surface. Her heart skipped a beat. This was different from anything she had seen before.

"What is that?" Milo asked, leaning in for a closer look.

Kaela didn't answer immediately, turning the device over in her hands. There were no markings, no labels, just a smooth surface that seemed to hum with a quiet yet extreme energy. She pressed a small button on the side, and the object clicked softly. A moment later, a holographic projection flickered to life above the desk.

At first, the image was blurry, the colors swirling like smoke, but then it began to take shape. A map. Her father's map. But this was different. It wasn't just filled with unknown markings, it was alive, shifting and rearranging before her eyes. The symbols on the map glowed faintly, pulsing as though they had a life of their own. The lines seemed to twist and turn, forming new patterns as if reacting to something Kaela couldn't understand. The map had begun to show more details than the previous map, details about what things were.

"What is this?" Kaela breathed, her voice barely above a whisper, as she stared at the holographic map. The symbols danced across the surface, shifting in patterns that felt alive, responding to her presence in ways she couldn't explain. The map, once a static blueprint of her father's work, now pulsed with an energy that made her heart race.

Milo, standing beside her, stared at the map in disbelief. His brows furrowed, his lips slightly parted in awe. "That's your dad's map, right? But . . . this isn't like anything I've seen before." His voice was filled with a mixture of wonder and confusion.

Kaela nodded, her fingers hovering over the glowing projection. Her pulse quickened as she traced the intricate lines of the map. "It's the same map, but it's . . . changing. It's not static. And it's responding to me." The words left her in a rush, as if she were trying to make sense of the strange pull she felt inside her, like something deep within was stirring.

Her fingers moved closer to the projection, almost as if drawn by an invisible force. The moment they neared the surface, the symbols shifted again, rearranging themselves in an intricate dance. It was subtle, but Kaela felt it, an undeniable tug, a thread of connection that linked her to the map, to the secrets hidden within it. It wasn't just a piece of her father's research, it felt like something more.

"Kaela," Milo's voice broke through her thoughts, low with uncertainty. "You've got to be careful. This doesn't look like something you can just play with."

But Kaela couldn't tear her eyes away. Her fingers trembled as she reached closer, drawn to the symbols as if they were calling her. "I don't think it's playing," she murmured, her voice distant, lost in the pull of the map. "I think it's trying to show me something. Something important."

As her hand inched closer, the hologram flickered, the symbols rearranging into a new configuration. Her breath hitched as one symbol, in particular, caught her eye. A circular shape surrounded by intricate markings, its center glowing with a soft, golden light. It felt familiar, almost like a memory tugging at the edge of her mind.

"Do you see that?" Kaela's voice shook as she pointed to the symbol. "That symbol. I think it's connected to the Garden."

Milo leaned in, squinting at the glowing projection. His expression was a mix of curiosity and skepticism. "It looks like it could be. But what does it mean? What's it pointing to?"

Kaela's heart pounded in her chest, the weight of the moment sinking in. She didn't have all the answers, but she knew this: whatever this was, it was tied to her father's disappearance, and in ways still unknown, it was tied to her. The strange connection she had felt with the plants outside, the way they had responded to her presence, it was all connected. But before she could study the map further, the hologram flickered one last time and then vanished, leaving only the faint hum of energy in the air.

"No, wait!" Kaela reached out, her fingers brushing the empty space where the map had been, but it was gone.

Milo looked at her, his brow furrowed in concern. "What just happened? It was like the map . . . just shut down."

Kaela's breath came in short bursts as she stood there, staring at the blank space where the map had been moments ago. The absence of it was palpable, like a physical weight pressing down on her chest. She could feel the void, the sense of unfinished business that gnawed at her. "It's locked," she murmured, her frustration creeping into her voice. "It won't stay on long enough for me to figure it out."

Milo glanced down at the device in her hand, his fingers hovering near it. "Is there any way to open it? Any other buttons?"

Kaela shook her head, the frustration building in her chest. "I don't think so. It's like it's responding to me somehow, but it won't stay still long enough for me to interact with it."

A heavy silence settled between them, thick with unspoken questions. Kaela's mind raced, trying to make sense of what had just happened, trying to connect the dots. And then, after a moment of hesitation, Milo spoke again, his voice quiet but earnest.

"Kaela . . ." He looked at her, his eyes searching hers with a mix of curiosity and concern. "I think I know what's going on."

She turned to him, confusion written on her face. "What do you mean?"

Milo took a step closer, his gaze unwavering. "You said the map responded to you, right? And the plants outside, they've been reacting to you too. And now this . . ." He gestured to the empty space where the map had been, his voice lowering. "Kaela, I think you've discovered something about yourself. Something . . . Important." Her heart skipped a beat, and her breath caught in her throat. She could feel the words hanging in the air, heavy with the weight of their implications. "What do you mean?" she whispered, her voice trembling. "You think I'm . . . connected to this somehow?"

Milo nodded slowly, his eyes serious. "I think you've got some kind of power, Kaela. I don't know how, but something's changing. Something's different in you." His words hung in the air like a revelation, something Kaela had never fully allowed herself to consider. She had always thought she was just like anyone else. An ordinary woman, caught in the whirlwind of her father's disappearance. But now, the possibility that she was somehow connected to all of this, that there was something inside her that could influence the world around her, was almost too much to grasp.

Kaela stood frozen, the weight of his words sinking in. "I don't know what's happening," she said quietly, more to herself than to Milo. Her mind swirled with the implications, with the terrifying and thrilling possibility that something inside her had awakened. She didn't understand it, didn't know how to control it, but she knew one thing for sure. She had to do something.

She looked at Milo, her gaze steady despite the storm of emotions raging inside her. "But I'm going to find out. Whatever this is, I need to understand it."

Milo met her gaze, his expression unwavering, his determination matching hers. "And I'll help you. Whatever it takes."

Kaela looked down at the small device in her hand, the cool metal smooth against her skin, but it was the faint hum that made her pulse quicken. It was barely noticeable, like a whisper in the back of her mind, but it was there, an undercurrent of energy that seemed to vibrate with a life of its own. She could feel it in her fingertips, deep in her bones, as though the device itself was calling to her, urging her to unlock its secrets.

Her breath caught in her throat as she stared at the tiny, flickering lights along its surface. The map, the strange symbols, the way they had shifted and responded to her touch, it all felt too significant to ignore. It was like the universe was handing her a key to something greater, something buried in the depths of her father's research, and now, somehow, it was tied to her. The connection to the Garden, the pull she had felt in the plants outside, the way the world seemed to shift around her, it was all becoming clearer, even as it remained frustratingly out of reach. A surge of emotion rose within her, frustration, awe, and an unfamiliar sense of purpose. She had spent so long in the shadow of her father's disappearance, haunted by the questions he left behind, but now . . . now she was standing at the edge of something far bigger than herself. The weight of it settled over her like a cloak, both exhilarating and terrifying. There was power in this, power she didn't understand but could feel, beating just beneath the surface, waiting to be unleashed. Kaela's heart thudded as she gripped the device tighter, the hum growing slightly louder, more insistent. She wasn't sure what it was, or why it had chosen her, but one thing was certain, she couldn't turn back now. The answers were out there, hidden in the secrets of the Garden, in the depths of her father's work, and now, in the power awakening inside her. It was all starting to weave together, a tapestry of mystery and possibility.

The fear that had gnawed at her for months, the fear of being lost, of never finding her father, of never understanding her place in all of this, began to fade. In its place was a quiet hopefulness. She wasn't just chasing shadows anymore. This was real. Whatever had begun in her father's absence was now unfolding before her, and she was determined to see it through. She wasn't going to let this slip through her fingers. Not this time. Her gaze lifted from the device, and for a moment, she felt as though she could see the path ahead of her more clearly. The Garden. The map. The powers. Her father. They were all tied together, and she was the key to unlocking it all. With a steady breath, Kaela tucked the device into her pocket, the faint hum still lingering in her senses. Whatever came next, she was ready. She had to be.

Chapter 4

The days blended together as Kaela and Milo worked habitually in the small, cluttered room, surrounded by stacks of papers, old books, and discarded tech. The map, her father's map, had become their obsession. Milo had spent hours studying it, trying to decipher its intricate symbols and unlock its secrets. He seemed to lose track of time entirely, only emerging from his frenzy of calculations and tinkering for brief moments, eyes wild with excitement and determination. Kaela, for her part, had never seen him so focused. She could almost feel the electricity vibrating in the air when he worked, the way his brain moved a mile a minute, sifting through theories and possibilities. But even Milo, brilliant as he was, had struggled with the map's cryptic energy. It refused to remain inert, slipping through his fingers like sand. Yet, he kept at it, determined, always finding new angles and new methods to try.

Kaela had been observant of Milo for hours, her eyes following his every movement, every frustrated gesture as he worked tirelessly on the map. But her mind wasn't fully on his methods or the strange device before them, it was on the aching feeling that had been growing steadily inside her, a quiet hum in the back of her mind. It was as though something was stirring, waking up inside her, and she couldn't ignore it anymore. It had been happening ever since she first laid eyes on the map, something in her, deep inside, seemed to respond to it. It wasn't just curiosity. It was a pull, an almost magnetic force, drawing her closer to the mystery, urging her to understand its meaning.

As Milo continued to work, Kaela found herself thinking back to the moment when she first touched the map. She had been so consumed by the search for answers, the fear of what she might uncover about her father, that she hadn't allowed herself to really feel it. But now, the memory came flooding back, how the symbols on the map had flickered when her hand had hovered over them, how the air had seemed to hum with energy, as if the map itself recognized her. It had been subtle at first, almost non-existent, but now it was undeniable. The way the map reacted to her, the way her body seemed to hum along in response, it was all connected. She wasn't just reading a map, she was somehow a part of it. The more she thought about it, the more the pieces began to fit together. Her father's disappearance, his obsession with the Garden, his secretive search for it, and the map that had led him on that journey had always felt like a mystery just out of reach. But now, it felt different. It was as if the map was more than just a clue. It was a bridge between her and something much bigger. She could almost feel the energy of it coursing through her veins, something ancient and powerful, like a thread that connected her to the Garden itself.

And then there was the strange connection she had been feeling to the plants outside, the way they seemed to respond in her presence, as if they knew her in some way. She had brushed it off as a coincidence at first, just another oddity in a world that seemed to be full of them. But now, with the map before her, the realization hit her like a lightning strike. The plants, the map, the strange hum in her chest, it was all tied together. She wasn't just a bystander in this story, she was meant to be a part of it. The Garden wasn't just a place her father had searched for, it was a place she was destined to find, a place that was calling to her. Her heart pounded as the weight of this realization settled over her. The more she thought about it, the more the connection felt undeniable. It was as if the map had been waiting for her, waiting for her to unlock its secrets, to follow the path her father had started but presumably never finished. It wasn't just about uncovering the truth about her father anymore, it was about something much bigger, something that could change everything.

The room around her seemed to spin as the weight of this

realization set in. She was standing at the edge of something monumental, something that could alter the course of her life forever. The pull was too strong now, the connection too real. She had no choice but to follow it, to discover what the map was truly leading her to. She glanced at Milo, who was still hunched over the desk, oblivious to her thoughts. He was so close, so close to unlocking the final piece of the puzzle. And she knew, without a doubt, that when he did, it wouldn't just be a discovery, it would be the key to everything. She could feel it in her bones, the certainty that the answers they were seeking weren't just about her father's disappearance. They were about her, about what was awakening inside her, and about the Garden that had always unknowingly been more than a legend.

Then, on the fourth day of their relentless study, as Kaela stood lost in her thoughts, something finally clicked. Milo leaned back in his chair with a deep sigh, rubbing his eyes, his hair more disheveled than ever. He had been at it for hours, mumbling under his breath, trying to make sense of the holographic map that had eluded them for so long. The map had resisted their every attempt, slipping through their fingers like a dream just out of reach. But now, it was finally happening. The pieces were falling into place.

Milo looked at her, his eyes wide with excitement, his voice barely above a whisper. "Kaela . . . I think I've got it."

Her heart skipped a beat. She wasn't sure what had changed,

but she could feel it too, the energy in the air, the subtle shift in the room. The map flickered to life once more, its symbols shifting and rearranging themselves in a fluid, graceful motion. It was no longer chaotic; it was clear, ordered, purposeful. And at the center of it all, there was something new, a glowing symbol, pulsing with a soft light. Kaela leaned forward, her breath catching in her throat as she recognized it. It was the symbol she had seen before, the one that had felt familiar, even though she didn't understand why. It was the symbol of the Garden, unmistakable in its design, its glow, its presence.

"This is it," Kaela whispered, her voice trembling with a mix of awe and disbelief. "This is the Garden. This is where it is."

And just like that, everything clicked into place. The map wasn't just a map. It was a guide. It was the key to finding the Garden, to understanding her father's disappearance, and to discovering what had always been waiting for her. And now, as the map's glow illuminated the room, Kaela knew that her journey was just beginning.

Kaela's breath caught in her throat as the map flickered, shifting before her eyes. For a moment, she thought it was another glitch, another fleeting image that would disappear just as quickly as it had appeared. But then, it stayed. The holographic projection stabilized, revealing something new, something she hadn't seen before. Her heart skipped a beat as the location materialized, the contours of the land becoming clear. A place she had never seen, yet somehow, she knew it. The faint lines of mountains, the winding rivers, the stretch of forest that seemed to go on forever—it all felt too familiar, as if she had seen it in a dream or felt its pull in her bones. The map had always been cryptic, a puzzle that refused to reveal its secrets. But now, it was different. The coordinates that had once been meaningless now clicked into place, each symbol, each line connecting to another with an eerie precision.

Kaela's stomach twisted, a mix of excitement and fear gnawing at her insides. The map was showing her something, something undeniably huge. The strange symbols, once indecipherable, now seemed to make perfect sense. It was as if a veil had been lifted, and the truth had suddenly been laid bare before her. She couldn't look away. The more she studied the map, the more she felt an overwhelming sense of recognition, a deep connection to the place it was showing her. And then, it hit her. The Garden.

She had heard the stories, the whispers that her father had chased for years. He had always talked about it as if it were more than a myth, more than just a tall tale. But Kaela had never truly believed, no matter how much she wanted to. Not until now. This was it. This was what he had been searching for, and it was more real than she could have ever imagined.

Her mind raced. The Garden was not just a legend, it was a destination, a place that was somehow tied to her father's disappearance. But it was more than that. It was connected to her. The pull she had felt earlier, the way the plants outside had responded to her, the strange energy that had hummed in her chest when she first touched the map, it was all connected. The Garden was calling to her, and she had no choice but to listen. She leaned in closer, her hand trembling as she hovered over the map. The coordinates, the glowing symbols, they all pointed to the same place, a place hidden beyond the reach of the dome. The Garden. And somehow, she was meant to find it.

But what did it mean for her? What did it mean for her father? Was this the key to understanding his disappearance? Was this why he had left, why he had been so obsessed with finding the Garden? And why was the map responding to her now, as if it recognized her, as if she was part of the puzzle?

Her heart pounded in her chest as the questions piled up, each one more urgent than the last. She didn't have all the answers yet, but one thing was clear, this was the beginning of something monumental. The Garden wasn't just a place to her father, it was a place she was meant to find. The pull she felt couldn't be a coincidence. It was a call to action, a call that she couldn't ignore. As the map flickered again, showing more details, rivers, valleys, and a forest that stretched for miles, Kaela's determination solidified. This was her path now. She had to follow it. There was no turning back.

Milo turned to her, his eyes wide with a mixture of wonder and concern. "Kaela . . . do you realize what this means? The Garden. It's real. It's out there. And your dad, he was trying to get to it. This could explain everything. Why he disappeared, why the map— why it's connected to you."

Kaela felt a surge of determination and purpose ripple through her. She had spent so long feeling lost, adrift in a world that no longer made sense. But now, with the Garden revealed, everything was falling into place. Her father had been onto something monumental, something that had been kept hidden from the world for a reason. And she was going to uncover it. She had to.

"I know," Kaela said softly, her voice steady, though her heart raced with anticipation. "It's like . . . it's like the pieces are finally coming together. My father, the Garden, the map. It's all connected. And I'm connected to it too."

Milo gave her a concerned glance, his brow furrowing. "Kaela, you've been acting different lately. The plants, the way the map responds to you . . . I don't know what's going on, but I think you've found something within yourself. Something that's tied to all of this."

Kaela's mind spun as she thought about the way the plants had reacted to her, the strange pulse she'd felt in her chest when she touched them, the humming energy she'd sensed when she stood in the garden. The way the map responded to her. It was all connected. Her father, the Garden, and whatever power was beginning to awaken inside her.

"I don't know what it is yet," she said, her voice quiet but firm, "but I need to find out. We need to get to the Garden."

Milo hesitated, clearly torn between supporting his friend and the obvious fear that gnawed at him. "Kaela, this is huge. If the Garden is real, if your dad really found it . . . we're talking about something that could change everything. And I don't even know if it's safe."

"I don't care," Kaela said, her voice hardening with resolve. "I've spent too long feeling like I'm just floating. I need answers, Milo. I need to know what happened to my dad, and I need to understand why all of this is happening to me."

Milo looked at her, pausing for a long moment, his expression softening. "Alright," he said finally, his voice full of quiet determination. "We'll figure this out. Together."

Kaela's heart swelled with gratitude for Milo's unwavering support, his determination to see this through alongside her. But that warmth was quickly overshadowed by a growing urgency. The Garden was out there, real, tangible, and waiting. She didn't know exactly what she would find, but deep down, she knew it held the answers to everything.

The pieces were falling into place, as if her entire life had been leading to this moment. She felt it in the way the map had responded to her touch, the way its glowing symbols had seemed to align perfectly with something buried deep within her. The Garden wasn't just a destination, it was the key. The key to her past, her future, and maybe even something greater than she could imagine.

Kaela pushed herself up from the desk, her legs unsteady beneath her as she stared at the softly glowing map. The faint hum of the device filled the room, a quiet reminder of how close they were. Her hand hovered over the projection for a moment, her fingers trembling. "Tomorrow," she said, her voice quiet but firm, filled with a sense of determination that even surprised her. "We leave tomorrow."

Milo looked up from where he was still tinkering with the device, his face lighting up with a mixture of excitement and determination. "Tomorrow," he echoed, nodding as though solidifying the decision.

Kaela glanced back at the map one last time, its soft light casting strange shadows across the room. Her mind raced with possibilities. What if the Garden wasn't just a place, but something alive? Something ancient, powerful, and tied to the strange connection she was beginning to feel? She didn't have all the answers, but she could feel the pull growing stronger, as if the Garden itself was calling to her, urging her to come.

Her stomach churned with a mix of anticipation and fear. Leaving the dome was no small thing. The world outside was unpredictable, dangerous, and unknown. But staying here, ignoring the pull of the Garden and the secrets it held, wasn't an option. Not anymore.

She turned to Milo, who was already scribbling notes and packing tools, his energy infectious. "This is it, Milo," she said softly. "We're really doing this."

He grinned, his eyes sparkling with excitement. "It's going to be amazing, Kaela. Whatever's out there, we'll find it. Together."

Kaela nodded, an unfamiliar smile tugging at her lips despite the storm of emotions swirling inside her. In a few days, they would step into the unknown, leaving behind the safety of the dome and the lives they had always known. It wasn't just her journey anymore, it was their adventure, and it was only just beginning. As she turned off the device and the room plunged into silence, Kaela felt the weight of the decision settle over her. In a few days from now, everything will change. And she was ready.

Chapter 5

Kaela loomed at her window, watching as the artificial sun rose into the sky of Dome 5. Its warm, golden light bathed the streets below, but it did little to ease the disorder within her. She'd barely slept, her mind consumed with thoughts of the map and the Garden. Her father had spent years chasing its secrets, and now she stood on the precipice of the same path, driven by the same questions. What had he been searching for? Why had he disappeared? And how was she connected to all of it?

Her fingers brushed against the device resting on her desk, its cool surface, a reminder of everything they had uncovered. The map had revealed the Garden's location, but it was more than a simple guide. It had responded to her, its symbols shifting and glowing as if it recognized her. That connection had ignited something deep inside her, something she didn't fully understand but couldn't ignore.

She closed her eyes, letting her mind wander back to the earliest memories of her father. He had always been a quiet, thoughtful man, his attention often drifting to things Kaela couldn't see. She remembered the late nights when he would sit at his desk, pouring over maps and journals, his face lit by the faint glow of his work. Back then, she hadn't understood the weight of his obsession. She'd only known that it had pulled him away from her, even when he was sitting right there. And then one day, he was gone.

Kaela's chest tightened. His disappearance had left a void in her life, one that had only grown larger with time. Her aunt had done her best to fill the gaps, but there were questions no one else could answer. And now, with the Garden calling to her, she felt closer to the truth than she ever had before. Her connection to the garden was a part of it, she was certain of that now. The way the plants had responded to her, the pull she felt when she was near the map, even the dreams she couldn't quite remember but woke from with a sense of purpose, it was all connected. The Garden wasn't just a place, it was a key, and she was meant to unlock it. An unexpected knock at the door broke her thoughts.

"Kaela?" Milo's voice was soft, but there was a familiar edge of excitement to it, a subtle tremor that always seemed to surface when he had something important, or reckless, on his mind. "You awake?"

Kaela stirred, blinking against the faint light filtering through the curtains. She pushed herself up, brushing a strand of copper hair from her face and squinting toward the door. "Yeah, come in."

The door creaked softly as Milo stepped inside, his usual energy subdued, like it was caught in the heavy undercurrent of everything they had planned. His dark blonde hair stuck up in unruly tufts, as though he's been running his hands through while deep in thought. Grease smudges streaked his palms and forearms, evidence of a late-night rendezvous with gears, wires, and whatever contraption he'd been obsessing over. His eyes, a sharp, clear blue, searched the room before landing on her. There was something else there, an unspoken question, maybe even hesitation, but milo being milo, he smothered it under a lopsided grin. "You look terrible."

Kaela rolled her eyes, suppressing a smile as she threw a pillow at him. "You're one to talk."

"You, okay?" Milo's voice was low and careful, his silhouette framed by the doorway as though he wasn't sure he should step inside. He leaned against the doorframe, his arms crossed loosely, but there was a softness in his eyes. A quiet concern that only Milo could wear so effortlessly.

Kaela nodded, though the movement felt hollow, her stomach churning like a storm just under the surface. She shifted in her chair, staring at the sleek map spread across her desk as though it might unravel its secrets on its own. "Just thinking."

"About the Garden?" Milo ventured, his tone gentle but knowing.

"About everything," she admitted, gesturing vaguely toward the map. Its edges were pulsating with a faint glow, as though signaling to Kaela that it understood her. "It feels like . . . like this is my only chance to understand what happened to him. To know why he left, what he was searching for."

Milo's expression softened, the sharp lines of his face easing as he stepped into the room. He didn't say anything right away, just let the silence stretch, a quiet acknowledgment of the weight her words carried. "You think the Garden has those answers?"

She hesitated, chewing on her bottom lip as she considered how to explain the feeling. Finally, she nodded. "I don't just think it. I feel it. It's like . . ." She swallowed, struggling to put the intangible into words. "It's like the Garden is calling to me, Milo. I know how it sounds, believe me, I know, but ever since we found the map, I can't shake this feeling that it's tied to him. And to me."

Milo crossed the room, his boots barely making a sound against the creaking floorboards. He stopped beside her, his eyes flicking to the map and then to her. "And your powers?"

Kaela exhaled slowly, the breath shaky, as though it carried the weight of a confession. She stared down at her hands, the faintest tingle of energy sparking beneath her skin, just out of reach. "They're part of it too. I don't know how, but I think my father knew.

He must have. He spent his whole life chasing the Garden, and now I'm . . ." Her voice caught, the words tangling with the ache in her throat.

Milo's hand came to rest gently on her shoulder, his grip firm but comforting, grounding her like an anchor in the storm. "You're not chasing it alone," he said softly, his voice steady and sure. "Whatever this is, we'll figure it out together."

She looked up, meeting his gaze. His blue eyes held none of the doubt she'd expected, only an unwavering loyalty that made her chest tighten with gratitude. "Thank you, Milo. I don't know what I'd do without you."

He smiled faintly, a corner of his mouth quirking up in that familiar, easy way. "Well, lucky for you, you don't have to find out."

The tension cracked just slightly, and Kaela let out a soft laugh, though it was fleeting. Her mind remained fixed on the map, on the Garden, on the gnawing need for answers that wouldn't let her go. It wasn't just a place to her anymore, it was a promise. A promise of understanding, of reclaiming the fragments of her father's life, of piecing together the tangled threads of her own identity.

"I know it's dangerous," she said after a moment, her voice low but sure. "I know we don't have all the answers, and I know leaving the dome is a risk. But I can't stay here, Milo. Not when the Garden is out there. Not when it could hold everything I've been searching for."

Milo studied her for a long beat, his expression unreadable. Then he nodded, his face set with a quiet determination that matched her own. "Then we'll go," he said firmly. "But let's be smart about it. We need to be prepared for whatever's out there."

Kaela's heart swelled with something she hadn't felt in years. Purpose. For so long, she'd been standing still, lost in the shadow of unanswered questions. But now, for the first time, she was moving forward. "Tomorrow," she said, the word like a vow, her voice steady. "We leave tomorrow."

Milo's smile returned, faint but reassuring, and he squeezed her shoulder once before letting his hand drop. "Tomorrow, then."

The room fell quiet again, but this time, it wasn't oppressive. The air seemed charged with the promise of what was to come, of answers waiting to be unearthed, of a journey neither of them could fully imagine. Kaela's gaze drifted back to the map, her fingers brushing its surface lightly. The Garden was out there, waiting for her. And she wouldn't stop until she found it.

As Milo's footsteps faded down the hall, the door clicked softly shut, leaving Kaela alone with the map and the weight of her thoughts. The faint hum of the device filled the silence, an almost imperceptible sound that seemed to pulse in rhythm with her own heartbeat. She turned back to the map, its soft, ethereal glow spilling across the desk and casting shifting patterns of light onto the walls. It looked alive, more than just the emanating glow of the glass, more than a mere relic of her father's search. The contours of the map were strange and unfamiliar, etched with landmarks that didn't exist in any place she'd ever known. Mountains twisted like sleeping giants; rivers wound like veins through uncharted lands; forests spread dark and sprawling, their outlines humming with mystery. It was a world she had never seen but one that felt startlingly familiar, as though it had been etched into her soul long before she'd ever touched it.

Kaela's fingers hovered just above the surface of the map, the tips tingling with the faint, electric pull she'd felt ever since they first uncovered it. She closed her eyes, letting herself breathe in deeply, slowly, as though the answers she sought might come on the exhale. And then she felt it, that pull again, a whispering current threading its way through her chest and down to her fingertips. It wasn't just a feeling. It was a call. The Garden. It tugged at her like an invisible tether, quiet but relentless, as if it had been waiting for her, for this moment, for years. I'm coming, she thought, the words ringing clear and steady in her mind. It wasn't a plea or a hope. It was determination and readiness.

Chapter 6

The morning light casted shadows through Kaela's window, forming soft shadows across her room. Her desk was cluttered with hastily scribbled notes, pieces of papers related to the map, and the device that had revealed the Garden's location. Today was the day. Kaela tightened her boots, her heart pounding in her chest as the realization of what they were about to do settled over her. She and Milo were leaving the safety of Dome 5, a place that had been both a sanctuary and a cage for as long as she could remember. The world beyond was a dangerous unknown, filled with rumors of savage landscapes, fractured domes, and people who didn't always welcome outsiders. Still, the pull of the Garden was stronger than her fear of any of it.

The room was a mess of movement, the quiet chaos of two people scrambling to prepare to leave behind everything they knew.

Bags lay half-packed on the floor, clothes and supplies scattered across the bed and desk, like a storm had blown through. The map, still glowing ever so faintly, rested in the center of it all, as though it were the eye of the whirlwind.

Kaela moved quickly, trying to focus on the task at hand instead of the knot of nerves twisting tighter with every passing moment. Her fingers hovered over a battered canvas bag before dropping in a rolled-up blanket, a few dried food packs, and a canteen. The items felt woefully inadequate, like they belonged to someone planning a picnic, not a journey into the unknown.

"Did you find the solar charger?" Milo's voice broke the silence. He stood on the other side of the room, rummaging through a pile of tools and devices he'd laid out across her desk. His dark blonde hair was messier than usual, sticking up at odd angles as he worked, and there were faint smudges of grease on his hands. Kaela recognized that it was a sure sign he'd been tinkering late into the night.

"Yeah, it's right here," Kaela replied, pulling the small, lightweight panel from a drawer and holding it up. "It's not much, but it should be enough to keep your gadgets running for a while."

Milo turned, offering a crooked grin. "More than enough. We'll make it work."

His confidence was reassuring, but Kaela couldn't shake the feeling of nervousness pressing down on her chest. She turned back to her bag, double-checking the contents. Along with the food and blanket, there was a small first aid kit, a fire starter, a utility knife, and a flashlight, items that felt both practical and woefully inadequate for what they might face.

Her gaze flicked to the map. Its glow seemed stronger today, casting a soft golden light across the room. It felt alive, like it was waiting for them. Calling to them. Today, she thought, the word sending a jolt through her. Today, we leave.

"Do you think this will be enough?" she asked, unable to stop herself. She turned to find Milo fitting tools into a compact roll of leather, each one chosen with deliberate care.

"For the first stretch? Yeah," Milo replied, though his tone was quieter now, more serious. He glanced up, his blue eyes meeting hers. "We don't know what's out there, Kaela. No one does. But we can't prepare for everything. We'll figure it out as we go."

Kaela nodded, but doubt gnawed at the edges of her resolve. The Garden felt like a promise, but it also felt like a threat. No one who'd gone searching for it had ever returned, not her father, not the others who had whispered of its magic. And yet, here they were, packing as though they could outwit the unknown with gadgets and rolled blankets. She turned back to her bag, pulling a worn jacket from her closet and tucking it inside. As she did, her eyes landed on a small, framed photograph on her bedside table. It was old, the edges fraying, but the image was still clear. It was her father's face, smiling as he held her in his arms, her copper hair a wild mess even then. She picked it up carefully, running her thumb over the glass.

"I'll find you," she whispered under her breath, the words more a vow than ever. Then, with a deep breath, she slid the photo into her bag, nestling it safely between layers of fabric.

Milo cleared his throat, breaking the moment. "I've got the essentials: tools, wire, the small soldering kit, and that old compass I've been fixing. Oh, and I found this." He held up a compact, metallic device, its surface smooth and black with a faint blue glow at the edges.

"What is it?" Kaela asked, frowning.

"Short-range signal jammer," Milo replied with a note of pride. "If anyone, or anything, tries to track us with a locator, this'll block it. It doesn't have a huge range, but it's better than nothing."

Kaela couldn't help but smile. "You think of everything."

"That's why you keep me around," Milo said with a grin, but it faded quickly. He dropped the device into his own bag and straightened, his expression serious again. "We'll need to be careful, though. Outside the domes, we're on our own."

The words hung in the air, stark and heavy. Kaela felt them settle into her chest like stones. She knew the risks. Outside the safety of Dome 5, the world was harsh and unpredictable, wild landscapes where unscheduled storms could last for days, old ruins filled with dangers no one had cataloged, and people who didn't take kindly to strangers.

"We'll be ready," she said quietly, though the words felt like they belonged to someone braver.

Milo studied her for a moment before nodding. "Yeah. We will."

Kaela turned to her desk, grabbing a scrap of paper and a pen. Her hand hesitated over the page, her mind suddenly blank. What could she possibly say? What was going to happen to Eila while she was gone?

"Leaving a note?" Milo asked softly.

"For Aunt Eila," Kaela replied. "She deserves . . . something." She stared at the paper a moment longer before the words finally came.

It wasn't enough, but it was all she could give. Kaela turned back to find Milo watching her. "Ready?" he asked, his voice soft.

She glanced around the room one last time. It looked strange, empty of her presence even though nothing had truly changed. The walls were still the same pale gray, the shelves still held her books, her sketches, her father's notes. But it felt hollow now, as though part of her had already left.

"Yeah," she said finally, slinging her bag over her shoulder. It was heavier than she expected, pulling against her muscles. "I'm ready."

Milo nodded, grabbing his own pack and the roll of tools. "Let's go. The tunnels are clear now, but we don't have much time."

Kaela slung her bag over her shoulder, the door physical and mental weight pressing down on her like a manifestation of everything she was leaving behind. She followed him to the door, her footsteps slow, reluctant. At the threshold, she hesitated, her hand lingering on the frame. She turned back, sweeping her gaze across the room, memorizing every corner. The cluttered desk, the sketches pinned to the walls, the small stack of her father's old journals. It felt unreal, as though she were looking at someone else's life, one that had been left behind years ago. The knot in her chest tightened, pulling hard against her ribs, but she swallowed it down. *This is the only way forward.*

Milo shifted in the hallway, his voice quiet. "Kaela . . ."

"I'm coming," she said softly, forcing her feet to move. She closed the door behind her with a finality that sent a shiver down her spine.

The house was dark, silent but for the faint creak of the floorboards beneath their boots. Kaela's breath felt too loud, her heartbeat pounding in her ears as they made their way to the back entrance. The air was heavy with stillness, as though the walls themselves knew what was happening and held their breath. Kaela paused at the kitchen table, her eyes catching the faint outline of her aunt's favorite mug sitting by the sink. Her chest tightened again. She set her pack down just long enough to pull out the note she had written earlier, unfolding it carefully. Her fingers trembled as she placed it on the table, weighed down by a smooth stone from her windowsill.

Eila,

I don't know how to explain this, but I have to go. I have to find him. I have to find the truth. Please don't worry about me. Milo is with me, and we'll be careful. I promise. I'll come back. I don't know when, but I will. Take care of yourself.

I love you.

Kaela

For a moment, she just stood there, staring at the note. It wasn't enough. Not for what she was doing, not for what she was leaving behind, but it would have to be. She couldn't allow herself to linger on the thought, it was time to go.

"Kaela." Milo's voice was urgent now, a quiet whisper from the doorway.

She nodded, slinging her pack over her shoulder again. The sterile morning air hit her as soon as she stepped outside, the curated wind cutting through the thin fabric of her jacket. The city stretched out before them, its lights glowing dimly against the haze, and the dome loomed overhead like a silent sentinel.

"This way," Milo said, leading her toward the shadows at the edge of the courtyard.

Kaela followed him, her boots crunching softly against the gravel. The darkness felt vast and consuming, pressing in on all sides, but it was better than the artificial brightness of the dome streets. Here, no one would see them. Here, they were just two figures slipping away into the shadows.

The tunnels lay at the edge of the sector, tucked away behind an abandoned maintenance building. Milo knelt beside a rusted grate, pulling it loose with an unnerving yet soft scrape of metal against stone. "It's clear," he whispered, glancing back at her.

Kaela crouched beside him, peering into the darkness below. A faint chill drifted up from the tunnel, carrying with it the scent of damp earth and rusted metal. Her pulse quickened. *No turning back now.* Milo climbed down first, landing quietly on the narrow path below. Kaela followed, the cold metal of the ladder biting into her palms as she descended. When her feet hit the ground, she took a deep breath, steadying herself.

"Light?" she whispered.

Milo flicked on a small flashlight, its beam cutting through the darkness and revealing the narrow, arched tunnel ahead. The walls were lined with old pipes, their surfaces corroded and dripping in places. The tunnel stretched out endlessly, disappearing into shadow. Kaela adjusted her pack, the straps digging into her shoulders. "How far do you think this goes?"

"Far enough to get us past the outer perimeter," Milo replied, keeping his voice low. "Once we're outside the dome, we'll head east."

"To the garden," Kaela said softly, more to herself than to him.

Milo glanced back, his face half-lit by the flashlight's glow. "To the garden."

The tunnel felt endless, their soggy footsteps echoing faintly against the walls as they walked. The further they went, the heavier the silence became, broken only by the occasional drip of water from overhead. Kaela's mind raced as she moved, her thoughts caught somewhere between fear and determination. She thought of her father, his face in the old photograph, his voice she could barely remember anymore. What had he been thinking when he left? Had he been afraid like she was now, or had he been so certain of what he would find that nothing else mattered? *I'll find you*, she thought, clutching the strap of her bag tightly. *I'll find the truth.*

Ahead of her, Milo moved steadily, his flashlight sweeping across the path. His presence was grounding, a quiet reassurance that she wasn't alone. He had always been there, her anchor, her partner in every reckless plan they'd ever dreamed up. And now, when it mattered most, he was here again.

"How are you so calm?" Kaela asked suddenly, her voice breaking the silence.

Milo glanced back, one eyebrow raised. "Who says I'm calm?"

"You look calm," she replied, a faint smile tugging at her lips despite herself.

"Well, someone has to be," Milo said, flashing her a quick

grin. "Trust me, my stomach is doing flips, too. But we'll get through this."

Kaela did not respond, but his words settled some of the tension in her chest. She focused on the sound of their footsteps, one after the other, carrying them forward. Minutes turned into an hour, or maybe more, it was impossible to tell in the dark. Finally, the tunnel sloped upward, the air growing colder and sharper. Milo stopped at a heavy, rusted door, his breath misting faintly in the glow of the flashlight.

"This is it," he said quietly, his voice laced with both excitement and caution. "Beyond here . . . we're out."

Kaela swallowed hard, her pulse quickening. She could feel the weight of the moment pressing down on her. This was the threshold, the line between the life she'd always known and the unknown world beyond the domes. The flips occurring in her stomach were a mixture of utter fear and excitement.

"Ready?" Milo asked, his hand on the door handle.

Kaela exhaled slowly, her breath shaking. "Ready."

Chapter 7

The creak of the door was sharp and metallic, a sound that sent a jolt of adrenaline through Kaela's chest. It wasn't loud, but here, in the dim and stifling quiet of the maintenance corridor, it seemed to echo off every surface, carrying with it the realization of finality. Kaela tightened her grip on the straps of her pack, watching as the seam in the dome's outer wall began to split. The crack of light widened slowly, stretching out like the first rays of dawn piercing a storm.

"Almost there," Milo whispered. His voice, though low, carried that unmistakable thread of excitement he always had when one of his gadgets was working. He was crouched beside the control panel, his small hacking terminal connected to the wall via a tangle of cables. The faint green glow of its display flickered across his face, highlighting the determined crease in his brow and the faint smudge of oil on his cheek.

Kaela gulped, her heart pounding vigorously against her ribs. The air inside the corridor felt heavy and stagnant, but as the door's opening grew wider, something new slipped through. A breeze. Raw, unfiltered air. It was faint, but unmistakable. Cool and crisp, with a strange edge that tingled against her skin. The outside.

"I hope you know what you're doing," she said, her voice steadier than she felt, the words tinged with a mixture of concern and skepticism. She crossed her arms, watching him as he fiddled with the small, intricate components in front of him. The faint hum of the gadgets he was assembling filled the space, but it did little to calm the unease that twisted in her stomach.

Milo didn't look up from his work, his brow furrowed in concentration. His fingers moved with practiced precision, the slight clicking of tools against metal the only sound in the otherwise still air. "Do you really want me to answer that?" he replied, his tone light, almost teasing, but there was an underlying seriousness to it.

Kaela exhaled sharply, a wry smile tugging at the corner of her lips despite herself. "Not particularly," she said, her voice carrying the weight of unspoken words of all the doubts, fears, and questions she couldn't quite voice. She shifted her weight, eyes still nervously glued on him, feeling the pull of both his confidence and her own uncertainty. There was something about his focus, his determination, that both reassured and unsettled her in equal measure.

The terminal beeped softly, and Milo gave the panel a light smack with the flat of his hand. "And . . . done!" He shot her a grin, bright and boyish, as the door groaned one final time and stopped moving. The seam was wide enough now for them to slip through, the edge of the opening framed by smooth, weathered metal.

Milo pushed to his feet, stuffing the terminal back into his pack with practiced efficiency. "After you," he said, gesturing grandly toward the light beyond.

Kaela hesitated, her feet suddenly rooted to the ground. This is it, she thought. She had spent her entire life inside Dome 5, surrounded by its glass-like walls and predictable order. The city was clean, safe, and familiar. And now, she was about to leave it all behind.

Beyond the opening, the world glowed softly with the pale gold of early morning. The light seemed almost too bright, and Kaela had to squint to make out the shapes beyond. Rolling fields of tall grass, their blades shimmering with dew. Above it all stretched a sky so vast and endless that it made her breath catch in her throat. The colors of the morning sky in the dome were undeniably dull compared to the beauty of the world outside.

Milo stepped up beside her, his shoulder brushing hers. "Kaela," he said quietly. There was no teasing in his voice this time, just understanding. "We can't stay here. If security finds out what we did

. . ."

"I know," she said, forcing herself to move.

Her boots hit the ground outside with a soft, muted crunch. The earth felt strange beneath her feet. Uneven and alive in a way the dome's perfectly polished floors never had. She staggered slightly, her balance thrown off by the unfamiliar texture, and Milo's hand shot out to steady her.

"Careful. Gravity's still the same out here, but the ground's a lot less predictable," he said, his voice laced with amusement.

Kaela shot him a glare, but there was no real anger behind it. She straightened, letting go of his arm, and turned to take in the world that stretched out before them. The morning was breathtaking. A light mist clung to the grasslands, the dew catching the sun and turning the landscape into a field of shimmering gold. The air smelled different, cool and sharp, with an earthy tang that filled her lungs and left her feeling more awake than she had ever been. A chill breeze rolled across the open space, rustling the grass and brushing against her face like a whisper.

"I can't believe this is real," she murmured, almost to herself.

Milo, now beside her, adjusted the straps of his pack and followed her gaze. "Yeah. They never tell you it looks like this, do they?"

Kaela shook her head, eyes wide with amazement. The dome's officials spoke of the wilderness as though it were something to be feared, a chaotic wasteland of ruin and decay. But here, outside the walls of their city, the world felt alive. Wild and untamed, yes, but not broken.

Milo reached into one of the many compartments of his oversized pack and pulled out a small, rectangular device. It hummed softly as he powered it on, a faint light flickering across its display. "Scanner's up," he said, turning in a slow circle as he held the device out in front of him. "Signal's weak, but it's there. The Garden's that way." He pointed toward a distant line of dark shapes on the horizon. Trees, Kaela realized. An entire forest.

"We're really doing this," she said quietly.

"Looks like it," Milo replied. He turned to her, his expression softening. "You, okay?"

Kaela nodded, though her chest felt tight. "Yeah. Let's go."

They started walking, leaving the dome and its glass-like surface behind. With every step, the sounds of the wilderness grew louder. The crunch of grass underfoot, the soft buzz of unseen insects, the distant calls of birds. It was overwhelming at first, like the world was alive with voices she had never heard before.

Kaela found herself glancing back at the rusted door more than once, half-expecting to see security drones swarming out of the dome to drag them back inside. But there was nothing. The door had sealed itself again, its surface smooth and featureless, as though it had never opened at all.

"We're clear," Milo said, his voice low but steady, eyes scanning the horizon as he checked over his shoulder. His hand hovered near his belt, fingers grazing the small, worn device that had just helped them slip past the dome's security. "If they notice the breach, it'll take them hours to figure out what happened." He sounded confident, but Kaela could sense the undercurrent of tension in his words, a silent acknowledgment that they were walking a razor-thin line.

Kaela gave a short, humorless laugh, trying to mask the knot of anxiety in her chest. "That's reassuring," she replied, her tone laced with dry sarcasm. She turned her gaze toward the vast expanse of wilderness stretching before them, the weight of their decision settling heavily in her chest. It was a world so different from the sterile, controlled environment they'd just left, and the uncertainty of what lay ahead was almost overwhelming.

Milo, ever the optimist, didn't seem phased. "Hey, give me some credit. It was my tech that got us out here, remember?" He flashed her a grin, a glimmer of pride in his eyes as he patted the small gadget on his belt, the one that had unlocked their way to freedom.

Kaela raised an eyebrow, her lips curling into a faint, skeptical smile. "Yeah, and let's hope your tech keeps us alive long enough to find the Garden," she shot back, the weight of their mission making her words more biting than she intended.

"Always so dramatic," Milo teased, a chuckle slipping from his lips. He pulled another device from his belt, this one more intricate and polished than the others. It was a small, mechanical orb, its surface smooth and metallic, with a series of faintly glowing rings that spun around its center, casting soft pulses of light into the darkening morning.

"Meet the Wayfinder 2.0," he announced proudly, his voice tinged with the excitement of a child showing off a new toy. "It'll track our direction, monitor air quality, and—"

"Explode if you drop it?" Kaela interrupted, a teasing glint in her eyes. She couldn't help herself, Milo's enthusiasm always made her want to push his buttons.

Milo rolled his eyes, though the grin on his face was unmistakable. "That happened once," he muttered with a mock sigh. "And for the record, it was a prototype." He handed the device to her, and Kaela took it gingerly, feeling the faint vibration of its inner mechanisms beneath her fingertips. The rings shifted subtly, almost as if acknowledging her touch, and the display blinked to life with a soft blue glow, the device coming alive in her hands. It was more than just a tool, it was a piece of Milo's genius, his obsession with perfecting his creations.

"Looks like it's working," Kaela said, her voice softer now as she handed the device back. There was a flicker of appreciation in her eyes, though she quickly masked it with a teasing tone. "I'll admit, you've got some impressive gadgets, even if they are prone to explosions."

Milo chuckled, slipping the Wayfinder into his pack with a satisfied nod. "Told you it was worth the risk," he said, clearly pleased with himself. He glanced up, his eyes scanning the distant treeline, where the shadows of towering trees beckoned them into the unknown.

"Come on," he urged, his voice growing more serious. "We've got a lot of ground to cover." His tone was filled with a quiet urgency now, as if the time for jokes had passed. Kaela nodded, her stomach churning at the thought of what lay ahead. The unknown wilderness stretched out before them, dark and mysterious, but with every step, they were moving closer to their goal.

Kaela felt a sense of both dread and exhilaration surge through her, the tension of their escape still hanging in the air, but now overshadowed by the promise of what they were about to face. The Garden, her father's legacy, was out there, waiting. As she fell into step beside Milo, the world around them seemed to come alive with the sounds of the wilderness. Distant birds calling, the rustle of leaves in the wind, and the faint hum of the device in her hand.

It was strange, this new world they were stepping into. It was raw and untamed, so different from the sterile, controlled life they had left behind. But Kaela couldn't shake the feeling that this was where she was meant to be. With Milo by her side and the unknown ahead, she couldn't help but feel that the answers she had been searching for were finally within reach.

They pressed on, the grasslands giving way to uneven, root-riddled terrain as they neared the forest. The air grew heavier here, filled with the damp scent of earth and wood. Shafts of sunlight filtered through the branches, breaking through the mist and scattering light across the ground in golden streaks. Kaela found herself staring up at the canopy, her neck craning as she took in the sheer height of the trees. Their trunks were massive, their bark rough and weathered, and their branches stretched so far overhead that they seemed to weave together like an ancient, protective net.

"Have you ever seen anything like this?" Kaela asked softly, her voice barely more than a whisper, as if the sheer magnitude of the forest demanded reverence. Her eyes swept over the towering trees, their gnarled trunks rising like ancient sentinels into the dimming sky. The canopy above seemed to stretch endlessly, a mosaic of shadows and light filtering through the thick layers of leaves. It was breathtaking, this untamed beauty that lay beyond the walls of the dome. But it was also overwhelming. There was something wild about it, something primal.

"Nope," Milo replied, his voice carrying the same awe that Kaela felt in the pit of her stomach. His gaze, too, was fixed on the forest, his eyes wide as they took in the sprawling wilderness. "It's . . . a lot bigger than I imagined," he added, his tone almost reverent, like a child seeing something new for the first time. The enormity of the place seemed to make even him, always so sure of himself, pause in wonder.

Kaela nodded, but her gaze shifted to the shadows pooling beneath the thick undergrowth. The sunlight that filtered through the leaves above did little to pierce the depths of the forest. It was beautiful, yes. So much more vibrant and alive than anything she had ever known, but it was also dark, a labyrinth of secrets waiting to be uncovered. Her heart fluttered with unease as her footsteps slowed, a flicker of doubt worming its way into her thoughts. The vastness of it was both mesmerizing and terrifying.

Milo must have sensed her hesitation because he looked over at her, his brow furrowing slightly, though his expression was still calm, reassuring. "Don't worry," he said, his voice soft but firm. "We'll be fine." His words, meant to comfort, barely brushed away the cold unease that had settled in her chest. She gave him a tight smile, but it didn't reach her eyes.

"You say that now," Kaela muttered, her words laced with a hint of irony, though she forced herself to keep walking. The forest seemed to close in around them as they moved deeper into the trees, its presence heavy and all-encompassing.

The world they had known, bright lights, constant motion, and the hum of tyrannized magic within the domes seemed a distant memory now. The only sounds that remained were the crunch of dry leaves underfoot and the occasional snap of a twig breaking in the distance. The grasslands they had left behind felt like a dream compared to the dense silence that surrounded them. It was a soundless world, except for the far-off calls of creatures that Kaela couldn't even begin to identify. They seemed to be everywhere and nowhere all at once.

Milo's scanner beeped intermittently, its soft hum a constant reminder of their mission. He glanced at the flickering device. The screen reflecting the dim light that filtered through the trees. The signal it was tracking was faint, like a whisper in the wind, but it was steady.

"How far do you think it is?" Kaela asked after a long stretch of silence, her voice barely above a murmur, as if speaking too loudly might disturb the fragile peace of the forest, and draw too much attention to themselves.

Milo didn't immediately answer, his eyes fixed on the scanner, the lines of concentration on his face deepening. After a moment, he looked up, his gaze meeting hers with a quiet determination. "Hard to say," he replied, his tone thoughtful. "The signal's weak, but it's steady. As long as we keep moving, we'll get there."

His words were simple and sharp. Yet, there was a confidence in them that Kaela couldn't help but desperately cling to. He had a way of making the impossible seem manageable, of turning uncertainty into something they could control. But still, she couldn't shake the feeling that the forest was watching them, its ancient eyes hidden in the shadows.

She glanced at the scanner, noting the way the small device flickered with every step they took, as if it were trying to guide them through the vastness of the unknown. They had little knowledge of the outside world, no clear path, only the faintest of signals and a sense of purpose driving them forward. The trees loomed taller now, their branches interwoven, blocking out more of the sky above. It was like walking into a cathedral made of wood, a place that seemed to have been untouched by time. Every step they took felt heavier, as if the forest itself were holding its breath, waiting for them to make the next move.

Kaela tightened her grip on the strap of her pack, the weight of their journey pressing down on her shoulders. The map was still safely tucked away, but the knowledge that they were walking into the unknown, into the very heart of the wilderness her father had once sought, made her pulse quicken. She was no longer just following in his footsteps. She was forging her own path, and the weight of that responsibility was both exhilarating and terrifying.

"I hope you're right," Kaela said, her voice quieter now, almost a whisper against the soft rustle of the leaves. "I hope we're really getting closer."

Milo didn't respond right away, but she could see the flicker of reassurance in his eyes, the same determination that had driven him to build all those gadgets that had helped them get this far. "We are," he said finally, his voice steady and calm, though there was a hint of excitement underneath. "I can feel it."

Kaela nodded, though her heart was racing. There was no turning back now. The wilderness stretched out before them, vast and wild, and in the distance, the faintest trace of the Garden called to her, a whisper that she couldn't ignore. The forest was dark, yes, and filled with secrets. But Kaela had secrets of her own, ones that she was now ready to uncover.

Kaela nodded, though the knot in her chest hadn't loosened. Every step deeper into the wilderness felt like stepping further into a story she wasn't sure she was ready to be a part of. And yet, she couldn't stop now. The Garden was out there, waiting. And so they walked.

Time stretched and blurred, the forest growing darker and more tangled the further they went. Kaela's muscles ached from the weight of her pack, but she didn't complain. Milo led the way, his gadgets humming softly as he scanned their surroundings and checked their progress. At one point, they stopped to rest beneath the massive roots of a fallen tree. Milo pulled out a small canister and twisted it open, revealing two thin bars of compressed protein. He tossed one to Kaela, who caught it with fumbling hands.

"It's not much," Milo said, biting into his ration bar with a satisfied crunch. "But it'll keep us going."

Kaela stared at the bar in her hands. Its dry, beige surface seemed almost too perfect, like it had been molded into shape by some unfeeling machine. She hesitated before taking a tentative bite. The taste hit her immediately. Bland, chalky, and dry, like she was chewing on a piece of compressed cardboard. She grimaced, struggling to swallow. "This tastes like cardboard," she muttered, her voice flat.

Milo chuckled, completely unfazed. He chewed another bite, the sound of his teeth crunching through the dense, tasteless bar oddly soothing. "Better than starving," he said with a shrug, his tone light, as if the tasteless food didn't bother him at all.

Kaela gave him a sidelong glance. "You're really not bothered by this, are you?"

Milo grinned, a spark of mischief in his eyes. "Not really. I've had worse." He took another bite, chewing thoughtfully. "Besides, it's kind of a challenge. Who can make the least disgusting face while eating these things?"

She rolled her eyes but couldn't help the small smile tugging at her lips. "You're ridiculous."

"I know," he replied, unfazed, popping the last bit of his bar into his mouth. He reached into his pack and pulled out another one, tossing it to her with a grin. "But at least it's keeping us going. You've got to admit, it's better than nothing."

Kaela caught the bar, holding it in her hand like it was some sort of strange object. She sighed dramatically before taking another reluctant bite, the texture making her want to gag. But she forced herself to chew, knowing there was no other choice. She looked around at the wilderness stretching out before them, letting the discomfort of the food fade into the background. She wasn't going to let something so trivial slow them down.

Milo was already packing up, tossing the wrapper into his bag with a carefree gesture. He seemed to be completely at ease, unaffected by the same discomfort that had Kaela cringing. He was always like that. Completely unfazed, finding humor even in the worst situations.

She swallowed the last of her bar, grimacing, and said quietly, "We'll find something better soon."

Milo shot her a quick, reassuring smile. "I'm counting on it. But until then, we've got this."

She made a face but took a bite anyway, chewing slowly as she looked out into the forest. The world beyond the domes was nothing like she had imagined. It was wilder, stranger, and more alive. And somewhere out there, the Garden was waiting. *I'm coming*, she thought, her resolve hardening. No matter what it takes.

The day stretched on, each hour blending into the next as Kaela and Milo pressed deeper into the forest. The trees, once towering giants, now seemed to crowd around them, their thick canopies casting deep shadows over the path. The air grew denser, cooler, as though the forest itself was holding its breath, waiting for something. Kaela finally allowed herself to really feel the uncanny connection to the world she had never thought existed. The weight of it all settled on Kaela's shoulders, but she refused to let it show.

Milo had become more focused as the landscape changed, his fingers never far from the devices he carried. The steady beeping of the scanner had become a comforting sound, like a pulse keeping them tethered to their goal. Every so often, he would stop, adjusting his gear or recalibrating the tracker, muttering to himself in a language Kaela couldn't quite understand. He seemed so at ease in this environment, his hands moving with the practiced precision of someone who had spent their entire life tinkering and inventing.

Kaela, on the other hand, felt out of place. She was used to the sleek, sterile walls of Dome 5, where every surface gleamed with perfection, the weather prescheduled, and Nothing ever out of the ordinary. Here, everything was unpredictable. The air smelled of damp earth and decaying leaves, and every rustle in the underbrush made her heart race. It was beautiful, but also terrifying in its vastness. She couldn't shake the feeling that the forest was watching them, its ancient presence hidden just beyond the veil of trees.

"How much farther?" she asked, breaking the silence. Her voice sounded strange, even to her own ears, small against the backdrop of the wilderness.

Milo glanced at the scanner, his eyes narrowing as he analyzed the data. "We're close," he said, his voice steady but with a hint of excitement. "The signal's getting stronger. We should be there soon."

Kaela nodded, though her nerves were starting to fray. The Garden had been nothing more than a myth to her. A legend passed down through hushed whispers. A dream wrapped in secrecy. Now, it was reality. A place that promised answers, but also dangers they could never have predicted. She had spent her entire life believing the Garden was a fairytale, something only her father had truly believed in. But here she was, walking toward it with Milo at her side, unsure of what they would find when they arrived.

The forest opened up before them suddenly, as if the trees had decided to part for them. Kaela's breath caught in her throat as she stepped into the clearing. The light was different here, softer and golden, as if the sun had found a way to filter through the dense canopy. The ground beneath her feet was softer, spongier, covered in a thick carpet of moss and wildflowers. In the center of the clearing stood a large, ancient stone archway, half-hidden by creeping vines and moss. It was tall, imposing, and covered in intricate carvings that Kaela couldn't begin to decipher. The air here felt charged, alive with something she couldn't name.

"Is this it?" Kaela whispered, her voice barely audible, as if speaking any louder might shatter the moment. Her eyes, wide with disbelief, scanned the ancient stone archway before them, the weight of the moment pressing down on her chest. The air felt thick, charged with an energy she couldn't explain, as though the very ground beneath her feet was alive with secrets waiting to be uncovered.

Milo stepped forward, his boots crunching softly against the moss-covered ground. His hand reached out, almost reverently, to trace the edge of the stone. His fingers hovered for a moment before making contact, and he shivered slightly, as though the touch alone sent a pulse of electricity through his body. "This is it," he said, his voice low and filled with awe. There was no mistaking the reverence in his tone. "The Garden . . . it's real."

Kaela's heart thundered in her chest, her pulse racing so loudly she could almost hear it in her ears. She had read about the Garden in her father's journals, studied the sketches he'd made of this very archway, each line and curve painstakingly drawn with the precision of a man obsessed. But standing here now, with the cool stone beneath her fingertips and the weight of the forest pressing in around them, it was nothing like the pages of a book. This was real. This was the place her father had believed in so fiercely, the place that had consumed his every waking thought. The Garden was no longer a myth, no longer a dream. It was tangible, breathing in the air around her.

Her breath caught in her throat as she stepped closer, her eyes drinking in the details of the arch. The stone was weathered, ancient, its surface etched with intricate carvings that seemed to shift and move in the flickering light. The air hummed with an energy she could feel deep in her bones, a strange warmth radiating from the archway as though it held the secrets of the universe within its walls. It was unlike anything she had ever experienced. No books, no stories, no warnings had prepared her for this.

Milo turned to her then, his face alight with excitement, his eyes wide and shining with a kind of joy Kaela had rarely seen from him. "We made it, Kaela," he said, his voice almost breathless with the enormity of it all. "This is it. We're standing at the threshold of something that no one could even begin to believe."

Kaela nodded, her mouth dry, the words caught in her throat. The overwhelming weight of the moment, the significance of their discovery, pressed down on her. It was like standing at the edge of a cliff, knowing that what lay ahead could change everything. But she wasn't sure if she was ready. Was anyone ready for this?

She swallowed hard, forcing herself to speak. "What now?" Her voice was quieter than she intended, laced with uncertainty. She had often imagined this moment, the moment they would finally find the Garden, but now that it was here, she wasn't sure what came next. Was there a door to open? A choice to make? Or was it as simple as stepping through?

Milo's gaze flickered to the archway, then back to her, his grin widening. "Now," he said, his voice steady but with an edge of excitement, "we step through. Together."

Without waiting for a response, Milo moved toward the archway, his steps quick and sure. Kaela hesitated for a moment, her eyes lingering on the intricate carvings that covered the stone. They were ancient, older than anything she had ever seen. Patterns that seemed to shift when she wasn't looking directly at them, like they were alive. She swallowed, gathering her courage, and followed Milo into the archway.

The moment she stepped through, the world seemed to change. The air grew warmer, richer with the scent of flowers and earth, and the ground beneath her feet shifted from soft moss to something smoother, almost like polished stone. The forest, the trees, everything outside had faded away, leaving only the vastness of the Garden in its place.

Kaela looked around in awe. The Garden stretched out before them, a landscape unlike anything she had ever imagined. Lush, vibrant greenery filled every inch of the space, with towering trees that seemed to reach the sky, their branches heavy with fruit that glowed faintly in the dim light. Flowers of every color bloomed in wild profusion, their petals shimmering with an ethereal light. The air was thick with the hum of life, the sounds of insects, birds, and the soft sound of a stream. It was a world unto itself, untouched by the hands of civilization.

"This is . . . incredible," Kaela whispered, her voice full of wonder.

Milo grinned, his eyes bright with excitement. "Told you. The Garden's not just a myth. It's a living, breathing place. But we're not here to admire the view. We've got work to do."

Kaela nodded, shaking herself from the daze of awe that had overtaken her. She could feel the weight of their mission settling back onto her shoulders. The Garden might be beautiful, but it was also a mystery, one that held the answers to her father's disappearance, to the powers that she was only beginning to understand. She needed to find those answers.

"Where do we start?" she asked, turning to Milo.

Milo pulled out the small device he had been using earlier, scanning the area with it. "The signal is stronger here, but it's still weak. We need to get deeper into the Garden. I think the source is somewhere in the center."

Kaela glanced around, her eyes scanning the dense undergrowth. "Let's go," she said, determination in her voice.

They moved deeper into the Garden, the lush foliage parting as they made their way through. Every step they took seemed to take them further from the world they knew, into a place where time didn't seem to matter. The air felt thick with magic, and Kaela could feel the pulse of it in her bones, a strange energy that thrummed through the ground and into her body. She didn't know what it was, but it was there, pressing in on her, making her skin tingle.

As they walked, the landscape around them seemed to shift and change. The trees grew taller yet more dull than before, their trunks twisted in intricate patterns. Flowers bloomed in slightly dull yet impossible colors, their petals glowing ever so faintly as if lit from within. Strange creatures, half-bird, half-insect, flitted through the air, their wings shimmering in the light. It was beautiful, yes, but there was something unsettling about it, too. The Garden felt as though it wasn't at its full potential, and Kaela couldn't shake the feeling that it was watching them, waiting for something.

They walked in silence for a while, the only sound the soft crunch of their footsteps on the smooth stone path. Kaela felt the weight of the Garden pressing in on her, its ancient power pulsing beneath her feet. She had no idea what they would find here, what answers lay hidden in this strange, otherworldly place, but she knew one thing for sure. The Garden was far more than just a place. It was alive with history, with secrets and it was calling to her.

"Kaela," Milo said suddenly, his voice cutting through the silence and snapping her from her thoughts. He stopped in his tracks, his face draining of color, a sheen of sweat starting to form on his brow. "Do you hear that?"

Kaela froze, her heart leaping into her throat, a cold shiver racing down her spine. There it was. A sound, distant yet unmistakable. A low, rhythmic thrum, like the deep, steady pulse of a heartbeat, vibrating through the air. It came from deep within the Garden, somewhere ahead of them, as though the very earth itself was alive.

"What is it?" Kaela whispered, her voice trembling, barely audible over the thrum that seemed to vibrate in her chest.

Milo didn't answer. His eyes narrowed, his expression tense as he scanned the dense, shadowed expanse before them. Without another word, he moved forward, his steps quickening, his breath shallow. "I think it's the source. Come on."

Kaela followed closely behind, her heart pounding vigorously in her chest, each beat echoing in her ears. The sound of her footsteps was muffled by the thick undergrowth, but the rhythmic thrum that had drawn them forward still hummed faintly in the air, growing louder with each step. She could feel the weight of the Garden around them, its ancient energy pressing in from all sides, its secrets waiting just beyond their reach. Whatever was ahead of them, whatever the Garden had been hiding for so long, Kaela could feel that they were drawing closer to it. The tension in her chest grew with each passing moment, a mix of fear and excitement tightening like a vice around her lungs. She didn't know what to expect, what they would find when they reached the source of that pulse, but she couldn't shake the feeling that whatever lay ahead, it would change everything. She wasn't sure if she was ready for it. Her mind raced with a thousand possibilities, each one more terrifying than the last. But there was no turning back now. They had come this far, and Kaela knew deep down that they had no choice but to face whatever the Garden was hiding.

Chapter 8

The ominous forest surrounding Kaela and Milo felt alive, as if the very air pulsed with energy. The trees loomed overhead, their gnarled branches twisting and stretching toward the sky, like ancient beings reaching for something far beyond their grasp. Thick vines clung to their trunks, slithering like serpents, and the underbrush was a labyrinth of dense ferns, moss, and wildflowers, each one whispering secrets in the wind. The scent of damp earth was rich and heady, mixed with the faint sweetness of hidden blossoms. The sounds of the forest were unlike anything Kaela had ever heard. Low murmurs of creatures lurking just out of sight, the rustling of leaves that seemed to respond to their presence, and the distant, haunting calls of unseen birds.

Each step Kaela took seemed to evoke the very land beneath her feet. The ground was soft, but it held a strange energy, like it was alive, watching them. The map in her hand flickered erratically, its light pulsing in rhythm with her heartbeat, as though the forest itself recognized her touch. It guided her forward, its glow dim but insistent, like a beacon calling her deeper into the heart of the wilderness. Milo was a few paces ahead, his energy scanner clicking and whirring in his hands, his brow furrowed in concentration. "We're getting closer," he murmured, not looking back. The scanner's lights blinked erratically, and he adjusted its settings with quick, practiced movements. "But there's something blocking the signal . . . I can't get a clear read."

Kaela barely heard him, her mind too preoccupied with the sensation growing inside her. It was a low hum, deep and resonant, like the pulse of the earth itself. It echoed through her veins, filling her with a strange warmth that spread through her chest and out to her fingertips. The further they went, the stronger the pull became, a magnetic force drawing her deeper into the forest, into the unknown. The path ahead was becoming more perilous, the ground uneven and cluttered with twisted roots and rocks that bulged up like the bones of some long-dead creature. But Kaela didn't notice. Her feet moved with purpose, her thoughts consumed by the growing connection she felt to the land, to the magic hidden within it. She could almost hear it now, a faint whisper in the breeze, a beckoning. Her father, the Garden, the power inside her, it was all starting to make sense, but only just. She didn't know how or why this was happening, but she knew one thing: she was meant to be here. The land, the forest, the magic, it was all calling to her, and she was finally listening.

Suddenly, the ground beneath Kaela's feet started to shift, and a low, guttural growl began reverberating through the earth. The trees trembled as the rumble grew louder, deep and ominous, like a warning from the very heart of the forest. Milo's head snapped around, his face draining of color. "What the hell was that?" His voice was sharp, almost frantic. Before Kaela could respond, the earth split open with a violent crack. Jagged rocks tumbling into the abyss below. The sound of the earth tearing apart was deafening, like the world itself was being torn in two. Kaela's heart slammed into her ribs, her body instinctively jerking back, but Milo. Milo wasn't fast enough. His foot caught on a twisted root, and with a startled gasp, he pitched forward, arms flailing as he fell toward the chasm. The world seemed to freeze, the air thick and suffocating with the weight of the moment.

"Milo!" Kaela screamed, the sound raw and desperate, her heart leaping into her throat as her mind screamed in panic. Her body acted before her thoughts could catch up. She reached out, instinctively, without thinking. Her fingers tingled with an unfamiliar, electric warmth, a jolt that shot up her arm, spreading through her veins like wildfire. The sensation was stronger now, more real, more urgent. It was the same feeling she had when she touched the map, but now it was raw, untamed. A rush of power surged through her body, a force so intense it felt like it could split her in two. The pulse of energy shot from her hand in a blinding flash of light. Time seemed to stretch, every second dragging on as the pulse wrapped around Milo, halting his fall just inches from the edge of the chasm. The air hummed with the power that radiated from her, the energy swirling like a storm, crackling with life. Kaela's breath hitched, her chest tight as she clung to the pulse, willing it to stay, to hold strong.

Her vision blurred at the edges as the power drained from her, like the light was being siphoned from her very soul. Her heartbeat thundered in her ears, every thrum of blood in her veins synchronized with the crackling energy that now surrounded Milo. The world felt like it was on the verge of breaking, as if she was teetering on the edge of something immense and incomprehensible.

With a grunt, Milo managed to shoot toward a nearby tree, his fingers desperately wrapping around the rough bark as his body shook with the effort. "Kaela, what did you just do?" His voice was strained, a mix of shock and awe, his wide eyes fixed on her.

Kaela's breath was ragged, her chest heaving with the effort it took to maintain the pulse. She felt lightheaded, the world tilting beneath her as the energy inside her flickered and faded. Her hand fell limp at her side, the power draining from her in an instant, leaving her breathless and shaky.

"I—I don't know," she whispered, her voice barely a breath. Her mind was spinning, trying to make sense of what had just happened. She had never felt anything like it before. Like the land itself had answered her, like the magic of the Garden had surged through her in that moment. "I didn't mean to . . . but I couldn't let you fall."

Milo stood slowly, his face pale, his eyes still wide with a mixture of speechlessness and awe. "That was . . . that was something," he muttered, shaking his head. "Whatever that was, Kaela, it's like nothing I've ever seen before." His voice cracked slightly, his hands trembling as he wiped them against his pants, as though trying to rid himself of the lingering sense of wonder and fear.

Kaela could only nod, still trying to wrap her mind around what had just happened. She had felt something, a deep, primal urge to protect, to save him. And somehow, her body had responded. But what was this power? And why had it manifested now, in this moment? She didn't have time to think about it further. The ground trembled again, more violently this time. The trees groaned as though they were being pulled from their roots.

"We need to move," Kaela said urgently, her voice trembling. "Now."

Each step Kaela took seemed to evoke the very land beneath her feet. The ground was soft, but it held a strange energy, like it was alive, watching them. The map in her hand flickered erratically, its light pulsing in rhythm with her heartbeat, as though the forest itself recognized her touch. It guided her forward, its glow dim but insistent, like a beacon calling her deeper into the heart of the wilderness.

Milo was a few paces ahead, his energy scanner clicking and whirring in his hands, his brow furrowed in concentration. "We're getting closer," he murmured, not looking back. The scanner's lights blinked erratically, and he adjusted its settings with quick, practiced movements. "But there's something blocking the signal . . . I can't get a clear read."

Kaela barely heard him, her mind too preoccupied with the sensation growing inside her. It was a low hum, deep and resonant, like the pulse of the earth itself. It echoed through her veins, filling her with a strange warmth that spread through her chest and out to her fingertips. The further they went, the stronger the pull became, a magnetic force drawing her deeper into the forest, into the unknown. The path ahead was becoming more perilous, the ground uneven and cluttered with twisted roots and rocks that bulged up like the bones of some long-dead creature. But Kaela didn't notice. Her feet moved with purpose, her thoughts consumed by the growing connection she felt to the land, to the magic hidden within it. She could almost hear it now, a faint whisper in the breeze, a beckoning. Her father, the Garden, the power inside her, it was all starting to make sense, but only just. She didn't know how or why this was happening, but she knew one thing: she was meant to be here. The land, the forest, the magic, it was all calling to her, and she was finally listening. Milo's voice broke through her thoughts. "You okay?" He glanced over his shoulder at her, his expression unreadable.

Kaela hesitated, her eyes still on the path ahead. "Yeah," she said softly. "I'm just . . . trying to make sense of all of this. It's like I'm connected to this place, to the magic. It feels . . . overwhelming."

Milo's brow furrowed in thought, his scanner clicking softly as he adjusted the settings again. "You're not the only one feeling it," he said, his voice quiet but tinged with concern. "Something's definitely off here. The forest is, well, it's not just a forest. There's something under the surface, something waiting."

Kaela gave him a faint smile, though it didn't reach her eyes. "I feel it too. It's like the air itself is alive."

They continued in silence for a few moments, the awkwardness between them palpable. The air grew thicker, the trees pressing closer as if they were watching their every move. Kaela's mind drifted back to her father, the garden, and the sudden surge of power she had felt earlier. She still didn't understand it, but it was real. It was inside her.

"I didn't even know I could do that," she said, her voice almost lost in the stillness of the forest. "Back there, with the chasm . . . It was like my body just acted without me even thinking. I don't know how I did it."

Milo paused for a moment, looking at her with a mixture of awe and concern. "I don't know what happened either. But I've never seen anything like it. That energy. It was like the whole forest responded to you."

Kaela looked down at her hands, as if expecting them to glow again, but they remained still. "I can't control it. I'm not even sure I want to. It's like—" She searched for the words, but they escaped her. "It's like I'm tapping into something I don't fully understand. Something powerful."

Milo nodded, his eyes softening. "I get it. It's scary. But you're not alone in this, Kaela. Whatever's happening, we'll figure it out. Together."

The sincerity in his voice caught her off guard, and for a moment, warmth spread through her chest. The tension, fear, and uncertainty she had been carrying seemed to melt away. His words, simple but genuine, made her feel lighter. In that instant, everything felt a little less heavy.

"Thanks, Milo," Kaela said, her voice barely above a whisper. She gave him a small, genuine smile. "I'm glad you're here with me."

Milo offered a small smile in return, his eyes meeting hers with understanding. "Wouldn't want to be anywhere else. Although it's dangerous, it's kinda awesome."

The forest around them seemed to shift, the sounds growing quieter, the trees more imposing. It was as though the very land was holding its breath, waiting for something to happen. Kaela felt the weight of it, but instead of fear, a strange sense of determination filled her. She didn't know what was ahead, but she knew one thing: she had to keep going. The map in her hand flickered again, its light more erratic now. But Kaela wasn't afraid. Whatever lay ahead, she was ready. She was connected to this place in a way she couldn't explain, and she was determined to understand why. The land called to her, the magic surged within her, and though she didn't have all the answers, she felt the pull of the Garden growing stronger with every step.

"We're getting closer," Kaela said, her voice steady now, her confidence slowly returning. "I can feel it."

Milo looked at her, his expression unreadable for a moment before his lips quirked into a faint smile. "I can feel it too," he said. "Let's just hope we don't run into any more surprises."

Kaela laughed softly, the sound almost drowned out by the whispering breeze that seemed to stir the trees around them. "If we do, we'll deal with them like we always do."

They continued onward, their steps in sync as they moved deeper into the forest, the air thick with the promise of what lay ahead. Kaela's mind raced with questions, but beneath it all, a sense of certainty blossomed in her chest. She was meant to be here, in this moment, on this path. The magic of the Garden was calling, and she was finally ready to listen.

Chapter 9

Kaela and Milo continued their journey through the decaying wilderness, each step taking them further from the safety of Dome 5 and into the unknown. The forest was eerily quiet, the silence interrupted only by the occasional rustle of leaves or the distant cry of a creature they couldn't see. The further they traveled, the more Kaela felt the weight of their mission pressing on her shoulders. The Garden was out there, waiting for them. But as each hour passed, she couldn't shake the nagging feeling that something, someone, was watching them.

Milo was a few steps ahead, his face focused and determined, but his eyes darting around with a mix of caution and curiosity. He had been silent since their encounter with the creature earlier, undoubtedly lost in thought, trying to make sense of what had happened with Kaela's powers. But there was something else in his expression now. A quiet alertness that told Kaela he felt it too.

The air felt different here, charged with something unseen, like static before a storm. And then, as if the forest had been waiting for this very moment, they stumbled upon something that made Kaela's blood run cold. The trees ahead had been pushed aside, their trunks scarred and splintered. At first, Kaela thought it was just another part of the natural decay, but as they drew closer, she saw something metallic gleaming in the dim light. The forest had been scarred by something much more unnatural than nature itself.

A structure, ruined, but unmistakable, lay half-buried in the underbrush. Its sleek, dark surfaces were covered in vines and moss, but the edges were sharp and angular, as if it had been built with precision. There were no windows, no doors. Only a series of smooth, overlapping panels that looked out of place in the natural surroundings. The structure hummed faintly, like it was still alive, though Kaela couldn't understand how.

"What is this?" Milo whispered, his voice filled with suspicion and curiosity.

Kaela's throat tightened as she took a cautious step forward. "Technomancer tech," she said, barely above a whisper. "It has to be. But how . . .? This doesn't belong here."

Milo looked at her, his brow furrowed. "But this is . . . it's outside the Dome. How could they have—"

"I don't know," Kaela interrupted, her voice trembling with unease. "But it's theirs. It's all theirs."

The two of them stood at the edge of the strange structure, the faint hum of energy growing louder as they approached. Kaela's heart beats faster in her chest, the feeling of something watching them intensifying with each passing second. She couldn't shake the sense that this place, this technology, was not just a remnant of the past. It was a warning. A message.

"Should we . . . should we go inside?" Milo asked, his voice hesitant.

Kaela shook her head. "I don't think we should. Not yet. We don't know what's inside or what it might do."

Milo didn't look convinced, but he nodded, his curiosity clearly warring with his caution. His eyes lingered on the strange structure, his fingers twitching as if itching to take it apart and study it. Kaela, however, couldn't shake the unease prickling at the back of her mind. Her instincts were screaming at her to tread carefully. The Technomancers never left their tech lying around by accident. This wasn't some forgotten outpost, a relic abandoned to time. This was deliberate, intentional. A trap, perhaps, or a warning.

They moved cautiously around the structure, their footsteps crunching softly on the overgrown ground. Every inch of the surface seemed to respond, shifting almost imperceptibly under their hands as they searched for a way in. The panels, sleek and dark, responded to their touch, humming faintly as though acknowledging their presence. Yet, despite the faint vibrations, they remained resolutely sealed, refusing to yield even a crack.

Kaela pressed her palm firmly against one of the panels, closing her eyes to focus. She tried to sense something, anything that might reveal the mechanism behind its design. The surface was unnervingly smooth, offering no clues, no hidden seams. Frustration welled up inside her, and she pulled her hand back with a sharp exhale, taking a step away to reassess. That's when she saw it.

A faint glow at the base of the structure caught her attention, its light barely visible beneath a tangle of moss and dirt. It was subtle, easy to miss, but something about it drew her in. Her heart quickened as she crouched down, brushing away the overgrowth with trembling fingers. The damp earth clung stubbornly to her hands, but as she cleared the debris, a small, circular indentation came into view.

It wasn't just a mark in the ground. It was alive. A soft hum pulsed from it, a rhythmic thrum that seemed to resonate deep in her chest. Kaela froze, her fingers hovering just above the indentation. There was something achingly familiar about the energy emanating from it, a faint whisper of recognition tugging at the edges of her mind.

"This . . . this feels familiar," she murmured under her breath, her voice barely audible over the hum. A memory stirred, unbidden, of her father's voice warning her about the Technomancers, about how their technology wasn't just machinery but something far more sinister. Alive in ways most couldn't understand. Her breath caught as a chill ran down her spine.

"Milo," she called, her voice breaking the heavy silence. "I think I've found something."

He was at her side in an instant, his expression cautious but loaded with curiosity. "What is it?" he asked, leaning in for a closer look.

Kaela didn't answer immediately. Instead, she pressed her hand into the indentation, the surface cool and unnervingly smooth against her palm. For a moment, nothing happened, and then the ground beneath her shuddered ever so slightly. A low, resonant hum echoed through the air as the panel in front of them shifted with a soft, mechanical groan.

A hidden compartment slid open, revealing something unexpected: a small, glowing orb nestled within. Its surface was perfectly smooth, almost crystalline, and it radiated a soft, pulsating light. The hum it emitted matched the rhythm of the structure itself, as if the two were connected, part of a larger, breathing system.

Milo leaned closer, his eyes wide with fascination. "What is that?" he whispered, his voice barely above a breath.

Kaela didn't answer immediately. Her fingers hovered over the orb, the energy it radiated thrumming against her skin. There was something unnervingly alive about it, as though it was watching, waiting. She hesitated, her instincts warring with her curiosity.

"I don't know," she finally admitted, her voice low. "But I think we just found a key."

"A key to what?" Milo asked, his eyes wide.

Kaela held the orb in her hand, its weight surprisingly light yet unnervingly significant. The low, pulsing glow emanating from its crystalline surface illuminated her face, casting strange, shifting shadows across her features. She stared at it with a mix of fear and fascination, her heart pounding as the hum it emitted seemed to sync with her own heartbeat.

"I think it's connected to the Garden," she said, her voice barely above a whisper, as if speaking louder might shatter the fragile moment. Her fingers tightened slightly around the orb as a wave of recognition washed over her, bringing with it a memory she hadn't realized she still carried. "And somehow . . . to my father. This is part of what he was searching for."

Milo glanced at her, his brows furrowed in confusion. "What makes you so sure?" he asked, crouching beside her, his gaze darting between her and the strange object.

Kaela didn't answer right away. Instead, she let her mind drift back, her thoughts tumbling through the years to the passing moments she had shared with her father before he vanished. She could almost hear his voice, low and filled with the quiet intensity he always carried when speaking about his work. He had never told her much, but she remembered the way his hands would linger over old maps, tracing lines that didn't seem to lead anywhere, his lips moving as though reciting a silent prayer.

"There's a pattern to everything," he had once said, his eyes distant, as if seeing something far beyond the walls of their home. "The Garden . . . it's not just a place, Kaela. It's alive. It calls those who are meant to find it."

And then there was the pendant he always wore, the one she had held in her hands after he disappeared. It bore a design etched into its surface, a swirling, intricate symbol she hadn't been able to decipher. Now, staring at the orb, her breath caught in her throat. That same symbol was faintly visible within the orb, shifting and shimmering like smoke trapped in glass.

Kaela swallowed hard, her fingers trembling as she tilted the orb slightly, the glow intensifying for a brief moment. "This symbol," she said, her voice steadier now as she pointed to the faint etching inside. "It's the same one on my father's pendant. He used to say it was the key to everything, that it would guide him to the Garden."

Milo's eyes widened, his curiosity overtaking his caution. "You think he left this here? That he knew we'd find it?"

"I don't know," Kaela admitted, her voice tinged with both hope and fear. "But I can feel it, Milo. This isn't just some random piece of tech. It's connected to him . . . and to me."

The orb's hum grew slightly louder, as if responding to her words, and a strange warmth spread through her hand, seeping into her skin. Kaela's heart raced as she looked up at Milo, her determination hardening. "Whatever this is, it's part of the puzzle he was trying to solve. And now . . . it's our turn."

They stood in silence for a long moment, the weight of their discovery heavy between them. The orb in Kaela's hand pulsed with a quiet urgency. She couldn't shake the feeling that it was waiting for something. Waiting for her to act.

"Kaela," Milo said softly, breaking the silence. "I think we need to get out of here. Whatever this is . . . it's not just a relic. It's alive. And I'm not sure it's something we should be messing with."

Kaela hesitated, the orb still humming faintly in her hand. Part of her wanted to keep studying it further, to understand what it meant. But Milo was right. There was something off about this place, something she couldn't explain. It felt wrong. She slipped the orb into her pack, her fingers lingering on it for a moment longer than necessary. She didn't know why, but she felt that she needed it. That it was somehow connected to the answers she sought.

"I know," Kaela said, her voice distant. "But we can't just leave it here. It's part of the puzzle. And I think it's the key to finding my father."

Milo nodded slowly, but there was a lingering concern in his eyes. "Alright. But we're not staying here any longer than we have to. Something about this place feels . . . off."

Kaela agreed, but there was something else gnawing at her, something deeper. As they turned to leave, Kaela felt a shiver run down her spine. She couldn't explain it, but she felt like they weren't alone. Like something was watching them, waiting. They started to move away from the structure, the air feeling heavier with each step. But just as they turned a corner, a distant sound made Kaela freeze in her tracks.

A low rumble echoed through the trees, reverberating through the dense forest like the growl of a slumbering beast. The sound vibrated the ground beneath their feet, sending a faint tremor up Kaela's legs. She froze, her breath hitching in her throat, and her heart thudding painfully against her ribs. The air around them seemed to thicken, heavy with the kind of silence that only came before something seemingly terrible.

The forest loomed on all sides, an endless expanse of towering trees with trunks so wide they looked like ancient sentinels standing guard. Their bark was rough and dark, mottled with patches of moss and glowing fungi that cast an eerie, bluish light over the undergrowth. Vines draped from the branches above like tangled threads of a forgotten web, swaying slightly even though the air was still. Shadows danced between the trees, shifting and morphing as if the forest itself were alive, watching, waiting.

Kaela's gaze darted around, her instincts screaming at her to run, but her feet felt rooted to the ground. The soft rustle of leaves overhead made her flinch, and her hand instinctively went to the dagger strapped to her side. She glanced at Milo, who stood just a few steps away, his jaw tight and his knuckles white as he gripped the handle of his satchel. His eyes flickered to hers, and though he didn't say a word, the fear in them mirrored her own.

The rumble came again, deeper this time, like a warning growl. It seemed to come from everywhere and nowhere all at once, wrapping around them and setting every nerve in Kaela's body on edge. The trees themselves seemed to respond, their branches creaking and groaning as if shifting under some unseen force.

Kaela turned slowly, scanning the forest for any sign of movement. The faint glow of the fungi barely penetrated the dense underbrush, leaving long, jagged shadows in its wake. Her eyes caught on the faint shimmer of dew clinging to the leaves, reflecting the eerie light like tiny, fractured stars. But beyond that, there was nothing. No movement, no sign of whatever had made the sound. And yet, the feeling persisted: they weren't alone.

A sudden gust of wind swept through the clearing, stirring the loose leaves and sending a chill down Kaela's spine. The scent of damp earth and decaying foliage filled her nose, but beneath it lingered something else. It was metallic and sharp, like the faint tang of blood. The realization set her on edge, her grip tightening instinctively. Her fingers tightened around the hilt of her dagger as she forced herself to speak, her voice low and strained. "Whatever it is . . . it's close."

Milo swallowed hard, his eyes scanning the darkness beyond the faint circle of light they stood in. "Do you think it's Technomancers?" he whispered, his voice barely audible over the distant hum of the forest.

A crack echoed to their left, sharp and sudden, breaking the tense silence. Both Kaela and Milo spun toward the sound, their breaths caught in their throats. The shadows seemed to shift again, and for a brief moment, Kaela thought she saw a glint of something. A pair of eyes, reflecting the faint glow of the fungi. But when she blinked, it was gone, swallowed by the darkness.

Kaela took a shaky step back, her voice trembling. "We need to keep moving."

Milo nodded, his movements jerky and uncertain, but he didn't argue. Together, they turned toward the faint path ahead, their steps careful and deliberate as they pushed through the thick underbrush. The rumble came again, closer this time, and Kaela couldn't shake the feeling that whatever was out there wasn't just following them. It was hunting them.

Kaela's heart pounded in her chest, the rapid rhythm drowning out the chaos of her thoughts. Her mind spun in a frantic whirl, searching for clarity but finding only fragments of understanding. She didn't have an answer, no explanation for the creeping tension that filled the air. All she knew, all she could grasp onto, was the undeniable truth pressing down on her like a weight: they once again, were no longer alone.

Chapter 10

The forest had grown darker. Though the sun was still up, its light barely penetrated the dense canopy of twisted branches and thick vines. The further Kaela and Milo ventured, the more suffocating the wilderness became. Every step felt heavier, every sound sharper, every shadow alive with the threat of the unknown.

Kaela walked a step behind Milo, her hand gripping the strap of her pack as her mind churned. The discovery of the Technomancer structure still weighed heavily on her. The orb nestled in her pack, humming faintly, almost imperceptibly, but enough for her to feel its presence. She hadn't told Milo, but touching it had left her with a lingering sensation. A warmth in her chest, as if the orb were somehow connected to her. To the Garden. To her father.

But the weight of the journey was beginning to press down on her. She had always imagined the wilderness outside Dome 5 was empty and lifeless. She had been wrong. This place wasn't just alive. It was wild, unpredictable, and filled with dangers she hadn't even begun to comprehend.

"Stay close," Milo said, his voice low and taut as it broke the uneasy silence. He glanced over his shoulder, his eyes darting through the dim light filtering down from the canopy above. In his hand, he clutched one of his inventions, a small, cylindrical device with a glowing blue core that pulsed faintly, casting a ghostly light across his knuckles.

Earlier, he had explained it was a type of sonar, designed to detect movement within a set radius. Kaela had watched it flicker a few times, its light dimming and flaring to indicate faint activity somewhere in the distance. Each time, Milo had waved it off, his tone calm, assuring her it was nothing more than wildlife. But now, his grip on the device was white-knuckled, and his pace had shifted from cautious curiosity to something sharper, more deliberate.

Kaela quickened her steps to keep up, the soft crunch of leaves beneath her boots sounding too loud in the oppressive quiet. The air around them felt heavy, like the forest itself was holding its breath. "You're tense," she said, trying to keep her voice steady, though the knot in her stomach betrayed her own growing unease.

Milo didn't look at her. "Because I'm not stupid," he muttered, his words clipped. His gaze swept the trees again, scanning the shadows that seemed to shift and twist just out of reach.

"Something's been trailing us since we left that structure."

Kaela's heart skipped a beat, her stomach twisting tighter. She had felt it too. The subtle prickling at the back of her neck, the sensation of being watched. The forest was alive with sounds, the creak of branches and the rustle of leaves, but beneath it all was something quieter, more deliberate, a presence she couldn't shake.

"You think it's . . . Technomancers?" she asked, her voice barely above a whisper, as though speaking the word might summon them.

Milo shook his head sharply, his jaw tightening. "If it were Technomancers, You think they'd let us keep moving?," he said, his tone grim. His eyes never stopped scanning, the faint blue glow of the device casting fleeting light on his face. "No, this feels . . . different."

Kaela swallowed hard, her mouth dry. That answer wasn't exactly comforting. She looked over her shoulder, her eyes searching the dense undergrowth behind them. The trees stood like silent sentinels, their gnarled branches draped with vines that swayed in the faint breeze. The light from the bioluminescent fungi scattered across the forest floor painted eerie patterns on the ground, but beyond that, the darkness was impenetrable.

The feeling of being hunted clung to her like a second skin. Whatever was out there wasn't just following them, it was watching, waiting. Kaela gripped the hilt of her dagger, her fingers slick with sweat. "Different how?" she pressed, her voice tight.

Milo hesitated, his brow furrowing as he finally slowed to a stop. He turned to face her, the glow of the sonar device reflecting in his wary eyes. "It's quieter. Smarter. Like it's deciding whether we're worth the trouble."

A chill ran down Kaela's spine as she took a step closer to him. Her instincts screamed at her to move, to run, to do something. Yet, she remained frozen, unable to act. Her eyes darted to the shadows, which seemed to deepen around them.

The device in Milo's hand pulsed brighter for a brief moment before dimming again. His expression darkened. "Whatever it is," he said quietly, "it's still out there. And it's not going away."

Kaela nodded, her throat tight, and forced herself to stay calm. As they started moving again, each step felt heavier than the last. She couldn't shake the feeling that they were being led somewhere. Into something they might not survive.

They pushed forward, the forest growing thicker and more tangled with each passing hour. The air was damp and heavy, carrying with it the faint smell of decay. Kaela's boots sank into the soft ground, and she found herself constantly pushing away low-hanging branches and thorny vines. The first attack came without warning.

A blur of motion erupted from the trees to their right, and before Kaela could react, something barreled into her, knocking her off her feet. She hit the ground hard, the air forced from her lungs as she rolled onto her back. A figure loomed over her, a gaunt man with wild eyes and tattered clothing, his face smeared with dirt. In his hand was a jagged blade that glinted in the dim light. Kaela's heart leapt into her throat. She scrambled backward, her hands clawing at the ground as the man lunged for her.

"Kaela!" Milo's voice rang out, followed by a loud crack.

The man jerked violently, his body seizing before collapsing to the ground. Kaela stared in shock, her breath caught in her throat. Smoke curled from the small stun device in Milo's hand. He didn't say a word, his grip tightening around the weapon.

"Get up!" Milo shouted, grabbing her arm and pulling her to her feet.

But there was no time to catch her breath. More figures emerged from the shadows. five, maybe six of them. each armed with crude weapons and a feral look in their eyes.

"Scavengers," Milo hissed, his voice filled with dread. "They'll strip us clean if we let them."

Kaela barely had time to process Milo's words before another attacker lunged at them, emerging from the shadows with feral speed. The scavenger's ragged clothing clung to his wiry frame, and his eyes glinted with a savage determination that sent a chill down Kaela's spine. Milo fired his stun device again, the glowing core flashing brightly, but this time the scavenger twisted to the side, dodging the shot with an agility that caught them both off guard.

The attacker closed the distance in an instant, his blade, a crude but deadly shard of metal, swinging in a vicious arc toward Kaela. She ducked, the blade slicing through the air just inches from her head, the sharp hiss making her heart slam against her ribs. Her breath came in short, panicked gasps as instinct took over. She dropped to the ground, her hand fumbling across the dirt and leaves until her fingers closed around the rough surface of a heavy branch.

With a desperate cry, Kaela surged upward and swung the branch with all her strength. It connected with the scavenger's chest, the impact sending a dull thud reverberating up her arms. He stumbled back, momentarily dazed, but the fury in his eyes didn't dim. His grip on the blade tightened, and he let out a guttural growl, his focus locking onto her like a predator ready to strike again.

"Run!" Milo shouted, his voice cutting through the chaos. He grabbed Kaela's arm and yanked her away before she could react.

Kaela stumbled but quickly found her footing, her legs pumping as she and Milo tore through the forest. The world around them became a blur of motion. The towering trees, their gnarled branches reaching like claws. The dense underbrush that snagged at their clothes. The uneven ground threatening to trip them at every step. The forest was alive with sound, their ragged breaths, the pounding of their boots, and the shouts of the scavengers behind them, growing louder with every passing second.

"They're not giving up!" Kaela shouted, risking a glance over her shoulder. Her stomach twisted as she saw at least three figures weaving through the trees, their movements relentless and predatory.

"Keep moving!" Milo barked, his voice tight with urgency. "I've got an idea!"

They broke through a wall of tangled vines and stumbled into a small clearing, the sudden openness almost disorienting. Moonlight filtered down in fragmented beams, casting an eerie, silver glow over the space. Milo skidded to a stop and dropped to one knee. His hands flew to his pack, searching for something fast.

"What are you doing?" Kaela demanded, her voice edged with panic as she glanced back toward the trees. The scavengers were closing in, their shadows flitting between the trunks.

"Buying us time," Milo said, his voice grim as he yanked out a small, spherical device. He pressed a series of buttons, the sphere coming to life with a faint hum, its surface glowing faintly blue.

"Cover your ears!" he shouted, throwing the device to the ground.

Kaela barely had time to obey, dropping to her knees and clamping her hands over her ears as tightly as she could. A blinding flash of light erupted from the sphere, turning the clearing into a searing white void. A deafening boom followed, the shockwave ripping through the air like a thunderclap, sending leaves and debris flying in all directions. The force of the blast knocked Kaela off balance, her body hitting the ground hard. Her ears rang painfully, the sound drowning out everything else, and her vision swam as she struggled to regain her bearings. She pushed herself up, her hands trembling, and turned to see the scavengers. They had stopped in their tracks, clutching their heads and staggering as if the explosion had scrambled their senses.

"Let's go!" Milo's voice cut through the haze, and Kaela felt his hand grab hers, pulling her to her feet.

They plunged back into the forest, the darkness closing in around them like a living thing. The shadows seemed deeper now, the trees leaning closer together as if trying to trap them. Kaela's lungs burned with every breath, and her legs felt like lead, but she forced herself to keep going. She could still hear the scavengers behind them, their disoriented cries giving way to renewed shouts as they began to recover. Branches whipped against Kaela's face, leaving stinging scratches, and roots jutted up from the ground, threatening to trip her. Her pack bounced heavily against her back, its weight a constant reminder of the supplies they couldn't afford to lose.

"Milo, how far—" she started, her voice breaking, but he cut her off.

"Just keep moving!" he shouted, his tone sharper than she'd ever heard.

The forest seemed endless, every direction blending into a

tangle of blackened trunks and shifting shadows. The faint bioluminescent fungi scattered across the ground gave the scene an otherworldly glow, but it did little to light their way. Kaela's body screamed for rest, her muscles aching with every step, but the sound of the scavengers' pursuit kept her moving. She risked another glance back, her heart plummeting as she saw the first of them emerge into the faint light behind them.

"They're catching up!" she gasped, her voice raw with fear.

Milo didn't respond this time, his focus locked on the path ahead. When he glanced back at her, the look in his eyes said everything. They were running out of options. And fast.

"We can't outrun them!" she gasped, clutching Milo's arm.

Milo glanced at her, his face pale and drenched in sweat. "We don't have a choice!"

But Kaela knew he was wrong. They couldn't keep running. The scavengers were faster, more familiar with the terrain. If they didn't do something, they wouldn't make it. And then she felt it. The same warmth she had felt when she touched the orb, the same energy that had surged through her when the vines had saved Milo from the crack in the ground. It was faint at first, like a whisper at the edge of her mind, but it grew stronger with each passing second.

Kaela skidded to a stop, her hand outstretched. "Milo, wait!"

"What are you doing?" Milo demanded, his voice filled with panic.

Kaela didn't answer. She closed her eyes, focusing on the energy coursing through her veins. She didn't know what she was doing, didn't fully understand how it worked, but she knew she had to try. The ground beneath her feet seemed to tremble, and then, as if in response to her unspoken command, the forest came alive. Vines shot out from the underbrush, twisting and coiling like serpents. They lashed out at the scavengers, wrapping around their arms and legs, pulling them to the ground. Kaela opened her eyes, her breath catching in her throat as she watched the scene unfold. The scavengers struggled against the vines, their cries of rage turning to panic as they were ensnared.

"Kaela . . ." Milo's voice was barely audible, thick with emotion.

She turned to him, her breath still ragged, her hands trembling uncontrollably. "We have to go," she said, her voice breaking. "Now."

They didn't stop running until the forest had swallowed the scavengers' shouts and the pounding of footsteps completely. The oppressive silence returned, broken only by the rasp of their labored breathing and the faint rustle of leaves overhead. Kaela stumbled to a halt and collapsed against a tree, her back sliding down the rough bark until she was sitting on the damp forest floor. Her chest heaved, and her lungs burned as she struggled to catch her breath. Milo paced a few steps away, his hands gripping the back of his head, his expression a storm of fear, disbelief, and something she couldn't quite name.

"What the hell was that?" he demanded, his voice sharp, cracking slightly at the edges.

Kaela dropped her gaze to her hands, staring at them as if they belonged to someone else. They still trembled from the surge of energy that had coursed through her, leaving a strange, buzzing sensation beneath her skin. "I . . . I don't know," she said finally, her voice barely above a whisper. "It just . . . happened."

"That's not good enough, Kaela!" Milo snapped, his frustration cutting through the stillness. He stopped pacing and turned to her, his eyes searching hers for answers she didn't have. "You. Those vines. They moved. They moved like they were alive, like they were listening to you!"

Kaela's throat tightened, her vision blurring with tears she refused to let fall. She pressed her palms against her thighs, as though grounding herself could make sense of what had just happened. "I don't understand it either," she admitted, her voice shaking. "But it's not the first time."

Milo froze. "What do you mean?"

She hesitated, her chest tightening as she forced herself to meet his gaze. "Back in the forest," she began, her voice trembling, "when you almost got pulled into the abyss. The vines. They saved you then, too. They moved on their own. Or maybe . . ." She swallowed hard, her voice dropping to a whisper. "Maybe it was me."

Milo stared at her, his face pale, his expression unreadable. He took a slow step toward her, his hands falling to his sides. "You're connected to this place," he said, his voice softer now, almost reverent. "To the Garden. To all of it. You can feel it, can't you?"

Kaela nodded, a tear slipping down her cheek before she could stop it. "I can," she whispered. "And it terrifies me, Milo. I don't know what's happening to me, but it's like . . . like the forest is alive, and it's inside me too. I can feel it changing me." She pressed a trembling hand to her chest. "And I think the Garden is at the heart of it. It's calling to me, Milo. I don't know why, but I can't ignore it."

Milo exhaled sharply, running a hand through his disheveled hair. He looked away for a moment, his jaw tightening, before turning back to her. "Then we need to get there," he said firmly. "Before something worse finds us. Before it's too late."

Kaela wiped at her face, nodding as she forced herself to her feet. Her legs felt like they might give out beneath her, but she steadied herself against the tree, her resolve hardening. The scavengers had been a brutal reminder of the dangers they faced, but they had also shown her something else. Her powers were real, and they were growing. If she was going to survive this journey, she would have to learn to control them. For her father. For the Garden. For herself.

Chapter 11

The air shifted as they moved further away from the chaos of the scavenger attack. The oppressive dampness of the forest began to lift, replaced by a strange stillness that made Kaela's skin prickle. The terrain was changing. She could feel it in the ground beneath her boots, in the way the light softened, spilling through the thinning canopy above.

Milo trudged ahead, his jaw set in quiet determination. His pack jingled faintly with the tools and gadgets he'd cobbled together for this journey, though his earlier energy had dimmed. Kaela couldn't blame him. The weight of what they had endured. The scavengers and her powers pressed heavily on them both.

Kaela adjusted the straps of her pack and glanced at the faintly glowing orb nestled inside. She could still feel its warmth through the fabric, a subtle pulse that seemed to sync with her own heartbeat. It was like the map was alive, guiding them not just with coordinates but with some unseen force.

The silence between them had stretched thin, heavy with tension, when Milo's voice broke through. "We should be there anytime now," he said, his tone low but steady.

Kaela blinked, pulled from her swirling thoughts by the weight of his words. She adjusted her grip on the orb, its faint warmth grounding her. "How can you tell?"

Milo stopped and turned toward her, holding up the cylindrical device he'd been using to track their path. The blue core at its center glowed brighter than before, casting an eerie light. A faint hum vibrated through the still air, resonating in her chest. It felt almost as if the device itself were alive, pulsing with energy.

"The readings are spiking," he explained, his gaze locked on the device. "Whatever's out here, it's massive. Bigger than anything I've ever picked up before. Then again, I've never really left the dome," she said jokingly, although Kaela could tell that Milo's nerves were still tense.

Kaela followed his line of sight for a moment before letting her gaze drift ahead. The dense forest around them was beginning to thin, the towering trees parting to reveal a vast, open expanse. Beyond the treeline, something loomed in the distance. A shimmering, luminous shape that defied logic. It felt alive, yet ancient, like it had always been there, hidden in plain sight.

Her breath hitched as the energy in the air shifted, growing heavier. The orb in her hand pulsed faintly, as if responding to whatever was out there. "Do you think it's the Garden?" she asked, her voice quiet.

Milo turned to her, his expression cautious but calm. The glow from the device illuminated the sharp lines of his face, making him look older than he was. "If it's not," he said slowly, "then I don't know what else it could be."

Kaela nodded, her stomach tightening as her thoughts churned. She had spent years listening to fragments of stories about the Garden, but standing here, so close to whatever this was, unease crept into her mind. What if they were wrong? What if this wasn't the Garden, but something far worse?

Milo noticed her hesitation and stepped closer, his voice softening. "We've come too far to stop now," he said.

She met his eyes, appreciating the quiet determination she saw there. Milo had always been her partner in every sense. Her problem-solver, her sounding board, her tether to reason when her mind ran wild. He didn't have to say anything more. His presence alone reminded her why they were here.

Kaela let out a slow breath and nodded again. "You're right. Let's keep moving."

They stepped forward together, the dense trees giving way to a strange, ethereal glow that bathed the landscape ahead. The orb in her hand grew warmer, its pulse syncing with the energy all around them. Whatever lay ahead was waiting for them, and Kaela knew, deep in her core, that this moment was part of a larger purpose. She glanced at Milo, who kept his focus trained ahead, the glowing device still clutched in his hand. They didn't need words. This wasn't just her journey, it was theirs. And together, they would face whatever waited beyond the treeline.

The forest's edge loomed closer with every step, and Kaela found herself gripping the straps of her pack tighter. Her mind was a swirl of emotions. Excitement, fear, curiosity. The map had been their guide, its glowing lines and shifting symbols leading them through the wilderness. But now, standing on the cusp of something entirely unknown, she couldn't help but feel a flicker of doubt. What if the Garden wasn't what they thought it was? What if it held no answers, only more questions? Kaela shook her head, forcing herself to focus. She had come too far to second-guess herself now.

"Milo," Kaela murmured, adjusting her pack as the faint glow of the orb cast shifting light over the trees. The air was cooler here, Lighter, and she found herself stealing glances at her oldest friend. His expression was set, serious, but his brow furrowed just slightly, a telltale sign that his mind was running faster than his feet.

He must have noticed her hesitation because he slowed his pace, glancing over his shoulder. "Kaela," he said, his voice softer now. "You, okay?"

The gentleness in his tone caught her off guard. She stopped, brushing a strand of copper hair from her face as she tried to steady her thoughts. "I'm fine," she replied, though her voice wavered slightly. "Just . . . trying to wrap my head around all of this."

Milo studied her for a moment, his gaze flicking briefly to the pack slung over her shoulder, where the orb pulsed faintly, as if alive. "You think your dad really found it? The Garden?"

The question hit her like a wave. She swallowed hard, her throat tightening as the memories rushed in. The countless nights she'd spent, staring at the stars, imagining what it would be like to hear her father's voice again. The moments when she swore she felt his presence, only to remember he was gone. The ache in her chest had dulled over the months, but it never truly left.

"I don't know," she admitted finally, her voice barely above a whisper. "I've been holding onto the idea that he did. That he found it, and maybe . . . maybe he left something behind. Something that can help us understand what's happening to me."

Milo's face softened, his usual quick wit replaced by something deeper, an understanding she wasn't sure anyone else could offer. He had been there through all of it. The whispered arguments between her father and her aunt, the empty promises, the silence that followed his disappearance. He had never once pushed her to talk about it, but he had always been there when she needed someone to listen.

"We'll figure it out," he said firmly, his voice steady but warm. "Whatever's out there. Whatever he was looking for, we'll find it. Together."

Kaela felt a flicker of gratitude in the chaos. She managed a small smile, the kind that didn't quite reach her eyes but carried the weight of her trust in him. "Thanks, Milo. For . . . everything."

He shrugged, but the corners of his mouth lifted just slightly. "Hey, someone's gotta keep you from running headfirst into trouble. Might as well be me." She let out a soft laugh, and for a moment, the tension in the air seemed to lift.

As they stepped out of the dense forest and into the open, the world seemed to transform before their eyes. The thick canopy that had shielded them from the sky parted, revealing a vast expanse above, painted in the warm, rich hues of gold and deep indigo. The air felt lighter, fresher, as though the weight of the forest had lifted with every step. Ahead, the ground sloped downward into a wide valley, its contours bathed in the soft glow of twilight. In the distance, something vast and luminous shimmered, its radiance almost ethereal against the darkening landscape.

Milo paused, his gaze fixed on the horizon. "Guess this is it," he said quietly.

Kaela nodded, her chest tightening as she stared at the faint glow in the distance. "Yeah. This is it." And as they stood there, side by side, Kaela felt the weight of what was to come, but also the comfort of knowing she wouldn't face it alone.

Kaela's breath caught in her throat as she stepped into the clearing, her eyes wide with wonder and disbelief. Before her stretched the Garden's outskirts, a landscape so impossibly beautiful it felt as though it were a dream. One too vivid to be real. The ground beneath her feet was no longer the damp, decaying soil of the forest, but a lush carpet of moss so vibrant it seemed to glow from within, shimmering with iridescent hues of green and gold as though it were alive, breathing with her every step. The soft, springy texture of it underfoot was like nothing she had ever felt before, as though the earth itself was welcoming her.

Towering plants, both alien and majestic, loomed around her, their long, slender stems twisting upward into the sky. Each leaf was a delicate crystal, translucent and glimmering in the soft light, their edges catching the sun's rays and scattering them into thousands of tiny, prismatic sparks. The air shimmered with a kaleidoscope of colors as the leaves swayed in an invisible breeze, their movements so fluid and graceful it was as though they were dancing in harmony with some silent, unseen rhythm.

And the flowers, strange, ethereal things, bloomed in vibrant clusters, their petals soft and glowing like the embers of a fire, casting a warm, pulsing light that bathed the ground in a gentle, golden glow. Each blossom seemed to pulse with life, its colors shifting slowly, almost imperceptibly, as though responding to the beat of Kaela's heart. Some flowers unfurled in intricate patterns, their petals opening and closing in time with the rhythmic pulse of the air, while others glowed with a soft, inner fire that reminded her of the warmth of a distant sun.

But it wasn't just the beauty that overwhelmed her. It was the energy, the power that radiated from the very ground she stood on. It was in the air, in the weight of the atmosphere, in the way the plants seemed to hum with life. She could feel it deep in her bones, like a subtle vibration that resonated through her entire body, drawing her in, beckoning her to come closer, to reach out and touch it. It was a pulse, a living heartbeat that thrummed in perfect sync with her own, as though the Garden itself was aware of her presence.

Kaela took a tentative step forward, her heart racing as she felt the energy surge around her. It was unlike anything she had ever experienced. An electric, almost tangible force that thrummed through the air and into her very soul. It resonated with something deep inside her, a connection she couldn't explain but felt with every fiber of her being. The power was alive here, not just in the plants and flowers, but in the very air, the very ground, in the pulse of the world itself.

Her eyes flicked to Milo, who stood beside her, equally mesmerized by the surreal beauty of the place. He was quiet, his gaze lost in the vastness of the Garden. She could sense the weight of the moment in the stillness between them, the unspoken understanding that this was something neither of them could fully comprehend yet. They had crossed into something beyond their wildest imaginations, something ancient, powerful, and alive. Kaela closed her eyes for a moment, letting the energy wash over her, feeling it deep inside, pulling at her, like a magnet drawing her toward something she couldn't yet see. Something that felt like home.

Milo let out a low whistle, his eyes wide with wonder. "This . . . this is insane. It's like stepping into another world."

Kaela nodded, unable to tear her gaze away from the landscape. "It's beautiful," she murmured, her voice barely above a whisper.

But it wasn't just the breathtaking beauty that gripped her, it was something deeper, something that resonated in her very core. There was a sense of recognition in the air, a silent acknowledgment that seemed to echo through the space around her. The energy that hummed so vibrantly didn't just surround her. It reached out, caressing her like a long-lost memory, as if the Garden itself knew her, understood her. It was as though the land had been waiting for her arrival, its pulse aligning with her own in a perfect, unspoken connection. The pull was undeniable, magnetic, tugging at her from within and drawing her forward with a force she couldn't resist. It was a call, ancient and familiar, whispering through the very fibers of her being, urging her to step closer, to trust the path unfolding before her.

Milo crouched down near a patch of moss, pulling out one of his scanning devices. "This stuff is . . . alive, but not like anything I've seen before. It's emitting some kind of bioelectric signal. I don't even know how to describe it."

Kaela knelt beside him, running her fingers over the moss. It was soft, almost warm to the touch, and it seemed to hum faintly under her fingertips. "It feels . . . alive," she said, echoing his words.

Milo's words hung in the air, heavy with a truth Kaela wasn't sure she was ready to face. His gaze lingered on her, a mixture of curiosity and concern in his eyes. "You're connected to this place, aren't you? Like, really connected."

Kaela froze, her fingers grazing the moss beneath her hand. The sensation of it was like a gentle hum beneath her skin, an energy she couldn't quite explain but could feel with every fiber of her being. She knew the truth of what he was saying, but saying It out loud made it all the more real, more terrifying. Her chest tightened, and for a moment, she couldn't find the words. How could she explain something she barely understood herself? The Garden was alive, and it was pulling her in, and she was afraid of what that meant.

"I don't know how or why, but . . . yes," she finally admitted, her voice a whisper that seemed to blend with the air around them. "It's like the Garden knows me. Like it's been waiting for me."

The words tasted strange on her tongue, but there was no

denying the pull she felt, the way the energy around her seemed to hum in response to her presence. It wasn't just a physical feeling; it was something deep within, like an old friend calling her home. She felt it in the depths of her bones, in the thrum of her heart, in the weight of the air around her.

Milo didn't say anything right away. Instead, he stood up, his gaze sweeping over the surreal landscape with a mix of awe and caution. His silence stretched between them, but Kaela didn't feel the need to fill it with more words. She was too lost in the sensation of the Garden's energy swirling around her, pulling at her thoughts, making her feel both incredibly small and impossibly significant at the same time.

"If this is just the outskirts," Milo said after a beat, his voice quiet but tinged with wonder, "imagine what the heart of the Garden looks like."

Kaela turned her gaze toward the path ahead, her stomach fluttering with a mix of anticipation and something darker, something that felt like unease curling deep inside her. The corridor of glowing plants before them beckoned, their soft light casting strange shadows across the path, as if the Garden itself was trying to show them the way. But with every step, a nagging feeling gnawed at her, like eyes were watching from the depths of the trees, like something was waiting just beyond their sight.

Her breath quickened as the sensation of being watched grew

stronger. It wasn't just the beauty of the place that overwhelmed her; it was the constant hum of energy, like the Garden itself was alive, aware of their every movement. The intoxicating beauty was like a siren's call, pulling her deeper, but beneath it, she could sense the danger that lingered just beyond the edges of her awareness.

"We need to be careful," Milo said, his voice low, his eyes scanning the trees around them with a wariness Kaela knew too well. "This place might be beautiful, but we don't know what's out here."

Kaela nodded, gripping the strap of her pack tightly, using its weight to anchor herself in the present. The danger that loomed was undeniable, but the pull of the Garden was just as real, drawing her in with an almost magnetic force. She couldn't ignore it now, not after coming this far. There was no turning back.

"I know," she said, her voice steady despite the uncertainty swirling inside her. "But we didn't come this far to turn back now."

She met his eyes, and for a brief moment, she saw something in them, something more than the usual camaraderie they shared. It was a glimmer of understanding, of trust. Milo had always been the one to keep her grounded, but now, in this strange place, it felt like they were both standing on the edge of something they couldn't quite comprehend. She wasn't sure if it was the Garden's power or something else, but the bond between them felt different now, stronger somehow.

Milo's lips curled into a faint smile, a small, familiar expression that made her heart beat a little faster. "That's the Kaela I know. Stubborn as ever."

She rolled her eyes but couldn't help but smile back. Despite everything, Milo's presence was a comfort. He was her anchor, her constant in a world that was quickly unraveling into the unknown. As they continued forward, the energy around them seemed to grow stronger, more concentrated. The plants became larger, more intricate, their glowing patterns shifting as if in response to their presence.

Kaela came to a sudden halt, her fingers grazing the smooth surface of the orb in her pack. It was warm, almost too warm, pulsing gently as if it had a heartbeat of its own. The sensation sent a shiver through her, an inexplicable pull that deepened with every passing moment. She pulled it out carefully, cradling it in her hands as it seemed to hum in response, the glow from within flickering like a distant star.

"It's reacting to something," she said, her voice barely above a whisper, the words laced with a sense of awe she couldn't hide.

Milo, who had been a few paces ahead, turned quickly at the sound of her voice. His gaze sharpened as he studied the orb, his eyes narrowing in concentration. "It's like it's . . . syncing with the environment. Maybe it's a key, or a guide."

Kaela's heart raced. The orb's pulse matched the rhythm of her own heartbeat, and she couldn't shake the feeling that it was more than just a simple object. There was a connection here, something ancient and powerful, calling to her in ways she didn't understand. "If it is . . . then it's leading us straight to the Garden."

The weight of her words hung in the air, thick with anticipation. The Garden had always been an abstract idea, a dream, a story her father had whispered about in fragments before he vanished. But now, it felt so close. She could almost taste it in the air, a promise just beyond the veil of reality.

They moved forward, drawn deeper into the heart of the Garden. As they neared a cluster of crystalline trees, their shimmering branches creating an almost ethereal canopy overhead, the world around them seemed to shift. The air was thick with the scent of something sweet and strange, and the ground beneath their feet seemed to pulse in time with the orb. It was as if the land itself was alive, aware of their presence.

Milo, never one to be distracted by beauty for long, dropped his pack with a soft thud and immediately began working with one of his gadgets, his muttered words barely audible over the sound of his own focus. "Calibrations . . . energy readings . . . levels off the charts . . ."

Kaela, still mesmerized by the orb's steady glow, sat down on the moss-covered ground. She cradled it carefully, her thoughts swirling like a storm. Her father's face flickered in her mind. His voice, his passion for the Garden, his obsession with its mysteries. And now, here she was, holding a piece of it in her hands, standing on the precipice of something that could change everything.

"Do you think he ever made it here?" she asked, her voice softer now, filled with a quiet longing that surprised her.

Milo paused mid-adjustment, looking up from his work with a rare, thoughtful expression. His eyes softened, and for a moment, Kaela could see the weight of the years they had spent together in his gaze. The shared memories, the unsaid words, the way he had always been there. "If anyone could, it'd be him. Your dad was . . . well, he was a genius. And stubborn, just like you."

A small, bittersweet smile tugged at the corners of Kaela's lips, but it didn't quite reach her eyes. She looked down at the orb, its glow steady in her hands, but it was the ache in her chest that dominated her thoughts. "I just hope we find something. A clue, a sign, anything that proves he was here."

Milo stood, brushing off his hands, and sat down beside her. He didn't speak, simply offering his presence as he settled next to her. The silence between them was familiar, comforting, yet now it carried an unspoken weight. A quiet understanding passed between them, acknowledging the gravity of their situation.

"We'll find him, Kaela. Or at least the answers he was looking for. I promise."

His words were simple, but they carried a weight of sincerity that made her heart tighten. He was right, there was no turning back now. The Garden was real. Her father was real. And whatever this place held, whatever secrets it had been guarding for so long, she was ready to face them.

Kaela nodded, the resolve hardening inside her like steel being forged in fire. The Garden was out there, waiting, and she wasn't about to let it slip through her fingers. Not now, not when she was so close. She could feel the pull in her chest, stronger than ever, and she knew with absolute certainty that whatever came next, she would face it with everything she had. For herself. For her father. For the truth.

Chapter 12

Kaela stood at the edge of the crystalline grove, her breath shallow as she gripped the orb in her hands. Its warmth blended into her palms, the steady pulse of magic a rhythmic thrum that seemed to echo in time with her heartbeat. The glow from the towering crystalline trees bathed her surroundings in an otherworldly light, their translucent branches shimmering like veins of light caught in the early morning fog. Each step she took sent a soft tremor through the ground, as if the very earth was aware of her presence.

But despite the beauty of the scene, the unease that had been growing in the pit of her stomach only intensified. The Garden around her was more than just a place; it was alive in ways that she couldn't quite comprehend. The air itself hummed with energy, thick and charged, as though the land itself was breathing. It felt ancient, ancient in a way that made her feel both small in comparison, yet deeply connected to what she was seeing, as if she were standing on the edge of something much larger than herself. Yet, for all its majesty, something about the place felt . . . unsettling. The silence was too perfect, the stillness too heavy. They weren't alone here.

Her fingers gripped the orb, and the pulse inside it quickened, as though responding to the mounting tension in the air. She glanced over her shoulder at Milo, who had been quiet for the past few minutes, his face etched with concentration as he studied the surrounding area. He, too, felt it. The weight of something unseen, something watching them from the shadows.

Kaela's eyes scanned the grove, the sparkling trees now towering above her like silent sentinels. Their soft glow illuminated the thick vines that wound around their trunks, twisting and spiraling in intricate patterns. The light seemed to dance off the branches, creating reflections that shimmered like stars in a vast, midnight sky. Yet the beauty of it only served to deepen her sense of foreboding. The grove, for all its otherworldly splendor, felt like it was holding its breath, waiting for something to happen.

And then, in the distance, she saw it. A flicker of movement, barely perceptible, but enough to make her heart skip a beat. Her eyes narrowed, focusing on the shadow that shifted just beyond the reach of the glowing trees. It was too fast to make out clearly, but the feeling of being watched, of being followed, was unmistakable. The hair on the back of her neck stood on end, and she instinctively took a step closer to Milo.

He noticed immediately, his gaze snapping to her. "What is it?" he asked, his voice low, tinged with concern.

Kaela didn't answer at first. Her heart was pounding now, the pulse of the orb matching the frantic beat of her chest. She knew, deep down, that they weren't alone. Not in this place. And whatever was watching them, it wasn't just the Garden. It was something else. Something that had been waiting for them. Her fingers tightened around the orb once more, and she could feel the energy within it surging in response, as though the artifact itself recognized the danger lurking in the shadows. It wasn't just reacting to her touch, it was responding to the presence that surrounded them.

"I don't know," she said finally, her voice barely above a whisper. "But we're not alone."

Milo's eyes darted to the darkened edge of the grove, his jaw tightening. He could feel it now, too. The weight of the silence, the sense of something just beyond the trees, watching, waiting. He took a step closer to Kaela, his expression unreadable, but his stance protective.

"We need to move," he said, his voice firm. "We're too exposed here."

Kaela nodded, her mind racing as she looked around, trying to make sense of the strange, unsettling feeling that clung to the air. The Garden might be alive, but it wasn't the only thing alive here.

Something, or someone, was watching them, waiting for them to make the wrong move. The pulse of the orb in her hands grew stronger, almost urgent now, as if it, too, sensed the growing danger. With a final, lingering glance at the shadows that seemed to move just beyond the trees, Kaela took a step forward, her heart pounding in her chest. Whatever was out there, it was time to face it.

"Milo," she said softly, her voice barely audible.

He looked up from his pack, where he'd been adjusting one of his scanners. "What is it?"

Before she could answer, a voice cut through the stillness. Smooth, deep, and laced with amusement.

"Well, this is unexpected."

Kaela spun around, her grip instinctively tightening around the orb as she sensed the presence of someone, something, just beyond her. From the shadows emerged a figure, tall and imposing, his movements effortless and fluid, like a creature born of the night. He stepped into the faint light of the grove, revealing a man whose very presence seemed to command the space around him.

His caramel skin glowed softly in the ethereal light, smooth and warm-toned, emphasizing the sharp elegance of his jawline and the high slant of his cheekbones. Thick, dark curls framed his face, artfully disheveled, their inky strands brushing against his forehead. His nose was straight and well-defined, lips full with a natural curve that hinted at amusement, or danger. But it was his eyes that held her captive. Golden-green, deep and unreadable, their feline sharpness exuding an intensity that sent a shiver through her. They studied her with an almost predatory patience, as if unraveling her with a single glance.

Dressed in dark, form-fitting clothes that accentuated his lean, athletic build, he moved with a grace that made him seem like part of the shadows themselves. Every shift of his body was deliberate, his presence both effortless and consuming. Even standing still, he radiated an air of quiet confidence, a smirk playing at the corner of his lips, as if he already knew exactly how this encounter would end.

For a moment, neither of them moved. The tension between them hung heavy in the air, thick with the weight of unspoken questions. Kaela's heart raced, a strange mix of caution and curiosity bubbling within her. The man before her wasn't just anyone. He was something more, something she has felt an instant, undeniable connection to. The orb pulsed in her hand to solidify this feeling.

He tilted his head slightly, as though sizing her up, his lips curling into a small, knowing smile. "You're not from here." he said, his voice low and rich, carrying an edge of both amusement and danger. The way he spoke made it clear that he already knew far more than he let on.

The man tilted his head, a slow, mischievous smile playing at the corners of his lips. "Uninvited guests, are we?" His voice dripped with amusement, as if he found the situation both intriguing and amusing. "I suppose I should be flattered."

Milo, ever the cautious one, took a step forward, his voice calm but laced with wariness. "We didn't mean to intrude. We're just passing through."

His golden-green eyes flicked to Milo, and his smile widened into something more dangerous. "Passing through? Into the Garden?" He chuckled darkly, the sound rich and full of knowing. "That's bold. Foolish, but bold. I do enjoy a little recklessness."

Kaela's heart thudded in her chest, a strange mixture of irritation and unease creeping in. There was something unsettling about the way the stranger moved, the way he spoke. It was as if he already knew their every move, their every thought, and was simply waiting for them to make the next misstep. She squared her shoulders, trying to keep her composure.

"Who are you?" she asked, her voice firm now, though the edge of uncertainty still lingered.

The man's smile shifted into a mock expression of surprise, as if her question was the most amusing thing he'd heard all day. "Ah, where are my manners?" He bowed his head slightly, an exaggerated gesture that somehow only added to his terrifying charm. "Ronan. And you are?"

Kaela's mind raced, the name echoing faintly in her memory, but she couldn't place it. She glanced at Milo, who gave a barely perceptible shake of his head, urging her to be cautious. She didn't trust this man. There was too much about him that she couldn't understand.

"We don't owe you our names," she said, her tone clipped, her eyes narrowing slightly.

Ronan raised an eyebrow, his smile turning more mischievous as he studied Kaela. "Fair enough," he said, his tone smooth, almost teasing. "But I should warn you, secrecy doesn't get you far out here." He took a leisurely step closer, hands still clasped behind his back, his gaze flicking between Kaela and Milo with a knowing glint. "You're not the first to come looking for the Garden. Most never make it past the outskirts. And those who do . . ." He paused, his lips curling into a smirk. "Well, let's just say their motives are rarely as pure as they claim."

Kaela's back stiffened, a spark of defiance flashing in her eyes. "You don't know anything about our motives," she shot back, her voice laced with quiet fire.

Ronan's grin only widened, a flicker of amusement dancing in his golden-green eyes. "Don't I?" he drawled, his voice low but playful. His gaze dropped to the orb in Kaela's hands, still glowing faintly in her grip. "That little trinket you're clutching so desperately, it's not just a map, you know. It's a key. And keys," he said, a wink accompanying his words, "tend to attract all sorts of attention."

Kaela's heart skipped a beat, but she didn't let it show. "Why do you care?" she asked, her tone sharp. "What's it to you if we're here?"

Ronan chuckled, the sound light and easy. "Why, Kaela, I care because—" he paused dramatically, eyes narrowing with a playful gleam. "I have a vested interest in who gets access to the Garden. You see, not everyone who wanders in here has good intentions. And you," he said, pointing at her with a teasing grin, "well, you don't exactly strike me as someone who knows what she's getting into."

Milo moved instinctively, stepping in front of Kaela, his protective stance firm. "We're not here to cause trouble," he said, his voice steady but cautious. "We just need answers."

Ronan's lips curled into a grin that could only be described as mischievous. "Answers?" He repeated the word like it was a joke only he understood, his gaze flicking between them, then lingering on Kaela with an almost amused curiosity. "And what makes you think the Garden has answers for you?"

Kaela hesitated, her thoughts a swirl of uncertainty. But the intensity of his gaze forced her to speak. "My father disappeared looking for this place," she said quietly, her voice tinged with a sadness she couldn't hide. "And I think . . . I think it's connected to me. To whatever's happening to me."

Ronan's expression softened for a quick moment, a flash of something almost sympathetic in his eyes, but it was quickly replaced with that same teasing glint. He stepped closer, his movements casual, as if he weren't in the middle of a tense standoff. "Ah, a missing father and a mystery to solve," he mused. "A classic. And here I thought you were just another wanderer lost in the woods." He flashed a grin at her. "But no, you've got more going on than I expected."

Milo tensed, his hand hovering near his pack, but Ronan seemed to sense it and tilted his head, amused. "Easy there, hero," he said, his voice light but carrying an edge. "I'm not your enemy. Not yet, anyway."

Kaela didn't flinch, her posture steady as she met his gaze. "If you're not our enemy, then what are you? Some kind of gatekeeper?"

Ronan's laugh was rich and genuine, a sound that seemed to echo in the air between them. "Gatekeeper?" he repeated, shaking his head in mock disbelief. "Hardly. But I've been around long enough to know the dangers, and the cost, of getting too close to the Garden." He leaned in slightly, lowering his voice. "And trust me, the Garden doesn't like visitors who don't know what they're doing."

Kaela's pulse quickened, the weight of his words sinking in. "What do you mean?" she asked, her voice softer now, almost a whisper.

Ronan's grin faded, replaced by a more serious expression, though his eyes still held a glimmer of amusement. "The Garden isn't some mystical paradise," he said, his voice steady, but with an edge of warning. "It's a place of power. Wild, ancient, and unpredictable power. People have died trying to claim it. And if you're not careful, you'll join them." He tilted his head slightly, studying her with a mixture of curiosity and caution. "So, if you're looking for answers, you'd better be ready for the price they come with."

The weight of Ronan's words hung in the air like a heavy fog, suffocating and unyielding. Kaela glanced at Milo, his expression tight with suspicion, his body coiled and ready to react. She could feel the tension in the air, thick and almost tangible, as Ronan's presence loomed over them like a shadow, neither friend nor foe. Yet.

"We don't need your warnings," Milo said, his voice sharp and laced with frustration. "We can handle ourselves."

Ronan's lips curved into a sly smile, the kind that promised mischief and danger in equal measure. His eyes beamed with an amusement that seemed at odds with the gravity of the situation. "Oh, I'm sure you can," he replied smoothly, his tone almost teasing. "That little gadget collection of yours is impressive, I'll admit. But out here? Technology only gets you so far."

Milo seethed, his hand instinctively reaching for his pack, but Kaela stepped forward, her feet firm against the ground. She met Ronan's gaze, unflinching. "Why are you here?" she demanded, her voice steady despite the unsettling tension coiling in her chest. "If you're not a gatekeeper, and you're not trying to stop us, then what do you want?"

Ronan regarded her with an unreadable look, his golden-green eyes scanning her face, as if weighing her very soul. He took a slow step closer, the air around him shifting, heavy with an invisible force. "Let's just say I'm . . . curious," he said, his voice soft, yet the words held a deeper weight. "You've made it further than most, and that's no small feat. I want to see how far you'll go."

Kaela's stomach churned, her mind racing. "And what happens if we keep going?" she asked, her voice quiet, though the uncertainty gnawed at her insides.

Ronan's smile faded slightly, his gaze turning sharper, more focused. "That depends on you." he said, his tone cool and measured. The words lingered in the air, like a challenge. A threat. Or maybe just a warning, one Kaela wasn't sure she could trust.

The silence lingered, thick with tension. Kaela could feel Milo's discomfort beside her, his body stiff with suspicion. She felt the pull of Ronan's gaze, and despite her wariness, there was something about him that kept her attention fixed on him. His presence was magnetic, compelling and dangerous, but strangely familiar, too.

Finally, Ronan stepped back, his posture easing, but his eyes remained intense, as if searching for something in her. "Well, I suppose I've said my piece," he said, his voice a little lighter now, though the edge of warning still lingered. "You've got a choice to make. Turn back now, or keep going and see what the Garden has in store for you."

Kaela's heart pounded in her chest. The Garden was ahead of them, and she wasn't about to back down now. They'd come this far, she wouldn't turn back. "We're not turning back," she said, her voice unwavering, her resolve hardening with each word.

Ronan's smile widened, though it didn't quite reach his eyes. There was something in his expression, a flicker of recognition, or perhaps just the thrill of the challenge. "I thought you'd say that," he murmured, his voice carrying a note of approval, or was it something else?

Kaela stood her ground, but an uneasy feeling lingered at the edges of her thoughts. Ronan's interest in their journey wasn't just curiosity, it was something more, something that tugged at her in a way she couldn't explain. His presence seemed to reach beyond the surface, like a thread pulling at something deep within her, something she hadn't yet fully recognized. She couldn't quite place it, but there was a weird feeling of familiarity to him, as if they were connected in ways that hadn't yet revealed themselves. The pull was subtle, elusive, but undeniable.

Ronan's grin faded, replaced by a more serious expression, though his eyes still held that glimmer of amusement, like a cat toying with its prey. "The Garden isn't some mystical paradise, Kaela." he said, his voice steady but edged with a quiet warning. "It's a place of power that's wild, ancient, and unpredictable. People have died here time and time again, and if you're not careful, you'll join them."

Kaela swallowed hard, but she didn't back down. "We're ready," she said, her voice steady, even as her heart raced. The weight of his words hung in the air, but she couldn't afford to doubt now. Not when the answers she needed were within reach.

Ronan's lips quirked upward, a teasing glint in his eyes. "Well, then," he said, the playfulness returning, "Let's see if the Garden's ready for you."

Kaela held his gaze, unease curling in her stomach. There was something about Ronan that set them on edge, yet kept them from walking away. He was obviously more than just some stray survivor, more than the smooth confidence he wore like armor. His words carried weight, personal and deliberate, as if he knew more about them than he should. She didn't trust him, not yet, but there was an unspoken thread between them, something neither she nor Milo could shake. And that, more than anything, unsettled her the most.

As Ronan turned to leave, Milo's voice rang out, sharp with suspicion. "If you think we're in over our heads, why not just stop us? Why let us go?"

Ronan paused, casting a quick glance over his shoulder. His expression was unreadable, but his words were steady, almost casual. "Because I'm not your keeper. You want to walk into the fire, be my guest. But don't expect me to drag you out when you get burned."

With a smirk tugging at the corner of his lips, he disappeared into the shadows, leaving the tension thick in the air. Kaela exhaled sharply, her heart pounding as the weight of his words settled over her. The Garden loomed ahead, a maze of beauty and danger, and his warning only made it more real. But there was no turning back. They had come too far, and something, someone, was waiting for her.

Milo turned to her, his brow furrowed with concern. "We can't trust him."

"I know," Kaela murmured, her voice steady despite the nagging feeling in her chest. "But we don't have to trust him. We just have to keep moving."

Milo gave her a reluctant nod, though his wariness remained. They gathered their things, the glowing path ahead pulling them deeper into the unknown. Kaela tightened her grip on the orb, its warmth seeping into her palms, grounding her. The questions that had haunted her since her father's disappearance burned brighter now. Whatever awaited them in the Garden, she was determined to face it. For him. For herself. For the answers that had always been just out of reach.

Chapter 13

The air became heavier as they ventured deeper into the Garden, bioluminescent plants casting long shadows on the ground. Kaela's grip tightened around the orb, its warmth a quiet comfort. Its pulse matched her heartbeat, steady and insistent. In the midst of so much uncertainty, it was the only thing that felt real.

Milo moved ahead, his usual effortless confidence now laced with unease. His steps were careful, measured, nothing like the reckless strides Kaela was used to. The silence between them was thick, stretching like a thread pulled too tight. His sharp gaze swept the unfamiliar terrain, cataloging every shadow, every shift in the undergrowth.

Kaela could feel it too. That creeping sense of uncertainty winding through her like a vine. Ronan's warning echoed in her mind, the words clinging to her like smoke. *Not your babysitter. Walk into the fire.* They had come too far to turn back now, yet with every step forward, the weight of the Garden's secrets pressed heavier against her chest. What *fire* had Ronan meant? And were they already walking straight into it?

"Do you think he's right?" Milo's voice cut through the silence, and Kaela's gaze shifted to him. He was glancing back at her, his expression unreadable. "About the danger? About . . . us getting burned?"

Kaela paused, turning his words over in her mind. "I'm not sure," she admitted. "But he's definitely keeping something from us." She exhaled, glancing ahead. "Either way, we can't stop now. We've come too far to turn back."

Milo's lips pressed into a thin line before going silent. "I don't trust him."

"I don't know either," Kaela said, keeping her voice steady despite the doubt creeping in. "But he knows this place, that much is clear. If he can help us get to the heart of the Garden faster, we should take the chance."

Milo didn't answer right away, his gaze flicking ahead. "Yeah. I guess we do. But we need to be careful."

Kaela nodded, her fingers curling tighter around the orb as a pulse of energy thrummed against her palm. They had stepped into a small clearing, but nothing about it felt open or inviting. The trees loomed unnaturally, their trunks bending at impossible angles, branches twisting like reaching hands. The air itself felt charged, thick with something ancient and powerful. It pressed against her skin, humming in her veins, vibrating through her very bones. The sensation was overwhelming, almost intoxicating, like a whispered promise of something just out of reach.

"You're both still here, I see." The voice broke the silence, smooth and dark. Kaela froze, her breath catching in her throat. She recognized the voice instantly. Ronan.

"You're still alive. Impressive." The smooth, unhurried voice cut through the silence, and Kaela stiffened. She knew that voice. Ronan.

He stepped out from the shadows, his movements effortless, like he belonged to the dark. His sharp gaze flicked over them, amusement glinting in his golden-green eyes. He carried himself like someone who knew more than he let on, like he was always one step ahead.

Kaela didn't flinch, but her grip on the orb tightened, pressing it against her chest as if it could shield her. "What do you want now?"

Ronan's lips twitched, almost a smile, but there was no warmth behind it. "Curiosity," he said simply. "I've seen plenty of people try to make it through here. Most don't last long."

Milo stepped closer to Kaela, his hand hovering near his pack, tense and ready. "And yet, you're still here," he said, his voice edged with suspicion. "Why?"

Ronan tilted his head slightly, like Milo had just asked the wrong question. Or maybe the right one. "Because the Garden isn't a place you just walk into and leave. It keeps you. Changes you." His gaze flicked back to Kaela. "You don't understand it yet. But you will."

Kaela frowned. "What's that supposed to mean? You're just standing around waiting for us to fail? Watching for fun?"

Ronan let out a quiet chuckle. "Something like that."

Ronan's expression shifted, the teasing glint in his eyes dimming into something more serious. He took a slow step closer, his gaze locking onto Kaela's. "No, I'm not waiting for you to fail. I'm waiting to see what you'll do next." His voice was quieter now, more measured. "The Garden isn't something you control. It changes, moves, and decides things for itself. But you . . . you have something the others didn't." His eyes flicked to the orb in her hands. "That's why I'm still here."

Kaela's grip tightened. "The orb? What do you know about It?"

Ronan didn't answer right away. Instead, he moved past them, stepping into the center of the clearing. "I know it's a key," he said finally, his voice almost distant. "And I know it's connected to you."

A slow unease coiled in Kaela's chest. "Connected to me *how*?"

Ronan hesitated just long enough to make her stomach tighten. Then he glanced at her over his shoulder. "You're not the first to come here with that orb," he said. "It's more than just a guide. It leads somewhere. And the deeper you go, the stronger the pull will get." His gaze sharpened. "It's like a tether, drawing you toward something that's been hidden for a long time."

Kaela glanced at Milo, catching the tightness in his jaw. His expression gave nothing away, but she could feel the tension rolling off him. He was on edge, ready for anything. She wasn't sure if it was Ronan or the Garden that unsettled him more.

"What is it?" she asked, her voice barely above a whisper.

Ronan turned back fully, his golden-green eyes unreadable. "That's the thing. I don't know exactly." His tone was steady, but there was something in it that made Kaela's pulse quicken. "But I *do* know this. The deeper you go, the more dangerous it becomes. The Garden isn't some mystical paradise, Kaela." His voice dropped slightly, carrying a weight she couldn't ignore. "It's a place of power. Old. Wild. Unforgiving."

Kaela swallowed hard, a chill creeping through her veins. The weight of everything pressed down on her, heavier than before. She was stepping into something vast and unpredictable. None of them truly understood what lay ahead.

She forced herself to hold his gaze. "Then how are you still here?"

For a moment, Ronan just looked at her, his expression unreadable. Then, his lips curled into a small, almost knowing smile. "I have my reasons." His voice was smooth, but there was something beneath it, something darker, something unsaid. "And I know this place better than most. I've seen what it can do." He exhaled through his nose, barely a laugh. "I've been through it before."

Milo, who had been standing rigidly beside Kaela, took a step forward. His suspicion was clear, his voice edged with frustration. "Then why help us?" He didn't bother hiding the sharpness in his tone. "What do you want?"

Ronan's eyes flicked briefly to him before settling back on Kaela. He straightened, his posture easy but charged with something unspoken. "What do I want?" he echoed, as if considering the question. His smile didn't quite reach his eyes. "I want to see how far you're willing to go. How much you're willing to risk. Because whatever it is you're looking for . . ." He tilted his head slightly. "It's going to cost you more than you think."

Kaela's breath caught. "What does that mean? That we're going to die if we keep going?"

Ronan let out a quiet chuckle, but there was no real humor in it. "Not necessarily." His expression softened just a fraction, but the warning in his gaze remained. "But you don't understand the price yet. The Garden doesn't just *give* answers." His voice dipped lower. "It *takes*."

A cold prickle ran down Kaela's spine. His words stirred something deep within her, making her feel uneasy. It was as if she were standing on the edge of something vast and beyond her comprehension. She hated the way it made her feel so small and vulnerable.

Kaela squared her shoulders, pushing the unease aside. "Why help us, then?" she asked, her voice a little steadier than she felt. "Why not just let us go on our own?"

Ronan's gaze lingered on her for a moment longer than necessary, his features unreadable, before he spoke softly, almost reluctantly. "Because I know what's at stake." His eyes flickered to the orb in her hands, then back to her, a trace of something darker passing through them. "I know the cost of walking into this place unprepared."

Milo's suspicion sharpened, but Kaela barely noticed, too caught in Ronan's gaze. "And what's that supposed to mean?" Milo asked, his tone thick with doubt.

Ronan exhaled slowly, his expression unreadable, though there was an edge to his voice. "It means that I've seen what the Garden can do to people. I've *felt* it." He took a step closer, his gaze still fixed on Kaela, as though there were something he was fighting not to say. "And if you're really going to push forward . . . you'll need more than answers. You'll need someone who's already been burned by it."

Kaela's stomach tightened, the weight of his words settling heavily in her chest. She didn't need him to say it outright, she already knew. The way he spoke, with that distant, haunted edge, made it clear he was speaking from his own painful experience. She could almost feel the unspoken history between them, something darker than she had imagined.

"Why would you help us, then?" she asked, her voice barely above a whisper. "After everything?"

Ronan's lips curled into a half-smile, but it didn't reach his eyes. "Because I owe it," he said simply, his voice a little too calm. "And because you *will* need help. Whether you want it or not."

Kaela's heart raced, a mix of curiosity and caution tightening in her chest. The way he spoke, casual but with a weight that lingered, unsettled her. She wanted to know more, to understand what lay behind his words, but she knew pushing too hard might make him pull away. They needed his help, but at what price?

Milo's voice broke the silence, his tone still laced with suspicion. "You want us to leave faster, why? What's your real game, Ronan?"

Ronan's eyes flicked to Milo for a moment, then back to Kaela. He shrugged nonchalantly, but there was something in his gaze that made Kaela's stomach tighten. "Because you don't want to know what happens when the Garden decides you've overstayed your welcome. And trust me, you don't want to find out. You can't control this place. The more you stay, the more it controls you." He stepped back, the shadows seeming to embrace him as he shifted slightly, his movements smooth and deliberate. "So, take my advice. Leave. Fast. The longer you linger, the more you risk. And once you cross certain lines . . . there's no turning back."

Kaela swallowed hard, her throat dry. There was something he wasn't saying, something hidden beneath the surface. But the pull of the Garden was undeniable, and she couldn't shake the feeling that whatever he knew, whatever connection there was between them, was far deeper than he was letting on.

She glanced at Milo, who was still on edge, but his eyes met hers, and for a moment, they were in sync, both of them feeling the same unease. "We don't trust him," Milo muttered, though his voice held less certainty than before. "But we need him."

Kaela nodded, but her stomach twisted. "I know. we don't have much choice."

Ronan was still watching them, his expression unreadable, as though he was waiting for them to make their decision. His gaze flickered again, just briefly, toward Kaela. And for a split second, she could have sworn she saw something in his eyes. Something that made her pulse quicken. A flash of recognition, of understanding, of something shared between them. But it was gone in an instant, replaced by that same cold, calculating expression.

"Well?" Ronan said, breaking the silence. "Do you want to find your answers or not?"

Kaela hesitated, her heart racing, but she could feel the weight of the Garden pressing in around her. "Fine," she said, her voice steady despite the unease swirling inside her. "We'll go. But if you're leading us into something worse, Ronan, I won't hesitate to turn on you."

Ronan's smile was almost predatory as he nodded. "I wouldn't expect anything less."

They began to move, Kaela and Milo trailing just behind him as he led them deeper into the Garden. But Kaela couldn't shake the feeling that this was just the beginning, and that Ronan, for all his mystery and dark charm, was hiding more than he was letting on. Kaela turned toward the path ahead, her resolve hardening. Whatever this place was, whatever Ronan's true intentions were, they had to keep moving forward. There was no turning back now.

Chapter 14

The Garden was alive, alive in a way that was more than just a forest. It pulsed, as if the earth itself had a heartbeat, a rhythm that Kaela could feel vibrating beneath her boots, matching the beat of her own pulse. She'd never imagined something so untamed, so strange, could exist here, hidden away from the cold, controlled world of Dome 5. Yet, every step she took seemed to draw her deeper into the Garden's strange embrace, as if it was pulling her in, alive with secrets she wasn't sure she was ready to uncover.

The sheer magnitude of it overwhelmed her senses. Trees stretched impossibly high, their trunks knotted with twisting vines that glowed faintly, as though lit from within. The leaves above shimmered like polished emeralds, catching the faint light filtering through in hues that shifted subtly, almost impossibly. The air was heavy, thick with the scent of damp earth, mingled with something faintly floral, sweet, but laced with a sharp bitterness that lingered at the edge of her awareness. It was the scent of something ancient, something that had been left to grow wild and unchecked, defying the sterile order of the world she knew.

Everywhere she looked, life swarmed in strange and wondrous forms. Flowers unfurled petals that glistened like jewels, their colors so vivid they almost seemed unreal. Faint trails of bioluminescent spores floated lazily through the air, glowing like tiny, drifting stars. Beneath her feet, the ground was soft, covered in a lush carpet of moss that pulsed faintly, as though it were alive, too. It felt like a place forgotten by time, untouched by the modern world, yet thriving in a way that seemed to defy all logic. And yet, Kaela couldn't shake the feeling that the Garden was watching her, waiting, as if it had a will of its own.

Ronan led the way, his strides fluid and deliberate, each movement exuding a confidence that seemed almost at odds with the chaos around them. He walked as if the Garden belonged to him, or perhaps, as if he belonged to it. His dark curls caught faint glimmers of the shifting light, and the sharp angles of his face seemed carved from the very shadows that danced across it. Kaela couldn't help but watch him, her gaze drawn to the way he moved, how his golden-green eyes flicked over the path ahead, scanning for unseen threats. His expression was as unreadable as ever, a mask that revealed nothing of what he might be thinking or feeling. It frustrated her as much as it intrigued her.

What secrets did he carry? And why, despite everything, did she feel that undeniable pull toward him? It wasn't just curiosity or caution, though they were there too. It was the way his gaze lingered on her a moment too long, the heat in his eyes that sent a flush creeping up her neck, and the way his voice, smooth and teasing, seemed to reach into places she didn't know were there. She could still remember the feel of his hand brushing hers earlier, casual, but somehow charged, like an electric current running between them.

Kaela had spent her life building walls, layers upon layers to keep everyone at arm's length, and she was good at it. But Ronan . . . he had this way of slipping through the cracks, unsettling her with just a look or a carefully chosen word, making her feel things she hadn't allowed herself to feel in years. Things that both terrified and excited her.

Milo followed close behind him, his movements less assured but no less determined. His eyes darted to every shadow, every flicker of movement, and his hand hovered near the array of gadgets strapped to his waist. He was ready to act at a moment's notice, his sharp mind already calculating contingencies for dangers they hadn't yet encountered. There was a tension in his shoulders, a protectiveness that Kaela knew was as much for her as it was for himself. It was comforting in its familiarity, but it also made her chest ache. Milo had always been there, her constant, her best friend. And yet now, walking behind Ronan, she couldn't ignore the subtle shift in the dynamic between them.

Kaela trailed just behind, her senses on high alert. The Garden seemed to press in on her from all sides, its presence palpable, like a great living thing watching their every move. The air felt heavy, thick with moisture and the scent of earth and life. Each step she took felt like it carried weight, as if the ground itself recognized her, pulling her deeper into its labyrinthine embrace. The moss beneath her boots was soft but uneven, its surface interrupted by gnarled roots and creeping vines that seemed to shift just out of sight, almost as though they were alive.

She couldn't shake the feeling that the Garden was testing them, its ancient power humming in her ears like a low, distant song. Her pulse quickened as she glanced at Ronan again. There was something about him that unsettled her, as if he, too, was a part of this place just as much as she. Wild, enigmatic, and utterly untamable. And yet, she couldn't deny the way her gaze lingered, drawn to the sharp line of his jaw, the faint smirk that tugged at the corner of his mouth when he caught her looking.

"Careful, Kaela," he said without turning around, his voice low and teasing. "The Garden doesn't take kindly to hesitation."

She bristled, her cheeks warming. "I'm not hesitating," she shot back, quick to cover the flicker of uncertainty in her tone.

Ronan chuckled softly, the sound barely audible over the

rustling leaves. The distant hum of unseen creatures filled the silence between them. It was infuriating how effortlessly he seemed to read her. Even worse was how easily he got under her skin.

Milo glanced back at her, concern flickering in his blue eyes. "You, okay?" he asked, his voice quieter than usual, as though he, too, could feel the weight of the Garden pressing down on them.

Kaela nodded, forcing a small smile. "Yeah. Just . . . trying to keep up."

As they pressed forward, the path narrowed, and the shadows grew deeper. Kaela couldn't shake the feeling that this journey wasn't just about finding answers in the Garden. It was also about unraveling the mysteries of the people she was with. Perhaps, it was even about discovering the ones hidden within herself.

The trees around them were towering and strange. Barks of deep purple, twisted and gnarled, their branches stretching up like arms reaching for the sky. Some trees bore fruits that glowed faintly in the dim light, while others had flowers blooming in impossible colors, their petals shimmering with iridescence. It was beautiful in a way that felt surreal, as though it were both an invitation and a warning. As they walked deeper into the Garden, Kaela couldn't help but be struck by the contrast between the lush, vibrant beauty and the decay that seemed to be slowly consuming everything. There were patches of earth where the ground had cracked open, revealing roots that twisted and writhed like serpents, dark and rotting. Some of the trees had withered, their branches bare, their trunks blackened as if burned by an unseen fire.

Yet, even in the decay, there was something captivating, a strange beauty woven into the ruin. At first, the Garden still held traces of its splendor, lush greenery, flowers clinging to life, but the deeper they walked, the more the decay took hold. Vines curled like withered veins around fractured stone, their leaves tinged with brown, as if drained of their vitality. The once-vibrant blooms grew sparse, their petals fragile and drooping, while the scent of damp earth thickened with the faint sting of rot. It was as if the Garden itself was caught in an unending battle, life struggling to persist even as death crept in, slowly tightening its grip.

Kaela's heart pounded in her chest, her breaths coming quick and shallow as she struggled to absorb the overwhelming sensations of the Garden. Every step she took seemed to draw her further into its thrall, as though invisible threads were winding around her, pulling her deeper into its embrace, calling for help. The more she saw, the stronger the feeling grew. A strange, unexplainable connection, as if the Garden knew her, as if it had been waiting for her all along.

Her fingers brushed against the orb hanging at her waist, its smooth surface warm to the touch. The warmth wasn't constant, it pulsed, faintly at first, but growing stronger the further they ventured. It was as though the orb was alive, reacting to the Garden in the same way she was. The sensation sent a shiver through her, not of fear, but of something far more unsettling: recognition.

"You feel it too, don't you?" Ronan's voice broke through the quiet, low and almost reverent, as if he were speaking to the Garden itself. It was soft, yet it carried weight, threading through the air like a melody that resonated in her chest.

Kaela's steps faltered as she looked up, meeting his gaze. He had slowed his pace, his sharp features softened by the faint glow of the bioluminescent flora around them. His golden-green eyes flickered with an intensity she couldn't quite place, like he was searching for something in her expression.

"I . . ." she hesitated, the words catching in her throat. How could she explain something she didn't fully understand? "It's like . . . the Garden is alive. It's calling to me."

Ronan's lips curved into a faint smile, though it was tempered by something deeper. Something almost sad. "That's the Garden for you," he said, his voice quiet but sure. "It's not just a place. It's a force. And when it chooses you, there's no escaping it. You're connected to it now, whether you like it or not."

Kaela's pulse quickened at his words, her hand tightening instinctively around the orb. "What do you mean, 'connected'? How can I be connected to something like this?"

His gaze lingered on her for a moment longer, unreadable, before he turned away. "You'll figure it out," he said, his tone lighter now, though the weight of his earlier words hung between them. "The Garden doesn't give you answers. It shows you truths. Whether you're ready for them or not."

Kaela didn't reply, but his words settled uneasily in her mind as they pressed on. The ground beneath her feet felt alive, the moss soft but faintly pulsating, almost like a heartbeat. The air around her seemed thicker, charged with an energy that made her skin tingle. And though she didn't look at Ronan again, she couldn't shake the knowledge that he, too, was part of this place, part of the same force that seemed to be awakening something deep within her. She felt it in the way the air seemed to shift when he was near, in the way his presence steadied her even as it unsettled her. There was something about him, something that tied him to the Garden in the same inexplicable way she felt tied to it. And yet, she couldn't bring herself to ask him about it. Not yet. For now, all she could do was follow, her senses stretched to their limits, as the Garden continued to draw her deeper into its mysteries.

Milo was the first to break the silence, his voice laced with frustration. "I don't like this. It feels like we're walking through a dream. Half of it's beautiful, and the other half's rotting away." He kicked at a vine that seemed to curl and recoil from his touch, its edges blackened and curling inward like a dying flower.

Ronan's gaze flicked to the vine, his expression briefly unreadable. "It's not as simple as it looks," he said quietly. "The

Garden has its own way of doing things."

Kaela glanced around, her unease growing with every step. The energy of the Garden was everywhere now, a low, insistent hum that seemed to vibrate beneath her skin, impossible to ignore. It was as though the air itself carried a charge, brushing against her senses and stirring something deep within her. She felt alive, more alive than she had in years, but at the same time, she couldn't shake the feeling that she was . . . different. Not quite herself. Her powers, usually distant and subdued, felt like they were stretching, reaching outward as if searching for something hidden in the depths of this place.

Almost without thinking, Kaela extended a hand toward a glowing flower beside the path. Its petals shimmered faintly in the dim light, their colors shifting like liquid trapped beneath the surface. As her fingers brushed against the soft petals, the flower seemed to react, quivering under her touch. Its hues began to shift, flowing through shades of deep blue and rich violet before settling into a pale, iridescent white that glowed softly against her skin.

Her breath hitched. The instant her fingers made contact, a spark of something powerful surged through her. A warmth that wasn't entirely her own. It was wild and uncontainable, coursing through her veins like a rush of wind. It wasn't just energy. It was as though the Garden itself was reaching out, acknowledging her, pulling her into its rhythm. Kaela snatched her hand back, staring at the flower as it slowly returned to its original hue. The spark lingered, faint but undeniable, somewhere deep inside her, leaving her shaken and unable to fully grasp what had just happened. The Garden wasn't just alive, it was aware. And somehow, it was aware of her.

"Kaela?" Milo's voice snapped her out of the trance, sharp and edged with alarm. His hand clamped down on her shoulder, pulling her back. "What are you doing?"

Her fingers recoiled from the flower, and the glow dimmed as the petals quivered, settling into stillness. But the sensation it had left behind was anything but gone. The pulse of the Garden hummed beneath her skin, steady and insistent, like it had become a part of her. She pressed her hand against her chest, trying to calm her racing heart, but something had shifted. She could feel it. Something inside her was awake now, stirring, stretching.

"I . . . I don't know," Kaela whispered, her voice shaking. She turned to Milo, her wide eyes betraying her confusion. "But I think the Garden is doing something to me. I can feel it, Milo. It's . . . it's triggering something."

Milo's frown deepened, his protective instincts flaring. His hand stayed firm on her shoulder, grounding her. "This place is unpredictable," he said, his voice low. "We don't know what it's capable of. You shouldn't just touch things."

Kaela didn't respond, her mind consumed by the lingering

energy coursing through her. It wasn't fear that gripped her, but something far deeper. The sensation was powerful and ancient, thrumming through her veins like a forgotten melody. It both terrified and thrilled her, as if she stood on the edge of something vast and unknowable.

"You felt it, didn't you?" Ronan's voice broke through the silence, smooth but laced with a knowing edge. He leaned against a tree, arms crossed, his golden-green eyes flicking to Kaela with that all-too-familiar smirk. There was something about the way he looked at her, like he knew exactly what was going through her mind, even if he wasn't going to share.

Kaela turned slowly, wary but refusing to show it. "What do you mean?"

"The Garden," Ronan said with a lazy wave of his hand, gesturing toward the flower. "It doesn't just sit there looking pretty. It reacts. It's . . . picky. It sensed something in you, and it did its thing."

Kaela's breath hitched. "Sensed something in me? What does that even mean? And stop talking like you've got some secret handbook for this place."

Ronan's grin grew wider, clearly amused. "Oh, I wish. No handbook, just lots of trial and error." He gave a mock salute before leaning in a little, his voice lowering. "What I'm saying is, the Garden's alive. Doesn't always play nice with everyone, but you? It's *definitely* paying attention. And you're not just walking through this place like a tourist. You've got its attention. Don't take it personally."

Kaela felt a knot tighten in her stomach. His words left a strange buzz in the air, but she was frustrated by how much he wasn't telling her. "You really know all this, don't you? Like you've got a map for this whole thing?"

Ronan's gaze softened for a fraction of a second, then he shrugged. "Well, I've spent some time here . . . Let's just say the Garden and I have a complicated relationship. It gives you just enough to keep you coming back for more. But it never tells you the whole story."

His tone was easy, almost too easy, like he'd been here a thousand times and knew exactly what to expect. It made Kaela want to push him further, to demand the answers she knew he was holding back. But there was something about the way he spoke, so sure of himself, so familiar with this place, that made her hesitate. It was like he had the keys to everything she needed to know, but he wasn't handing them over. She glanced away, her gaze falling back to the flower. Its glow had dulled, but she could still feel the hum in the air, its rhythm syncing with her pulse. She didn't know what was happening to her, but one thing was certain: this was just the beginning. The Garden had chosen her, and whether she liked it or not, she was already tangled up in its pull.

They continued on, the Garden's strange beauty and decay unfolding around them like a living, breathing puzzle. The deeper they went, the more Kaela felt the weight of her powers growing, her senses heightening. She could feel the subtle vibrations in the air, the way the trees seemed to shift and move just out of the corner of her eye, the way the earth beneath her feet hummed with life. It was intoxicating, overwhelming, and yet she couldn't bring herself to pull away. It felt like the Garden was becoming a part of her, like her powers were feeding off it, growing stronger the longer they stayed.

They emerged into a clearing, the air dense with the scent of damp moss and decaying leaves. In the center of the space loomed a tree unlike any Kaela had ever seen. Its bark shimmered with a deep, almost black shade of purple, veins of silvery light coursing through its surface like rivers of starlight. Its roots sprawled outward in tangled knots, gripping the earth as though holding the entire clearing in place. The gnarled branches above twisted into the sky, their shapes jagged yet elegant, like frozen lightning.

At the heart of the tree, hanging from a low-hanging branch, was a single, glowing fruit. Its light pulsed faintly, and Kaela's breath hitched as she realized it matched the rhythm of her heartbeat. It was mesmerizing, otherworldly, and impossibly inviting. She stepped forward without thinking, her hand lifting instinctively toward the fruit.

"Don't even think about it." Ronan's voice sliced through the air, calm but with a sharpness that made her pause. He strolled casually into her path, his gaze flicking from the glowing fruit to her, his golden-green eyes reflecting the same mix of mischief and seriousness.

Kaela hesitated, her fingers just inches from the fruit. "Why not?" she asked, raising an eyebrow. "What's the harm? It looks . . . tempting."

Ronan let out a breath, his lips twitching into a half-smile. "Oh, it's tempting alright. Tempting enough to make you forget your own name," he said, his tone almost teasing but with a certain edge. "That tree? It's older than most of the crap in this Garden, and its fruit . . . well, let's just say it *can* give you what you want, but it'll ask for something in return. And trust me, you don't want to find out what that *something* is."

Kaela's hand hovered in the air, the pull of the fruit still there, soft but persistent. "What kind of price?" she asked, her voice dipping with both curiosity and caution.

Ronan gave her a look, a quiet seriousness slipping past his usual playful demeanor. "Something you'll never forget. Some things in this Garden? They're better left alone." He smirked then, but there was no humor in it, just a quiet warning. "Take my advice, don't go poking around where you don't belong."

Milo shifted beside her, his hand brushing against the gadgets strapped to his waist. He was silent, but the tension in his posture was unmistakable. His gaze darted between Kaela and Ronan, his unease palpable. "We should keep moving," Milo said finally, his voice tight. "Whatever this thing is, it's not what we came for."

Kaela nodded, though her gaze lingered on the fruit for a moment longer. The air around the tree crackled with an energy she couldn't quite grasp. It beckoned to her, a pull she couldn't shake, even as she stepped back. She knew the memory of it would stay with her, haunting her every step.

As they moved past the tree, Ronan fell into step beside her, his usual air of teasing confidence replaced by something quieter, more contemplative. "You're not like the others who've been here," he said softly, his voice just loud enough for her to hear.

Kaela glanced at him, startled by the vulnerability in his tone. "What do you mean?"

He hesitated, his gaze fixed ahead. "The Garden doesn't pull at just anyone," he said finally. "It sees something in you. It knows."

"Knows what?" she pressed, her frustration bubbling to the surface.

Ronan gave her a sidelong glance, his expression unreadable once more. "That's for you to figure out."

The cryptic answer only deepened her confusion, but the way he said it made her heart ache with a strange mix of anticipation and fear. There was more to Ronan than he let on. More to the Garden, too. And as much as she wanted to understand it all, she wasn't sure she was ready for the answers. Behind her, Milo walked in tense silence, his eyes scanning the path ahead. She could feel his protective presence like a shield at her back, steady and unwavering. Between Ronan's mystery and Milo's quiet strength, Kaela felt caught in the pull of something larger than herself. The Garden seemed to hum around her, alive and watchful. Whatever secrets it held, Kaela knew they were only just beginning to unravel.

Chapter 15

The fire crackled softly, its flames licking the air and casting flickering shadows on the gnarled walls of the hollowed-out tree that had become their shelter. The warmth of the fire contrasted sharply with the chill of the night, wrapping them in a fragile cocoon. Outside, the Garden whispered in its eerie, constant hum. A deep, rhythmic pulse that vibrated through the very ground beneath them, a reminder of the power that thrummed in every leaf and vine. Yet here, in the heart of the ancient tree, the noise seemed distant, muffled, as though the tree itself shielded them from the Garden's relentless presence, offering a brief, uneasy reprieve in its hollow embrace.

Kaela sat cross-legged by the fire, her fingers curled around a tin cup of water that Milo had carefully boiled, the heat from the metal sinking into her skin like a quiet anchor. The warmth spread through her, grounding her in the moment, but her mind remained adrift, tangled in thoughts she couldn't untangle. Her eyes drifted to the flames, their vibrant dance of reds and oranges flickering wildly, a mirror to the restlessness clawing inside her. Still, no matter how hard she tried to lose herself in the fire's hypnotic dance, her senses couldn't escape the man who stood just beyond the flickering light, his presence like an unspoken weight against the tree's twisted bark

Ronan lounged with an almost unnatural ease, as if the strange, pulsating Garden around them was just another backdrop for his effortlessly cool demeanor. One leg stretched out lazily, the other bent at the knee, his arm slung casually across it like he had all the time in the world. The firelight flickered over his face, casting playful shadows that sharpened his cheekbones and made his golden-green eyes glint with a curious mix of mischief and danger. Kaela found herself sneaking glances at him, more than she intended, her eyes catching on the way his fingers absently rolled a small, smooth stone, as if he hadn't a care in the world. But even in his relaxed posture, there was something about him, an almost imperceptible tension, a readiness that hinted at more than just his flippant attitude. He felt like he was here, but also somewhere far away, like a riddle waiting to be unraveled.

Across from her, Milo was the stark contrast to Ronan's relaxed ease. His posture was stiff, his back straight as a board, and his tools were carefully laid out in neat rows before him, their polished surfaces catching the warm glow of the fire. Every now and then, his eyes would flick toward Ronan, his expression a mix of suspicion and irritation, like a simmering storm just beneath the surface. His fingers twitched restlessly, as if he wanted to reach for something, anything, to distract himself from the words he was clearly holding back, his jaw set tight, as though biting down on the retorts that were threatening to escape.

Kaela felt the weight of their unspoken tension, a taut thread strung between the three of them. It pressed on her like the Garden's pulse, making the small space feel even more confined. The hollowed-out tree provided a sense of security, its ancient bark thick and gnarled, wrapping around them like a protective embrace. The scent of damp wood mixed with the earthy aroma of the forest floor, grounding them in the present moment. Outside, the wind whispered through the leaves, a soft susurration that seemed to carry secrets from the depths of the Garden.

The fire crackled, its flickering light casting long shadows that danced on the tree's twisted walls, making the night feel alive with quiet secrets. Despite the warmth, Kaela couldn't shake the feeling that the Garden itself was watching them, a silent observer in the dark, weighing their every movement. The air between them felt thick, as if the space around them held all the unspoken things they weren't yet ready to confront. Milo was absorbed in his tools, his sharp movements betraying a mind that was as restless as ever, while Ronan sat with an unnerving ease, his eyes catching the firelight in a way that made them seem almost too intense.

It was Kaela who finally broke the silence, her voice cutting through the stillness like a blade. "You've been through the Garden before."

Ronan's gaze shifted to her, a flicker of amusement lighting up his golden-green eyes. "You catch on quick," he drawled, the teasing tone barely masking something darker beneath. "A few times, actually."

Kaela's fingers tightened around her cup, the cold metal grounding her as she leaned in, her voice low but sharp. "Why?"

His shoulders shifted in an almost lazy shrug, but there was a flicker of something unreadable in his expression, something that made her question if she was about to hear more than he intended to say. "Let's just say . . . the Garden and I have a history." His words were soft, but they hung in the air with a weight that felt far too heavy for casual conversation.

Milo scoffed from across the fire, his eyes never leaving Ronan as he muttered, "History? Is that what we're calling it?" His voice was laced with disbelief, and his gaze was sharp, like a hawk sizing up its prey. "You act like you've got some kind of claim to this place."

Ronan's lips curled into a knowing grin, the playful edge never quite reaching his eyes. "I don't *own* it," he said, his tone casual but with a bite of something darker lurking beneath. "But I know it, better than most. And that's why you're still alive. So, you're welcome."

The air thickened between them, Kaela's curiosity pushing the silence into something almost unbearable. She could feel Milo's tension too, the way his fingers twitched at his tools as if he were holding back a snide remark. But she didn't let the simmering tension distract her. She needed answers, needed to understand who this man really was. "You said you were a Technomancer," she said, her voice steady but low, like the weight of her words would shift the very air between them. "What does that mean? And why are you hiding here?"

Ronan paused, his gaze flickering for just a moment, like a shadow passing over his face. The smirk that had been a fixture on his lips faltered, and something darker passed through his golden-green eyes. "Hiding? That's one way to put it," he said, his voice suddenly quiet, almost as if he were talking to himself. "Technomancer is a title, sure. But it's not something you can just walk away from, no matter how much you want to."

Kaela leaned forward slightly, pressing him for more. "And what did you want to walk away from?" she asked, her tone sharper than she intended.

Ronan's lips quirked into a wry smile, but there was no humor in it. "It's not that simple, Kaela," he said, a strange mix of weariness and deflection in his voice. "It's a little too . . . complicated to explain over a campfire." He leaned back slightly, letting his gaze slide toward the fire, though his attention never fully left her. "Let's just say that Technomancers don't exactly have the best reputation when it comes to playing by the rules. And I . . . well, I didn't exactly follow the rules. Not even close."

The unspoken weight of his words settled heavily over them, and Kaela could feel the sudden shift in the air. This wasn't the Ronan who had been joking and bantering earlier. This was someone else. Someone far more complicated, far more dangerous.

Milo snorted from across the fire, his voice cutting through the tension. "Oh, great. So you were one of them." His tone was thick with distrust, his brow furrowed as he stared at Ronan. "How do we know you're not just using us?"

Ronan's gaze flicked to Milo, then back to Kaela, his expression unreadable. He wasn't rattled, not in the slightest, but Kaela could see the faintest flicker of something in his eyes—a mix of amusement and annoyance. "Using you?" Ronan echoed, his voice cool but edged with something darker. "If I were using you, trust me, you'd know it by now."

There was a beat of silence, and Kaela's pulse quickened. She was starting to piece together fragments, but there was still so much left unsaid. "Then why are you here?" she asked again, more softly this time. "Why stick around if you've got this complicated past?"

Ronan let out a sigh, the hint of a smile returning to his lips. "I'm here because I owe someone. The Garden, I guess. And I'm here

because . . . well, maybe I'm just trying to figure things out myself."
He looked at her then, his gaze steady. "But I'm not here to drag you down with me, Kaela. If that's what you're thinking."

Milo wasn't convinced, his skepticism still thick in the air, but Kaela felt the weight of Ronan's words in a way that made her hesitate. There was more to this man than he was letting on, and though she still didn't fully trust him, part of her wondered if maybe, just maybe, she was starting to understand him.

Milo muttered under his breath, his suspicion thickening the air between them, but Kaela's attention never wavered from Ronan. Her pulse fluttered erratically, a strange mix of caution and something deeper. Something she couldn't quite put a name to.

Ronan's voice dropped, the usual bravado gone, leaving a quiet weight in his words. "I was a Technomancer," he began, his gaze distant, as if he were mentally pulling himself back from somewhere darker. "But not like the ones in the Domes. Those guys, they're all about flaunting old tech, pretending they're gods. Me? I was part of something . . . bigger. And a lot more dangerous."

Kaela's breath caught, a chill crawling up her spine as the implications of his words hit her. She leaned in slightly, unable to stop herself. "What kind of dangerous?" she asked, her voice barely above a whisper, like saying the words might pull something awful into the air.

Ronan's smile tightened, turning into something thin and bitter.

The firelight flickered across his face, casting shadows that made him look unfamiliar, like someone who had walked through too many ghosts. "The kind of dangerous that destroys worlds," he murmured, as if the very memory of it still burned him. "The kind that takes power and twists it until it's nothing like what you thought it was. We thought we were building a better world. But all we did was dig our own graves."

There was a weight in his voice, raw and unguarded, that made Kaela swallow hard. This wasn't the cocky, teasing Ronan she was used to. It was something darker, something real. She couldn't tell if he was playing a game or speaking the truth, but the sincerity in his eyes made her believe him, at least for now.

"What happened?" she asked, quieter this time, almost afraid of the answer but needing to hear it anyway.

Ronan's gaze flickered briefly before his expression tightened, his lips pressing into a thin line. For the first time since she'd met him, there was uncertainty in his eyes, a vulnerability he clearly didn't want to show. "Let's just say I figured it out too late," he said, his voice rough, the words like they'd been dragged out of him. "And when I tried to leave . . . Well, hiding here seemed like the only way to stay alive." He glanced out at the Garden, his eyes shadowed, the unspoken weight of it all hanging in the air between them.

Milo's frown deepened, his suspicion mounting as he processed Ronan's words. "So, you're running. From who?"

Ronan's gaze shifted toward the horizon, his jaw tightening slightly. "People who don't take kindly to betrayal," he said flatly. "Trust me, you don't want to meet them."

Kaela studied him, her mind racing with questions. His past felt like a puzzle, pieces scattered just beyond her grasp. Every glance she stole at him only deepened the mystery. She couldn't shake the feeling that there was more lurking beneath the surface, waiting to be uncovered.

"You're not telling us everything," she said quietly, her voice steady but carrying a quiet demand for the truth.

Ronan's lips curved into a teasing grin, his eyes glinting with mischief. "Of course not," he replied, his tone light, but there was a sharpness behind his smile. "Where's the fun in that?"

Milo muttered something under his breath, his tone edged with bitterness. "Typical." But Kaela didn't respond, her attention still caught by Ronan, by the way his gaze lingered on her. It was as if he was peeling back layers she didn't even know existed, his eyes unsettling in their intensity. She wanted to look away, to hide, but she didn't. She couldn't let him have that control.

Ronan, sensing the shift in the air, broke the silence, his voice casual but with an undercurrent that made Kaela's pulse quicken. "And you?" he asked, his gaze still on her. "What's your reason for being here? Answers? Power? Revenge?"

The question caught her off guard. She wasn't prepared for him to turn the tables. She opened her mouth, but for a second, nothing came out. "That's none of your business," she said finally, her voice firmer than she felt.

Ronan's grin widened, but there was a knowing gleam in his eyes. "Fair enough," he said smoothly, though his gaze never wavered. "But whatever it is, you should know the Garden doesn't care about your reasons. It takes what it wants, whether you're ready or not."

The words sent a chill through Kaela. Her heart picked up pace, and the air between them thickened with something unspoken. The Garden. She had heard the warnings, but they hadn't felt real until now. Still, she squared her shoulders and met his gaze, forcing her voice to remain steady. "We're not here to take anything. We're here to find answers."

Ronan's expression shifted, the teasing gone, replaced by something more intense. His eyes darkened, and for a brief moment, she saw the weight of the past in them. "Answers," he murmured, almost to himself. "They come at a price. The Garden doesn't give them freely."

Kaela couldn't tell if he was speaking from experience or just trying to unsettle her, but his words lingered in the air, thick with something she couldn't quite place. There was an edge to them, a weight that felt personal. She found herself wanting to ask more, but something in his tone held her back. It was as if he was daring her to dig deeper, yet warning her not to.

The air between them thickened, heavy with the weight of his words. Kaela opened her mouth, but no sound came out. What could she say? The Garden had already shown its power and its cost, and now she feared that answers might come with an even steeper price.

The crackling of the fire was the only sound, filling the space with its rhythmic crackle. The flames danced across Ronan's features, casting shadows that made him look even more elusive, more dangerous. Despite the tension, despite the distrust gnawing at her, Kaela found herself drawn to him. There was something magnetic in his presence, something that made her want to uncover the layers he kept hidden, even as she dreaded what she might find.

"Why are you really helping us?" Kaela asked, the words slipping out before she could stop them, her voice barely above a whisper.

Ronan leaned back slightly, that familiar smirk still dancing on his lips, but something softer flickered behind his eyes. "Curiosity," he said, his voice low, a touch of something darker in it. "Maybe I see a little of myself in you. Who knows?"

Kaela held his gaze, the weight of his words settling heavy in her chest. She didn't know whether to be intrigued or cautious. There was a rawness in him she hadn't expected, a glimpse of something more than the usual arrogance. But even so, the guarded part of her whispered that there was always a price.

Milo, who'd been silent up until now, finally spoke, his voice tight with suspicion. "And what's in it for you?"

Ronan's gaze flicked to Milo for a moment before he answered, his smile turning more mischievous. "What's in it for me?" he repeated, leaning forward slightly, his eyes glinting. "I'm not in it for your reasons. But I'm not one to sit back when there's a game to be played." He turned back to Kaela. "Just don't mistake my help for loyalty."

Kaela felt a surge of defiance rise in her chest, but she tamped it down, forcing herself to stay calm. "Fine," she said, her voice steady despite the undercurrent of tension. "But if you betray us, I'll make sure you regret it."

For a split second, Ronan's smirk wavered, and Kaela saw something. Genuine amusement, maybe even respect. "I wouldn't expect anything less," he said, the playful edge back in his voice.

There was a shift in the air then, a moment between them that wasn't quite trust but not outright distrust either. It was an understanding. Silent and fragile, like an unspoken pact. For now, they were allies, but Kaela couldn't shake the feeling that things were far from settled.

Milo shifted again, his hand brushing against one of his gadgets, the subtle movement sharp with tension. Kaela could feel his gaze on her, like a weight at the back of her neck, but she didn't meet his eyes. The conversation with Ronan had taken an unexpected turn, leaving her with more questions than answers, and now she needed space to process it all, the danger, the enigma of Ronan, and the way he seemed to slip under her skin in ways she hadn't expected.

The fire crackled softly in the silence, the only sound that filled the air as Kaela sat there, her mind spinning. The Garden, their search for answers, and Ronan's cryptic promises twisted together in her thoughts, each thread tangled with the next. She couldn't make sense of it all, not yet, but one thing was clear: this journey was going to change everything. And when it came time to face the truth, she would have to decide just how far she was willing to go— and what, or who, she was willing to risk.

Chapter 16

The air in the Garden shifted abruptly, as if the ancient, living place had taken a deep, shuddering breath. The subtle hum Kaela had grown used to. The constant, rhythmic pulse of unseen life seemed to falter, like a heartbeat caught in a moment of hesitation. The leaves of the towering trees stilled, their edges no longer trembling in the breeze, and the soft rustling of distant creatures paused as if holding their breath. A profound stillness followed, thick and heavy, pressing in from all sides like a weight she couldn't shake. It felt like the moments before a storm, silent but charged, the kind of quiet that makes the air taste different, thick with anticipation. The ground beneath her feet seemed to hum with a strange energy, a warning, though she couldn't place why. It was as though the Garden itself was aware of something, a shift in the very fabric of its existence that Kaela couldn't yet comprehend.

Kaela's eyes flicked to Ronan, who leaned against a jagged

boulder, exuding his usual nonchalance, though there was something in his posture that didn't sit right. His gaze was sharp, scanning the trees with an intensity that made her skin prickle, as if he could sense something she couldn't. Even Milo, ever the skeptic, had set down the gadget he'd been tinkering with, his fingers now curled into tight fists. It was a rare show of discomfort from him, and Kaela knew that whatever was looming in the air was enough to unsettle them both.

"What's wrong?" Kaela asked, her voice low and cautious, a sense of foreboding creeping into her words.

"Not wrong," Ronan murmured, his golden-green eyes narrowing as they tracked the shifting shadows ahead. "Just . . . different."

Before Kaela could press him further, a soft glow began to pulse from the twisted roots of a gnarled, ancient tree. At first, it was just a faint shimmer, like moonlight skimming the surface of water, barely visible in the dim forest. But it grew, steadily and unrelentingly, blossoming into a brilliant light that seemed to hum with an energy that wasn't of this world. As the glow intensified, it coalesced into the shape of a woman, moving with a fluid grace, as though she were made of the very air itself. Her presence was magnetic, pulling at the space around her, making the forest feel smaller, as if everything in it had shifted to accommodate her.

She stepped forward, and the air seemed to bend in response to her movement, the light casting shifting patterns across the ground. Her silver hair flowed like liquid metal, catching the light with every movement, and her robe shimmered with the colors of the Garden. Rich greens, deep blues, and soft purples woven together in a way that made her seem like an extension of the world itself. It was as if the Garden had come alive, wrapping itself around her, binding her to its very essence. The world seemed to pause, holding its breath in her wake.

Her eyes, pale and luminous like twin stars, bore into Kaela with a piercing intensity. It felt as though the woman was not just looking at her, but through her, dissecting every hidden thought, every buried fear. Kaela's breath caught in her throat, as if the weight of those eyes was pressing against her chest, making her feel exposed and vulnerable in a way she had never experienced. She couldn't tear her gaze away, but it left her feeling small and fragile, as though her very existence were nothing more than a fleeting shadow in the face of something far greater.

Ronan straightened, the casual ease in his posture vanishing as his smirk fell away. He pushed off the boulder, his stance shifting into something more guarded, his expression unreadable. Kaela's heart skipped, a flutter of unease rising in her chest. Even Milo, normally the skeptic, instinctively took a half step back, his fingers hovering near the tools at his belt, prepared for whatever came next.

Aelera's gaze swept over them, lingering on Kaela just a beat longer than necessary, before flicking to Ronan. Her presence was commanding, yet there was an ethereal serenity to it, as if she belonged to a world far older than their own, timeless and untouchable. When she spoke, her voice was soft but rich with an ancient authority that seemed to resonate with the very air. "You walk upon sacred ground," she said, her accent strange, almost melodic, in a way Kaela couldn't quite place. "Do you truly understand what you've stumbled into?"

Kaela's throat tightened, her voice barely rising above a whisper. "We're looking for answers," she said, her words unsure, as if she feared their own inadequacy.

Aelera's lips curled into a faint, enigmatic smile that never quite reached her eyes. "Answers," she murmured, her gaze now flicking to Ronan, "that is what they all seek. But some are more prepared for the cost than others."

Ronan stiffened but didn't break eye contact with Aelera. His jaw clenched, the muscles in his neck tightening. "Aelera," he said, his voice steady, though it carried an edge that Kaela couldn't place.

"You remember me, then?" Aelera asked, her tone carrying a sharpness that was barely contained. "Good. It will save us time."

Kaela exchanged a glance with Milo, both of them equally confused. She leaned toward him and whispered, "Who is she?"

Ronan's eyes never left Aelera. "The Garden's guardian, its protector. If you believe in such things."

Aelera's gaze turned toward him, narrowing slightly as something ancient flickered in her expression. "Believe, Ronan? You of all people should know better than to question my existence." Her voice was calm, but the weight of her words hit like a storm. "Or have you forgotten what this place once was?"

Kaela stepped forward cautiously, drawn by an unspoken need to understand. "You're the guardian," she said slowly, her voice trembling with a mix of awe and curiosity. "Guardian of what?"

Aelera's eyes fixed on Kaela, and for a heartbeat, Kaela felt as though the air itself had turned still, heavy with something unspoken. Aelera's presence pulled at the very air, and Kaela's breath faltered as she met the woman's gaze. "Of life," Aelera's voice rang low and strong, as if her very words were woven from the fabric of the earth itself. "Of magic. Of balance." She let her words settle before continuing. "This place, the Garden, is older than your Domes. Older than the machines that poison your world. It is a sanctuary . . . but it is fragile."

The mood around them shifted. Aelera's expression darkened, and the light surrounding her seemed to dim as though her words had taken weight. "And it is dying," she said, the gravity of her words sinking into Kaela's chest like a stone.

"Dying?" Kaela breathed, the question escaping before she could stop it. Her stomach churned with fear, unfamiliar and deep.

Aelera's eyes flicked briefly to Ronan, her gaze piercing. "The

Garden is not what it once was. Its magic, its lifeblood, is being drained. Taken," she paused, and the silence between them seemed to stretch, thick and suffocating. "You know who is responsible," she said, her eyes locking with Ronan's in a way that made Kaela's heart race, sensing a story untold, one that connected them all in ways none of them fully understood yet.

Ronan shifted his posture just slightly, but his face remained unreadable. "I know what you're about to say," he said, his voice low, giving away nothing.

Kaela turned toward him, frustration rising in her chest, mingled with confusion. "What does she mean? Who's taking the magic?"

Aelera's gaze softened, just a little, as she turned to Kaela. "The Technomancers," she replied, the words dripping with disdain. "They've learned how to tap into the power of this place, but they don't understand it. They drain its essence, using it for their own purposes, with no care for the damage they're causing."

Milo scoffed from behind them, his voice thick with disbelief. "You mean the Domes?"

"No," Ronan said flatly, shaking his head. "The Technomancers don't operate within the Domes. They're something else. Something outside of all that."

Aelera's expression grew harder, and she nodded gravely. "They were once like you, seekers of knowledge, driven by ambition. But ambition without wisdom is a dangerous thing. They came here, discovered the Garden's power, and instead of protecting it, they tried to control it. They built machines to siphon its magic, to fuel their own creations. In doing so, they began the Garden's unraveling."

Kaela felt a shiver crawl up her spine, her skin growing cold. "If the Garden is dying, why are we still alive? Why hasn't it . . . stopped us?"

"The Garden is resilient," Aelera said, her voice taking on a quieter, more somber tone. "But its patience is not endless. It allowed you to enter because it sensed something in you, Kaela. Something . . . familiar." Her gaze lingered on Kaela, as if trying to read something deep within her. "You are not like the others who've come before."

Kaela's heart thudded heavily in her chest. "I don't know what you mean."

"You will," Aelera said simply, her words final and heavy with meaning. The weight of them settled over Kaela like a shadow.

Aelera turned her gaze to Ronan then, her expression sharpening. "And you," she said, voice cutting through the stillness, "you've witnessed the destruction they've caused. You know what they are. And still, you hesitate."

Ronan's lips twisted into a faint, bitter smile, though it never touched his eyes. "I don't hesitate," he said, his voice steady, but there was an uncertainty lurking beneath the surface. "I just . . .

don't know if there's anything left worth saving in a world that's already burned." His gaze flickered toward the Garden, a flicker of doubt clouding his features before he quickly masked it with indifference.

Aelera's eyes flared, and for a moment, the light around her brightened, almost blinding in its intensity. "That is not yours to decide."

The tension in the air thickened, crackling with the weight of their unspoken conflict. Kaela stepped forward, her voice breaking through the charged silence. "What are we supposed to do? If the Garden is dying, how do we stop it?"

Aelera's gaze landed on Kaela, and for the first time, there was a softness there, a glimmer of something unspoken. "The path you must walk is your own, Kaela. But know this: the Garden will not survive if the Technomancers' machines are not stopped. And if the Garden falls, so too will the last hope for your world." She paused, then shifted her focus to Ronan, her eyes lingering for a moment longer than was comfortable. "You both have a part to play in this, whether you understand it yet or not."

Kaela's stomach tightened as she stole a glance at Ronan, her gaze flickering to his clenched jaw. There was something behind his unreadable expression, something that spoke of a struggle he hadn't voiced. An echo of doubt hung in the air, as though he was wrestling with a truth he hadn't yet accepted. For a brief moment, she saw the faintest flicker of recognition. Something about the words Aelera had spoken had landed somewhere deep within him, but he quickly masked it, his features hardening once more.

"What happens if we fail?" Milo asked, his voice quieter than usual, tinged with a rare vulnerability.

Aelera's eyes darkened, her voice like the chill of winter. "Then the Garden will die, and with it, the balance that sustains your world. The Technomancers will take what they can, but they will find only ruin. And all that remains will wither and fade, until there is nothing left."

Kaela's heart hammered in her chest, the enormity of their task pressing down on her. Yet even as fear coiled around her, a flicker of determination sparked deep within her. They couldn't let that happen. They couldn't fail.

Aelera stepped back, her form beginning to fade into the shadows, her presence still lingering in the air. "The Garden has chosen you," she said, her voice carrying a weighty finality. "It sees something in you, in both of you, that you do not yet understand. Trust in it, and it will guide you."

Before Kaela could respond, the light around Aelera flickered, gradually dimming until she vanished entirely, leaving nothing but the lingering echo of her presence. The forest stood in stunned silence, as if the air itself was holding its breath. Kaela's mind raced, the weight of Aelera's words pressing down on her with an intensity that made her feel as though she were standing at the edge of a precipice. The world around them felt unnervingly still, as if time had momentarily frozen, and all that remained was the crushing uncertainty of what was to come.

"Well," Milo said finally, his voice shaky but trying to lighten the mood. "That was . . . something." He let out a breath, glancing between Kaela and Ronan as though unsure of how to proceed.

Kaela didn't answer right away. Her mind was still reeling from the weight of Aelera's words. Frustration churned inside her, mingled with a deep sense of betrayal. She turned to Ronan, her voice sharp. "You knew about this. The Technomancers, the destruction they're causing. Why didn't you tell us?"

Ronan met her gaze, his expression unreadable, but there was something more in his golden-green eyes, a flicker of something vulnerable, even uncertain. "I knew enough," he said quietly, his tone calm but edged with something deeper.

Kaela's pulse quickened, her anger bubbling over. "Why didn't you tell us?" The question had been building for days, maybe even longer, as the tension between them mounted.

Ronan sighed, his shoulders tensing slightly, though he stayed composed. "Would you have believed me?" he asked, the words carrying an edge of regret, but also a guarded sort of honesty.

Before Kaela could respond, Ronan pushed off from the tree he had been leaning against. His demeanor shifted, the casualness gone. He stepped forward, his eyes sharpening, focused. "We've wasted enough time," he said, his voice steady but urgent. "The Garden doesn't wait for anyone. We need to move."

Kaela hesitated, the knot in her chest tightening. She wanted to keep pressing him, to demand more answers, but she couldn't ignore the truth in his words. Aelera's warning echoed in her mind. The Garden was dying, and they didn't have time to waste.

"Fine," Kaela said, her voice firm despite the uncertainty gnawing at her. "But we're not done talking about this."

Ronan smirked, a flicker of the familiar confidence returning to his expression. "Looking forward to it," he teased, his tone lighter, but the subtle weight of something unsaid still lingered in his eyes.

Milo watched them both for a moment, sensing the shift in the air between Kaela and Ronan. He could see it now, the tension fading and something else settling into place. They needed to work together if they were going to stand a chance. With a sigh, he cleared his throat, his voice more steady than before. "Let's just get moving then. No time to waste, right?"

Ronan gave a silent nod, then turned and began walking toward the deeper part of the Garden, his strides purposeful. Kaela and Milo exchanged a brief glance before following, the unspoken tension between them lingering. But there was no time for confrontation now; the urgency of their task pressed on them like a weight. They had a world to save, and every step counted.

Kaela stood for a moment, fists clenched, her frustration simmering beneath the surface. Milo, ever steady, placed a hand on her shoulder, his touch steadying her. He didn't say a word, but it was enough to quiet the storm in her mind. She knew he felt it too, the betrayal, the confusion, the hurt. Wordlessly, they followed Ronan, the thick silence of the Garden pressing in on them. As they walked deeper into the twisting, vibrant landscape, Kaela found herself glancing at Ronan more than she wanted to. His easy confidence, once intriguing, now felt like a wall keeping her at a distance. The more she thought about it, the more unsettled she became. There were parts of him she didn't understand, and now, after Aelera's revelation, she couldn't shake the feeling that those parts held the answers she needed. Why had he kept so much from them? Was it to protect them, or because he didn't trust them?

As they moved deeper into the Garden, Kaela found herself walking a little faster to keep up with Ronan. She wanted answers, but more than that, she wanted to understand the man who had become an undeniable part of their group. Despite the uncertainty that hung between them, there was something about him. Something that made her heart race, something she couldn't ignore.

Milo glanced at Kaela, sensing the change in her. Falling back a step, he walked beside her, his voice quiet. "You, okay?"

Kaela gave a small, tight smile, though it didn't reach her eyes. "I don't know," she admitted. "I feel like I don't know anything anymore."

Milo's gaze softened, a quiet understanding passing between them. "I get it. But whatever happens, we're in this together. You're not alone in it."

Kaela nodded, grateful for his presence, though the words felt hollow in her chest. They had always been a team. She, Milo, and even now Ronan, though that was a relationship fraught with more tension than she cared to admit. But the more she thought about Aelera's cryptic warning, the more she realized that the stakes were higher than they had ever imagined. This wasn't just about the Garden. This wasn't just about their mission. It was about something much bigger, and the consequences of failure were unimaginable.

They continued their trek, the dense foliage of the Garden closing in around them, as though the place itself was alive and watching. With every step, the weight of Aelera's words seemed to grow heavier on Kaela's shoulders. She wasn't just carrying the responsibility of their mission, she was carrying the weight of the world. And if Ronan was right, the Garden might be the only thing standing between them and total destruction.

Ronan's voice sliced through the silence, low and tense. "Stay alert," he called, not bothering to look back but making it clear that the warning was meant for all of them. "We're not alone out here."

Kaela's pulse spiked, and Milo's hand drifted to the tools at his belt, his body coiling with the sudden shift in the air. A thick, suffocating tension settled over them, something dangerous lurking just beyond the shadows of the Garden. Kaela's eyes flickered toward Ronan, but he remained focused on the path ahead, his posture stiff with vigilance.

What was waiting for them? Kaela couldn't shake the feeling that they were about to face something far worse than they had anticipated. One thing was clear: they couldn't afford any more missteps, not with the Technomancers on their trail, and certainly not with the fate of the Garden hanging in the balance. The unspoken words between them lingered, their connection fraying but still holding strong. Whatever lay ahead, Kaela knew it would push them to their limits, and that fragile trust they had? It would either bind them together or break them beyond repair.

Chapter 17

The Garden felt different today, like the very air was charged with something she couldn't quite touch. The trees swayed restlessly, their leaves whispering to the wind as if they too sensed the shift. It wasn't just the Technomancers looming ahead, it was something deeper, something stirring within her. Kaela stood at the edge of a small clearing, her eyes drawn to Ronan, who was a few paces ahead, scanning the sky with an intensity that mirrored the strange energy pulsing through the air. Every fiber of her being felt the hum of it, that crackling current of power that seemed alive, teasing her, always just out of reach. The connection to the Garden was there, so clear, so strong. But no matter how she tried to grasp it, it slipped through her fingers, like trying to catch the wind.

Ronan didn't turn around when he spoke, his gaze still fixed on the darkening sky, but his voice sliced through the tension like a blade. "You can't force it, Kaela. You have to feel it." His tone was calm, steady, like he was talking to someone who might not understand but could get there if they just stopped trying so hard. "The Garden's magic isn't something you wield. It's alive. It's a thread that runs through everything. Through you. Through me."

Kaela's frustration surged, impatience spilling over. "I'm trying!" she snapped, sharper than she meant, her voice trembling with the weight of everything she didn't understand. "I'm trying, and nothing is working."

Ronan turned then, his expression unreadable. His golden-green eyes flashed with that same maddening mix of amusement and something else, something she couldn't quite place. Something that made her pulse quicken. He gave her that smile, the one that always made her want to punch him and kiss him in the same breath. "You're trying too hard," he said with that familiar, infuriating smirk. "That's your problem. You're thinking too much."

Kaela's frustration flared, and she stepped forward, the dry brush crunching under her boots. "Maybe I *need* to think," she shot back, her voice a little too sharp. "If I don't get control of this, we're screwed. I'm screwed."

Ronan's gaze softened just a fraction, and for a split second, she could have sworn she saw something in his eyes that wasn't there before. It wasn't the usual cocky deflection, but something deeper. Protective, even. The shift was gone almost as quickly as it came, but it lingered in the space between them. "I know," he said, his voice lowering, almost reluctant. The change in his tone was subtle but noticeable. "And I'm trying to help you."

Kaela clenched her fists, the frustration bubbling again. "Then teach me," she demanded, the words spilling out before she could stop them. She took another step forward, closing the distance between them. "Stop talking in riddles. I need more than that."

Ronan's eyes lingered on her, narrowing just slightly as he took in the raw edge of her voice, the tension in her words. He said nothing, his gaze steady and unreadable, like he was weighing something in his mind. The silence stretched between them, thick and thickening. Then, finally, he nodded, once, his expression sharpening again. But there was something there, just beneath the surface. Something unspoken, maybe even reluctant, that softened the sharpness. It was subtle, fleeting, but Kaela couldn't shake the feeling that he was seeing her in a way he hadn't before.

"Fine," Ronan said, his voice lower than usual, more serious. "But you need to understand something first."

Kaela's patience snapped, and she took a step forward, her tone sharp. "What?"

Ronan's gaze held hers, steady and unwavering. "The power isn't just in you, Kaela. It's in the Garden too. The three of us are connected. How or why, I can't say. But one thing's for sure: the Garden chose us."

Her frown deepened as confusion twisted in her gut. "What do you mean?"

Ronan closed the space between them, his presence suddenly more imposing, and Kaela could feel the shift in the air, charged, like a storm was coming. There was something about him now, something that made her hyper aware of the proximity between them. It wasn't just the Garden's magic that hummed beneath the surface; it was him, his intensity, his gravity. Then he spoke again, his voice low, like he was revealing a secret.

"You're not just some random person the Garden chose. You're connected to it, the same way I am. It's ancient. It's powerful. It's in you, Kaela. In us."

For a moment, his gaze flickered down to her lips, and Kaela's breath caught in her chest. It wasn't just the brief, fleeting look that had her heart racing, but the way his words lingered in the air. The weight of the word *us* settled between them, hanging heavy with meaning neither of them was ready to unpack. She could feel the unspoken tension, a strange connection pulling them closer, though neither of them acknowledged it aloud.

Kaela's mind raced, but before she could speak, Ronan held up a hand. His fingers hovered, just a breath away, and his voice dropped to a near-whisper, a quiet command that cut through her thoughts. "Let me show you. Trust me."

She didn't know why, but she did. She didn't know why his words, or the way he stood there, dangerous, but not entirely threatening, pulled her in. But in that moment, she couldn't look away. And somehow, she didn't need to understand it. Not yet.

Ronan reached out, his fingers brushing gently against her arm. The touch was light, but it left an unmistakable mark. A shock of warmth ran through her, sharp and electric, and in that fleeting moment, the world seemed to vanish. The rustling leaves, the soft hum of the wind, all fell away until there was only the sound of her heart thudding in her chest. She became hyper-aware of everything, of him, of the pulse of energy that seemed to reverberate in the space between them. For an instant, it felt like nothing else existed but the space they shared, the air between them charged with something unspoken.

Ronan's voice was barely audible, his breath warm against her skin. "Close your eyes," he murmured, his words gentle but insistent. "Let the Garden speak to you."

Kaela hesitated, her mind racing with a thousand questions, but her body moved before she could stop it. Slowly, she closed her eyes, her pulse quickening as she allowed herself to feel what she could not yet understand. The Garden opened to her, not as something she needed to control or grasp, but as something alive. It wasn't distant or foreign. It was part of her. The air hummed with its ancient energy, a current running through the earth, the wind, the very breath in her lungs. The connection was undeniable, profound. A force that was both overwhelming and comforting. She could feel it deep inside her, wrapping around her heart like something she'd known all her life, though she hadn't known it until now.

And then, just as suddenly as it had come, the sensation faded, leaving her gasping, her chest rising and falling with each breath. She opened her eyes, blinking through the blur of emotion and magic, trying to make sense of what had just happened. The world had shifted in ways she didn't fully understand, and yet, for the first time, she felt it all, like a part of something bigger than herself, something that had always been waiting for her.

Ronan stood before her, his hand still suspended in the air where it had touched her. His gaze remained locked on hers, a quiet intensity that made her heart race. The space between them seemed to hum with unspoken words, heavy with something neither of them dared to name. Kaela couldn't look away, caught in the pull of his attention.

"Did you feel that?" he asked, his voice low, the weight of the question hanging in the air.

Kaela's throat tightened, and she swallowed hard, struggling to steady her breath. She nodded slowly, barely able to whisper, "I . . . I did."

Ronan's lips curved into a small, knowing smile. It still held that playful edge, but there was something more beneath it, something that felt too close, too intense. "Good," he said, his voice dropping even lower. "We're just getting started."

Kaela stood in the clearing, still reeling from the intensity of the moment. Her heart raced, her skin still tingling where Ronan's fingers had brushed against her. The magic of the Garden hummed through her veins, an unfamiliar warmth that made her feel both alive and unmoored. She had felt it, the undeniable connection between them, but as much as she wanted to embrace it, something about the whole situation left her unsettled. She glanced at Ronan, but his gaze was fixed on the horizon, distant and unreadable, as though the moment had already slipped away.

"Are you always this cryptic?" she asked, attempting to lighten the mood, but her voice came out sharper than she meant. She wasn't sure whether her frustration was with the magic, her own confusion, or Ronan himself, who seemed to hold all the answers but never shared them easily.

Ronan's lips twitched into a half-smile, his voice laced with amusement. "Only when it suits me," he replied smoothly, as if their moment hadn't just shifted something between them. "You'll learn. It's all about patience, Kaela."

"Patience?" Kaela scoffed, crossing her arms over her chest. "That's your answer? After all that? You want me to just . . . wait?" Her frustration flared again, the heat of it rising in her chest. "I don't have time for patience. We're on the clock here, Ronan."

For a moment, his usual smirk faltered, and Kaela saw a flicker of something, maybe concern, in his eyes before it vanished. "You think I don't know that?" he said softly, his voice matching the edge in hers. "I didn't ask for this either, Kaela. But we don't control the Garden. We work with it. We have to trust it, just like we have to trust each other."

Before Kaela could respond, a familiar voice broke through the tension. "Alright, you two," Milo called out, his tone light and teasing as he stepped into the clearing, his messy dark blonde hair bouncing with each step. He glanced between them, his expression equal parts amused and concerned. "You're about to start a fight, aren't you?"

Kaela let out a breath, caught between relief and irritation. She turned to Milo, grateful for the distraction, even as frustration still simmered beneath the surface. There was something steady about him, something grounding, that made everything feel a little less complicated. With him, there were no unspoken tensions, no unanswered questions, just an easy familiarity she could rely on.

"I'm not starting anything," Kaela said quickly, forcing a grin as she turned to Milo. "Just getting some sage advice from Ronan. You know, patience and all that."

Milo raised an eyebrow, glancing between her and Ronan with an amused smirk. "Patience?" He let out a low chuckle. "I thought the Garden was supposed to be all about instant results. Who knew it was actually some mystical lesson in inner zen?"

Ronan shot Milo a look, but there was no real malice in it, just that ever-present playful edge. "You should try it sometime, Milo. You might actually learn something."

Milo held up his hands in mock surrender. "Oh, don't worry. I'll leave the magical enlightenment to you two. I'm just here for tech support." His grin was easy, but Kaela knew him too well. Beneath the teasing, he was watching them, reading between the lines, the way he always did when things got too heavy.

"Tech support, huh?" Ronan mused, smirking. "Is that what you're calling yourself now? Last I checked, magic wasn't exactly your area of expertise."

Milo's grin widened, and he shot back with a wink. "Hey, magic is just science we don't understand yet. And if you ever need someone to invent a way to control this whole 'Garden connection' situation, you know where to find me."

Kaela laughed despite herself, the tension between her and Ronan momentarily lifting. Having Milo here, grounding her with his easy humor, reminded her that she wasn't alone in this. No matter how strange things got, how tangled the magic became, he was still by her side. He always had been, in ways she hadn't fully appreciated until now, and that steadiness was something she wasn't willing to take for granted.

"Good to know I'm not the only one who thinks this is a little . . . insane," she admitted, her voice lighter now. "You really think you can invent something to make this magic less unpredictable?"

Milo's eyes sparkled with mischief. "If anyone can, it's me." He paused, glancing between her and Ronan, something unreadable flickering across his face. "But hey, don't go thinking I'm the third wheel here. I'm just here to help . . . with whatever you two need."

Ronan shot him a sidelong glance, his lips twitching like he had a sharp retort lined up, but instead, he just nodded, his expression light. "Don't worry, Milo," he said, voice laced with amusement. "We'll make sure you're not left out of the fun."

Milo gave him a mock shove. "Fun, huh? I'll believe it when I see it. Just don't start getting all intense on me. I'm not ready for that level of drama."

Kaela rolled her eyes but couldn't stop the grin pulling at her lips. "You're one to talk. You're usually the one who gets us into trouble."

Milo shrugged, his teasing smile softening into something more sincere. "Hey, someone's got to keep you two from taking things too seriously. It's a dangerous world out there, Kaela. If we can't laugh at the chaos, what's the point?"

Ronan, who had been listening quietly, nodded, his usual playful edge giving way to something steadier. "Milo's right," he said, his voice thoughtful. "We need to stick together. Whatever's coming, we face it as a team."

The words settled over Kaela like a weight and a comfort all at once. No matter how uncertain the path ahead was, no matter how tangled her connection with Ronan or the Garden became, one thing was clear. They weren't in this alone. That knowledge didn't erase her fears, but it gave her something to hold onto, a reason to keep moving forward.

"Together," she murmured, more to herself than anyone else.

The three of them stood in the clearing, the Garden stretching endlessly around them, its ancient energy thrumming beneath their feet. The tension from before had softened, leaving behind something unspoken but understood. Whatever came next, they would face it side by side. And for now, that was enough.

Chapter 18

The air in the Garden pulsed, alive with something unseen, as if the land itself was whispering beneath the surface. Kaela stood in the clearing, fingers grazing the rough bark of an ancient tree, grounding herself in its quiet strength. Time felt strange here, weightless and stretched thin, but she couldn't let herself get lost in the wonder of it. As breathtaking as the Garden was, there was no time for awe.

The Technomancers were still out there. The thought settled like a stone in her chest, heavy and unshakable. The awareness of them lingered beneath everything, a quiet hum of dread that never truly faded. They were hunting her. Hunting all of them. Every rustling leaf and every shifting shadow sent a jolt of unease through her, tightening her grip on the knife at her belt. The Technomancers were methodical, relentless, and no matter how much the Garden had shielded them, Kaela could feel it. Something was changing.

The magic that once pulsed so strongly here now felt thinner. The energy holding them in this fragile sanctuary was unraveling, stretching too far to conceal them much longer. She didn't know how or why, but she could sense it deep in her bones. The Garden was no longer impenetrable. If it failed them, if it let the Technomancers through, there would be nowhere left to run.

She clenched her jaw, her fingers tightening around the strap of her pack. They needed answers. They needed a way out. But where did they even begin? The weight of uncertainty pressed down on her, turning every breath shallow and every step heavier. She cast a glance at Ronan, standing just ahead, his back to her as he studied the path before them. His posture was rigid and his shoulders tense. She knew he felt it too. The pressure. The silent, unspoken knowledge that time was running out.

Behind her, Milo was quieter than usual, his easy grin missing. He kept glancing over his shoulder, his restlessness bleeding through the cracks in his usual bravado. Kaela had known him long enough to tell when he was uneasy. Right now, he was as on edge as she was.

They were all feeling it. The slow tightening of the noose and the creeping realization that the Garden's protection was unraveling. If they did not act soon, their time here would end, whether they were ready or not. There would be no choice, no control over their fate. They would be dragged from this place, and the only question was when.

Kaela's gaze shifted back to the path ahead. The Garden, for all its beauty and power, was not their forever home. They had to leave. They had to step beyond its walls and face whatever waited for them in the unknown. The only question was how.

How would they outrun the Technomancers? How would they survive beyond this fading sanctuary? The answers felt just out of reach, but Kaela knew one thing for certain. The Garden had given them something. A connection. A bond. And with that, maybe they could find the strength to escape before the magic protecting them disappeared for good.

Milo shifted beside her, his usual humor dimmed by the thick weight of uncertainty. Ronan stood a short distance away, unmoving, but she could sense the tension radiating from him. His sharp, calculating gaze flickered between the horizon and the others, as if expecting something he could not quite name. His stillness was misleading. Beneath it, she knew, was the same restless energy that gripped them all.

Then, as if the very air around them had summoned her, Aelera appeared, cutting through the tension like a blade. She moved with an effortless grace, her presence commanding yet strangely soothing, as though she carried the weight of centuries in her steady gaze. The magic of the Garden seemed to stir around her, bending to her will, acknowledging her in a way that made Kaela's breath catch. In that moment, it was clear. Aelera was not just part of the Garden. She was woven into its very essence.

Aelera's presence was nothing short of captivating, drawing every bit of attention as she stepped into the clearing. Her silver hair caught the last rays of the dying sunlight, shimmering like the first stars of evening, casting an otherworldly glow around her. Her eyes, glowing with a soft but undeniable radiance, fixed on Kaela with an intensity that seemed to see beyond her, straight into the heart of her very being. The air around them seemed to still, as if nature itself held its breath, honoring Aelera's every movement. In that moment, Kaela felt small, insignificant, as though she was standing in the shadow of something ancient and immeasurable.

Milo, usually full of his usual witty energy, stood frozen. The ease he wore like a second skin was absent, replaced by a quiet intensity as he stared at Aelera, his eyes following her with an almost reverent attention. Kaela caught a fleeting glance between them, and in that brief exchange, she saw something unfamiliar in Milo's expression. A mix of admiration, perhaps even wonder. It was gone as quickly as it appeared, but it hadn't escaped Aelera's notice. Her gaze flicked to him, a knowing smile curving at the corner of her lips, before she turned back to Kaela.

"Kaela," Aelera's voice rang out, low and resonant, like a call that came from both within the earth and from the sky above. "You have felt it, haven't you? The pull of the magic. The Garden has begun to reveal its secrets to you."

Kaela's heart skipped at the mention of the magic, her pulse quickening. She nodded, a weight settling deep in her chest. "I don't understand it," she confessed, her voice betraying the uncertainty gnawing at her. "I feel it. This power. But I can't control it. I don't even know where to begin."

Aelera's gaze softened, though her face remained serious, marked by centuries of knowing. "Control is a myth, child," she said, her voice gentle but firm. "The Garden does not yield to force. It yields to trust."

Kaela frowned, struggling to comprehend. "Trust? How can I trust something I don't understand?"

Aelera moved closer, her presence exuding a warmth that seemed to reach deep inside Kaela, calming her when nothing else could. "The Garden is not an enemy, Kaela. It is a part of you. It calls to you because it recognizes something in you. Something worth protecting. But to wield its power, you must first learn to understand it. And to understand it, you must trust it. Let it guide you, and it will show you the way."

Kaela's mind raced, trying to piece together the meaning of Aelera's words, but the more she thought about them, the more they resonated. There was something deep inside her, a flicker of recognition, like a memory she couldn't fully grasp but somehow knew was true. For the first time, she felt a pull to believe in what

Aelera said, a call to trust in the magic, and in herself.

"I don't know how," Kaela whispered, her voice trembling with doubt. The weight of her uncertainty pressed down on her, each word carrying the heaviness of everything she didn't understand. "I don't even know where to start."

Aelera's smile was soft, yet imbued with a quiet power that seemed to hum in the air around them. "The magic is already inside you, Kaela. It always has been. You must learn to listen. To feel it in your bones, in your heart. The more you trust yourself, the more the magic will respond. The Garden is alive, but it is also a reflection of you."

Kaela nodded slowly, the force of Aelera's words settling deep in her chest, like an ancient truth she wasn't yet ready to fully grasp. It felt like a riddle with no clear answer, but one she had to try to solve. For herself, for Ronan, for Milo. There was too much at stake now to turn back.

Aelera's voice shifted, growing darker with an urgency that sent a shiver through Kaela's spine. "You must go," she said, her words carrying the weight of something that couldn't be ignored. "The path ahead will be perilous. The Garden will protect you, but only if you are prepared. You will leave soon, and the journey will be unforgiving. You will need more than strength. You will need your wits, and you will need to trust each other."

Kaela turned to Ronan, his face a mask of unreadable emotion, but his eyes, his eyes betrayed him. There was something there, a flicker of doubt or perhaps reluctance, something he wasn't ready to share. She didn't know if he feared what lay ahead or if the idea of leaving unsettled him, but there was a quiet storm in his silence.

"We're leaving," Kaela said, her voice steady with resolve. "We need to find answers, and we need to move before the Technomancers catch up to us."

Ronan didn't answer right away, but after a long pause, he gave the smallest nod. His gaze briefly flicked to Aelera before settling back on Kaela, and when he spoke, his voice was low, laden with the weight of the moment. "I'll guide you," he said, his words firm, deliberate. "But don't mistake this for easy. The wilderness is unforgiving. It's not just the land you have to worry about. The creatures . . . there are things that hide in the shadows."

Milo, who had been quiet up until now, spoke up, his voice brimming with a confidence that matched Kaela's growing determination. "We'll manage," he said, a spark of something Kaela couldn't quite place flashing in his eyes. "I've got supplies, tools, everything we need to survive. Right, Kaela?"

Kaela turned to him, her eyes meeting his with a shared resolve. "Right," she affirmed, her voice steady, her earlier doubts now slipping away. "We'll be fine. We just need to stay focused."

Aelera took a step back, her gaze lingering on them for a moment longer, unreadable as ever, before she turned toward the dense, mist-covered forest ahead. "The dome you seek lies ahead," she said, her voice laced with a prophetic finality. "It is not far, but the journey will test you. The path will not be straight, and the Garden will shift as you move through it. You must trust each other, and you must trust yourselves."

With those final words, she faded into the mist, her figure dissolving like a whisper carried away by the wind. Kaela stood still for a moment, the weight of Aelera's departure sinking in, the echo of her words still vibrating in the air. The path ahead was uncertain, but the words "trust" and "understand" continued to hum in her mind, urging her forward into the unknown, where the Garden awaited them all.

Milo seemed to snap back to himself, his eyes flickering between Kaela and Ronan, and then he grinned, his usual energy returning. But underneath it, there was something deeper. Something not quite in place. "Well then," he said, his voice laced with both determination and an unspoken edge. "Let's get moving. This is definitely going to be one for the books."

Kaela caught Ronan's gaze. He was already scanning the horizon, his expression unreadable, but she saw it. The weight of the choice that loomed over them. There was no turning back now. A surge of determination swept through Kaela, settling her thoughts like a heavy stone. Aelera's words had anchored themselves deep within her, grounding her in this moment. The uncertainty that had clouded her mind earlier was gone, replaced by something quieter. Stronger. She didn't understand everything. The magic, the Garden, the path ahead, but she knew they couldn't stay here. The Garden had offered them shelter, but it was a temporary reprieve. The answers they needed were out there, and she would find them.

Her eyes drifted across the landscape. The trees, vibrant and tangled, swayed gently in the evening breeze, their leaves whispering secrets she couldn't hear. The golden light of the setting sun cast long, shifting shadows over the ground, and the air was thick with the scent of damp earth and the hum of ancient, untapped power. Yet, in the stillness, Kaela couldn't help but feel small. A single thread in a vast, living tapestry. As she turned back to Ronan and Milo, their faces mirrored her resolve, and something deep within her told her this was the right choice. The Garden had given them temporary safety, but the Technomancers were coming. They needed to leave. There was too much at stake.

"We're ready," Kaela said, her voice steady despite the whirl of thoughts spinning through her mind. "Let's go."

The journey into the wilderness beyond the Garden was nothing like Kaela had imagined. She had expected a path, challenging yet manageable. Difficult but not impossible. The reality, however, was far more daunting. The air was thick with humidity, clinging to her skin as if trying to hold her back. The ground beneath their feet was uneven, treacherous, with roots that seemed to rise up from the earth and thick underbrush that snagged at their clothes. Each step felt like they were plunging deeper into a realm both alien and ancient, as though the earth itself was alive and watching them. The deeper they went, the more Kaela felt the pull of something larger than any of them. A force, a presence, ancient and powerful, guiding them forward, or perhaps drawing them in.

Ronan moved ahead, his pace fluid and confident despite the obstacles. His dark curls bounced with each stride, his golden-green eyes sharp as he scanned their surroundings, always alert. Kaela couldn't help but admire him, the way he navigated the thick foliage with ease, as if he had been walking through forests like this his entire life. It was both comforting and unsettling. Ronan was their guide, but Kaela sensed something in him that wasn't quite at ease. Even he, it seemed, wasn't fully comfortable in this untamed wilderness.

Kaela kept close behind, every sense heightened. Her eyes darted from tree to tree, her pulse quickening as the constant hum of unfamiliar energy buzzed through the air. Milo walked beside her, his usual exuberance subdued, his focus sharp. He wasn't the same Milo she had known, his playful energy muted, replaced by a quiet intensity. The ever-present alertness in him reminded her this wasn't just an adventure anymore. This was a journey into the unknown, into danger. And the stakes were much higher than they had anticipated.

The forest around them seemed to close in as the trees towered above like silent sentinels, their gnarled trunks twisted by centuries of growth. Their canopy was so dense that only slivers of light managed to break through, casting strange, flickering shadows on the forest floor. The air was thick with the smell of moss and earth, but there was something else. A faint sweetness, like flowers Kaela had never seen before, mingling with the dampness of the forest. The scents wrapped around her, dizzying and overwhelming, as if the forest was breathing with them.

Time seemed to slow here. The air held weight, as if it carried memories and secrets buried deep within the earth. Kaela could feel it. The pulse of something ancient beneath her feet. This was no ordinary forest. This was the Garden, and it wasn't just watching them. It was alive in ways she couldn't yet understand. And she couldn't shake the feeling that they were trespassers in a realm that wasn't meant to be disturbed.

As they ventured deeper into the wilderness, a growing sense of isolation washed over Kaela. The world outside seemed to fade away, as though they had stepped into a realm all their own. There was no sign of civilization. No distant chatter, no hum of human life. The only sounds were the whispering leaves, the snap of twigs underfoot, and the occasional call of unseen creatures, their voices strange and unfamiliar. The air felt thick, heavy with something ancient, as if the forest itself were holding its breath. Kaela couldn't shake the feeling that they weren't just walking through a forgotten part of the world, they were trespassing in a place far older and far more alive than they could comprehend.

"We need to keep moving," Ronan said, his voice low but sharp with that same edge Kaela had come to expect. His gaze swept over the landscape, scanning every shadow as though danger could spring from any direction. "The dome isn't far, but we need to make sure we're not followed. The last thing we need is to be caught out here with no way back."

Kaela nodded, the words hanging in the air, heavy with the weight of their journey. The Garden had been their shelter, a fragile calm before the storm, and now that they were leaving it behind, Kaela felt the world outside pressing in on them. She trusted Ronan's instincts, but a knot of unease settled in her chest. She glanced over her shoulder at the path they had traveled, the way the trees closed in behind them like silent watchers. "Do you think they're already out there?" she asked, her voice barely above a whisper.

Ronan shot her a quick, wry glance, a flicker of humor in his eyes despite the tension that rippled through him. His grin was fleeting, replaced by the sharp focus she had come to know well. "If they are, they're probably just as lost as we are," he replied, his tone light but undercut with something darker. "We can't afford to take chances. Let's keep moving."

Milo, ever the practical one, adjusted his pack with methodical precision. He checked their supplies, muttering about food and water rations. "We've got enough to last us a few days," he said, his voice steady but with an edge of caution. "But we need to be careful. The wilderness isn't kind, and we don't know what we'll run into out here." He looked up, his eyes narrowing, as though seeing more than just the trees. "Whatever's out there, I'm guessing it's not something you want to cross paths with."

Kaela's chest tightened, a mixture of gratitude and concern washing over her. She'd always known Milo was resourceful, but in this moment, his foresight felt like a lifeline. She smiled at him, though the unease that lingered in her chest hadn't quite loosened its grip. "We'll manage," she said, her voice steady, but it was more for herself than him. "We'll make it work."

Ronan's voice cut through the moment, low and commanding. "Keep your eyes open. We'll make camp soon. The night will be colder than you expect." His tone had an air of finality, but there was also that touch of wit Kaela had grown so used to. "And don't even think about finding some nice warm rock to sleep on, Kaela," he added, a teasing smirk tugging at the corner of his lips. "We all need to stay alert tonight."

Kaela rolled her eyes, but a small laugh escaped her despite the gravity of their situation. "I'll keep that in mind," she replied, her voice lighter than it had been moments before. Even in the midst of everything, there was something comforting about the way Ronan's teasing cut through the tension. Something that made her feel, for just a moment, like they were still a team. A family, facing this together.

They walked for hours, the landscape shifting with every step as they ventured deeper into the wilderness. The trees grew taller, their twisted branches weaving into a dense canopy that blocked out most of the sunlight, leaving the forest dim and shadowed. The air grew thick with the scent of damp earth, moss, and flowers Kaela didn't recognize. This place felt different. Alive in a way that made the hairs on the back of her neck stand on end. The farther they went, the more distant the Garden's protective energy seemed, and the more Kaela felt like they were entering a realm that was untamed and unpredictable. The stillness was unsettling, as if the land itself was waiting for something, watching them from the shadows.

"We need to set up camp," Milo said, his voice cutting through the quiet. "We're losing daylight." His tone wasn't just practical, it carried a warning. "We don't know what's out here, and I'm not taking chances by staying out in the open once it gets dark."

Ronan nodded, his face unreadable. "Agreed. We need shelter before nightfall. We can't afford to be exposed out here."

The three of them moved quickly, scanning the dense forest for a safe place to make camp. As they worked, Kaela's mind drifted back to Aelera's words. The Garden had chosen her, but now she had to learn to listen to it, to trust it. Aelera had said the magic had always been inside her, she just had to find it. Kaela felt the weight of that responsibility settle heavily on her chest. There was no turning back now. She had to figure this out, for herself, for Ronan, and for Milo.

Kaela found a large rock and sat, closing her eyes, trying to focus. The sounds of the forest surrounded her. The rustling of leaves, the distant calls of strange creatures, and the steady hum of magic that seemed to vibrate through the air. She couldn't see it, couldn't touch it, but she felt it, an invisible current, flowing just beneath the surface of everything. It was subtle and elusive, but it was there. Kaela took a deep breath, trying to center herself, to connect with that energy. She didn't know how yet, but she had to learn. It was the only way forward.

Nearby, the fire crackled. Kaela opened her eyes to see Milo and Ronan working together, setting up camp. There was a quiet ease to their movements, a shared understanding between them that Kaela envied. They had been through so much already, and now they had each other to rely on. She didn't have that confidence yet, not like they did. But she would. She had to.

As the night drew closer, a chill began to settle in the air, biting at Kaela's skin. She pulled her cloak tighter around her shoulders, the weight of the journey ahead pressing on her. But she wasn't alone. She had Ronan, with his quiet strength, and Milo, with his sharp mind. Together, they would face whatever came next. For now, that was enough.

The night fell over the wilderness, bringing with it a heavy stillness. The temperature dropped sharply, and the cool air seemed to seep into their bones, forcing Kaela to draw her cloak tighter. The trees, now dark silhouettes against the fading sky, loomed overhead like silent sentinels, their branches creaking in the wind as though they were whispering secrets she couldn't understand. The wilderness felt vast, yet suffocating, its quiet broken only by the crackling of their campfire. The flames danced, casting long, flickering shadows across the trio. The shadows stretched and shifted, as if alive, as if they, too, were watching.

Ronan moved around the camp with effortless precision, his every movement fluid and deliberate, as though he belonged to the wilderness itself. He didn't need to speak to command. They all knew what had to be done. With practiced hands, he set up traps and signals, his eyes constantly scanning the shadows, alert to any shift in the dense forest. His body moved in rhythm with the land, his presence as natural as the wind rustling through the trees. He was a man shaped by years in the wild, attuned to the silence and the dangers it concealed. He worked without a word, his focus unwavering, as if this was nothing more than another night in a life he had long accepted.

Milo, by contrast, was a whirlwind of energy. Now that they had a moment to catch their breath, his usual enthusiasm returned, and he dove into his pack with an excited flurry. Gadgets, tools, survival gear tumbled out in a rapid cascade, his hands moving so quickly that Kaela could barely keep up. His voice was a steady stream of plans and observations. "We've got rations, but they won't last forever," he said, his tone practical, though a spark of excitement danced in his eyes. "Tomorrow, we need to find fresh water. And I've got some extra stuff for navigation. Compasses, flares, some tech that might help us communicate if we get too separated." He paused, looking up from his pack with a grin that could light up the darkest night. "But the Garden . . . it's messing with signals, so if things go south, we might be on our own. No big deal," he added with a shrug. "We always manage."

Kaela smiled despite herself, touched by his optimism. Milo had always been the one to lighten the mood, to bring balance when everything seemed too heavy. His confidence was contagious, and for a moment, it almost made her believe things would be fine. But even as his words rang with certainty, Kaela felt the weight of their situation settle deeper in her chest. The wilderness around them seemed vast and uninviting, stretching on endlessly beyond the firelight. With every gust of wind, the trees seemed to whisper, as though something, or someone, was waiting.

She stared into the fire, the flames flickering and crackling, but the unease that had tightened her chest since leaving the Garden only deepened. It was an invisible pressure, slowly building, as though the wilderness itself was pressing in on her. She couldn't shake the feeling of being watched, of being observed by something just out of reach. It wasn't the usual unease that came with the unknown. No, this was different. This was a presence. Something lingering, just beyond the firelight, like a shadow that refused to move.

Kaela found herself glancing over her shoulder repeatedly, expecting to see movement in the darkness. But each time, there was nothing, only the stillness of the wilderness, the endless stretch of trees that seemed to go on forever. Every snap of a twig, every rustle of leaves sent her heart racing, but when she turned to look, there was nothing there. The night felt endless, the forest stretching in every direction, as though time itself had forgotten to stop. And still, that feeling clung to the air. Heavy, unshakable. They weren't alone. She could feel it, even if she couldn't see it.

Kaela's gaze drifted to Ronan, his face bathed in the flickering glow of the fire. His expression was unreadable, his posture relaxed, but Kaela could see the tension in his eyes. He was alert, scanning the dark edges of their camp, waiting for something to break the stillness, just as she was. Milo, however, was oblivious to the simmering tension. He was already back to his usual whirlwind, pulling out tools, muttering about the routes they might take the next day. Kaela couldn't help but envy how effortlessly Milo compartmentalized his worries, his mind always bouncing between plans, optimism, and a thousand ideas. How did he do it? How could he remain so unfazed in the face of everything that loomed over them?

The fire crackled again, the sound sharp and invasive in the quiet of the wilderness. Kaela exhaled slowly, trying to shake off the restlessness that had settled in her chest. They were here. They were together. And for now, they had a plan. But deep down, Kaela couldn't ignore the feeling that this was just the beginning, that the hardest part was still to come. And the wilderness, whatever it had in store, wasn't going to let them walk through it easily.

Ronan moved closer to the fire, settling down beside it with the ease of someone who had spent years living in the wild. His body was relaxed, but his eyes never stopped scanning, always alert. The flames danced over his features, casting shifting shadows across his jawline and making him look both at peace and ready for anything. His presence, commanding as always, seemed to grow stronger in the quiet of the night. He turned his head slightly, meeting Kaela's gaze with an intensity that made her pulse skip. She fought to keep her expression neutral.

His voice broke the silence, low and steady. "Tomorrow, we head for the dome. We move quickly, stay low, and avoid anything that looks . . . too alive."

Kaela raised an eyebrow, her curiosity piqued. "Too alive?"

Ronan's lips quirked into a half-smile, a glint of mischief in his eyes, but his tone remained serious. "The wilderness here isn't just plants and trees. Some of the creatures are far worse than anything you've seen in the Garden. There are predators that hunt in packs, creatures that can mimic sound, and others . . . older than they should be." He leaned forward slightly, his gaze never leaving hers, as if testing her reaction. "You'll learn to recognize the signs, but until then, trust your instincts."

A chill ran down Kaela's spine. His words lingered in the air, heavy with the reality of what they were about to face. She glanced over at Milo, hoping for some of his usual bravado to lighten the mood. Instead, he snorted, a grin tugging at his lips. "I'm more worried about surviving without Wi-Fi."

Kaela laughed, the sound light but relieving. Milo's humor was a much-needed distraction, easing the tension in her shoulders. But as the laughter died down, the gravity of their situation settled back in, like a weight pressing against her chest. The fire crackled between them, but it did little to chase away the uncertainty that gnawed at her. Ronan's warning echoed in her mind: This wasn't the Garden. They were stepping into something far older, far more dangerous. And if they weren't careful, the wilderness would swallow them whole.

Kaela couldn't help but glance at Ronan again, his face partly illuminated by the firelight, the flickering shadows accentuating the sharp lines of his jaw and the intensity in his eyes. There was something about him, something magnetic that she couldn't quite explain. He was their guide, their protector, and yet there was an undeniable connection between them. Raw, unspoken, but palpable. His confidence settled over her like a warm cloak, but it also stirred something deeper within her. A flutter of unease mixed with a strange, unshakable trust. She didn't understand it, but she felt it in her bones. She trusted him, even when every rational part of her mind told her to be cautious. It unsettled her, but it also gave her a strange sense of peace.

"We'll stick together," Kaela said, her voice steady despite the flutter of uncertainty that still lingered in her chest. "We're not getting separated. Not now, not ever."

Milo, ever the optimist, flashed her a grin so wide it was impossible not to feel the warmth of it. "We've got this," he said, his voice light, but there was an unspoken promise behind his words. He wasn't just trying to keep their spirits up, he believed it, truly believed it.

Kaela met his gaze, feeling the weight of their bond, the quiet reassurance in his words, and nodded. Milo's optimism had always been a grounding force for her, the steady presence that kept the world from feeling too heavy. But even with him at her side, the path ahead felt uncertain, like they were on the verge of something that could change everything. Still, the three of them, together, was a solid foundation. They had each other, and that had to be enough.

The night wore on in quiet preparation, the trio slipping into an unspoken rhythm. They ate their rations, checked their gear, and made final adjustments to their packs. The sounds of the forest around them were muted, yet everything seemed to hum with an energy that made Kaela's skin prickle. She tried to focus, to keep her mind on the task at hand, but Aelera's cryptic words kept echoing in her thoughts: *Trust the magic. Trust the Garden.* But how could she trust something she barely understood? Magic had always been a distant hum in the background of her life, a soft whisper at the edge of her senses, but now, with everything on the line, it felt more like a weight she had to carry.

As she lay on her bedroll later that night, the sounds of the forest pressing in around her, Kaela closed her eyes and let the cool air wash over her skin. She tried to clear her mind, to find some peace amidst the chaos that churned inside her. But the pulse of energy within her was undeniable. It was there, constant and thrumming, like the beat of her heart. The magic that had always been a part of her was now a force she could feel more clearly, a current running beneath the surface of everything. The more she focused on it, the more she realized that this wasn't just a gift. It was a responsibility. A responsibility she couldn't afford to ignore.

Kaela knew Ronan had warned them of the dangers that lurked in this wilderness. He had seen them before. Creatures that could tear them apart if they weren't careful. But what if the real danger wasn't out there in the dark? What if it was the magic inside her? If she couldn't learn to control it, to wield it, then the threats Ronan spoke of wouldn't just be dangers—they would be their downfall. Kaela couldn't afford to fail. The weight of that responsibility settled over her like a cloak, heavier than anything she had carried before. But as she lay there, the firelight flickering softly beside her, she realized something else too—she wasn't alone. Ronan, Milo—they were with her. And maybe, just maybe, that was enough to keep them safe

The morning light filtered through the dense canopy of trees, casting long, jagged shadows across the forest floor. Kaela stirred, the soft rustling of leaves and distant bird calls pulling her from sleep. The cool, quiet stillness of the early morning wrapped around her like a blanket. She stretched, feeling the stiffness in her muscles from a restless night spent on the hard ground. The weight of their journey pressed heavily on her, but she shook off the grogginess and pushed herself up, gathering her bearings as her eyes scanned the campsite. Everything was packed away, ready for the day ahead.

Milo was already up, crouched beside his gear, his hands moving with practiced speed as he tinkered with a small device. His wild hair looked even messier than usual, sticking out in all directions, but it didn't seem to bother him in the least. His eyes gleamed with the same enthusiasm that never seemed to fade, even in the face of danger, his mind already racing ahead to the next challenge. Despite the tension in the air, his energy was a constant, like a spark that couldn't be extinguished, and it made Kaela feel momentarily lighter.

Ronan stood at the edge of the clearing, his posture tense, eyes scanning the horizon. He was a study in quiet focus, unaffected by the morning chill, every inch of him alert. His gaze flicked over to Kaela for a brief moment, sharp and unreadable. He took in everything at once, like a predator in its element. But there was something else in his vigilance, a subtle, protective edge, as if he carried the weight of the world on his shoulders and would never let anything happen to them.

"Ready?" His voice broke the stillness, steady yet laced with an intensity Kaela couldn't quite ignore. He was always like this. Commanding, a little teasing, but never giving her more than she could handle. And still, there was a part of her that wanted to lean into that, to let him take the lead.

Kaela felt that familiar surge of determination rise within her. There was no turning back now. "Let's do this," she said, her voice firm, pushing aside the remnants of doubt.

They packed quickly, the weight of the journey ahead settling over them. The forest was unnervingly quiet, the usual hum of wildlife muted, as though even the land itself was holding its breath. Milo's voice filled the silence, a constant stream of low commentary as he tucked away gadgets, muttering about routes and survival plans. Ronan moved with quiet precision, his eyes flickering over the treeline, scanning every inch of the wilderness around them. It was like he could sense danger before it even appeared, and it made Kaela feel oddly safe . . . and a little unsettled at the same time.

Once everything was packed and they'd ensured they left no trace, they set off. Ronan led the way, his movements confident and sure, like the terrain was second nature to him. The path ahead was rough. Dense underbrush and uneven ground that slowed Kaela's pace, but Ronan barely seemed to notice. He glided through the wilderness, every step effortless, as if the forest itself bent to his will. Kaela struggled to keep up, her legs aching with each step, but she pushed herself, refusing to fall behind.

And yet, no matter how hard she tried, she couldn't shake the feeling that Ronan was waiting for her to catch up. His pace didn't change, but there was something in the way he moved, a deliberate ease that kept her just a little behind. She caught herself glancing at him more often than she should, trying to read the unreadable, to figure out what was lurking behind those teasing eyes of his.

"Keep up, Kaela," Ronan called over his shoulder, his voice laced with playful challenge. "I wouldn't want to have to carry you."

She bristled at his words, but a small, unbidden smile tugged at her lips. "I'm not some damsel in distress," she shot back, forcing her legs to move faster.

He glanced back at her, his lips curling into a teasing smile that made her heart skip a beat. "I never said you were. Just don't slow me down." His tone was light, but the edge of something else lingered underneath, something that left her wondering if he was just playing with her, or if it was something more. With each step, the distance between them seemed to grow smaller.

Milo kept pace beside her, his voice a constant presence as he rambled on about their plans. "We'll need to find shelter before nightfall," he said, his tone laced with concern. "I've got a thermal blanket in my pack, but if it gets too cold, we'll be in trouble. The temperature drops fast after sunset. And if the weather shifts, we'll have bigger problems." He trailed off, glancing around as if mentally calculating their next move. "We need to be careful."

Kaela nodded, her gaze sweeping over the changing landscape. The deeper they ventured into the wilderness, the more unsettling it became. The trees were enormous, their trunks twisted and gnarled, as though the forest itself had been here long before they arrived. The thick canopy above blocked out most of the sunlight, casting the forest floor in a muted twilight. The air felt different here. Denser, alive with an ancient energy that made her skin prickle.

Strange plants dotted their path. Some with flowers that glowed faintly, others with leaves that shimmered like glass. Kaela's fingers itched to touch one of the glowing petals, and when she did, a sharp jolt of energy surged through her, as if the plant had recognized her touch. She pulled back, startled, the strange hum of magic lingering in her fingertips.

"Careful with that," Milo called over his shoulder. His usual teasing tone was gone, replaced with a rare note of caution. "We don't know what these things do. They're not exactly . . . friendly."

Kaela glanced back at the plant, her curiosity still piqued, the lingering hum of magic tingling in her fingertips. The deeper they ventured, the more the landscape seemed to shift, as if the forest itself were watching, waiting. Shadows stretched unnaturally beneath the thick canopy, and the air carried an eerie stillness that set her on edge. It felt less like they were passing through the land and more like the land was measuring them, testing their worth.

She looked at Milo, who was walking ahead, eyes scanning the path. "How do you know so much about this place?" she asked, her curiosity getting the best of her. "You talk like you've been here before."

Milo hesitated for a moment, a flicker of something in his eyes that Kaela couldn't quite place. Then, with a half-shrug, he answered, "My family had a cabin out here. A little place no one knew about, deep in the forest." He said it so casually that Kaela almost didn't notice the subtle shift in his tone. "It was . . . a secret, I guess. I didn't talk about it much."

Kaela blinked in surprise. "You never mentioned it."

Milo shrugged again, his walls coming up. "There's not much to say. It was just a place where we could get away. My parents were big on keeping things private, and the cabin was part of that." He gave a half-hearted laugh, but it didn't quite reach his eyes. "I used to spend a lot of time there, learning about the land, how to survive in it. My dad showed me a few things. But after everything that happened . . . well, I just didn't think it was something worth talking about."

Kaela frowned, the weight of his unspoken words settling between them. She didn't press, knowing that Milo's secrets were never easily shared. Still, the idea of a hidden cabin. Something so personal he'd never told her about, felt like a small but significant piece of a puzzle she wasn't quite allowed to see. Instead, she nodded, choosing to let it go. "Sounds like it helped."

"Yeah," Milo said, his voice lightening, the familiar grin returning to his face. "Came in handy. Now, let's just hope I remember everything." He flashed her a grin, and despite the heaviness of their situation, Kaela couldn't help but smile back, grateful for the brief moment of levity.

As they pressed on, Ronan moved through the wilderness with a quiet, effortless confidence, his pace never faltering. There was something about the way he carried himself. Calm, alert, like he belonged to the wild just as much as the trees and shadows around them. Kaela couldn't fully explain it, but there was a comfort in it, a sense of security she hadn't realized she'd been craving. The land around them shifted as they ventured deeper, the air thick with something unspoken, something ancient.

Despite the beauty of the forest, unease curled in Kaela's chest, growing heavier with every step. The towering trees, their gnarled trunks wrapped in thick vines, cast long, shifting shadows, turning the path ahead into a labyrinth of light and dark. It was breathtaking, in a way, but it felt wrong. Like the forest was watching, waiting. She glanced over her shoulder, but there was nothing there, only the rustling of leaves and the whisper of the wind through the canopy.

Still, the sensation of unseen eyes on her refused to fade. The further they went, the more the forest seemed to close in, like it was testing them, waiting for them to prove themselves, or fail. Her instincts screamed that they weren't alone, but when she scanned the underbrush, there was nothing. She pushed the feeling aside, focusing on the path ahead. They had a destination. They had a purpose. But the tension in the air told her they weren't the only ones who knew it.

After hours of travel, the landscape began to change. The towering trees thinned, their trunks twisted and skeletal, their leaves sparse as though they had withered under an unseen force. The ground turned rocky, uneven, forcing them to pick their steps carefully. The air grew colder. Not the natural chill of nightfall, but something deeper, unnatural, seeping into her bones like a warning. Every snap of a twig, every rustle in the underbrush felt amplified in the silence, each sound sending a fresh wave of adrenaline through her.

Finally, the trees parted, revealing a clearing bathed in pale, filtered light. At its center stood the remnants of a structure. Stone walls half-consumed by nature, their once-sharp edges softened by time. Moss and vines crept over the ruins, but even in its decay, the shape was unmistakable. A dome.

The air around him felt charged, as if he could sense something lurking just beyond their sight. Every muscle in his body was coiled, ready to strike at the first sign of danger. Kaela watched him closely, unease creeping up her spine. If Ronan was on edge, there was a reason. The ruins were silent, but the tension in the air was deafening.

"We're close," he murmured, his voice low, laced with something unreadable. "Stay alert."

The weight of unspoken fears settled between them, heavier than the humid air around them. Milo gave a small, reassuring nod, but it did little to ease the tension tightening in Kaela's chest. She could tell he felt it too. The sense that they were standing on the edge of something they couldn't turn back from. With a steadying breath, she tightened her grip on her pack and forced herself to move forward.

The air shifted the moment they stepped inside. A chill swept through the ruins, carrying the faint scent of decay of time long forgotten. Strange symbols covered the walls, their carved edges glowing faintly in the dim light. Some were familiar, others entirely foreign, but all of them pulsed with an energy Kaela could feel thrumming beneath her skin.

Milo moved toward the markings, his fingers trailing just shy of the stone. "These are ancient," he muttered, eyes narrowing. "But they don't make sense. Some of these symbols . . . they aren't from any language I know."

Kaela barely heard him. A pull, deep and undeniable, drew her forward. The symbols seemed to hum in her presence, their glow intensifying as she reached toward them. The moment her fingertips met the stone, the magic surged. A pulse of energy rippled through her, raw and electric, setting her heart pounding. The symbols rearranged themselves before her eyes, shifting, twisting, revealing a message hidden beneath centuries of dust and time. Her breath caught as she whispered the words aloud, the weight of them settling into her bones.

"This is the way. Follow the path. Trust the magic." The words hung in the air, vibrating like an unspoken command, like a promise.

Kaela's pulse thundered in her ears. The power of the Garden wasn't just legend. It was real. And it was waiting for them. There was no turning back now.

Chapter 19

The air inside the dome felt heavier now, thick with the weight of secrets just out of reach. The symbols still pulsed faintly on the stone, their glow like embers refusing to die, a lingering echo of the magic that had surged through Kaela moments before. *This is the way. Follow the path. Trust the magic.* The words had unveiled a truth, but instead of clarity, they had left her with more questions. Questions that gnawed at the edges of her thoughts.

Kaela's fingers hovered over the wall, her skin still tingling from the energy that had coursed through her. The Garden wasn't just a sanctuary; she could feel it now, something deeper, something far greater than any of them had realized. But what *was* it? And why had its secrets been buried beneath time and silence?

Milo's voice cut through Kaela's thoughts, low and intent as he traced the symbols with careful precision. His fingers hovered just above the stone, following patterns that seemed to pulse beneath his touch. "These aren't just instructions," he murmured, his brow furrowing. "This is a map. A map to something else. Something the Technomancers have been searching for." His voice trailed off, the weight of his realization settling over them like a storm on the horizon.

Kaela's heart skipped a beat. *The Technomancers.* The ones who had hunted Ronan, twisted her father's research, and corrupted the Garden's magic for their own ends. The truth about them had always loomed at the edges of her mind, half-formed and distant. But now, it was crystallizing, sharp and undeniable, cutting through her like a blade.

The walls of the dome seemed to press in, the air thick with something unspoken. The hum of the symbols resonated through her skin, sending a shiver down her spine. This wasn't just about unlocking secrets anymore. This was about survival.

Ronan stepped closer, his movements quiet, deliberate. His golden-green eyes flickered over the symbols, his expression unreadable, but Kaela could feel the shift in him. An intensity that hadn't been there before. He wasn't just observing; he *understood* in a way she didn't yet. Beneath his usual calm, there was something darker, something knowing. A flicker of warning or maybe certainty, and she felt drawn to it, drawn to *him*. The heat of his presence sent a ripple through her, but she forced herself to focus. There was too much at stake.

Ronan reached out, his fingers gliding over the wall with deliberate precision. There was something in the way he touched the symbols, an unspoken familiarity, as if he was attuned to the magic in a way Kaela could only begin to grasp. The markings shifted in response, their glow deepening, revealing hidden layers beneath the surface. The air thickened with power, and Kaela's breath caught in her throat.

"There's more," Ronan murmured, his voice edged with a dark certainty, as though he had already glimpsed the truth long before this moment. "The Technomancers didn't just want the Garden. They wanted to control it. Control *everything.*" His fingers hesitated over one of the symbols before he turned to face Kaela and Milo. His golden-green eyes burned with an unsettling knowing, a weight that seemed to reach into Kaela's very core. "They've been searching for a way to manipulate the Garden's magic. *To weaponize* it."

The words sliced through Kaela like cold steel, the realization settling deep. The Technomancers weren't just power-hungry. They weren't simply scavengers of lost magic. They were something far worse. Calculating, relentless, willing to twist the very fabric of the world to suit their will. And they would stop at nothing to claim what they sought.

Milo cursed under his breath, tension coiled tight in his shoulders. "So they've been hunting the Garden, not just for its power, but to *control* it?"

Ronan nodded, his jaw tightening, fury simmering just beneath the surface. "Exactly. And whoever controls the Garden, controls *everything.*" His voice was low, edged with something dangerous, something personal. "That's why they've been after me. I was part of their plans, once." His golden-green eyes flicked to Kaela, dark and unreadable. "But now . . . now they want *you.*"

The words slammed into her, knocking the breath from her lungs. She had always known the Technomancers were dangerous, but this was something else. They weren't just hoarding power. They were weaving a noose around the world, tightening their grip on everything, *everyone.* And now she was at the center of it. Not just as an obstacle, but as a piece of their plan. A resource to be controlled. The thought sent ice slicing through her veins, anger and fear tangling in her chest like a vice.

"We can't let them get their hands on it." Kaela's voice was steady, but her fingers dug into the stone wall, grounding herself in the weight of the moment. "We can't let them twist the magic. Not after everything they've done."

Ronan's gaze softened, just for a second, an ember of quiet understanding beneath the storm. His hand found her shoulder, a light touch, but solid, *anchoring.* A silent promise. She hadn't realized how much she needed it until now. "We won't," he murmured, his voice firm, certain. "We'll stop them. *Together.*"

Beside them, Milo exhaled sharply, shaking his head. His usual restless energy was gone, replaced by something heavier, sharper. "But we need to know more. How deep this goes. What they're planning next. And we need allies." His gaze swept between them, determination hardening his features. "Because if we try to take them on alone, we won't win."

Kaela's eyes met Ronan's, and for a moment, the world narrowed to just the two of them. His gaze was steady, intense, and in it, she saw the same realization that was tightening in her own chest. They weren't just searching for answers anymore. They were stepping into a war. One that would decide not only the fate of the Garden but the fate of everything they knew. The weight of it pressed down on her like a gathering storm, heavy and inescapable. The path ahead was uncertain, but one thing was clear: there was no turning back.

"We need to go deeper," Ronan said, his voice low, resolute. His fingers traced the symbols again, as if searching for a hidden truth within their glow. "There's an old network of allies, people who fought the Technomancers long before we ever got caught in this. They've been forced into the shadows, but they're still out there."

Milo's brow furrowed, the spark of curiosity flashing in his eyes. He was always the one chasing knowledge, drawn to questions like a moth to flame. "Who are they? And where do we find them?"

Ronan hesitated, the weight of history hanging in the silence between them. His gaze drifted toward the overgrown ruins beyond the dome, as if measuring the distance between past and present. "The Guardians," he said at last, his voice thick with meaning. "They were the ones who protected the Garden before it fell into the wrong hands. They've been waiting for someone to awaken the magic again. *They're the key to stopping the Technomancers."*

The name sent a ripple through Kaela's chest, a thread of recognition pulling at something deep within her. Aelera's words echoed in her mind. *You will need allies.* Had she meant the Guardians? The thought settled over her like a lock clicking into place. Fear still coiled in her gut, but beneath it, something steadier took root. Determination.

The air around them thickened, the last traces of daylight stretching the shadows long across the clearing. Kaela exhaled slowly, gripping the edge of the stone as if bracing herself. This was no longer just a search for truth. This was a fight for survival. And the battle had already begun.

"Where do we find them?" Kaela asked, keeping her voice steady despite the storm of emotions tightening in her chest. There was no turning back now.

Ronan turned toward the forest, his gaze sharp as he studied the darkening horizon. The trees swayed in the rising wind, their branches whispering like secrets carried through the night. The world beyond the dome felt different now. Charged, expectant, as if the land itself was bracing for what was to come. The weight of their discovery settled over them like a heavy shroud, but beneath it, Kaela felt something else. A spark of hope.

"We head north," Ronan said, meeting her eyes. "Deep in the mountains, there's a stronghold. That's where the Guardians have been waiting."

The mention of the mountains sent a flood of images through Kaela's mind. Jagged peaks cutting into the sky, ancient stone worn by time, and whispers of secrets buried beneath layers of rock and history. The stronghold was more than just hidden; it was veiled in mystery, tucked away in a place few knew of and even fewer could reach. It existed outside the grasp of the world, a sanctuary for those who had once stood as protectors of the Garden.

Kaela exhaled slowly, nodding as she tried to steady the whirlwind of thoughts racing through her mind. The path ahead had never been clearer, yet the weight of it settled over her like a heavy cloak. There was no turning back now. They had to move fast and stay ahead of the Technomancers, reach the Guardians before it was too late.

As they gathered their things, the urgency of the moment pressed down on them. The air felt charged, the forest unnervingly still, as if the land itself sensed the coming storm. Kaela's pulse pounded in her ears, her magic stirring beneath her skin, restless and alert. The Technomancers were closer than they realized, and their reach would only tighten unless they stopped them.

"We need to move. Now," Milo said, his voice firm as he secured his bag, his usual easygoing nature replaced by sharp focus. "If we don't, they'll be on us before we even get close."

Ronan's gaze flicked to him, his expression unreadable, but the slight clench of his jaw spoke volumes. He was already anticipating the worst. "We won't let that happen," he said, his voice quiet but edged with certainty. "We can't afford to."

The world around them felt suspended in time, the air thick with anticipation as they prepared to leave. What had once been a quiet, hidden sanctuary now felt like the ruins of a battlefield, haunted by the ghosts of its past, bracing for the storm to come. The remnants of the dome loomed in the fading light, silent sentinels standing watch as if bearing witness to the choice they had made. Kaela's pulse quickened. They had uncovered so much, yet the deeper they dug, the more the truth unraveled. More questions, more uncertainty. But hesitation was a luxury they couldn't afford. The path ahead was dark, but there was no turning back.

Ronan moved with quiet urgency, every motion precise, calculated. But there was a grace to him, an effortless confidence that made the very air around him feel charged. Kaela tried to ignore it, tried to focus on the road ahead, but the pull of him was undeniable, a presence that unsettled something deep within her. A force she didn't fully understand but couldn't shake.

The forest swallowed them as they pressed forward, its towering trees weaving together into a canopy that closed them off from the world outside. The ground was uneven beneath their feet, the air sharp with the scent of earth and pine. Somewhere in the distance, water rushed over stone, a sound that felt both soothing and ominous. Kaela's thoughts churned with the weight of everything they had learned. The Technomancers were out there, hunting them. The Guardians were their only hope, but what if they had been gone for too long? What if there was nothing left to find? The uncertainty gnawed at her, but there was no room for doubt. Not now.

As they climbed higher into the mountains, the journey became an endless test of will. The cold bit through their layers, the air thinning with every step. The trees grew sparse, their skeletal branches reaching for the sky like clawed fingers. The wind howled through the rocky passes, a chilling reminder that they were stepping deeper into the unknown. Kaela's muscles ached from the relentless terrain, her breath coming in sharp bursts, but she pushed forward. Stopping wasn't an option. The Technomancers were closing in, and every second wasted brought them closer to danger.

By the time they found a small, sheltered cave for the night, darkness had swallowed the sky, and the cold had seeped into their bones. Their fire crackled weakly, its flickering light barely holding back the creeping shadows. Kaela sat close to the flames, hugging her knees to her chest, trying to absorb whatever warmth she could. Across from her, Ronan sat at the cave's entrance, his silhouette outlined against the night, his gaze locked on the horizon. Always watching. Always waiting. His presence was like a shield, steady and unyielding, yet something unspoken hung between them. An invisible thread pulled taut.

Tonight, something had shifted. The tension wasn't just from the cold or the danger lurking beyond the fire's glow. It was something else. Something neither of them dared to name.

"We'll be there in two days," Ronan said, breaking the silence. His voice was low, steady. "If we keep this pace, we should reach the stronghold by midday."

The words should have eased some of the weight pressing down on Kaela's chest, but instead, they only made it worse. Two days. It wasn't enough time. She had no idea what they'd find when they reached the Guardians, or what dangers waited for them along the way. But there was no turning back now.

Milo sat beside her, staring into the fire. He'd been quiet for hours, his usual easy banter replaced by an unsettling stillness. The shift in him gnawed at Kaela. His shoulders were tense, his gaze distant. She could feel the weight of whatever was on his mind, thick and heavy in the air between them.

"Milo?" she asked, her voice barely above a whisper, nearly lost in the crackle of the flames. "What's wrong?"

He didn't answer right away. When he finally looked at her, it was only for a second before his eyes dropped back to the fire. His jaw tightened. "I just . . ." He exhaled sharply, shaking his head. "I didn't think we'd be here. Not like this. I thought I understood what was happening, what was coming. But this—" He gestured vaguely around them, at the cave, the fire, the vast unknown beyond. "This is bigger than anything I could've prepared for."

A knot tightened in Kaela's chest. She understood. None of them had expected any of this. The magic, the secrets, the impossible choices. But they had no choice now. They had to keep moving.

She reached out, squeezing his shoulder. "We're in this together," she said, offering a small smile. "All of us."

For a moment, Milo's shoulders relaxed, and his expression softened. He gave a small nod, but the tension lingered. The storm inside him hadn't passed. Not yet.

Across the fire, Ronan's gaze flickered toward them, his eyes sharp in the dim light. He didn't speak immediately, letting the silence stretch between them, but his presence was grounding, unwavering. There was a quiet strength in the way he sat, his confidence radiating without a single word. When he finally did speak, his voice was steady, sure, carrying the weight of someone who had seen the path ahead and knew what needed to be done.

"We'll find the Guardians," he said, his words quiet but firm. "We'll stop the Technomancers. And we'll do it together."

The certainty in his voice sent a warmth through Kaela's chest, like a spark catching fire. But it wasn't just his words that made her pulse quicken. Something had shifted between them. Something unspoken, something just beneath the surface. And Kaela wasn't sure if it was the weight of their mission . . . or something else entirely.

The fire crackled softly, casting dancing shadows across the cave walls, while the wind howled outside, its fury muffled by the shelter of their temporary refuge. The world beyond felt distant, irrelevant. It was just them now, the space between her and Ronan thick with something unspoken. His gaze lingered on her, an intensity that made her heart race, and for the first time, she let herself acknowledge the pull between them.

Ronan rose from his seat, moving toward her with an easy grace that both captivated and unsettled her. His presence was magnetic, drawing her in without a word. The moment stretched, the air between them charged, and Kaela felt her breath hitch as he reached out, brushing her hand with his. The electric jolt of the touch seemed to send her spinning, and for a heartbeat, the world outside the cave disappeared.

Ronan leaned in slightly, his breath warm against her cheek, and she felt the heat of his body, the way her pulse raced in response. Just when it felt like the space between them would disappear completely, something flickered in his eyes. A hesitation. He pulled back abruptly, his jaw tightening as he cleared his throat, and for the first time in a long while, Kaela saw something uncertain in him.

"Sorry," he murmured, running a hand through his hair, and the moment was gone as quickly as it had arrived.

Kaela's heart still pounded in her chest as she tried to make sense of what had just happened. The room felt colder now, even with the fire crackling in the center of the cave. Was it a slip? A moment of vulnerability from him? She didn't know. She had never thought of him that way. Or at least, she never let herself. But now, the pull between them felt undeniable, and she couldn't ignore it.

The silence stretched until Milo's voice cut through, steady but tinged with a vulnerability of his own. "We'll figure this out," he said, his words grounding, though she could hear the faint tremor beneath them. "Together."

Kaela could feel the promise in his words, but even as it lingered in the air, she couldn't shake the tension between her and Ronan. It was there, thick and heavy, and Kaela wasn't sure what it meant, what it would mean for the journey ahead. The night stretched on, the wind outside whipping through the trees, but in the cave, everything felt too still, too quiet.

As Kaela lay on her bedroll, her mind was consumed with the unsettling mixture of their proximity, the charged silence between them. Every time she closed her eyes, she could still feel the warmth of Ronan's presence, the weight of his gaze lingering on her. She hadn't expected it to feel so intimate, so consuming.

Her thoughts kept circling back to him. She could almost feel him in the stillness of the night, like a shadow looming at the edge of her consciousness. She hadn't allowed herself to think of him that way, hadn't allowed herself to even entertain the idea. But there was something about the way he had held her gaze, the way his body had been so close to hers, that made it impossible to ignore. It was as if they were both holding back, both caught in something that neither could name.

Ronan was always so unreadable, so guarded, like a storm held within. She could see it now, the storm inside him. He was at war with himself. And though he never let it show, she could almost feel it in the air around them.

His voice broke the silence, low and steady, as though he was speaking to himself. "We're not out of the woods yet. The Technomancers will come for us. They always do."

Kaela's heart tightened. She wanted to reassure him, to say something, but the words felt hollow. Instead, she shifted closer to the fire, catching his gaze for a brief moment. There was something in his eyes, something vulnerable, that made her chest tighten, and in that moment, she understood, whatever this was between them, it wasn't going to be simple.

"I know," she said softly, her voice barely above a whisper. "We'll keep moving. We'll find the Guardians."

Ronan's lips curved into a half-smile, but it never reached his eyes. "I hope so," he murmured, the words heavy with a quiet sorrow. "But sometimes, hope just isn't enough."

Kaela studied him, her chest tight with something she couldn't quite name. She knew he wasn't talking about the journey. There was something more beneath his words, something deeper, something personal. She wanted to reach out to him, to close the distance between them, but she knew it wouldn't matter. He wouldn't let her in. He never did. There was a wall around him, a quiet, invisible barrier that he kept locked in place. She wondered what had caused it. What was it he was hiding, what had he sacrificed for this life of loneliness? What was he running from?

She didn't have the answers, but the questions twisted inside her like a knot. She thought of the bargain he had made with the Garden, of the scars it had left on him, and wondered if they were the reason he kept everyone at arm's length. He cared, she could see it in the way he watched her, in the way his attention never wavered, but it was like he couldn't bring himself to love, to let anyone close enough to hurt him again. It made her heart ache for him, but she couldn't tell if it was pity or something else, something raw that she couldn't fully understand.

The wind howled outside, pulling Kaela from her thoughts. She shivered and tugged her cloak tighter around her shoulders, though the cold gnawed at her from the inside as much as the out. It wasn't just the chill of the night; it was the weight of the uncertainty that hung between them, a heavy fog that seemed to press in on her chest. She couldn't shake the feeling that something was changing, something between them, something she couldn't put her finger on, but she felt it growing, like a storm waiting to break.

"Get some rest," Ronan said, his voice rough, but there was a tenderness in it that caught her off guard. "We'll leave at first light."

Kaela nodded, but the ache in her chest didn't subside. Sleep felt impossible. She closed her eyes, but even in the dark, his presence lingered, a constant hum in the back of her mind. It was like he was there, even when he wasn't. As she drifted into an uneasy sleep, she couldn't shake the sense that everything was about to change. That the storm Ronan had been holding inside for so long was finally reaching its breaking point. And somehow, she knew it would pull her in with it.

Chapter 20

The sun had just begun to rise when they set out again. The cold mountain air nipped at their skin, but Kaela barely felt it. The night had been restless, filled with strange dreams and even stranger thoughts of Ronan. She couldn't shake the feeling that something was shifting between them, but every time she tried to face it, her mind seemed to block her out. She was too focused on the road ahead, on the Technomancers closing in. But there was something else, something quietly pulsing beneath the surface of her thoughts. It was the whisper of a truth she hadn't yet figured out. A puzzle that felt just out of reach, the pieces scattered, waiting to fall into place.

Ronan, ever the quiet sentinel, led the way with smooth, confident movements, navigating the rugged path like someone who had crossed these mountains a hundred times before. Each step was measured and deliberate, as if the terrain were an extension of him. His long strides carried him over the uneven ground, boots firm against the jagged rocks that jutted from the earth. The cold wind bit at the air, but Ronan didn't flinch; his sharp gaze was always scanning the horizon, vigilant and alert.

The mountains rose around them like ancient giants, their jagged peaks scraping the sky, silent witnesses to the passage of time. The air was thin and biting, and the world felt smaller, as if it had shrunk to just the three of them. The weight of their mission pressed on their shoulders with every step. The Technomancers hadn't shown themselves yet, but Kaela could feel them, an electric hum beneath the surface, like a storm gathering in the distance. She glanced at Ronan, watching the way his eyes narrowed as he studied the cliffs. He wasn't just looking for danger; he was sensing it. He was attuned to the land, to the pulse of the world in a way Kaela couldn't quite understand but couldn't help but admire. There was a stillness about him, a calm that was both reassuring and unnerving. She envied it in a way, how he could face danger and still seem as if the world was unfolding exactly as he expected it to.

"We're close," Ronan said after several hours of travel, his voice low but steady, cutting through the silence. Kaela didn't need to ask what he meant. They all knew. The Guardians were within reach. Their only hope for stopping the Technomancers. It was all leading up to this moment, this trek through the unforgiving mountains, to whatever lay ahead in the hidden stronghold Ronan had promised would be their salvation. The weight of it settled heavily on Kaela's chest, the magnitude of the task pressing on her. She couldn't afford to let herself dwell on the uncertainty. Too many lives were at stake. Too many people depended on their success.

Milo, who had been walking slightly behind them, hadn't said much since the night in the cave. His usual chatter was gone, replaced by a quiet intensity that Kaela couldn't ignore. She noticed it in the stiffness of his posture, the way his movements had become more deliberate, controlled. He was still Milo, but something had shifted. Something was eating at him, more than just the weight of the journey itself. It was deeper. Kaela glanced over her shoulder, her brow furrowing as she slowed her pace, falling in step with him. She had always been able to read him, she knew the unspoken language between them better than anyone else. But now, there was something between them, an invisible wall she couldn't quite break down.

"Milo," she called softly, her voice barely rising above the wind as she fell into step beside him. "What's going on? You've been distant."

He didn't respond right away, and Kaela could see him shift uncomfortably, adjusting the strap of his pack. His eyes darted over the craggy cliffs and trees, scanning the world around them like there was something hidden out there, waiting. But Kaela didn't see the fear in his eyes that came from facing the Technomancers. No, this was something else. Something more internal, more personal. There was a tension there, one that had nothing to do with the danger they faced on the outside, but everything to do with what was happening inside of him.

"I'm fine," he muttered, his voice tight, the words pushed out like they were being forced through clenched teeth. He kept his gaze fixed ahead, avoiding her eyes. "Just thinking."

Kaela knew he was lying, but she didn't press. She understood Milo better than anyone; she knew when he needed space, when he needed silence to wrestle with whatever burden was gnawing at him. Sometimes the best thing she could do was let him be, let him figure it out on his own. So, she shifted her focus to the journey ahead. The wind picked up again, howling through the narrow pass, swirling around the jagged peaks. The cold was creeping deeper into her bones, but she pushed through it. They were close now. The Guardians. This was it. The ones who could help them stop the Technomancers. They had to be. She had to believe it.

But even as Kaela clung to that belief, something unsettled her. There was a subtle shift in the air, something she couldn't quite place. Maybe it was the wind, the way it seemed to howl with a new urgency. Maybe it was the sense that the mountains were closing in on them, tightening their grip with every step. Whatever it was, Kaela couldn't shake the feeling that something was waiting. Something just out of reach. Something that wasn't yet clear, but felt inevitable.

Ronan had stopped up ahead, his back to them, his head slightly turned as he surveyed the path. He didn't seem to notice the tension between Kaela and Milo, or maybe he just chose not to. He was always so attuned to the world around him, so focused on what lay ahead, that the personal dynamics between them rarely seemed to register.

"We're getting close," Ronan said, his voice breaking the silence once again. His tone was steady, almost reassuring, but Kaela could hear the undercurrent of urgency beneath it. "Stay alert."

She nodded, trying to steady her breath, trying to focus. There was too much at stake to let anything distract her now. But as she glanced at Milo again, his shoulders still hunched, his eyes distant, she couldn't shake the worry gnawing at her. What was weighing so heavily on him? Kaela shook her head, forcing the thought aside. They had to keep moving. They had to trust Ronan. They had to trust each other.

The path ahead narrowed, the jagged cliffs closing in around them as they ascended higher into the mountains. The air grew thinner, colder, but they pressed on, each step bringing them closer to the unknown. The Guardians. The hope of stopping the Technomancers. Kaela could feel the weight of it all pressing down on her, but she kept moving, one foot in front of the other. When Ronan spoke again, his voice barely rising above the wind, there was a quiet promise in it. They were almost there. Almost at the end of this journey.

"We're close," he repeated, his voice barely audible above the wind. But to Kaela, it was a beacon of hope. The sound of something they had all been waiting for.

The path grew steeper as they neared the heart of the mountains. The air had become thin, brittle, each breath feeling like it was drawn from the very edge of the world. It stung Kaela's lungs, but she pressed on, determined. The promise of the Guardians, the hope that they could be the key to stopping the Technomancers, kept her feet steady. But as the landscape changed, something else inside her shifted, too. The closer they got to their destination, the heavier the air seemed to grow.

Ronan was always ahead, moving with fluid, instinctive grace. Each step was taken with quiet confidence, as though the incline was nothing more than a gentle slope. But Kaela could tell something was different today. His usual ease was gone, replaced by a tension that radiated from him like heat off desert sand. She watched him closely, noting how his eyes narrowed slightly, how his hands hovered just above the weapons at his sides. He was on high alert, like a predator that had caught the scent of danger.

They moved on in silence, the only sound the crunch of boots against rocky ground and the whisper of wind through the trees. After hours of trekking, they reached a clearing, and the world seemed to open up before them. The valley stretched out, nestled between towering peaks that seemed to close in on the world like ancient sentinels. At first glance, it looked like little more than an abandoned ruin. Stone buildings crumbled and were overtaken by moss and vines.

But there was something in the air that made Kaela pause. Something alive. The ground beneath her feet hummed with a strange energy, a subtle vibration that resonated through her bones. The air itself seemed thick with it, as though the valley were breathing, waiting for something.

Ronan halted at the edge of the clearing, his eyes scanning the surroundings with a practiced intensity. His shoulders were squared, his stance rigid. He didn't speak, didn't move, but Kaela could feel the shift in him. He wasn't just observing the valley; he was feeling it. She could see the tension in his jaw, the way his eyes flicked over the ruins. Sharp, calculating. The playful, teasing man she'd come to know had slipped away, replaced by someone colder, harder. A warrior. A man who had been through too much to trust easily, and someone who had learned to trust only his instincts.

Kaela's gaze lingered on him longer than she intended. She felt the pull of the silence between them, the distance that had quietly crept in since their moment in the cave. It was as though an invisible wall had formed between them, one that neither dared acknowledge. She couldn't help but wonder why it was there. Why, after everything they'd shared, everything they had almost shared, he remained distant. His eyes never lingered on her for too long, never met hers with the same intensity they once had. There was no spark, no hint of the chemistry that had once crackled between them. Just an unreadable calm, as though he was holding something back, something deep inside that he refused to let her see.

A mixture of confusion and frustration tightened in her chest. She wanted to ask him about it, demanding an explanation on why he had pulled away, but the words stuck in her throat. Maybe it was the way he seemed to close off every time she came near, the way he locked everything about himself up tight, like a treasure chest buried beneath layers of cold stone. But even as she fought the knot in her stomach, she knew one thing for certain: he mattered. Not just for the mission, not just because he held the answers they needed, but because something about him, something deep, pulled her in. She wanted to understand him. She ached to break through the walls he'd built around himself. But that was the problem, wasn't it? He didn't want anyone breaking through. He was a man who kept his secrets close to his chest, who hid his true feelings behind a mask of calm control. And yet, Kaela couldn't ignore the flutter of unease in her chest, the feeling that something was happening between them, something she couldn't stop or fully understand.

But she also knew this. Whatever connection was growing between them couldn't distract her, not now. Not when they were so close to finding the Guardians. Not when they had a chance to finally take down the Technomancers.

Ronan turned to face her, his gaze flicking over her briefly before returning to the valley ahead. "We're here," he said, his voice low, tone flat. He didn't meet her eyes again, didn't offer any explanation, but Kaela could feel the weight of this moment. The weight of everything they'd been through, pressing down on him just as heavily as it was on her.

The stillness between them felt unbearable. But she didn't break it. Instead, she nodded, the tension in her shoulders easing just slightly as she prepared to step forward. She wasn't going to let him drag her down with his distance. She had her own path to follow, her own role to play. She wasn't going to waste time wondering about things she couldn't change.

As they ventured deeper into the valley, Kaela couldn't shake the feeling that something was waiting for them, hidden beneath the surface, buried in the very air around them. The energy here was thick, almost suffocating, crackling with a power that tugged at her senses. The Guardians were close. But so were the Technomancers. And they would stop at nothing to find them. Kaela's mind raced, her thoughts tangled with the reality of what lay ahead. Whatever came next, they would face it together. Even if Ronan refused to let her in, even if he continued to hold himself at a distance. Whatever pull there was between them, whatever bond had begun to form, it would have to wait. There was a war to fight. And the Technomancers would destroy everything they had fought for if given the chance.

"They're here," Ronan said quietly, his voice low but carrying a weight that sent a chill down Kaela's spine. His words were simple, but they held an unspoken understanding, something ancient, something Kaela couldn't quite grasp. He wasn't just stating the obvious. He was acknowledging something deeper, something Kaela didn't fully understand but felt stirring in the pit of her stomach. He knew this place. And it was clear that it wasn't the first time he had been here, or that something about this place had called to him. A part of him that Kaela still hadn't uncovered.

They pressed forward cautiously, each step measured and deliberate. The path ahead was choked with thick vines and moss, the stone buildings around them almost consumed by the relentless march of nature. As they neared the first of the ruins, Kaela's attention was drawn to the carvings on the walls. They weren't just markings, they were symbols, strange and familiar all at once. Symbols she recognized from the Garden, faintly glowing in the dim light, like whispers on the edge of her awareness.

"Guardians," she whispered, the word slipping out before she could stop it, a strange awe threading through her voice. The Guardians. The ones they had come here for. The ones who held the key to stopping the Technomancers.

Ronan's eyes flicked to her, his expression grim, but there was something else there, too. A flicker of something deep, something Kaela couldn't name. "They've been waiting," he murmured, as if the words held a weight only he fully understood.

Before Kaela could respond, the faint hum that had been in the air grew louder, vibrating through the ground beneath them. It wasn't quite a sound, not exactly. It was more like an energy, alive, pulsing through the earth beneath their feet. The hum resonated in her bones, vibrating deep within her chest. She stopped instinctively, her gaze sweeping the clearing. The world around them felt too still, too quiet, as though everything was holding its breath.

"Stay close," Ronan ordered, his voice steady but carrying an edge of caution that made Kaela's pulse quicken. His gaze swept the clearing, his eyes narrowing slightly as he scanned the surroundings. There was a tension in his stance now, a readiness Kaela hadn't seen before. She'd grown used to the easy-going Ronan. The one who teased, who bantered, but now, in the presence of the Guardians, she saw something else. The warrior in him. The one who had fought. The one who had survived.

They moved through the courtyard, the hum growing stronger with each step, until figures began to materialize from the shadows. Tall, cloaked beings, their faces hidden beneath hoods. But their eyes, they glowed, just like the symbols carved into the walls. Kaela's breath caught in her throat. The Guardians were real. They were here, waiting for them.

One of the figures stepped forward, his cloak billowing like smoke in the still air. Though his face was obscured, Kaela could feel his gaze on her, heavy and unwavering. When he spoke, his voice rumbled deep and ancient, carrying the weight of centuries. "You've come for us," he said, not asking, but stating with certainty. "And you've come at the right time."

Ronan didn't hesitate. He stepped forward, his movements fluid yet purposeful. "We need your help. The Technomancers are coming, and we can't stop them alone."

The Guardian studied Ronan for a long moment, his glowing eyes sharp and piercing. The silence between them stretched, thick with unspoken meaning. Finally, after what felt like an eternity, the Guardian nodded slowly, his gaze flicking to Kaela and Milo. "We've been watching. We know what's at stake."

Kaela's heart hammered in her chest as the weight of his words sank in. They had been watching. They knew. And the knowledge sent a chill through her, making the gravity of their mission feel even more overwhelming. They weren't just fighting a war against the Technomancers. They were part of something much bigger, something far older.

Ronan's jaw clenched, but he remained silent, his gaze briefly meeting Kaela's. There was something in his eyes, something unspoken, but he didn't voice it. He just stood there, steady and composed, his presence as unwavering as the mountains around them. And Kaela, though her emotions were a storm inside, knew one thing: they were about to face something beyond anything they had imagined. Whatever came next, they would face it together, whether they were ready or not.

The Guardian leader gave a subtle nod, his cloak sweeping behind him as he turned and began to lead them into the first building. The moment they stepped inside, Kaela was struck by a wave of ancient energy that seemed to pulse through the very air. The space was vast, cavernous, with towering stone walls that seemed to breathe with history. Shadows clung to every corner, deepening the mystery that hung thick in the air.

Inside, relics of a forgotten age filled the room. Scrolls, intricately carved tablets, and strange, unfamiliar devices that Kaela couldn't even begin to understand. The scent of aged parchment mixed with something deeper, something earthy and organic, pulling at her chest. It reminded her of the Garden, but there was something different here, something that felt both connected to and separate from its magic.

As they ventured deeper into the heart of the stronghold, the silence grew even more intense. The walls were lined with shelves filled with long-forgotten knowledge, each item a testament to a history they could barely comprehend. The stone floor beneath them was worn smooth, evidence of countless footsteps through the ages. The faint hum from earlier still pulsed through the air, vibrating in Kaela's bones, a constant reminder that they were standing in the presence of something far greater than they could yet grasp.

Milo, who had been walking a few steps ahead, suddenly stopped. His boots scraped against the stone floor as he froze in place, his eyes scanning the walls with a look of disbelief. He stepped forward slowly, his breath catching in his chest, drawn to a cluttered table covered in scraps of old technology. Wires, half-dismantled gadgets, and tools scattered as though left in haste. But it wasn't the disarray that caught his attention. It was one small, seemingly insignificant device sitting at the edge of the table, partially hidden beneath the pile of forgotten debris.

Kaela noticed how his fingers twitched, how his whole body seemed to stiffen, as if he were fighting the urge to dive in and start fixing what had been abandoned. But this wasn't just any piece of forgotten technology. As he stepped closer, his face drained of color. His gaze locked onto the device, and for a moment, it felt as though time had stopped. It was sleek, compact, and smooth, its edges catching the dim light of the room, but it was the markings etched into its surface that made Milo's heart stutter. He knew this symbol. It was a design he'd seen many times before, on his parents' private journals, on hidden documents locked away in drawers, untouched for years.

His fingers hovered over it, trembling. The weight of the moment hit him like a tidal wave. His breath caught in his throat, his chest tightening as he realized the full implication of what he was holding. This wasn't just a relic. This was a connection, a link to something his parents had been involved in, something he had never known about until now. The world seemed to tilt beneath him. How long had they been hiding this from him? And why?

He picked up the device carefully, his hands shaking as he turned it over, examining it with a mixture of reverence and suspicion. His mind raced, trying to make sense of everything. *This was the key.* The key to understanding what his parents had been involved in all along, the truth behind everything.

"Milo?" Kaela's voice was gentle but laced with concern, drawing him out of his thoughts. He hadn't realized how tightly he was gripping the device until her voice broke the silence. He turned toward her, his expression haunted, eyes filled with disbelief.

"This . . ." he whispered, barely able to form the words, his voice a mix of awe and shock. "This is . . . my parents' work."

Kaela stepped closer, her brow furrowing in confusion. "What do you mean? What is it?"

Milo didn't respond right away. His fingers trembled as they hovered above the device, as though he feared it would slip through his grasp. When he finally picked it up fully, his movements were slow and deliberate, as if he were handling something fragile.

Something that could unravel everything. He turned it over in his hands, scanning the markings, his eyes widening in recognition. "I don't know," he said quietly, his voice hollow, barely a whisper. "But this tech . . . it's connected to the search for the Garden. I've seen designs like this before. My parents . . . they were involved."

Kaela's breath caught in her chest, the realization hitting her like a shockwave. Milo's parents, the two people who had always kept their past carefully veiled, had been tied to the very mission that had brought them here. To the Garden. To the Technomancers. To everything. She stepped back, her mind reeling as the truth unfolded before her. She had never known how deep Milo's family's involvement went, but now, the answer was right in front of them.

Milo's hands tightened around the device, his fingers white against its dark surface. His expression darkened, a storm of emotions swirling in his eyes, confusion, anger, hurt. "Why didn't they tell me?" he whispered, his voice breaking. "Why didn't they trust me with this?"

Kaela's heart ached for him. She could see the betrayal etched across his face, the weight of the secrets his parents had kept from him. She knew how much he valued honesty, how fiercely he tried to protect those he loved. And now, he was faced with the painful truth that even those closest to him had kept him in the dark. Secrets that could change everything.

She reached out, placing a gentle hand on his shoulder. "We'll figure this out, Milo," she said softly, her voice steady but filled with the strength she wished she could give him. "We will."

But Milo didn't seem to hear her. His gaze was fixed on the device, his jaw clenched so tightly that the muscles in his neck stood out. Kaela could feel the tension in him, the internal battle to reconcile the man he had always trusted with the painful truth he was now forced to face.

Before Kaela could speak, Ronan's voice cut through the air, low and urgent. "We don't have time for this. The Technomancers are coming. We need to focus on the here and now, and on what's ahead."

Milo didn't respond right away. He nodded stiffly, but his eyes remained distant, clouded with confusion. His gaze never lifted, as if the weight of what he was holding, what it represented, was too much for him to bear. Kaela could see the slight sag in his shoulders, a visible sign of how crushed he felt in that moment.

Her heart ached for him. She could feel the weight of everything closing in on them, the lives they'd once known, slipping further away with each passing second. It wasn't just about survival anymore. They were tangled in something far larger, something darker than they'd ever imagined. The lies and secrets were piling up, and they were right in the middle of it all, with no way to escape.

Ronan's voice sliced through her thoughts, sharp and unwavering. "Milo, Kaela, we don't have time to lose. The

Technomancers are moving faster than we thought. We need to stay focused."

Milo's head jerked up at Ronan's words. Their eyes locked for just a moment, but then Milo turned back to the device in his hands, his gaze still heavy with unspoken pain. He heard the urgency in Ronan's voice, but the hurt in his eyes remained. Kaela could feel the tension between them. Ronan's determination, his unwavering focus, and Milo's frustration, raw and unspoken. There was no room to unpack it all. Not now.

"We're in this together," Kaela said softly, but firmly. "We'll take it one step at a time. We'll get through this."

As the words left her mouth, she knew deep down that nothing would ever be the same. Their fight was no longer just about survival. It was about the truth. About the answers they'd been searching for. And about a future none of them had seen coming.

The Guardians led them deeper into the stronghold, guiding them to the heart of it all, where an ancient map sprawled across a large table. The map was covered in intricate symbols and markings, some of which were unfamiliar to Kaela, others unsettlingly familiar. The Guardians, silent and steadfast, encircled the map, their presence commanding and ancient, their eyes glowing with the weight of knowledge accumulated over centuries. They had been tracking the Technomancers' every move, waiting for this moment. And now, it was time to fight.

Kaela felt the gravity of their discovery settle over the room like a storm cloud. The map before them was not just a tool. It was a key, a puzzle. And in that moment, Kaela could feel the air thick with something deeper, something unspoken. The Guardians, though standing still, radiated purpose, as though they were more than just warriors. They were keepers of secrets, of a past Kaela could barely grasp.

Milo leaned over the map, his brow furrowed in concentration. His fingers traced the symbols as if he had seen them before, as if they were etched into his very bones. The map itself was old, its edges worn and fragile, but the weight of its significance was clear. It held the answers, answers that had eluded them for so long.

He reached for the device still pulsing faintly in his hand, the hum vibrating through his fingers. It felt alive, its rhythm syncing with his heartbeat, as though it were calling him, pulling him toward something just beyond reach. His mind raced, piecing together fragments of his parents' past. Their hidden involvement in the search for the Garden, and the symbols now sprawled before him.

Every line on the map seemed to pulse with meaning, urging him to dig deeper. His fingers moved restlessly, tracing paths and markings, as if the map itself was guiding him to the answers. When his eyes locked on one particular region, his pulse quickened. It was far off, buried beneath jagged mountains and thick forests, but something about it felt significant, important. As if this place, these lines, were calling to him.

He followed the path with his finger, an instinctive sense of knowing taking over. The map wasn't just a drawing. It was a bridge to the past, to a time he couldn't fully remember but somehow felt connected to. He was certain this was the answer they'd been seeking. This was the key.

"I've seen these symbols before," Milo muttered, almost to himself. "This place . . . it's not just part of the Garden's magic. It's something bigger. My parents . . . they were searching for it, too."

Kaela looked at Ronan, searching for some reaction. But his expression was unreadable. The easy, teasing smirk that usually played at the edges of his lips was gone, replaced by a quiet intensity that seemed to swallow the air around him. His gaze was distant, his jaw set in a hard line, and Kaela could almost feel the storm brewing inside him. There was something simmering beneath the surface, a tension that Kaela couldn't quite place. It unsettled her, leaving her with a knot in her stomach, a feeling that something was shifting between them.

For a moment, she opened her mouth to say something, anything, to break the silence, but the words wouldn't come. Instead, she reached out, her hand finding Milo's shoulder. His skin was warm beneath her touch, but the tremble of his muscles, the strain in his posture, was impossible to miss. He was no longer present with her, or Ronan. His focus was entirely on the map, his fingers brushing the symbols as though he were trying to unlock a secret only he could see. He was lost in the past, in the truth he had only just begun to understand, and for a moment, it felt as though he had crossed into a world that didn't have room for her or Ronan.

Milo had become a stranger, absorbed in something that had always been just out of reach, and Kaela felt the gulf between them widen. It wasn't just the physical distance, it was the chasm opening between the past and the present. Between what they had thought they knew and what they were learning now. She reached for him, but the distance felt insurmountable, like a wall made of years of secrets and silent pain. The air in the room felt heavier, the silence more suffocating, as though they were all being pulled in different directions by forces beyond their control.

Ronan's voice cut through the tension, low and urgent. "Milo's right. This is bigger than we thought. The Technomancers haven't just been after the Garden. They're hunting for something more. An artifact. A key to unlocking the true power of the Garden."

Kaela's heart pounded as the weight of Ronan's words sank in. The Technomancers had been manipulating the Garden for years, but now they were after something even more dangerous. Something that could control the very fabric of magic itself.

"We can't let them find it," Kaela said, her voice sharp with newfound resolve. "We can't let them have that kind of power."

Ronan nodded, his eyes scanning the map with a determined

focus. "The Guardians have tracked the Technomancers' every move. They know where the artifact is. We just need to get there before they do."

The gravity of his words hung heavy in the air, a cold weight pressing down on them all. The room seemed to grow colder, the hum of the Guardians' presence vibrating through Kaela's chest. She could feel it, an overwhelming sense of inevitability. They were standing on the edge of something immense, something far beyond anything they had faced before.

Milo's attention was fixed on the device, his fingers tracing the faint markings on its surface. His touch was gentle but insistent, as though he were trying to unlock something buried deep within it. "This tech," he murmured, his voice tight with emotion, "It's connected to my parents' research. They weren't just after the Garden. They were looking for the key to controlling it."

A cold shiver ran down Kaela's spine, settling deep in her bones. The words hit her like a blow. Milo's parents, always so distant, so careful, had been involved in something far darker than she could have imagined. Not only had they been part of the Technomancers' search for the Garden, but they had been hunting for the means to control it. The very magic that could shape the world, and they wanted to wield it. The thought made her stomach churn.

She glanced at Milo, watching as he continued to study the device, his brow furrowed in concentration. He looked lost in the flood of revelations crashing over him. He was unraveling a past that had been hidden from him, a past tied to secrets that were now surfacing. The device pulsed faintly in his hand, as though it were reacting to his thoughts, and Kaela couldn't shake the feeling that the truth was just beyond their reach, slipping away like sand through her fingers.

Swallowing hard, Kaela forced herself to speak. "But . . . if they were looking for control, what does that mean for us? For the Garden?"

Milo didn't answer right away. His gaze remained fixed on the device, his fingers tracing its sleek surface as if it held the answers. When he finally spoke, his voice was soft, almost to himself. "I don't know. But it's more than just magic. They wanted something. Something bigger than any of us realized. They thought they could control the Garden, shape it to their will." He clenched his jaw, his fingers tightening around the device. "And they weren't the only ones. My parents were working with others . . . people with their own agenda. People I didn't even know about. People who—"

He stopped suddenly, cutting himself off, his face going hard with the weight of his own words. Kaela could feel the unspoken truths lingering in the silence, the painful realization that Milo's parents had been part of something far more complex and dangerous than she had ever imagined.

Kaela's mind raced, the pieces of the puzzle beginning to fall into place. Milo's parents, those enigmatic figures who had always kept their secrets, had been part of a web far beyond their understanding. But there was something else, something she couldn't shake. Her own father. The man who had disappeared without a trace. The man whose disappearance had set her on this path. What if . . . what if he had known about this? Had he been working with Milo's parents? Had he been part of this same search?

Her heart hammered in her chest as the connection between her father and Milo's parents became impossible to ignore. She hadn't made the link before, but now it seemed too strong to be a coincidence. Her father, Milo's parents, the Technomancers, the Garden. It was all tied together. And that meant the stakes were higher than they had ever imagined.

"Milo," she said, her voice trembling slightly, "What if my dad . . . What if he was involved too?"

Milo's head snapped up, his eyes meeting hers for the first time in what felt like ages. His expression was unreadable, but there was a flicker of something in his gaze, a hint of realization, or something darker. "I don't know," he replied, his voice rough with emotion. "But we can't ignore it. We can't pretend that this is just about us anymore. It's bigger than that. It always has been."

Kaela's heart raced, the weight of their situation crashing down on her. Everything was connected. Her father, Milo's parents, the Garden, and the Technomancers. She could feel the past catching up with them, dragging them into a fight they couldn't ignore. A fight for something far more dangerous than they had realized.

As Milo turned back to the device, Kaela's mind drifted back to the cave, to the moment when her father's name had echoed through her thoughts, the lingering sense that his disappearance was more than just a mystery, it was the key to everything. She had to know more. She had to uncover the truth about what he had been a part of. And no matter how painful, she had to confront it.

The weight of the moment pressed down on Kaela, and for a fleeting second, she wished she could turn back to a time when things were simpler, when their lives hadn't become so tangled with forces beyond their control. But there was no going back now. They were too deep into this. The answers they sought were out there, waiting to be uncovered. The only question was whether they were ready to face the truth when it came.

Milo's voice interrupted her thoughts, soft and uncertain. "We have to keep moving, don't we?"

Kaela lifted her gaze to meet his, her heart heavy with the knowledge that they couldn't stop now. Not when they were so close. Not when the answers were within reach. "Yeah," she said, her voice steady despite the storm brewing inside her. "We keep moving. We have no choice."

"They were part of it," Kaela whispered, the words tasting like betrayal. "They were working with the Technomancers all along."

Milo's eyes flicked to hers, dark with the weight of his own disbelief. "I didn't know," he said, his voice tight. "I thought they were just scientists. I thought they were trying to help. But they were looking for something more. Something that could control the magic."

Ronan's gaze shifted between them, his expression hard. "This isn't the time for doubt, Milo. We need to focus on what comes next."

Milo nodded, but his mind seemed elsewhere. Kaela could see the struggle in him. The confusion and anger bubbling beneath the surface. He had trusted his parents and believed in their intentions. Now, it felt like the ground was crumbling beneath him. But there was no time to dwell on the past. The future was too uncertain, and the Technomancers loomed larger than ever.

The Guardian leader, who had been silent until now, stepped forward. His voice resonated with ancient authority. "You've seen the map. You've seen the path the Technomancers are taking. If you want to stop them, you must go now. The artifact is hidden in the old temple, deep within the mountains. You must reach it before they do."

Kaela's heart pounded, each beat echoing the gravity of their mission. The path ahead was filled with danger, unknown threats that could tear them apart, but she knew there was no other choice. They had come too far to turn back now. Every step from here would bring them closer to a reckoning, one that could change everything.

"We'll go," Ronan said, his voice unwavering. "We'll get to the temple first."

The Guardians nodded subtly, their eyes heavy with unspoken understanding. Kaela couldn't shake the feeling that they knew something she didn't. Their glances exchanged with Ronan made her wonder if there was something more between them. Something deeper than their mission. Ronan's quiet confidence, the way he held himself like a man who had seen too much, clearly left an impression on them. But Kaela didn't ask. Not yet. She wasn't ready for whatever truth they might reveal. Not when so much was at stake.

As they left the stronghold, the weight of their mission settled over her like a cloak. The air outside was sharp, biting, with the promise of a storm in the distance. The mountain path ahead felt even more daunting now, every jagged rock beneath her feet reminding her of the peril they faced. Still, she couldn't afford to slow down. Not when they were so close, not when every step could mean the difference between success and failure.

With each step, Kaela found herself glancing at Ronan more often than she'd like to admit. There was a tension between them she couldn't ignore, a subtle undercurrent that threaded through their interactions. His eyes would occasionally meet hers, and she could feel the weight of those moments, a quiet recognition of something unspoken. It was like a spark in the air, an electricity barely contained between them. Every time their hands brushed, it was as if the world held its breath. The pull between them was undeniable, but something kept them apart, something unspoken that neither had dared to address.

But Kaela couldn't afford to focus on that now. Not with the stakes so high, not when everything they were fighting for hung in the balance. They were standing on the edge of something monumental, and there was no room for distractions, not even the ones that tugged at her heart when she least expected it. She shoved her feelings down, burying them beneath the weight of their mission, determined to focus on what lay ahead. The Garden, the Technomancers, the fight for survival. They were her priorities now.

The climb grew steeper, the wind whipping around them with a vicious chill. Each step felt heavier as the path became more treacherous. The mountain was alive with the sounds of wind howling through craggy cliffs, the distant echo of stones tumbling down into the abyss below. But still, they pressed on, the temple drawing nearer.

In the distance, hidden in the shadows of the towering peaks, the temple loomed, its ancient stone walls barely visible through the thickening atmosphere, a silhouette against the darkening sky. The temple stood unmoving, as though it had weathered centuries of storms and secrets. The mountain seemed to guard it, like the land itself knew the weight of what was held within those walls. Kaela's heart quickened at the sight. The temple was the key. But what would they find inside?

As they neared, the air shifted. The wind that had whipped around them relentlessly suddenly stilled. The atmosphere thickened, as if the world was holding its breath. The ground beneath them hummed, a low pulse that vibrated in Kaela's chest. A strange, familiar sensation she couldn't quite place. It was like a memory just out of reach, like the same energy she'd felt when she first entered the Garden.

Her senses heightened. Her pulse quickened. Something ancient and powerful lingered in the air. The temple wasn't just a structure; it was a force, an entity, pulsing with untold power. The energy was calling to her, pulling her in like a tide she couldn't escape. It had been waiting for her all along.

Then, as they drew even closer, the ground trembled beneath their feet. At first, it was a faint quiver, like the earth awakening from a long slumber. But quickly, it grew stronger, a rumble that vibrated through their boots, sending a shiver up Kaela's spine. The temple seemed to react, as if the very stones had sensed their approach. The air grew charged with an electric hum, making her skin tingle.

Something was waiting for them. Kaela stopped, breath catching in her throat. The tremors beneath her feet intensified. The energy coiled around her like a storm, crackling in the air. What had they awakened? What force had they disturbed?

Ronan, who had been leading the way, paused too. His sharp gaze swept over the temple, his body tense. Kaela could tell he felt it too. The shift in the air, the heavy tension. But he didn't speak. He just motioned for them to move forward, his face hardening with determination. Kaela couldn't shake the feeling that they were walking into something far beyond their understanding. Whatever it was, it was waiting for them to make the next move.

Chapter 21

The storm that had threatened all day finally erupted as the group neared the entrance to the hidden temple. Dark clouds swirled ominously above, casting a thick, suffocating gloom over the mountain pass. The wind howled between the jagged peaks, biting at their exposed skin like a thousand tiny daggers. The rugged terrain stretched out before them, unforgiving, wild, and seemingly alive with danger. But amidst the chaos of the storm, there was something else in the air. Something electric. It surged through Kaela, making her skin prickle and her heart race. It was a sharp, restless energy that left her feeling both on edge and oddly alive, as if the mountain itself was awakening.

They moved cautiously, the terrain growing more treacherous with each step. As they reached a narrow pass, Ronan suddenly raised his hand, signaling for them to stop. His eyes swept over the shadowed cliffs, narrowing as though he had sensed something long before they had. The wind howled around them, but there was a stillness in Ronan's posture, a tension that told Kaela he was waiting for something.

"Stay alert," he said, his voice low, laced with a sharp edge. "There's something off about this place."

The words hung in the air, their weight pressing down on Kaela. A cold shiver crawled down her spine as she absorbed his warning. Whatever lay ahead, it was more than just the temple they needed to fear. The feeling in the air had shifted, and it was as if the mountain itself was holding its breath.

Kaela's eyes flicked to Ronan, her heart thundering in her chest as the air between them thickened with unspoken tension. Every glance, every accidental brush of their hands seemed to deepen the connection, leaving her breathless. Ronan's protectiveness was palpable, his gaze constantly on her, his posture alert, ready to step in front of her at any sign of danger. She could feel the weight of it all. The electric pull that hummed just beneath the surface, but it was buried beneath layers of restraint, a silent understanding that neither of them dared to confront. He was always too close, and yet, the moments between them were fleeting, too short to unravel the feelings stirring between them.

As much as Kaela longed to confront it, she shoved the emotion aside. The mission came first. They had no room for distractions. The path ahead was growing more dangerous with every step, and she couldn't let the storm inside her distract her from the greater one they were walking straight into. But still, as she forced her focus on the mission, part of her wondered: How much longer could they pretend nothing was happening between them? How much longer could they ignore the undeniable spark that simmered in the spaces between them?

Milo, walking just ahead, seemed lost in his own thoughts, his fingers fiddling with the strange device his parents had left him. Every now and then, he'd glance at the symbols etched into its surface, as if searching for meaning in the cryptic carvings. Kaela wanted to ask him what it meant, but the words always caught in her throat. There was a growing distance between them now, one neither of them knew how to bridge.

"Over there," Ronan suddenly said, pointing to a darkened alcove off to their left. His voice was steady, but Kaela could see the tension in his posture, the way his shoulders were squared and his hand hovered near the blade at his side.

Before anyone could speak, two figures emerged from the shadows of the forest, their movements nearly silent, like wraiths slipping through the trees. The taller of the two, broad-shouldered and imposing, stepped forward first, his dark cloak blending with the night, while the other lingered just a step behind, his sharp gaze flicking between them like he was assessing every possible threat.

They were dressed in layers of well-worn fabric, built for survival rather than comfort, their gear reinforced with scavenged metal and leather. These were men who knew how to navigate the wilds, how to endure without the comforts of the domes. There was something about them, an edge, a quiet resilience, that made it clear they belonged to the world outside of civilization.

The taller one, his hood partially drawn back to reveal sharp features and storm-gray eyes, spoke first. "Are you the ones they've been talking about?" His voice was calm, but there was an undercurrent to it, a tension beneath the surface. "The ones trying to stop the Technomancers?"

Kaela felt a flicker of both hope and caution. Whoever these men were, they knew something. But that didn't mean they could be trusted. The Technomancers had spies everywhere.

"We are," Ronan answered, his tone measured. "Who are you?"

The second man, leaner and sharper in his stance, smirked slightly but didn't let it reach his eyes. "We should be the ones asking that question." He crossed his arms, studying them for a long moment before finally giving an answer. "I'm Theo. This is my brother, Kallen."

Milo frowned, his grip tightening around the device in his hand. "And we're supposed to just believe you're on our side?"

Theo huffed a quiet laugh. "We didn't say we were on your side." His gaze flicked to Kaela. "But we do have information you need."

Kaela exchanged a glance with Ronan, his expression

unreadable. The air between them felt charged, thick with something unspoken. She wasn't sure if it was tension, hesitation, or something deeper neither of them wanted to acknowledge. Whatever it was, it lingered between them, impossible to ignore.

"What kind of information?" she asked cautiously.

Kallen finally spoke, his voice lower than his brother's, smoother but no less guarded. "The Technomancers aren't just after the Garden. They're searching for something even more dangerous, an artifact that will give them complete control over magic itself. If they find it, they won't just reshape the world. They'll own it."

A cold weight settled in Kaela's chest. "Where is it?"

Theo's eyes flicked toward the distant mountains. "It's hidden in the temple you're heading toward. But it's protected. The Technomancers can't get to it alone. They need someone connected to the Garden."

Kaela's stomach twisted. "You're saying they need me."

Kallen's expression darkened. "Not just you. Your power. They've been watching you, Kaela. If they can use you, they'll have everything they need to break through the magic keeping the artifact locked away."

A chill ran down her spine. She could feel Ronan shift beside her, his presence grounding her, but also humming with tension. His hand brushed against hers, just for a moment, but the silent reassurance was enough to steady her thoughts.

"We can't let them get to it first," Ronan said, his voice rough with conviction.

Theo and Kallen exchanged a glance. Whatever passed between them was silent but understood. Finally, Theo gave a slow nod. "Then you need to move fast."

Kaela narrowed her eyes slightly. "You said you've been fighting the Technomancers. What do you know about their operations?"

Kallen hesitated, just for a fraction of a second. "They've infiltrated everything. Governments, corporations, there isn't a system they haven't touched. They control the flow of technology, of resources, of power. And they're hunting anyone who stands against them."

Milo's voice was quieter when he spoke. "And my parents?"

Kallen's gaze flicked to him, unreadable. "They were involved in ways you might not be ready to hear."

Milo's hands curled into fists, his knuckles turning white. His jaw tightened, but he remained silent. Tension radiated from him, unspoken words hanging in the air. Still, he held them back, swallowing whatever anger or frustration threatened to spill out.

Kaela exhaled slowly, trying to piece it all together. "And you?" she asked, studying them carefully. "Where do you come from?"

For the first time, something flickered in Theo's expression, something almost hesitant. "We come from a village outside the domes."

Kaela frowned. A village? People surviving out here, beyond the reach of the Technomancers? That was nearly unheard of.

"You'll see it soon enough," Kallen added. His tone was casual, but there was an edge beneath it, something hidden, something careful.

Something wasn't right. It was then that Kaela noticed it. The way neither of them had looked directly at Ronan. Not once. Their gazes skirted him, their words never directly addressing him, the tension between them laced with something more than just wariness. It was personal. Kaela's pulse quickened as realization struck. They knew who Ronan was, and they hated him for it. But they weren't going to say it outright. Not yet.

Theo shifted, his fingers twitching at his side as if holding back words he wasn't sure he should say. His eyes flickered to Kallen, who gave him the smallest of nods. Whatever silent decision passed between them was made quickly.

"We've told you all we can," Theo said finally, turning to Kaela. "But we need to get back before nightfall. Our village doesn't take kindly to strangers, and we've been gone too long as it is."

Kallen adjusted the strap of his pack and gave a sharp nod. "You'd be wise to keep moving, too. The longer you stay out here, the more eyes you'll draw."

Kaela hesitated, glancing between them. There was so much left unsaid, so much tension still hanging thick in the air. She wanted to push, to demand answers about what they knew of Ronan, about what he had done to make them regard him with such quiet fury. But now wasn't the time.

Instead, she nodded. "Thank you. For the advice."

Theo's expression was unreadable, but there was something heavy in his gaze. "Just be careful who you trust." And with that, he turned, Kallen close behind him as they disappeared into the trees, heading back toward their village.

Kaela exhaled slowly, turning toward Ronan. He was watching them go, his jaw tight, his golden-green eyes dark with something she couldn't quite name. He knew. And he wasn't saying anything either.

Chapter 22

The moon hung high above the mountain pass, its silvery glow casting an eerie light over the jagged peaks and the treacherous path ahead. Shadows stretched long and restless across the desolate landscape, as if the earth itself conspired against them. The air was thin and biting, the wind slicing through the night like a blade, leaving Kaela, Ronan, and Milo gasping for breath with each step. The only sounds were the distant chirp of crickets and the rustling of unseen creatures in the trees, sounds that felt almost too serene for the storm of danger that loomed just beyond the horizon.

They had barely made it a mile past the hidden temple when a sharp prickle ran down Kaela's spine. A warning. The hairs on the back of her neck stood on end, a sensation as if the very air had thickened, charged with something unseen. She cast a glance at Ronan, who was already scanning their surroundings, his body poised, every movement laced with a predator's instinct. He felt it too.

"I don't like this," he muttered, voice low and edged with tension. His hand hovered near the hilt of his blade, fingers flexing. "We're being followed."

Milo, hunched over his latest invention, barely looked up, but his fingers stilled over the small device in his hand. Blue lights flickered across its surface, casting faint glows against his furrowed brow. He swept his gaze across the jagged cliffs, the thick trees lining their path. "I don't see anything," he said, though his tone betrayed uncertainty. His eyes lingered on the dark expanse, as if trying to decipher an invisible threat. "But . . . something's off."

Kaela felt it too. The shift in the air, the crackling hum just beneath the stillness, subtle yet undeniable. It was as if the very earth vibrated with anticipation, like the mountains themselves were bracing for something inevitable. She turned, glancing back down the winding path they had just crossed, but there was nothing. No shifting shadows. No rustling leaves. Not even the distant cry of an animal. The silence pressed in, suffocating, unnatural. The world was holding its breath.

Then Ronan moved. A single step forward, his muscles coiled, his golden-green eyes flashing with sharp awareness. "Get ready," he warned, his voice urgent. "They're close."

Kaela barely had time to react before the ground beneath them trembled. A low, guttural rumble that sent a jolt through her bones. A warning. Then, from the darkness ahead, a burst of white-hot light exploded into the night, searing the landscape. The air filled with the sharp hum of machines powering up, a sound that sent icy dread racing down her spine.

Figures emerged from the trees, shrouded in dark, tactical gear, their faces obscured by reflective visors. They moved in unison, their steps calculated, purposeful. The glint of metallic implants gleamed beneath the moonlight. Technomancers. Dozens of them. Kaela's pulse pounded. The chase was over. The fight had begun.

Kaela's heart pounded, a wild, frantic rhythm that filled her ears as the magic inside her stirred, restless and untamed. It pulsed beneath her skin, searing hot, as if it were alive. Raw, unpredictable, and still beyond her control. She wasn't ready. Not yet. The power of the Garden hummed within her veins, flickering like a spark struggling to catch, and the weight of it, of her own inadequacy, pressed down on her like a vice. A storm was coming.

"We need to move!" Ronan's voice cut through the chaos, sharp and commanding. He was already sprinting toward the cover of the rocks, his movements swift and fluid, a shadow slipping through the darkness. "Follow me!"

Milo was right behind him, his mind racing even as his feet struggled to keep up. His device flickered with erratic signals, unfamiliar warnings flashing across its surface. He shot one last glance at Kaela, his chest tight with urgency. Then, without hesitation, he bolted after Ronan.

Kaela ran. Her breath came in sharp, ragged bursts as they tore across the rugged terrain, the Technomancers closing in behind them with unnerving precision. Their movements were eerily synchronized, their pursuit relentless. The night filled with the crunch of boots against loose gravel, the metallic clank of weapons being readied, and the eerie hum of their advanced tech charging to strike.

Then, light. A crackling bolt of energy streaked through the air, a hair's breadth from Kaela's head. She ducked, barely in time. The heat of it scorched the air, leaving a sharp, acrid scent in its wake. A second too late, and she would have been nothing more than ash. Keep moving. Don't stop.

The narrow pass loomed ahead, jagged cliffs rising like walls on either side, the path tightening until there was nowhere left to run but forward. Ronan was already calculating, scanning their surroundings in that sharp, instinctual way of his. In one swift motion, he grabbed a handful of loose stones and hurled them down the path, sending a cascade of rocks tumbling into their wake. It wouldn't stop the Technomancers. Not for long. But it would slow them down. And right now, every second mattered.

"They'll be on us in seconds," Ronan said, his voice sharp with urgency as his gaze cut across the rugged terrain. "We need to move.

There's a cave system beyond that ridge, it's our only chance."

Milo's breath came fast, but his mind was already working through calculations. "Can we hold them off long enough to get there?"

Ronan didn't answer immediately, his eyes scanning the fast-approaching figures. The Technomancers moved with chilling precision, their weapons humming with lethal energy. "We'll have to," he said finally, his voice edged with cold certainty. "I've got a plan, but you need to trust me."

Kaela's pulse pounded against her ribs. She had trusted Ronan before, but this wasn't just about outmaneuvering their enemies. This was survival. If they didn't make it to that cave, they would be surrounded, trapped like prey with nowhere to run.

"What's the plan?" she asked, keeping her voice steady despite the adrenaline surging through her veins.

Ronan's eyes locked onto hers, unwavering. "We split up. I'll lead them away while you and Milo make it to the cave. Once you're inside, I'll meet you there."

Milo's expression darkened. "You want us to leave you behind?"

A smirk ghosted across Ronan's lips, his signature confidence cutting through the tension. "I can handle myself, Milo. Just get to the cave."

Kaela's chest tightened at the thought of leaving him behind, every instinct urging her to stay. But deep down, she knew Ronan was right. If they hesitated, they would be caught. Gritting her teeth, she forced herself to move.

"Go!" Ronan commanded, already turning on his heel and sprinting into the darkness.

Kaela and Milo exchanged a quick, unspoken agreement before taking off toward the ridge. The air pulsed with urgency, the sound of their pounding footsteps drowned out only by the whine of Technomancer weapons charging behind them. Light flashed against the rock walls as energy blasts whizzed past, the heat searing through the cold night air. Kaela ducked, her breath ragged, every muscle in her body coiled with tension.

As they reached the ridge, Kaela felt it, the magic stirring inside her, stronger now, restless and demanding. It crackled beneath her skin, hot and volatile, pulsing against the restraint she fought to maintain. Her vision blurred for a moment as power surged, and her knees nearly buckled. She wasn't ready, not yet. But the energy inside her didn't seem to care.

In the distance, Ronan's voice rang out, a taunting challenge that lured the Technomancers away. It was a calculated risk, one he had taken without hesitation. The distraction worked, buying them precious seconds to escape. But even as they ran, Kaela couldn't shake the feeling that the storm was far from over.

"Now!" she whispered, shoving Milo forward.

They slipped into the mouth of the cave, the air inside damp and cold, wrapping around them like a living thing. They didn't stop running until the darkness swallowed them completely, the echoes of their hurried breaths bouncing off the stone walls. Kaela pressed a hand against the rough rock, grounding herself, forcing her mind to focus. But the weight of everything settled in like an iron band around her ribs. Ronan was still out there. Alone.

Milo's voice broke through the suffocating silence. "He'll be fine," he said, his breath uneven but firm. "Ronan's got more tricks up his sleeve than he lets on."

Kaela nodded, but doubt clawed at her gut. The Technomancers had been too close. Too relentless. And her magic . . . it was still too unstable, too unpredictable.

She exhaled, steadying herself. "We wait for him. But we can't stay here long. If they track us, we need to be ready."

Milo glanced toward the cave's entrance, where the faintest sliver of moonlight trickled in, illuminating the jagged stone. "Yeah," he muttered. "Something tells me this isn't over."

They pressed deeper into the twisting tunnels, their footsteps muffled by stone and shadows. The air grew colder with every step, the weight of the cave pressing in, thick with silence. Just when Kaela began to wonder if they were wandering blind, the path opened into a small, natural chamber. Crystals lined the walls, pulsing with an eerie glow, their faint light casting fractured reflections across the stone.

Milo halted, fingers flying over his device. "I'm picking up something," he muttered, brow furrowed. "There's a signal here. A hidden network."

Kaela frowned. "A network? In a cave?"

Milo knelt beside a cluster of crystals, his voice tight with concentration. "It's not the crystals. There's something else, something tech-based. I think it's a transmission."

As he adjusted the settings, his device emitted a soft whirring sound. The crystals flickered in response, as though waking up. The air shifted. Heavy. Unnatural.

A prickle of unease crawled up Kaela's spine, the feeling of being watched sinking deep into her gut. Her instincts flared, warning her before her eyes could catch up. A shadow stirred at the far end of the chamber. Then, a figure emerged, silent and deliberate.

Cloaked in dark fabric, their face obscured beneath a hood, they moved with effortless silence. Every step was calculated, too smooth, too deliberate. A presence that felt predatory, as though they were always aware of their surroundings. The air seemed to grow colder in their wake, the tension thickening with each step.

Milo's hand twitched toward his belt, but Kaela lifted a hand, her voice barely above a whisper. "Wait."

The figure's eyes gleamed beneath the hood, sharp and knowing. When they spoke, their voice was low, roughened by age or hardship. "I knew you would come."

Kaela's breath hitched. The words sent a jolt of recognition through her, though she couldn't place why. "Who are you?"

Cloaked in layers of shadowed fabric, their face hidden beneath a deep, concealing hood, they glided through the darkness with unnerving silence. Each movement was fluid and precise, like a predator stalking its prey, their body a seamless blend with the night. The air seemed to thicken, an almost tangible weight pressing down, as if the very space around them bent to their will. Their presence exuded a chilling calm, as though they were both the hunter and the hunted in a world of their own making.

"I'm not here to fight," the woman said, her voice edged with an accent Kaela didn't recognize. "I'm here to help."

Milo's jaw tightened. "Help? How?"

The woman's gaze flicked to his device. "Your parents were involved with the Garden's research." A pause, deliberate. "I know because I've been tracking their work. And I've been tracking you."

Kaela's stomach twisted. "Tracking us?"

A faint smile ghosted the woman's lips. Something between amusement and grim acknowledgment. "Your parents weren't just researchers, Milo. They were rebels. Part of a network that opposed the Technomancers long before you were born. And they left behind something critical. Clues that could bring the Technomancers down for good."

Milo paled. "My parents . . . they were part of the resistance?"

The woman nodded, her expression unreadable. "They had information. More than anyone realized. They were close to uncovering the Technomancers' true goal. And they were silenced before they could share it."

Kaela stepped forward, pulse hammering. "What goal? What are they really after?"

The woman's gaze locked onto hers, unwavering. "Not just power. Control." She took a slow breath, as if weighing her words. "They want the Garden itself. The source of all magic, all energy. If they succeed, the balance will be shattered. The world as you know it will fall."

Milo's fingers curled into fists. "So, they've been hunting the Garden not just to destroy it, but to own it?"

A grim nod. "And your parents were the last ones who stood in their way."

A chill ran through Kaela, deeper than the cave's cold. "Then we're next."

The woman's expression darkened. "Unless you finish what they started."

Kaela exchanged a quick glance with Milo, her heart racing as disbelief swirled in her chest. She had always known the Technomancers were a threat, but standing here now, face to face with the woman who held the answers, the reality was darker, far more suffocating, than she could have ever imagined. The weight of their mission felt like a physical burden, pressing heavily on her chest, as if every breath she took was a reminder of the danger they faced. This wasn't just about surviving. This was a battle against something much darker, something so insidious it had the power to destroy everything they had fought for and more.

"We need to stop them," Kaela said, her voice unwavering despite the storm of emotions raging inside her. "We need to find the heart of the Garden before they do."

The woman's lips pressed into a thin, hard line, her gaze unwavering as she studied them. "I can help you," she said, her voice low, but with a cold precision that cut through the tension in the air. "But first, you need to know the truth about your parents, Milo. And you need to understand the full gravity of what you're about to face."

Milo's jaw clenched, his eyes darkening as he took in her words. "Tell me everything."

The woman inhaled deeply, as if bracing herself for the weight of the truth she was about to impart. "It's time to finish what they started," she said, her voice thick with resolve. "The fight is only just beginning."

Chapter 23

The cave was cold and silent, the only sounds the crackling of a low fire and the distant, rhythmic drip of water from the stone walls. Kaela sat with her back pressed against the rough surface, her knees drawn up to her chest, fingers tightly clutching the edges of her jacket. Her body ached from the battle, the tension in her muscles, the pounding in her head, all reminders of the toll the magic had taken on her. Each time she tapped into it, the weight felt heavier, as though it were demanding more from her than she could give, draining her in ways she still didn't fully understand.

Across from her, Milo sat still, his face drawn and weary, his hands resting in his lap. The firelight flickered in his eyes, casting shadows that seemed to deepen the lines of exhaustion on his features. Since the ambush, he had said little, his mind clearly consumed with everything Melana had revealed. The truth about his parents had hit him hard. They hadn't been just researchers, as he'd always believed. They had been rebels, part of a secret network fighting against the Technomancers, working toward something far greater than he could have ever imagined. They had been on the verge of uncovering the heart of the Garden, the key that could tip the scales in the war against the Technomancers. And now, Melana had placed that weight on his shoulders, asking him to finish what his parents had started.

A pang of guilt twisted in Kaela's chest. She had always seen Milo as the steady one, the reliable friend who could shoulder any burden, but now, seeing him so still, so distant, she wasn't sure how he would carry this new weight. She longed to comfort him, to say something, anything, that might ease his pain, but deep down, she knew there was nothing she could say that would make it easier. This was something he had to process on his own.

The fire flickered, casting a warm, dancing glow over the group, but Kaela's mind was elsewhere, lost in the weight of what they were up against. The Technomancers weren't just after the Garden, they were after its power, its magic, the very force that kept the world in balance. And they would destroy anything in their path to control it. The more Kaela thought about it, the clearer the stakes became. This wasn't just a fight for survival. It was a battle for the future of everything they knew.

But they weren't alone in this fight. Kaela's gaze shifted to

Ronan, standing by the cave entrance, his silhouette outlined by the pale light of dawn. His sharp features were set in a hard line, his posture tense as he scanned the horizon. The air around him felt charged, as if danger itself clung to him like a second skin. He was a former Technomancer, and although he had turned his back on them, Kaela knew his past was a double-edged sword. It was something he was always trying to outrun, always trying to escape, but it had a way of catching up with him.

Ronan's eyes flicked to hers for the briefest of moments, and Kaela felt a flicker of something in his gaze, something she couldn't quite place. It was as though he was silently asking her to understand something deeper, something unspoken between them. He stood still, watchful, but there was a tension in the way he held himself, an energy she couldn't ignore. She knew he had been a Technomancer, but what had led him to leave that life behind was still a mystery. There was more to his connection to the Garden than he was willing to share, something tied to his past, something he wasn't ready to reveal.

Before Kaela could let herself dwell on it any longer, she heard footsteps approaching from the shadows. She turned, her breath catching in her throat as the figure of Melana emerged from the darkness. Melana's presence seemed to fill the cave with an unspoken tension. She wasn't tall, but her posture was straight, every movement deliberate, controlled. Her dark hair fell in loose waves around her face, and her eyes, sharp and calculating, locked onto Kaela and Milo as she stepped closer. Her expression was unreadable, but there was an undeniable strength in the way she carried herself. She wasn't here to make friends, Kaela realized. She was here to deliver a message.

Milo shifted uncomfortably as Melana approached, his gaze sharp, guarded. Everything had been chaos since they uncovered the map, and now this stranger claimed to know things about his parents that even he didn't. She had been tracking them, watching from the shadows. Kaela wasn't sure how much of that she believed, or wanted to, but there was no denying the air of authority Melana carried, as if she had lived through the kind of truths they were only beginning to uncover.

"I'm not here to fight," Melana said, her voice calm but resolute, the slight lilt of her accent unfamiliar to Kaela. "I'm here to help."

Milo's eyes narrowed, suspicion etched across his face. "Help? By stalking us? That doesn't exactly inspire confidence."

Melana stopped a few paces away, her gaze flickering to the device in Milo's hand. "That device," she said softly, her voice almost reverent, "is more than just a key. It's a piece of a puzzle your parents spent their lives trying to solve. I've been following their work, trying to make sense of what they left behind when everything fell apart."

Kaela's stomach tightened. She'd heard enough cryptic talk

about secrets and legacies to last a lifetime, but something in Melana's tone made her pause. "Why were you following them?" she asked cautiously.

"Because I believed in their mission," Melana replied, turning her attention to Kaela. "Your parents were more than just rebels, Milo. They were among the few who truly understood what the Garden meant. Not just as a source of power, but as something that could tip the balance of our world. They knew what the Technomancers were capable of and how far they'd go to control it."

Milo's jaw clenched, his voice low with frustration. "I already know my parents were part of the resistance. I know they were fighting to protect the Garden. What I don't understand is why you've been watching me."

Melana hesitated for a moment, her gaze flicking briefly to Kaela before returning to Milo. "Because the Technomancers aren't just after the Garden . . . They're after the heart of it. The source of its power. And your parents were closer to finding it than anyone else."

Kaela's pulse quickened, but she remained silent, sensing a deeper layer to Melana's words. There was something unspoken in the way she spoke, a weight to her tone that suggested more than she was revealing. The tension in the air thickened as the unspoken truth lingered. Kaela could feel it pressing in on her, but she had no idea what it meant yet.

Milo's voice cut through the tension. "Closer how? They left me with this device, but they didn't leave any answers. Just fragments."

Melana's lips pressed into a thin line. "Because they didn't have time to finish what they started. The Technomancers silenced them before they could. But they didn't work alone."

Kaela caught the faint shift in Melana's tone, the way her words seemed to hang in the air. It wasn't the first time she'd felt the absence of her father so sharply, like a shadow in the room, a ghost tied to the Garden's mysteries. But this wasn't about him. Not yet.

Milo's expression darkened. "So, you're saying they left a trail, but not the answers? That it's up to me to figure it out?"

Melana stepped closer, her voice low but firm. "Your parents didn't just leave a trail. They left a way to stop the Technomancers, to protect the Garden from falling into their hands. And I can help you find it. But we don't have much time. The Technomancers are closer than you realize."

Kaela exchanged a glance with Milo, the weight of unspoken questions pressing heavily between them. Tension coiled in her chest, sharp and unrelenting, as she studied the stranger before them. Melana had brought answers, but they only raised more questions. About their parents, the Garden, and the true extent of the danger they faced. Trust was fragile, and Kaela had learned the hard way not to give it freely. Too much remained unsaid, too many pieces of the puzzle scattered, and Melana's sudden arrival felt like another tangled thread in an already chaotic web. Yet beneath her wariness, a quiet voice reminded her they couldn't do this alone. The Garden, the Technomancers, the stakes. They were bigger than anything she and Milo had faced. If Melana was telling the truth, they might not have a choice but to trust her. And if she wasn't, the consequences could be catastrophic.

Chapter 24

The evening air was cool, thick with the scent of pine and damp earth, and as the sun dipped behind the horizon, the sky bled into shades of purple and indigo. Long shadows stretched across the dense forest, and the only sounds were the occasional snap of a twig beneath their boots. The group moved in silence, each lost in their own thoughts. Milo trailed just behind, his face etched with a quiet, contemplative frown, and Kaela could feel the weight of his thoughts hanging between them, though she wasn't sure how to ask about it.

Melana walked beside her, her movements nearly imperceptible in the fading light. Kaela couldn't help but study her, noting the fluid way she navigated the terrain, as if the forest were as familiar as her own skin. Her coiled hair was pulled tightly back, revealing faint scars on her olive-toned skin. Her gaze was sharp, but there was a softness to it, a quiet intensity born of experience, both in battle and life.

Melana was different. Older, perhaps in her late twenties or early thirties, she carried a gravity that Kaela hadn't yet fully understood. The way she moved, the way she spoke, it was all laced with a seasoned assurance, a stark contrast to the uncertainty that still clung to Kaela and Milo.

Ahead of them, Ronan moved with a purposeful grace, his golden-green eyes scanning the landscape, constantly assessing their surroundings. Kaela watched him more often than she cared to admit, but each time their eyes met, he quickly looked away, his expression unreadable. For days now, he had kept his distance, the usual playful banter replaced with cool silence. It unsettled her. Ronan had always been the one to tease and provoke, but now . . . now, he felt like a stranger, retreating behind an invisible wall, one Kaela couldn't seem to breach.

Her mind wandered back to the morning's conversation. Milo's unease had been palpable, impossible to ignore. Since discovering the device his parents had left behind, he had been different, quiet, withdrawn. Kaela could sense the turmoil simmering beneath his calm exterior, something deeper than the usual battles they faced. And with Melana now in their midst, someone who seemed to know more about the resistance than they had realized, Kaela couldn't help but wonder whether things were about to get easier, or much more complicated.

Milo's voice broke through her thoughts, low and almost lost in the rustling of the wind. "Do you think they were always hiding things from me?"

Kaela glanced at him, startled by the question. She hadn't expected him to speak, especially not about his parents. She knew the discovery of the device had unsettled him, but she hadn't realized how deeply it was affecting him.

"What do you mean?" she asked softly, slowing her pace so that she could walk beside him.

Milo kept his eyes on the ground, his fingers idly brushing against the strap of his pack. "I don't know. I thought I knew them, you know? But now, everything feels like it's built on lies. They were part of the resistance, and I didn't even know. I don't know who they were anymore."

Kaela bit her lip, unsure of how to respond. She could feel the weight of his words, the confusion and hurt that laced them. It was a kind of betrayal, even if it wasn't intentional. Milo had always seen his parents as paragons of truth, but now, with the revelation of their secret involvement with the resistance, it was as if the ground beneath him was crumbling.

"I'm sorry," she said quietly. "That's a lot to take in."

Milo gave her a small, weary smile. "Yeah. It is."

They walked in silence for a while, the crackling of the underbrush beneath their feet the only sound between them. Kaela could sense that Milo was struggling to process everything, but there was something else there, too. A determination, a quiet resolve that had always been part of him. She wasn't sure if it was enough to face the truth about his parents, but she hoped it would be.

From up ahead, Ronan's voice cut through the quiet. "We should set up camp soon."

Kaela's heart stuttered at the sound of him, her gaze snapping to his. There was no teasing glint or lazy smirk, only a shuttered expression and cold, distant eyes. Before she could speak, he turned away. Without a word, he headed toward the tree line to gather firewood.

Milo shot her a subtle, questioning look. He'd noticed it too. Ronan had been off for days. Something was wrong, but neither of them knew why.

Melana, walking beside Kaela, slowed her pace, her sharp amber eyes flicking between them. "He's different," she murmured, her voice nearly lost to the wind.

Kaela exhaled, keeping her voice low. "Yeah. It's like he's shutting me out."

Melana studied her for a beat, unreadable. Then, with a knowing sort of amusement, she said, "He's not the easiest, is he?"

Kaela huffed out something between a sigh and a laugh. "No. And I have no idea what's going on with him."

Melana let out a quiet chuckle, rich with experience. "Men," she muttered, shaking her head.

Kaela blinked, caught between surprise and reluctant amusement. Melana just shrugged, the faintest grin tugging at her lips. "Don't worry," she said. "He'll come around. They always do."

By the time they reached the clearing, Ronan had already begun building the fire. His movements were quick, efficient, too practiced, as if he were trying to keep his hands busy, his mind elsewhere. Shadows danced across his face, but his expression was unreadable, his focus locked on the task at hand. Kaela couldn't shake the feeling that he was keeping something from them, something important.

Milo lowered himself near the fire, his gaze heavy with unspoken thoughts. Melana sat a little farther off, her sharp eyes flicking between the two men. The silence pressed down on them, thick and unyielding. Kaela eased down beside Milo, hoping to break it.

"You're quiet," she said gently.

Milo glanced at her, his tired eyes barely meeting hers. "I'm always quiet."

"Not like this." Her voice was soft, careful. "You've got a lot on your mind, don't you?"

He didn't answer right away. Instead, his fingers absently traced the edge of his pack, his focus still lost in the fire. "Yeah. A lot."

The flames crackled, throwing shifting light across their faces, deepening the quiet between them. Kaela could feel the tension thick in the air. Ronan's distance, Milo's unease, the unspoken weight pressing down on all of them. Something was changing, something she couldn't quite grasp, and with every passing day, it felt like Ronan was slipping further away.

Her gaze drifted to Milo and Melana, seated off to the side, their voices low, their conversation easy. There was a warmth between them, a quiet understanding that stood in stark contrast to the cold silence stretching between her and Ronan. Melana had begun to fit into their group effortlessly, and Kaela had noticed the way she and Milo worked together, their bond shifting from strategy to shared memories, to pieces of their pasts only they understood. It was good to see Milo connect with someone like that. She was happy for him. But still, a lingering unease settled in her chest. She wasn't jealous, not really. Yet with every passing day, the space between her and the people she cared about seemed to widen, and she wasn't sure how to close it.

With her gaze returning to Ronan, Kaela's frustration finally boiled over. "Ronan," she said, sharper than she meant to. "What's going on with you?"

He barely looked at her, his gaze locked on the fire as if the flames might give him an answer. "I'm not pulling away," he muttered, but there was no weight behind the words.

Kaela stepped closer, arms crossed. "Don't do that. Don't lie to me." Her voice softened, but the hurt was still there. "You've been distant. I can feel it. And if you won't tell me why, what am I supposed to think?"

Ronan's jaw tightened, his muscles shifting as if he were physically holding something back. The fire crackled between them, sending flickering shadows across his face, but he remained silent, his gaze fixed on the flames. Kaela's heart pounded, each second stretching unbearably as she waited, willing him to say something, anything. The weight of unspoken words hung thick in the air, and she could almost feel the battle waging inside him. Whatever he was hiding, it was clawing at him, just as much as his silence was clawing at her.

Then, at last, he exhaled, his voice low and hesitant. "I made a bargain with the Garden." He said it slowly, like he was still testing the weight of it. "When I escaped the Technomancers, I struck a deal to survive. But the price . . ." He hesitated, his fingers curling into fists. "The price was high."

Kaela's pulse quickened. "What did you give up?"

His eyes met hers then. Raw, conflicted. "I never thought I'd have it again, so it didn't seem like a loss." He took a deep breath and swallowed hard, avoiding eye contact. "I had to give up my true love."

The words landed like a blow. Kaela's breath caught. "Ronan . . ."

"I didn't think it mattered," he went on, voice thick. "I didn't think I would ever care about anyone like that. But now . . ." He trailed off, shaking his head. "Now, I feel something for you. And I can't—" He exhaled sharply. "I can't risk it."

Kaela stared at him, her chest tight, her thoughts spinning. "So that's why," she murmured. "That's why you've been keeping your distance."

Ronan turned back to the fire. "It's not just a bargain. It's a curse. If I let myself love you, if I let myself feel . . . I don't know what will happen. I don't know what the Garden will take."

Silence stretched between them, thick with unspoken words. It felt fragile, like the slightest push would shatter it, yet neither of them moved to break it. The fire crackled, filling the space where their voices should have been. Kaela swallowed hard, waiting, hoping he would say something first.

Kaela stepped closer, her voice quiet but firm. "We can figure this out. We can face whatever comes . . . Together."

Ronan shook his head. "I can't. If anything happened to you because of me—" His voice broke off, his fists clenching. "I won't let that happen."

Kaela hesitated before reaching out, her fingers grazing his with the lightest touch. Ronan flinched, his body tensing, but he didn't pull away. Encouraged, she curled her fingers around his, offering a silent reassurance. She gave his hand a gentle squeeze, anchoring them both in the moment.

"You don't get to decide that for me," she said softly. "You don't have to do this alone."

Ronan let out a shaky breath, his grip tightening for just a second before he pulled away. His eyes flickered with something she couldn't quite read. Fear, longing, something in between. The space between them remained, but Kaela wasn't letting him disappear into it. Not this time.

Meanwhile, Milo and Melana had fallen into an easy conversation. The fire crackled softly between them, and their words were low but carried a quiet sincerity. Milo had always kept to himself, hiding behind humor and quick wit to avoid revealing too much. But with Melana, something was different. Her calm presence seemed to draw him out, making him feel like he could speak his mind without fear of judgment.

"So," Melana said, her voice playful, "tell me about your inventions. I've got to know how your mind works."

Milo chuckled, rubbing the back of his neck. "I wouldn't call them 'brilliant.' More like 'frustratingly complicated.' I get lost in the details and forget to take a step back sometimes."

Melana raised an eyebrow. "I get that. It's easy to get wrapped up in the planning. But at some point, you've got to trust the people around you to handle the rest."

Milo glanced at her, surprised by how much her words resonated. "Yeah, I guess you're right. I've always been a lone wolf, you know? Hard to let go of control."

Melana's gaze softened, her tone gentle. "I understand. But you don't have to carry it all on your own. We're all in this together."

Milo let the silence hang for a moment before offering a small, appreciative smile. "Thanks, Melana. That means more than you know."

Their bond had been growing slowly, but it was there now, a quiet understanding between them. It wasn't rushed or forced, just a comforting mutual respect. For the first time in a while, Milo didn't feel like he was carrying the weight of the world alone. Kaela had been by his side his whole life, but there was something about Melana that made him feel understood in a way he hadn't expected.

As Kaela and Ronan talked, her thoughts drifted back to their journey ahead. The bond between them was undeniable, but it was clear they both had their own battles to face. They couldn't do it alone, they'd need to trust each other, no matter how complicated things got. It wouldn't be easy, but it was the only way forward.

The fire crackled softly as the night settled in around them, the darkness growing thicker with each passing minute. The group fell into a quiet, uneasy stillness, each of them caught in their own thoughts, the weight of the journey ahead pressing on their shoulders. Kaela glanced at the others, a sense of resolve settling in her chest. Whatever came next, they were stronger together. No matter how uncertain the path, they'd face it as a team, and that gave her a quiet confidence she hadn't realized she needed.

Chapter 25

The morning air was sharp, the kind of cold that bit at your skin, with frost clinging to the leaves like jagged shards of glass in the pale light of the rising sun. Kaela stood at the edge of the clearing, her arms wrapped around herself as she stared out into the woods. The camp behind her was still, broken only by the soft crackle of the dying fire and Milo's quiet muttering as he tinkered with a piece of scavenged tech. His hands moved with precision, but Kaela could tell his focus wasn't entirely on the task, his mind was elsewhere, just like hers.

The tension in the air had settled between her and Ronan over the last few days, thick and unspoken. His presence was like a weight, constant and unshakable. She could feel him before she saw him, the faint rustle of his boots on the frozen ground pulling her attention. He didn't speak at first, just leaned against a tree a few paces away, his posture deceptively relaxed. But Kaela knew better than to mistake his stillness for indifference. Ronan was always watching, always waiting. Now, with the knowledge of the bargain he had made with the Garden, she could feel the distance between them more than ever, the weight of his secret pressing on her from all sides.

"You've been quiet," Ronan said finally, his voice low, a hint of something unreadable beneath the surface.

Kaela glanced over her shoulder, meeting his golden-green eyes, but she didn't say anything right away. "Just thinking," she replied, her tone guarded. She wasn't about to open up, not when she wasn't even sure how to express the frustration that had been building inside her.

Ronan stepped closer, his gaze never leaving her face. "About what?"

Kaela took a deep breath, turning fully to face him, the morning air biting at her skin. "About how we can't keep doing this," she said, her voice stronger now. "We can't keep running, reacting, always one step behind. We need to change the way we fight back."

Ronan tilted his head slightly, his expression unreadable, though there was a spark of something curious in his eyes. "And what do you suggest?" His tone was teasing, but there was a sharp edge to it. "You want us to march straight into Technomancer territory and see how that goes?"

Kaela felt her frustration flare. "No," she snapped, voice sharper than she intended. "But we can't keep hiding, waiting for them to find us. We need to take control."

He studied her for a long moment, his gaze steady. "Control," he echoed, a faint, almost imperceptible smile tugging at the corner of his lips. "It's a nice thought. But it's never that simple."

Kaela crossed her arms, her jaw tightening. "It's better than doing nothing."

Ronan moved closer, a subtle shift in his stance that made her acutely aware of the space between them. "I'm not saying we do nothing," he said, voice quieter now, more thoughtful. "But there's a fine line between being bold and being reckless. We can't afford to make a move without knowing what's coming."

Kaela's chest tightened. She knew he was right, but the idea of just continuing to run, it was suffocating. "We've survived this long, haven't we?" she said, her voice steady despite the uncertainty creeping in.

Ronan's lips quirked into a faint smile, but it didn't quite reach his eyes. "We have," he agreed. "But surviving isn't the same as winning. And I'd rather not gamble with your life, or anyone else's, unless I know we've got a fighting chance."

The sincerity in his voice caught her off guard, more than she expected. His words lingered between them, heavy and unspoken. Kaela swallowed hard, feeling the weight of the moment. Something unspoken passed between them, a tension she couldn't ignore.

"I'm not afraid of the risk," she said softly, her voice quieter now.

Ronan's gaze softened, but there was something in his expression, something closed off, a guarded flicker of something he wasn't ready to share. "Maybe you should be," he said, almost to himself, as if the words were meant for him just as much as for her.

Kaela frowned, her thoughts swirling, but before she could press Ronan further, Milo's voice broke the moment. "Hey! Are we going to strategize or just stare at each other all day?"

Kaela turned away quickly, a faint flush creeping up her neck as she muttered something under her breath. Ronan's laughter followed her, soft and husky, pulling at something deep inside her. It wasn't just a laugh, it was warm, low, and unexpectedly intimate, curling around her like a thread she couldn't shake. The sound unsettled her, sending a shiver down her spine, as if he knew exactly how to throw her off balance without even trying. She picked up her pace toward the camp, trying to push the feeling aside, but the tension between them hung in the air, thick and unspoken.

Once they regrouped around the campfire, Kaela couldn't ignore the nagging feeling that something more lay beneath Ronan's guarded demeanor. She knew about his bargain with the Garden, the price he'd paid to stay safe, but there was more to it than that. It was in the way he held back, in the flicker of something heavy in his eyes whenever their plans were discussed. It wasn't the usual wariness she'd come to expect from him. It was as if he was holding something back, something important that he wasn't ready to share.

Meanwhile, Ronan found himself watching her a little longer than he intended, his golden-green eyes tracing the lines of her face, the way her copper hair caught the light. He hadn't meant to linger, but the tension in her presence, the weight of the conversation they'd had earlier, kept pulling him in. There was something about her, something that made him forget his resolve. His own secrets. His bargain with the Garden, the cost of his safety, the promise he'd made, pressed heavier on him with every passing second. He knew he couldn't let her in, but it was becoming harder to keep the walls up.

The campfire crackled softly as the group gathered, the early morning silence stretching between them. Milo sat cross-legged, his tools spread out like a protective barrier, his focus absolute. His hands moved with practiced precision, working on a piece of scavenged tech. The firelight flickered off the metal parts, casting shifting shadows across his face as he tinkered, lost in the rhythm of his task.

Melana sat a little apart, her posture relaxed but watchful, eyes scanning the woods with a quiet alertness. Kaela couldn't help but notice the bond forming between her and Milo, though it was different from the connection she shared with him. Their bond felt grounded, quieter, more intellectual, based on mutual respect. It wasn't rushed, but each day it seemed to grow stronger, especially as they worked side by side.

Milo broke the silence, his voice cutting through the stillness. "Alright, I've got something. It's not much, but it's better than nothing."

Kaela leaned forward, curiosity piqued. "What is it?"

He held up a small, rectangular device, its surface worn and scratched. "This is a Technomancer relay. Or part of one, anyway. It's used for short-range communication, so if I can get it working, we might be able to tap into their transmissions."

"That's a big 'if,'" Ronan said, his tone laced with skepticism. He leaned back against a rock, arms crossed over his chest, his golden-green eyes sharp and calculating.

Milo shot him a look. "And yet, here I am, trying to make it work. Unless you've got a better idea?"

Kaela met Ronan's unreadable gaze, a sense of something deeper lingering between them. There was always something about him that made her wonder what he was hiding, beyond just the weight of their mission. She could feel it, a tension in the air that never quite settled. It was elusive, something she couldn't grasp, but it was always there.

"Milo's right," Kaela said, cutting through the tension. "If we can get their communications, it could give us an edge. It's worth a shot."

Ronan's eyes flicked to hers, and for a moment, there was something softer between them, something unspoken. He nodded slowly. "Fine. But don't expect miracles."

Milo muttered under his breath as he turned back to the relay, his hands moving quicker now. Kaela watched him, her mind drifting to her earlier conversation with Ronan. She couldn't shake the feeling that there was more to Ronan than he was letting on. The hum of the relay snapped her back to the present, and Milo's eyes widened as he made a quick adjustment.

"Got it!" he exclaimed, his excitement infectious. "It's not perfect, but I'm picking up something."

The team fell silent, all their attention fixed on Milo as they waited for the next step. The air was thick with anticipation, every eye trained on the relay. Tension buzzed around them, as if the next moment could change everything. In the quiet, each person seemed to hold their breath, waiting for the signal.

A distorted voice crackled through the device, faint but unmistakable. The group fell into a tense silence, leaning in to catch every word. ". . . sector seven . . . recon unit . . . secure perimeter . . ." The message was fragmented by static, but it was clear enough. The Technomancers were closing in, searching for something or someone.

Kaela's stomach twisted with unease. "They're still looking for us," she said quietly, her voice barely above a whisper.

Ronan's jaw clenched, his gaze darkening. "Of course they are. They won't stop until they have what they want."

Milo's voice was sharper than usual. "And what exactly is that? Kaela? The Garden? Or both?"

Ronan hesitated, his posture tense as he stood and began pacing. His voice was tight when he finally spoke. "It's bigger than just the Garden," he said. "They want control. Over magic, over technology, over everything. And Kaela . . . she's the key."

Kaela's chest tightened at his words, the weight of them sinking in. She had always known she was tied to the Garden in some way, but hearing it put so bluntly made it feel far more personal. The realization that she was at the heart of the Technomancers' plans pressed heavily on her. It wasn't just a distant threat anymore. It was her, the target, the key to everything.

"We need to move," Ronan said, his voice leaving no room for debate. "If they're this close, it's only a matter of time before they find us."

Kaela stood, nodding. "Agreed. But we need a plan. Running without one won't do us any good."

Ronan hesitated for a moment, his eyes locking with hers. There was a flicker in them, something like admiration, maybe even respect. "You're right," he said, his voice quieter now. "We'll figure it out. Together."

The words hung in the air, thick with unspoken meaning. Kaela's pulse quickened, warmth spreading through her. She forced herself to focus on what needed to be done, pushing the feeling aside. Still, the tension between them lingered, unacknowledged, between every word.

As they packed up their camp, Milo pulled Kaela aside, his face tight with concern. "Hey," he said softly, keeping his voice low, like he was afraid someone might overhear. "You, okay?"

Kaela forced a smile, but it felt thin. "I'm fine. Why?"

Milo's eyes flicked to Ronan, his unspoken question clear. "You and him . . . there's something there, isn't there?"

Her heart skipped, her cheeks flushing with a mix of embarrassment and confusion. She shook her head quickly, more to convince herself than him. "No. I don't know. We're just trying to stay alive."

Milo didn't press further, but his silence said enough. Kaela ran her fingers through her hair, the tension in her chest growing. She didn't know what was happening between her and Ronan, but she couldn't deny it was becoming harder to ignore. But survival came first, and she pushed all the feelings aside, focusing on what mattered.

As the group prepared to leave, Ronan approached, his expression unreadable. "You ready?"

Kaela nodded, her mind steeling itself. "Always."

Together, they moved into the woods, the silence between them thick with unspoken tension, a quiet understanding neither of them dared address. Each step felt heavier than the last, as though the weight of their unsaid thoughts clung to them, pulling them down with every stride. The trees seemed to close in tighter, shadows stretching long as the path ahead grew murkier, and Kaela couldn't shake the sense that the greatest trials and truths still lay ahead. The air grew thick with anticipation, her pulse quickening as an unsettling chill crept over her, a foreboding whisper that the forest held more than they were prepared for.

Chapter 26

The forest began to thin as the group pressed on, the towering trees gradually giving way to jagged cliffs and rugged paths carved into the stone. The canopy overhead loosened, letting in more light but also exposing them to the harsh wind that cut through the mountain pass. The air grew colder with each step, the sharp bite of it catching in Kaela's lungs. Her breath fogged in front of her as they ascended, the weight of the climb sinking into her muscles. Still, she didn't slow down, her eyes fixed ahead on Ronan, whose every stride seemed to eat up the distance effortlessly. His golden-green gaze flicked over every shadow, scanning for danger with a quiet intensity that made her step a little faster to keep up.

Beside her, Melana moved like a shadow. Silent, purposeful, and always watchful. Her amber eyes, sharp as ever, seemed to see everything, catching every rustle of the wind, every creak of the branches around them. Despite the palpable tension between the group, there was something calming about Melana's presence, a steady force that grounded them. It was clear to Kaela that Melana was no mere bystander in this journey. She was a force in her own right, one they'd come to rely on more than they realized.

"Are you sure we're close?" Milo asked, his voice tight with frustration as he shifted his pack, his steps growing heavier with each passing minute. He glanced around, trying to pierce the thick woods, but everything looked the same, endless trees and frozen earth.

Ronan gave a quick look over his shoulder, his expression unreadable. "Close enough. The camp is hidden, but the markers are here."

Kaela frowned, her brow furrowing in confusion. "Markers?" she asked, slowing her pace to catch up with him.

Ronan stopped suddenly, crouching down beside a gnarled tree, his gloved fingers brushing away the frost from its bark. Beneath the icy layer, Kaela could see a faint spiral etched within a triangle, the symbol worn but still distinct. Melana stepped forward, her gaze sharp as she studied the markings. "The rebels use these symbols," she said in a low, measured tone. "They've been evading the Technomancers for years. If we follow these, we're on the right path."

Milo leaned in, squinting at the mark, his face drawn in

suspicion. "Why haven't the Technomancers found them yet?"

"They don't believe the rebels are an actual threat," Ronan replied, his voice flat and dismissive. "To the Technomancers, they're nothing more than a nuisance. Barely worth their attention."

Kaela exchanged a glance with Milo, a silent question passing between them. If the rebels had been able to stay hidden this long, they must be formidable, but could they trust them? The wind picked up again, biting at their skin, and the forest seemed to grow darker and colder. The faint scent of smoke lingered in the air, an unsettling sign that they were nearing something, and Kaela's pulse quickened in response.

"We're close," Ronan said again, his voice tight with something unspoken.

Minutes later, they rounded a bend and found themselves on a hidden plateau, sheltered between towering rock formations that blocked the wind. At first, the area appeared deserted, a vast, untouched blanket of snow stretching across the ground. But as Kaela's eyes adjusted, she noticed the subtle signs of life: faint footprints etched into the snow, the glint of metal half-hidden under jagged rocks, and the faint shimmer of what might have been a hidden barrier flickering at the edge of her vision.

"Stay close," Ronan murmured.

As they stepped onto the plateau, a sharp whistle split the silence. Kaela froze, her hand instinctively brushing the hilt of her dagger. Figures emerged from the shadows, moving with practiced speed and stealth. Five of them, clad in mismatched armor and cloaks that seemed to melt into the landscape, each holding a weapon. Bows, daggers, even a rifle, and their eyes sharp, scanning the group with suspicion.

"State your business," a woman called out as she stepped forward. She was tall and lean, her brown and grey hair pulled back into a tight braid. Her sharp eyes swept over the group, briefly lingering on Ronan.

"We're here to talk," Ronan said, his tone even but unwavering.

The woman raised an eyebrow. "Talk? With who?"

"With your leader," Ronan replied, his voice firm. "Tell them Ronan's here."

The mention of his name caused a noticeable shift in the air. The woman's eyes narrowed, her suspicion palpable. A low murmur rippled through the group, whispers passing like a current. The tension in the atmosphere thickened, everyone waiting for the next move.

"Ronan," she repeated, suspicion dripping from her voice. "You've got some nerve showing up here."

"I'm not here to cause trouble," Ronan said, his gaze steady. "But I've got information you'll want to hear."

The woman studied him for a beat, then nodded to one of the others. "Take them in."

They were escorted deeper into the camp, past makeshift tents and crude fortifications. Kaela noticed the rebels' resourcefulness— salvaged materials repurposed into weapons, hidden defenses built into the terrain. These people weren't just surviving; they were preparing for war. Finally, they were brought to a large tent at the center of the camp. Inside, a man stood by a table covered in maps and notes. He was older, his face weathered but strong, his gray hair tied back.

"Ronan," the man said, his voice heavy with both recognition and caution. "It's been a long time."

"Cyrus," Ronan replied, inclining his head.

Kaela and Milo exchanged a look, their unease reflected in each other's eyes. It was clear there was some history between Ronan and these rebels, one thick with tension and unspoken words. The air around them felt charged, an invisible thread tying Ronan to this place and its people, something neither Kaela nor Milo could ignore. They didn't ask, but the weight of it hung between them, impossible to shake.

Cyrus's gaze shifted to Kaela, Milo, and Melana. "And who are they?"

"Allies," Ronan replied, his tone flat. "We're here because the Technomancers are closer than you think. They've stepped up their search for the Garden."

Cyrus's expression darkened. "And why should we trust you?"

"Because I've been on the inside," Ronan said. "I know their plans, their weaknesses. And I know they're hunting Kaela."

At the mention of her name, every eye in the room snapped to Kaela, their gaze like a physical weight pressing down on her. For a heartbeat, the air thickened with a mix of judgment and intense curiosity, but she refused to back down. She straightened, holding their stares without flinching, her heart pounding in her chest, though her expression remained calm. Whatever doubts they had, whatever suspicions they carried, she would face them head-on, unshaken.

"And why are they hunting you?" Cyrus asked, his voice low but carrying a sharp edge.

Kaela hesitated, her mind racing to find the right words. The silence stretched, heavy and suffocating, each passing second only deepening the tension. She glanced at Ronan, searching his face for reassurance. His steady gaze met hers, calm and unwavering, a quiet strength in his eyes that steadied her. It wasn't just encouragement; it was a promise that she wasn't alone, that he believed in her. In that moment, she drew a deep breath, feeling a surge of courage stir within her.

"Because of the Garden," she said, her voice steady despite the storm brewing inside her. "I'm connected to it, somehow. They think I'm the key to controlling its magic."

Cyrus's eyes narrowed, his suspicion thickening the air, but after a long pause, he nodded slowly. "If what you're saying is true, you're in more danger than you realize. The Technomancers won't stop until they have you."

"Which is why we need your help," Ronan interjected. "You have the numbers, the resources. Together, we can stop them."

Cyrus's face remained unreadable. "You think it's that simple? You think we haven't fought them before?"

"I'm not saying it's simple," Ronan's voice grew sharper, the frustration beneath the calm rising. "But you've survived this long for a reason. You know how to fight back. And now, we have something they don't. A way to exploit their weaknesses."

Cyrus studied Ronan for a long moment, eyes calculating, before he finally gave a stiff nod. "We'll hear you out. But don't think for a second we trust you."

Ronan inclined his head slightly, acknowledging the unspoken challenge. "Fair enough."

As the meeting dragged on, Kaela's thoughts spun in a chaotic blur. The rebels were a potential ally, yes, but their mistrust of Ronan was impossible to ignore. She couldn't shake the gnawing feeling that their very presence had already attracted the Technomancers' attention. The weight of that realization settled in her chest, making it hard to breathe. When the meeting finally ended, they were escorted to a small tent for rest, though Kaela hardly felt like she could relax.

She sank down onto a rough blanket, her gaze drifting to Ronan. He stood by the entrance, his posture tense, eyes unfocused as if lost in thought. The silence between them stretched before she finally spoke, breaking the quiet with a question that had been clawing at her mind. "Do you think they'll help us?"

Ronan's voice was low, almost too soft for her to hear over the noise of the camp outside. "They don't have a choice. If they don't, they'll fall, just like everyone else."

A shiver ran down Kaela's spine, but it wasn't from the cold. Ronan's words hung in the air like a warning, dark and heavy with truth. The stakes were higher than she'd realized, and the road ahead felt even more treacherous than before. But there was a strange weight lifted, too. At least they weren't facing this alone.

Melana, who had been quietly observing, spoke up, her voice sharp and decisive. "If we're going to fight, we need more than just trust. We need strategy." She turned to Kaela, her amber eyes intense, like a hawk sizing up its prey. "We need to know the rebels' strengths and weaknesses. We can't afford mistakes."

Kaela nodded, her mind sharpening as Melana's words echoed in her thoughts. As the camp bustled with preparation, rebels moving with grim purpose, the uneasy tension in Kaela's chest only grew. It was becoming undeniable. This journey wasn't just about surviving. They were tangled in something far bigger, something none of them had fully prepared for.

Later that night, the stillness of the camp was shattered by a sharp whistle slicing through the cold air. Kaela's breath caught, her muscles tensing as she exchanged a wary glance with Milo. Around them, the rebels froze mid-motion, their hushed conversations and preparations falling silent. The air thickened with tension, every face turning toward the sound. Ronan, ever alert, was already on the move, his steps quick and deliberate, as if expecting trouble. Without hesitation, Kaela, Milo, and Melana followed, weaving through the cluster of makeshift tents toward the central fire.

There, under the flickering glow of the flames, stood Cyrus, his expression grim as he held up a large, rectangular piece of tech. The device gleamed ominously, its smooth metal surface catching the firelight. Kaela noticed Milo stiffen beside her, his wide-eyed stare locked on the object, recognition and unease written across his face. Whatever this was, it wasn't just another piece of scavenged technology. It was something far more significant, something Milo clearly knew all too well.

As the rest of the camp gathered around, murmurs rippled through the crowd. Theo and Kalen, who had been absent until now, emerged from the shadows. They had found the surveillance drone, its hidden mechanism still faintly humming. The brothers' presence seemed to shift the mood of the rebels, like a door reopening, and suddenly Kaela understood. This wasn't just a discovery, it was the catalyst for something larger.

"This was found on the eastern perimeter," Cyrus announced, his voice grim. "It's a Technomancer surveillance drone. They're closer than we thought."

Milo stepped forward, his eyes narrowing as he studied the drone. "Wait, let me see that." He examined it carefully, his brow furrowing. "This isn't just a surveillance drone," he said, his voice sharp. "It's modified. Someone's tampered with it."

Kaela moved closer, confusion lacing her features. "What does that mean?"

Milo pointed to a small insignia etched into the metal. "This symbol. It's the same one my parents used on their old prototypes. They used to work on tech like this."

Kaela's stomach twisted. "Are you saying your parents were working with the Technomancers?"

Milo shook his head, his face hardening. "No, but if their designs ended up here . . ." His voice trailed off, the weight of the thought sinking in.

Ronan placed a steady hand on Milo's shoulder. "We'll figure it out. But right now, we need to focus. If the Technomancers are using this tech, they're watching for us."

Kaela turned to Melana, who stood with a hard, determined look on her face. "We can't let them catch us off guard," Melana said quietly. "We need to strike first."

The days in the rebel camp passed in a blur of strategy meetings, exhausting training sessions, and quiet moments of tentative connection. While their shared mission to resist the Technomancers united them, there was an undeniable tension surrounding Ronan. It wasn't just that he had been a Technomancer. It was something deeper, a shadow from his past that seemed to follow him wherever he went. Kaela felt it most during the rare moments when the rebels gathered around the fire to share stories or rest. While they welcomed her, Milo, and Melana with a cautious warmth, their glances toward Ronan were colder, weighed down with an unspoken mistrust. Even Theo and Kalen, the two brothers who had given them valuable information, grew quiet when Ronan approached, their smiles tight, as though holding back unspoken thoughts.

One evening, Kaela sat with Theo, Kalen, and Milo by the fire, the flickering flames casting long shadows over their faces. Her curiosity finally pushed her to ask. She glanced toward Ronan, who was sharpening his blade a few paces away, his face unreadable. "Why is everyone so tense around Ronan?" she asked quietly, leaning toward the brothers.

Theo exchanged a glance with Kalen, then looked back at her. "It's not just because of his past with the Technomancers," he said, his voice low. "It's what he did before he left them."

Kaela frowned, her thoughts spinning. "What do you mean?"

Kalen shifted uncomfortably, his gaze flicking briefly to Ronan before continuing. "A few years ago, during one of the largest offensives the Technomancers launched against the resistance, Ronan was leading their forces. He wasn't just following orders. He was planning attacks, setting traps. He made sure the resistance took heavy losses. So many good people died because of him." His voice dropped to a near whisper. "Our parents included. They were protecting our community when the Technomancers attacked. They didn't stand a chance."

Kaela's chest tightened as the weight of the story settled over her. She glanced at Ronan again, his focus still on his work. He seemed unaware of the tension, but Kaela couldn't shake the feeling that he was listening to every word. The silence between them felt heavy, charged with unspoken understanding.

"He was ruthless," Theo added, his face hardening. "Then, just like that, he disappeared. We thought he was dead, but months later, we heard rumors that he'd left the Technomancers. Most of us didn't believe it. How could someone like him just walk away?"

Milo shifted beside her, his tone defensive. "And now he's here, fighting with us. Doesn't that count for something?"

Theo shook his head slowly. "It's not that simple, Milo. You don't just undo that kind of damage. He might be on our side now, but we're not sure if we can ever trust him completely. Not after what he's done."

Kaela sat back, her mind a whirlwind of conflicting thoughts. She replayed the moments when Ronan had stepped in to protect her,

Milo, and Melana. His actions had been driven by something deeper than just duty. Something raw and instinctive. He hadn't hesitated when the danger had been real, his reflexes sharp, but there had also been those fleeting moments of quiet vulnerability. In those rare instances, his guard had slipped, his eyes softening as if he were lost in a battle only he could see.

She couldn't reconcile these two sides of him. The man capable of destruction and the one who had shown them tenderness. Could someone like him really change? The question gnawed at her, but she pushed it aside.

Later that night, as the camp settled into an uneasy quiet, Kaela found Ronan standing alone at the edge of the clearing. His figure was silhouetted against the moonlit trees, his posture stiff, shoulders taut as though bracing for something unseen. There was a weight to him that went beyond the physical, a burden Kaela couldn't quite understand. He stood there like someone who had lived through too many battles, each one leaving its mark, each one adding to the invisible load he carried. She hesitated for a moment, unsure of what to say, but the need to understand him, to understand why he was the way he was, pushed her forward.

"You don't make it easy to defend you, you know," Kaela said, stepping closer to him.

Ronan turned to face her, his golden-green eyes meeting hers without a hint of his usual teasing. Instead, his expression was worn, his shoulders heavy with exhaustion. "Let me guess," he muttered. "They told you all about my glorious past."

Kaela crossed her arms. "They told me what you did. What you led. But they didn't tell me why."

Ronan's gaze shifted away, his jaw tightening. "Does it really matter?"

"It matters to me," Kaela replied, her voice firm. "You're here now, fighting with us. But if I don't understand why you left them, how am I supposed to trust you?"

There was a long pause before Ronan let out a sharp breath, running a hand through his dark curls. "I didn't leave because I suddenly grew a conscience," he said, the bitterness clear in his voice. "I left because I couldn't do it anymore. The things they asked of me . . . the things I did . . . I told myself it was for the greater good, that I was protecting the domes, keeping order. But all I was doing was destroying lives."

His voice wavered, and Kaela noticed the rawness behind his words. "There was one mission," he continued, quieter now, his eyes shadowed with the memory. "A village hiding resistance fighters. They told me to burn it to the ground. No survivors. I . . . I followed orders. But when I saw what I had done, when I looked at the destruction . . . I couldn't stomach it. I left that night. Never went back."

Kaela's chest tightened with a mix of anger and something

darker as she listened, the weight of his words pressing against her. She wanted to hate him, to feel nothing but rage for the lives he had destroyed, for the blood on his hands. Every instinct screamed at her to turn away, to cast him aside as the monster he had once been. But as she looked at the man standing before her, she saw the cracks in his façade. The way his eyes darted to the ground, the tremor in his voice when he spoke of his past.

This wasn't the same person who had carried out those brutal orders, not anymore. The man in front of her was broken, shattered by the weight of the choices he had made, haunted by the ghosts of those he'd killed. There was a vulnerability in him now, a weariness that spoke of sleepless nights and battles fought in the silence of his own mind. She couldn't deny that, despite everything, he was human, and that realization twisted something inside her.

"And now?" Kaela asked softly. "Why are you here, fighting with us?"

Ronan met her gaze, and for the first time, she saw a flicker of something in his eyes. Determination, maybe, or hope. "Because I want to make things right," he said, his voice low. "I know I can't undo the past, but if I can stop the Technomancers, if I can save even one life . . . maybe that'll count for something."

Kaela nodded slowly, her heart heavy but resolute. "It does mean something," she said, her voice steady.

Ronan gave a small, almost sad smile. "You're too forgiving,

Kaela. One day, that's going to get you in trouble."

"Maybe," she replied, stepping a little closer. "But I'd rather believe people can change than give up on them."

Just then, voices called them back to the camp, breaking the moment. Kaela turned to leave, but paused and glanced back at Ronan. "You're not the same person you were," she said quietly. "And neither are we."

For the first time that night, his smile reached his eyes. "I hope you're right," he said softly.

As they made their way back to camp, the crunch of snow beneath their boots was the only sound breaking the stillness of the night. Kaela's mind swirled with conflicting thoughts. Despite the tension between them, there was something undeniably different in the air. She couldn't shake the feeling that they were heading toward something greater than survival.

Despite the unspoken tension between them and the scars of past betrayals, something felt different in the air. It wasn't just the quiet resolve in Ronan's steps or the way Melana's sharp gaze softened when she met Kaela's eyes. There was a subtle shift, a sense of purpose that seemed to gather around them. A fragile thread wove them together, even after everything that had come before.

In that moment, Kaela felt it. A glimmer of hope, fragile but undeniable. They were all headed toward something greater than survival. They weren't just fighting for the Garden, or the rebellion, or even their own safety. They were fighting for something worth the sacrifice, something that might heal the brokenness they all carried. Something that could reshape their futures in ways they couldn't yet imagine.

Chapter 27

The camp buzzed with activity as dawn's pale light broke through the trees, casting long shadows over the snow-covered ground. Rebels moved with practiced efficiency, their murmurs blending with the clatter of weapons in the crisp morning air. Tension lingered, but their steady movements spoke of discipline and purpose. Each action was a quiet promise, they were ready for whatever came next.

For Kaela, the morning offered a rare moment of stillness. She stood at the edge of the camp, watching the others work, feeling the weight of everything that had brought her here. Not long ago, she had been just a girl searching for answers about her father, about the strange power stirring inside her. Now, she was something more. Not just an outsider looking in, but a part of this fight. A soldier, an ally, and maybe, just maybe, someone who could make a difference.

That thought settled deep within her, both thrilling and

terrifying. The battle ahead was uncertain, its outcome impossible to predict. But for the first time, she wasn't standing at the edge of it alone. She had allies, and that made all the difference.

Ronan's presence beside her was a constant reminder of how much had changed. The bond between them was undeniable, but Kaela couldn't shake the unease that lingered beneath it. The man who fought beside her now, who protected her without hesitation and filled the silence with sharp-witted remarks, was not the same as the Technomancer who had once served the enemy. She had seen the weight he carried, the ghosts of his past lurking in the shadows of his golden-green eyes. And yet, there was something else there, too. A quiet tenderness, a softness that surfaced when he thought no one was watching. It unsettled her as much as it pulled her in, leaving her caught between trust and the fear that one day, she might regret it.

As they trained with the rebels, Kaela's thoughts drifted to him more than she wanted to admit. They moved side by side, testing their skills in combat, learning the rhythms of battle together, yet something unspoken stretched between them, both fragile and heavy. She noticed the way his gaze lingered when he thought she wouldn't notice, the way his stance shifted just slightly when danger was near, always making sure she was safe before throwing himself into the fray. She found herself drawn to him in ways she hadn't expected, but part of her resisted, knowing that whatever was building between them could be just as dangerous as the fight ahead.

Milo, ever the steady presence, seemed to be growing closer to Melana in a way that surprised Kaela. The two often huddled together in the evenings, deep in discussion over strategies, survival tactics, and the ever-present threat of the Technomancers. Melana's sharp mind and quick instincts made her an invaluable ally, and it didn't take long for Milo to start respecting her as more than just another rebel. He admired her strength, the quiet confidence with which she carried herself, as if nothing could break her. But Kaela also noticed the way Melana's guarded expression softened when she looked at him, the subtle shift in her posture when he spoke.

They were an unlikely pair. Reserved, thoughtful, yet fiercely capable, but there was something undeniable between them. Not romance, not yet, but a quiet understanding that ran deeper than simple camaraderie. Kaela noticed the way Milo listened when Melana spoke, how he respected her insight in a way he rarely did with others. And Melana, who kept most people at arm's length, seemed to trust him in a way that was rare for her. It wasn't just necessity that drew them together, it was something unspoken, something steady, something that, given time, might grow into more than either of them had anticipated.

That night, after a long day of training and strategizing, Kaela lay in her bedroll, trying to block out the sounds of the camp. The low murmur of voices, the distant crackle of the fire, the wind whistling through the trees. It all felt louder in the stillness. Sleep didn't come easily, her mind tangled with thoughts of the Garden, the rebellion, and the weight of the choices she had yet to make. But exhaustion won out, and eventually, her eyes fluttered shut.

At first, there was nothing. Just the deep, dreamless abyss of sleep. Then, like a ripple through still water, something shifted. The cold of the night melted away, replaced by warmth, by the scent of earth and blooming flowers. When she opened her eyes, she was no longer in the camp. The Garden stretched out before her, more vivid than any memory, its towering trees heavy with shimmering fruit, its glowing flowers casting soft, golden light. The air thrummed with magic, wrapping around her like an old friend, and for the first time in days, she felt at peace.

But the peace was fleeting. Aelera emerged from the shadows, moving with an unnatural grace that sent a shiver down Kaela's spine. Her golden eyes locked onto Kaela's, filled with ancient wisdom and urgency. The sight was mesmerizing, yet deeply unsettling.

"You are not ready, Kaela," Aelera's voice was barely more than a whisper, yet it sliced through the stillness like a blade. "The Garden's peril grows, and you must act before it's too late."

Kaela's pulse quickened, her breath catching in her throat. She took a step forward, reaching out as if she could anchor herself to the guardian. But Aelera only shook her head, sorrow and determination warring in her gaze. The distance between them felt impossibly vast, no matter how close Kaela tried to get.

"You are not alone, but you must take risks," she warned, her voice low but unwavering. "The Garden is dying, and with it, everything you hold dear. Be bold, Kaela. Face the darkness, or it will consume you all."

The words wrapped around her like vines, tightening with each syllable. Before Kaela could respond, the dream began to unravel. Aelera's form dissolved into mist, her presence fading into nothing. The lush glow of the Garden was swallowed by shadows, leaving Kaela alone in the dark.

Kaela jolted awake, her heart pounding in her chest. The guardian's final words echoed in her mind, sharp and urgent. Time was slipping away, and hesitation was no longer an option. She knew what she had to do, even if the cost was unknown.

As Kaela sat up, the cold air of the camp bit at her skin, but it was nothing compared to the fire that burned within her. She had to act. There was no room for hesitation, no matter the cost. And Ronan . . . she couldn't help but wonder if he was the key to what they needed. But even as his image lingered in her thoughts, doubt crept in. Could she trust him fully? Was he truly the ally she hoped for, or was he still bound by the ghosts of his past? Kaela shook her head, clearing the fog from her mind. There was no time for uncertainty. She had a mission to complete.

Later that morning, as the group gathered around the fire, Kaela stood beside Ronan, the tension between them almost palpable. The air felt charged with unspoken words, heavy and thick. Ronan turned to her, his golden-green eyes sharp, as if sensing the turmoil swirling inside her. In that brief moment, a flicker of understanding passed between them, and Kaela couldn't look away.

"What's on your mind?" he asked, his voice low and hushed, the sound of it sending an unexpected shiver down her spine.

Kaela hesitated, her heart pounding as her thoughts spiraled. She opened her mouth, but it took a moment before the words came, steady despite the chaos swirling inside her. "I had a vision," she said, her voice tight with the weight of it. "Aelera. She warned me . . . warned us. The Garden's in danger. We have to act, and soon."

Ronan's expression darkened immediately, his jaw clenching, and the shift in his demeanor didn't go unnoticed. "I knew it wasn't just about survival," he muttered under his breath. "The stakes are higher than we thought."

Before she could respond, Milo and Melana appeared, their faces grim, the tension in the air palpable even to them. Melana's sharp eyes flicked between Kaela and Ronan, noticing the silent weight hanging between them. "What did she say?" Melana asked, her voice steady but edged with concern.

"The Garden's dying," Kaela replied, her throat tight as the truth settled heavily in her chest. "We need to take risks. We need to move faster, or it'll be too late."

The group fell into a heavy silence, the words sinking deep, pressing against their hearts like an unbearable weight. Finally, Ronan broke the stillness, his voice low but filled with quiet resolve. "Then we move. No more hesitation."

Kaela met his gaze, and in that moment, the tension between them was still there, raw and unresolved, but there was something else, too. A shared understanding, a quiet bond forged in the fire of everything they had endured. Despite everything that had happened between them, despite the doubts that still lingered, they were in this together. And together, they would face whatever came next.

The air around the camp was thick with anticipation as Kaela's words lingered in the silence. The weight of Aelera's warning pressed on them all, and even the rebels, who had been working with relentless determination, seemed to feel the shift in the atmosphere. They gathered around the fire, each turning the same thoughts over in their minds, the stakes of their mission clearer than ever. For Kaela, the decision was made. Waiting was no longer an option.

Ronan's voice broke the silence, cutting through the unease with quiet command. "We start tonight. Gather your things. We move at first light."

Kaela's heart raced at the urgency in his tone. There was no hesitation now, no shadow of the past that had so often kept him distant. He was with them fully. It was both a relief and a stark reminder of how much was riding on their next move. She met his gaze and saw not just resolve, but something softer too. He wasn't just fighting for survival anymore. There was a fire in him now, one that mirrored her own. He had his demons, yes. But so did she. Together, they just might stand a chance against whatever darkness lay ahead.

As the group dispersed to prepare, Kaela found herself standing beside Melana, the soft crackling of the fire filling the space between them. The woman's expression remained calm, a mask of controlled composure, but Kaela could see the subtle tension in her posture. Melana had always been one to guard her emotions closely, her sharp mind working in silence, but Kaela had come to understand the quiet language of her body. The slight flex of her hands at her sides, the tightness in her shoulders, it was all too familiar. Kaela knew her well enough now to see when something troubled her.

"You're not sure about this, are you?" Kaela asked, her voice a quiet murmur meant only for Melana's ears.

Melana turned to her, a flicker of a smile tugging at her lips, but it didn't quite reach her eyes. Her amber gaze softened for a moment before she spoke, the weight of unspoken thoughts behind her words. "No, I'm not. But it's not my job to be sure. It's my job to follow orders, and right now, those orders are to keep everyone alive. We don't have the luxury of doubt." Her tone was matter-of-fact, but there was an edge to it. An undertone of something more, something Kaela couldn't quite place.

Kaela nodded, feeling a surge of gratitude for Melana's steady presence. There was something reassuring in the woman's unwavering focus, a quiet strength that grounded Kaela even when the uncertainty of their mission gnawed at her. "We'll make it," Kaela said, her voice firm despite the doubt lingering in the back of her mind. She knew she had to believe it, for both of them. There was no turning back now. The unknown loomed ahead, vast and uncharted, but if anyone could navigate it, it was this group. Melana's pragmatic resolve, Milo's steady presence, Ronan's fire, and Kaela's own determination. Together, they were stronger than the sum of their parts.

The hours that followed blurred into a whirlwind of preparation. The rebels moved swiftly, gathering weapons, supplies, and intel on the surrounding terrain. What had once been a safe haven now felt like a fleeting moment of calm. They were about to plunge into something much larger and far more dangerous.

Milo approached Kaela as she finished securing her gear, his usual easy smile absent. His face was drawn tight with concern, and Kaela could feel the weight of the situation pressing down on him. Though he'd always been the one to keep their spirits lifted, the one who held the group together with humor and lightness, Kaela could sense that something had shifted in him. He carried a burden that went beyond the rebellion. One that wasn't easy for him to shake off. She wanted to ask him about it, but now wasn't the time.

"You sure you're ready for this?" Kaela asked, her voice softer than usual, trying to gauge where he was mentally.

Milo hesitated, the small pause speaking volumes before he gave a small nod. "I don't have a choice, do I? None of us do." His words were flat, as though they had been weighed down by more than just the mission ahead.

Kaela studied him for a moment, noting the absence of his usual easy going nature. Instead, there was a grim determination in his eyes, a sharpness that wasn't there before. She could see how much he'd grown into his role as not only an ally but a protector, a warrior in his own right. It was strange to think of him as anything but her best friend, but with each passing day, she felt the shift. Milo was becoming someone the group needed. Someone vital.

"Just . . . be careful," she said, her voice barely above a whisper, the weight of their unspoken connection hanging between them.

Milo's lips quirked into a small smile, but it didn't quite reach his eyes. "You too, Kaela. You're the one with the big job. Just don't do anything reckless, okay?"

Kaela chuckled, though the sound was tight with nerves. "No promises."

As the evening deepened, Kaela couldn't shake the feeling that this was the calm before the storm. The rebels moved through their routines with quiet efficiency, but beneath the surface, there was an undeniable tension that seemed to pulse through the camp. The crackling of the campfires seemed muffled against the growing weight in the air, and even the stars above appeared distant, as if watching, waiting for something to unfold. Kaela wrapped her arms around herself, her thoughts drifting uneasily between the looming mission and the complex, unspoken connection with Ronan.

Later, as the camp settled into a tense stillness, Kaela lay awake in her bedroll, staring up at the canopy of trees above. The sounds of the night blended into the background as her gaze shifted toward Ronan. He sat alone by the fire, his dark figure almost blending into the shadows, his eyes distant, lost in thought. Kaela hesitated for a moment, considering whether to approach him, but something held her back. The space between them wasn't just physical, it felt like an emotional chasm, one she wasn't sure how to bridge.

Then, unexpectedly, Ronan rose from his seat and walked toward her with deliberate, measured steps. Kaela's heart raced, caught off guard by his sudden movement, but she didn't speak, didn't move. He stopped beside her, close enough that she could feel the warmth of his presence, but still far enough to maintain a barrier between them. The silence stretched, charged with an unspoken tension, as if both of them were waiting for something.

Waiting for the right moment to break the stillness that had hung between them for so long.

"I've been thinking about what you said earlier," Ronan's voice was low, rough with an edge of something Kaela couldn't quite place. "About the Garden. About the danger we're facing."

Kaela glanced over at him, meeting his gaze. "And?"

"I agree with you," he said, his words steady but heavy with meaning. "We can't keep waiting. Something's off, I can feel it too. The urgency. Whatever's happening in the Garden is only going to get worse if we don't act. But we can't just rush in without a plan."

Kaela's heart clenched as she processed his words. She had known Ronan had his doubts, but hearing him admit it struck deeper than she expected. It wasn't just the words, but the unspoken understanding between them, that they were both feeling the weight of it all. In that moment, everything felt more real, more urgent than ever.

"I'm not asking us to rush in blindly," she said softly, her voice carrying a quiet intensity. "But we can't keep waiting. We have to take the first step."

Ronan's eyes locked with hers, unwavering and intense. "Then we take it together."

In that moment, Kaela felt something shift between them. It wasn't just trust. It was an unspoken recognition, an understanding that their fates were tangled together in ways neither of them fully grasped. They had faced too many dangers, survived too much, for their bond to be anything less than one forged in the heat of their shared struggles. As the first light of dawn painted the sky in gold and crimson, Kaela knew they were ready. The path ahead was uncertain, but they would face it side by side, unyielding and united against whatever came their way.

The morning sun filtered through the trees, casting long shadows over the camp as Kaela moved between the tents, steeling herself for the mission ahead. The air was thick with anticipation, everyone knew the next few days would decide their fate. There was no turning back now, no room for hesitation. The risks they'd been avoiding were suddenly unavoidable, but even as she focused on the bigger picture, her thoughts kept circling back to the device Milo had been working on.

Milo had secluded himself in a corner of the camp for days, focused on a project that could change everything. Kaela had overheard snippets of his plan. A device that could disrupt the Technomancers' technology and level the playing field. It was a long shot, but it was the only hope they had. The weight of it all hung heavily between them.

She found him hunched over his workbench, brow furrowed in deep concentration. His usual messy appearance was even more disheveled, with rumpled clothes and wild hair. But amid the chaos, there was a calmness about him, this was the one thing that made sense to him. In that moment, it was the only thing that mattered.

"How's it coming?" Kaela asked, stepping closer.

Milo didn't look up at first, his hands moving deftly as he adjusted the wiring. "Almost there," he muttered. "I just need to fine-tune the signal and get the frequency right to disrupt their systems without frying everything. If I can pull it off, their comms will go down, and they won't be able to track us."

Kaela leaned in, watching him work. The energy in the air was palpable. The kind that hummed when someone was on the edge of a breakthrough. She could feel how much this meant to him, how desperate he was to make a real difference. The idea that Milo, the inventor, might be the one to tip the scales filled her with equal parts pride and anxiety.

"Do you think it'll work?" she asked quietly.

Milo paused, glancing up at her with a small, uncertain smile. "I hope so. But you know how it is. Nothing's certain with this stuff. It's all trial and error until it's been tested."

Kaela nodded, her chest heavy with the weight of their situation. The Technomancers were powerful, their technology ruthless and deadly. If Milo's device worked, it would change everything. But if it didn't, she couldn't afford to dwell on the consequences.

"Do you need any help?" she asked, attempting to lighten the mood.

Milo shook his head without looking up. "Nah, I've got it. You focus on getting ready. We're going to need everyone sharp for what's coming."

Kaela hesitated, watching him work for a moment longer. "I know you're doing your best, Milo. I just . . . I don't want to lose anyone."

He met her gaze, and his expression softened. "I don't want to lose anyone either. But we can't keep waiting. We have to act, Kaela. We can't keep running from them."

Her chest tightened at the truth of his words. They were out of options, and there was no turning back. Running was no longer an option, only fighting. It was the only choice they had left.

Later that day, as the camp buzzed with preparations for their move, Kaela found herself thinking about the bond she shared with Milo. It wasn't a romantic connection, not by any means, but there was something about the way they understood each other, an unspoken history that made their friendship feel unshakable. She had always been able to rely on Milo, and despite the tension in the air, that was something she found herself grateful for. It wasn't the same with Ronan, though. With Ronan, it was different. There was a charge between them, an unspoken pull that neither of them had fully addressed yet. She didn't know where it was headed, but she couldn't ignore it, no matter how much she tried to push it aside.

As evening fell and the camp settled into a tense quiet, Kaela found herself once again drawn to the place where Milo was working. The firelight flickered in his eyes as he carefully adjusted the final components of the device, his fingers moving with practiced precision. His focus was absolute, and for a moment, Kaela allowed herself to watch him, to admire the way he had grown into his role as not just an inventor, but a crucial member of their fight.

The device, a small, compact mix of wires, metal, and tech, glowed faintly in front of Milo as he completed the final touches. Kaela could see the exhaustion in his eyes, the toll of sleepless nights spent tinkering and adjusting, but there was also a quiet pride in the way he handled it. This was his contribution, his way of fighting back.

"I think it's ready," he said quietly, glancing up at Kaela. "But I'll need a volunteer to test it."

Kaela raised an eyebrow. "Volunteer? You're not testing it yourself?"

Milo chuckled, but it was hollow, forced. "I've done enough testing already. It's time for someone else to take the risk."

She saw the hesitation in his eyes. The same fear she'd noticed earlier. He didn't want to put anyone else in danger, but he knew it was necessary. Kaela stepped forward without a second thought.

"I'll do it."

Milo's expression softened, gratitude and concern flickering across his face. "Kaela, I don't want to—"

"It's fine, Milo. I trust you. And I trust this."

He hesitated for a moment longer before handing her the

device. "Alright. Just be careful."

As Kaela held the device in her hands, she felt a surge of determination. This was their chance. Milo had made something that could tip the scales in their favor, and she wasn't about to back down. She took the device and moved toward the edge of the camp, where the rebels had set up a small test area. With Ronan by her side, watching with quiet intensity, she activated the device.

For a heartbeat, nothing happened. Then, the device hummed to life, a low buzzing sound filling the air. A small spark shot out from the device, and for a moment, Kaela's heart stopped. But then, with a loud crackle, the nearby tech, an old comms unit they had salvaged, sputtered and died, its lights flickering out.

It worked. The sense of relief that flooded Kaela was almost overwhelming. She looked back at Milo, who was watching her with wide eyes, a look of disbelief crossing his face. He had done it. The device had worked.

"We have a chance," Kaela said softly, turning back to the group.

Milo nodded, a smile slowly spreading across his face. "Yeah. We do."

And for the first time in days, Kaela felt a spark of hope. The weight of uncertainty still loomed, but it no longer crushed her. She didn't know what the future held, only that they weren't out of the fight yet. In that moment, they had a chance. A real, fighting chance.

Chapter 28

The rebel camp was alive with hushed murmurs, each person moving with quiet urgency as they prepared for the journey ahead. Kaela stood near the edge of the camp, the crisp air biting at her skin, her thoughts clouded with the weight of what was to come. They hadn't yet infiltrated the Technomancer facility, but they were getting closer, closer to a confrontation that would test them all. Her eyes flicked to the distant horizon, the faint glow of dawn barely breaking through the trees. It felt like the calm before a storm.

Beside her, Melana was sharpening her sword with careful precision, her amber eyes scanning the camp with a practiced ease. "The Technomancers will know we're coming," Melana said, her voice low, almost too calm for the tension hanging between them. "We need to be ready for anything."

Kaela nodded, though the pit in her stomach remained. She had learned over the past few weeks that Melana wasn't one to waste words. Her quiet confidence was both reassuring and unsettling, and Kaela knew she could rely on the woman when things got rough. But that didn't mean she wasn't nervous.

Milo, always busy with some invention or another, was crouched near a stack of supplies, tweaking one of his devices. His brow furrowed in concentration as he soldered a small piece of tech together. Kaela approached him, her steps quiet. "How's the device coming along?" she asked, her voice laced with a quiet sense of hope.

Milo looked up, his usual easy smile replaced with a look of intense focus. "It's coming," he said, holding up the small device. "This should disrupt their tech long enough to give us an edge. I just hope it's enough."

Kaela's heart tightened. The Technomancers had a way of manipulating technology with ease, and if they couldn't disrupt that control, they were at a serious disadvantage. She took a deep breath and forced herself to focus. This wasn't the time for doubt.

As she turned away, her gaze fell on Ronan. He stood a little further from the group, his dark curls blowing in the wind, his eyes distant. Kaela had learned not to ask too many questions about his past. He was a former Technomancer, and the weight of that history hung heavy between them. Despite their shared purpose, their uneasy alliance was fraught with unspoken tension. But today, something in the way he carried himself made Kaela feel the shift in the air, the undeniable pull between them.

Ronan's eyes met hers across the camp, and for a moment, everything else faded. There was a quiet understanding in his gaze, a shared weight of the coming days. He had always been guarded, his emotions locked away behind a wall of wit and teasing, but in that instant, Kaela saw something else, something raw and unspoken.

Without breaking eye contact, he turned and began walking toward the treeline, motioning for her to follow. "We should get moving," he said, his voice low, the usual teasing edge absent. "The sooner we start, the sooner we'll be done."

Kaela hesitated, but something inside her stirred. She knew the journey ahead wouldn't be easy. But with Ronan at her side, there was a part of her that believed they might actually stand a chance.

She followed him into the woods, the rest of the group falling in behind them. The weight of their mission was heavy, but there was also a strange sense of unity in their movement, a silent promise that they would see this through together.

The path through the trees was treacherous, the terrain uneven and steep. The group moved quickly, but there was no rushing through the wilderness. Every step brought them closer to the Technomancers and closer to whatever awaited them on the other side. As they moved deeper into the forest, the air grew thick with tension. Kaela's thoughts were a whirlwind, her mind flickering between the dangers ahead and the unexpected pull she felt toward Ronan.

As they stopped to make camp for the night, the atmosphere was quiet but tense. Kaela could feel the weight of everyone's eyes on her, as if they were waiting for something to break, waiting for the moment when everything would change. But she wasn't sure what that moment would look like.

The fire crackled softly as they gathered around it, the glow casting shadows on their faces. Ronan sat closest to her, his eyes flicking between the others as they spoke in low voices. He seemed more at ease in the quiet of the camp, his guard slightly lowered. Kaela's gaze lingered on him for a moment, and when he caught her watching, a faint smirk tugged at the corner of his lips.

"What?" he asked, his voice low, teasing.

Kaela shook her head, the corners of her mouth twitching in spite of herself. "Nothing," she said, but there was an underlying tension in her voice, one she couldn't shake. "Just thinking."

Ronan's gaze softened, though only slightly. "About what?" His voice was quieter now, less playful, more serious.

She met his eyes, feeling the pull between them more than ever. "About what comes next. What we're up against." She hesitated, her words faltering. "And about what you've sacrificed. I—" She broke off, unsure of what to say. The truth of his past, the price he had paid to escape the Technomancers, lingered between them, unspoken.

Ronan studied her for a moment, his expression unreadable. Then, slowly, he spoke. "I'm not the man I was," he said, his voice barely above a whisper. "I can't undo what I've done, but I'll fight with everything I have to make it right."

His words hit her like a punch to the gut, heavy with unspoken pain. She couldn't ignore the depth of his sacrifice or the guilt that still clung to him. And yet, despite everything, he remained unwavering. He was here, ready to risk it all once more.

Kaela swallowed hard, the knot in her chest tightening. "You don't have to do this alone," she said softly, the words coming out more vulnerable than she intended.

Ronan's gaze softened even more, his usual bravado slipping away. "I'm not alone," he murmured, his voice barely audible. "Not anymore."

Kaela's heart raced, her pulse quickening in the silence. The air between them felt heavy, charged with something unspoken. For the first time, she let herself fully acknowledge the pull between them. The tension was undeniable, growing stronger with every passing moment.

But before either of them could speak again, the crackling of the fire interrupted the moment, and the camp's atmosphere shifted. The others were stirring, their faces shadowed with exhaustion and determination. The mission ahead was clear. There would be no turning back.

Kaela stood, her legs stiff from sitting too long. "We'll need to be ready for anything," she said, her voice steady. "The Technomancers won't make it easy."

Ronan stood with her, his hand brushing hers in a fleeting touch. "We're ready," he said, his voice a quiet promise. "We'll face it together."

His words hung between them, carrying the weight of what lay ahead. Kaela's chest tightened, her breath hitching. The future was uncertain, filled with danger and unknowns. But standing beside Ronan, she felt like they might have a chance.

The road ahead was uncertain. As the fire flickered out, Kaela felt a growing sense of unease. She knew the real test was just beginning. The journey would be harder than anything they had faced before.

The early morning air was thick with the scent of wet earth, a sign of the coming rain. Kaela stood near the edge of the camp, her arms folded across her chest, her gaze lingering on the path they would soon take. The rebels were packing up, their movements sharp and purposeful, a sense of urgency hanging in the air. Milo's device was safely stowed in a secure pack, ready for its moment of use, but Kaela knew they weren't out of danger yet. The Technomancers were never far behind.

A low hum vibrated through the air, and Kaela's heart skipped a beat. She turned to see Ronan, his dark gaze fixed on her, his expression unreadable. The tension between them, simmering since the night he had sacrificed himself to protect the group, had only grown. She could feel it in the way his eyes lingered a moment longer than necessary, in the subtle shifts of his body as if he was aware of every inch of space between them.

"Ronan," Kaela began, her voice softer than she intended, "the Technomancer patrol from earlier. What do you think their next move will be?"

He didn't look away from her, his eyes locking onto hers with an intensity that made her pulse quicken. "They're getting more aggressive. That last patrol we saw was a warning, not just a sweep." He paused, his jaw tightening as if remembering the close call they had earlier. "They're circling us. If we don't make our move soon, they'll tighten their grip on the whole area."

Kaela felt the weight of his words settle on her chest. The patrol they had encountered earlier had been too close for comfort. As they had approached the outskirts of the camp, the faint hum of their Technomancer tech had reached Kaela's ears, signaling their arrival. Ronan had been the first to spot them, and without hesitation, he had led the group into the shadows, out of sight. But the encounter had been a close call. One misstep, and they would have been caught.

The memory of the moment still clung to her. Ronan had stood between her and the advancing patrol, his body poised and ready to fight. She had seen the way his eyes had narrowed, the way he had shifted, calculating his next move. He had been ready to sacrifice himself for the group. But it hadn't come to that. Not yet.

Kaela shook herself from the memory, her fingers brushing the strap of her pack. "So we're still going through with it then? We're going to infiltrate the Technomancer facility?"

Ronan gave a slow nod, his lips curling into a half-smile, though there was no humor in it. "We don't have much choice. The longer we wait, the more likely they'll find us first."

Behind them, Melana's voice broke through the quiet. "We need to be careful. The Technomancers have eyes everywhere." She stepped closer, her amber eyes sharp, her body moving with the silent grace Kaela had come to recognize. "If we get too close to their stronghold, they'll know. They'll be waiting for us."

Kaela turned to Melana, grateful for her insight. Melana had proven herself to be more than just an ally. She was a strategist, a quiet force of nature. Every word she spoke carried weight, every plan she proposed had depth. She had seen firsthand what the Technomancers were capable of, and Kaela had come to trust her judgment above all else.

Milo joined them then, his face alight with excitement. "I think we've got a shot," he said, holding up the device he had spent countless hours perfecting. "This should disrupt their tech long enough for us to slip through undetected."

Kaela's gaze fell on the device, sleek and compact. It was Milo's masterpiece, the result of countless hours of tinkering. If it worked, it could be the key to getting past the Technomancers' defenses. The simplicity of its design belied its deadly potential.

"Good," she said, her voice steady despite the flutter of nerves in her stomach. "We move at night. It's our best chance."

The group fell silent, each of them processing the enormity of what lay ahead. The path was treacherous, but they had no choice. It was a matter of survival. They had to move forward, no matter the cost.

As the day wore on, the camp grew quieter. The rebels had completed their preparations, and the time to move was fast approaching. Kaela found herself standing at the edge of the camp again, this time with Ronan by her side. He was quiet, his gaze fixed on the horizon, but Kaela could feel the tension radiating off him.

"You know," she said, breaking the silence, "I never thought I'd be here, doing this. Fighting the Technomancers, planning a mission like this." Her voice faltered for a moment, and she looked away, her heart thudding in her chest. "It feels too big, too dangerous."

Ronan's gaze softened, and he stepped closer, the warmth of his presence comforting in the chill of the evening air. "You're not alone in this, Kaela," he said, his voice low, steady. "None of us are."

She met his gaze then, and for a moment, everything else faded.

There was something in his eyes, something that spoke of the sacrifices he had made, of the risks he was willing to take. She could see it clearly now, the way he had put himself in danger to protect them, the way he would do it again if necessary. And yet, there was more. There was something between them, something unspoken, a tension that neither of them could deny.

"Ronan," Kaela began, her voice barely a whisper, "you didn't have to do what you did back there. You didn't have to risk yourself for us."

Ronan's expression darkened, but there was no bitterness in his gaze. "I would do it again," he said, his voice raw with an emotion Kaela couldn't place. "I would do anything to keep you safe."

The words hung between them, thick with unspoken meaning. Kaela's heart raced, her chest tightening. She could feel the pull between them, the undeniable connection that had been growing ever since they'd met. But there was still so much between them, so many things left unsaid and unresolved. Before she could speak again, a sharp whistle cut through the air. The group sprang into action immediately. The time had come. They were ready to move forward. Kaela turned away, her heart pounding in her chest. As she moved to join the others, she felt Ronan's eyes on her. The weight of his gaze settled over her like a promise. The journey ahead would be dangerous, but with Ronan at her side, she knew she wouldn't face it alone.

Chapter 29

The journey to the Technomancer facility had taken longer than they'd anticipated. The landscape had shifted from dense forest to jagged mountains, the path winding through narrow passes that were almost too treacherous to navigate. Every step felt like a test of endurance, and the deeper they traveled, the more the weight of their mission pressed on them. Kaela couldn't help but feel the tension in the air, like the world itself was holding its breath, waiting for something.

As they moved through the rugged terrain, Kaela found herself watching Ronan more than she cared to admit. His presence was a constant, an undercurrent that pulsed through every moment. He moved with the confidence of someone who had seen too much, someone who had lived through things Kaela couldn't quite understand. Yet there was something about him, something unspoken, that drew her in. His quiet intensity, the way his eyes always seemed to be scanning their surroundings, never resting, never quite at ease. She caught his gaze once, his eyes flickering with something unreadable before he turned his attention back to the path ahead. Kaela's heart skipped a beat, but she quickly pushed the thought aside. They had bigger things to focus on now.

Milo, ever the inventor, had been keeping to himself, his mind consumed with his device. It was their best hope to disable the Technomancers' technology once they reached the facility. The small, portable device was designed to disrupt the signal frequencies that powered their tech, rendering their weapons and security systems useless. Milo had worked tirelessly to perfect it, and now, it was their only advantage.

Melana, on the other hand, was the glue that held them all together. She had been here before, infiltrating similar facilities during her time with the resistance. She was a master of stealth, and her ability to navigate enemy territory without being detected was unmatched. Kaela had grown to trust her instincts, relying on her quiet guidance more than she cared to admit. Melana's eyes were sharp, constantly scanning the environment for threats, and her demeanor was calm, almost too calm for someone about to walk straight into the heart of the enemy's lair.

As they neared the facility, the tension became palpable. The once serene wilderness now felt suffocating, like they were walking straight into the belly of the beast. Kaela's mind raced with questions about her father, the Garden, the Technomancers, and their relentless pursuit of power. But most of all, she thought about Ronan. What had he meant when he said they were connected to the Garden? Was that the key to everything? And if so, why hadn't he told her sooner?

The facility loomed in the distance, a cold, imposing structure nestled between two jagged cliffs. It was heavily fortified, the kind of place that seemed impenetrable. But they had no choice. This was where the answers lay.

Melana led them to a hidden entrance, a narrow, nearly invisible tunnel that led into the facility's underground level. She had scouted it earlier, making sure the guards were far enough away for them to slip through undetected. The air inside the tunnel was dank and cold, the walls slick with moisture. It smelled like old metal and decay.

Kaela's breath came in short bursts as they crawled through the tunnel, the weight of their mission settling heavily on her shoulders. She couldn't help but glance over at Ronan again, who was walking just behind her. His gaze was steady, but there was a flicker of something in his eyes, something that made her heart race. She wanted to say something, to ask him what was really going on between them, but the words caught in her throat. They had more pressing matters to deal with, and yet, the pull between them felt undeniable.

Once they reached the facility's lower level, the atmosphere grew tense, the air humming faintly with the facility's hidden power. The walls were lined with sleek, dark panels, glowing softly with the pulsing rhythm of technomantic energy. Melana crouched at the front of the group, her sharp amber eyes darting between the corridors. She raised a hand, signaling for them to stay back as she crept forward.

At the next junction, a grid of surveillance cameras and motion sensors glinted faintly in the low light. The steady blink of a nearby security panel reflected off the cold, metallic surfaces. Without hesitation, Melana pulled a compact toolkit from her belt, fingers moving with deft precision. She removed a slim device, placing it carefully against the security panel. The faint whir of her tool filled the silence as she bypassed the cameras, her hands moving quickly to splice wires and reroute the power. The motion sensors flickered once before dimming entirely.

"Cameras are looped, sensors are offline," she murmured, her voice low but confident. With a glance over her shoulder, she gestured for the others to follow. "Stay close and step exactly where I do."

Kaela glanced at Ronan, their shared look reflecting admiration for Melana's skill. The group followed closely, each step light and deliberate. Guided by Melana, they moved deeper into the facility, the oppressive silence amplifying their focus. The security systems remained unaware of their presence, leaving them undetected.

Kaela's mind was on high alert, her senses heightened as they moved through the facility's corridors. The walls were lined with cold metal, the floors gleaming under the harsh fluorescent lights. It felt sterile, like a place built for efficiency, not humanity. But it was the people who made Kaela's skin crawl. The Technomancers, their faces hidden behind masks, moved in and out of the rooms, their steps purposeful and calculated. They were always watching, always waiting. They had to move fast.

Kaela's pulse quickened as they neared the central control room. This was where they would find the answers. But it wasn't going to be easy. The room was guarded, and the doors were reinforced with layers of security.

Milo stepped forward, his device in hand. "This is it," he whispered. "Once I disable the system, we'll have a window of about five minutes. That's all the time we'll have before the backup systems kick In."

Melana nodded, her eyes sharp. "We need to be in and out, fast. No mistakes."

Kaela took a deep breath, steeling herself. "Let's do it."

As Milo set to work on the device, Ronan moved to cover the perimeter, his eyes scanning the hallways for any signs of movement. Kaela couldn't help but notice how effortlessly he moved, like a shadow, his every motion fluid and precise. She wanted to ask him what was going through his mind, but she didn't dare. The tension between them was thick, and she knew he was just as focused on the task at hand as she was. Then, a noise. The sound of footsteps approaching from around the corner.

"Get down," Melana hissed, her voice low but urgent.

They all ducked into the shadows, holding their breath as the guards passed by, oblivious to their presence. Kaela's heart pounded in her chest, and she felt Ronan's body close behind hers, his breath warm against her neck. For a moment, it was just the two of them, alone in the silence, the weight of everything pressing in on them. Kaela could feel the tension in the air, the unspoken words hanging between them. She was acutely aware of his proximity, the way his hand brushed hers as they crouched together in the darkness. It was dangerous, the way their bodies seemed to draw closer despite the mission. But Kaela couldn't help herself. There was something about him, something she couldn't shake, no matter how hard she tried.

When the guards finally passed, they moved quickly, reaching the control room without further incident. Milo activated the device, and the facility's security systems flickered and died. The door to the control room slid open with a soft hiss, revealing the heart of the Technomancer operations. They were inside. But as Kaela stepped over the threshold, she couldn't shake the feeling that something, or someone, was watching them.

The control room was cold and sterile, lit by flickering overhead lights that hummed in the silence. Kaela's eyes darted over the rows of consoles and terminals, each one brimming with data, flashing lights, and an overwhelming sense of urgency. This was the heart of the Technomancer operation, the place where the strings of power were pulled. And here, Kaela was about to uncover the truth. Milo moved quickly to one of the terminals, his fingers flying over the keys as he bypassed the security measures. He didn't speak, but the look of concentration on his face was clear. This was his domain, and he was in control.

Melana was at the door, her back to the wall, eyes scanning the hallway for any signs of trouble. Her posture was tense, every muscle coiled and ready for action. She was always alert, always prepared, and Kaela admired that about her. Despite everything that had happened, Melana had remained a steady presence, and Kaela couldn't help but feel grateful for her guidance.

Ronan stood beside Kaela, his presence a quiet reassurance. He had positioned himself at the far side of the room, watching their surroundings with a quiet intensity. His eyes flickered to Kaela for a brief moment, and she caught the unspoken words in his gaze. An acknowledgment, a connection that neither of them had fully explored yet.

Kaela swallowed hard, her pulse quickening. This was it. The moment when everything would change. As Milo worked, Kaela's thoughts raced. Her mind kept drifting back to the vision of Aelera, the mysterious guardian of the Garden, urging her to take risks, to trust in herself and the journey ahead. But it wasn't just Aelera's words that echoed in her mind. It was the unspoken truth about her connection to the Garden, to Ronan. Was their bond really what she thought it was? Could it be that the answers she sought had been with her all along?

"Got it," Milo said suddenly, breaking Kaela from her thoughts. He stepped back from the terminal, his face pale but triumphant. "I've accessed the central database. We have everything we need."

Kaela's heart skipped a beat. "Show me."

Milo pulled up a series of images and data files on the screen, each one more cryptic than the last. But as Kaela's eyes scanned the information, one thing became painfully clear: the connection between her and Ronan was far deeper than either of them had realized. The Garden wasn't just a place of magic, it was a nexus, a focal point of immense power, and they were both tied to it in ways that defied understanding.

Ronan stepped closer, his eyes narrowing as he examined the screen. "This . . . this is why they're after us," he murmured, his voice low, almost to himself.

Kaela felt a chill run down her spine. "What do you mean?"

Ronan turned to face her, his gaze steady and intense. "The Technomancers want the Garden's power, but it's not just the magic they're after. They want to control the people who are connected to it. People like you and me."

Kaela's breath caught in her throat. "So they've been hunting us all along . . . because of the Garden?"

"Yes," Ronan said softly. "But there's more. They don't just want to control us. They want to use the Garden's power to reshape the world, to make it theirs. They've been searching for a way to manipulate its magic, and we're the key."

Kaela's mind spun. Everything she thought she knew was shifting beneath her feet. "But why didn't you tell me? Why didn't you tell me sooner?"

Ronan hesitated, his jaw tightening. "Because I didn't understand it myself. I didn't know what it meant until now. And now . . ." His voice faltered for a moment, before he squared his shoulders. "Now I do."

The room was silent for a moment, the weight of his words hanging in the air between them. Kaela's heart raced, her thoughts a whirlwind. The connection between them, the one she had sensed growing stronger with every passing day, it wasn't just physical or emotional. It was something deeper, something far more powerful. But before Kaela could say anything else, a sudden noise broke the silence. A low hum, followed by a series of clicks. The backup systems had activated.

"Shit," Melana hissed. "We're not alone."

Ronan's eyes flicked toward the door, his posture shifting into something more dangerous. "We need to move. Now."

Milo grabbed the device, stuffing it into his bag, his hands trembling. "I've downloaded everything we need. Let's go."

Kaela nodded, her heart pounding in her chest. They had what they came for, but now they had to escape before the Technomancers realized what had happened. She didn't need to look at Ronan to know he was already thinking three steps ahead, calculating their next move. As they slipped out of the control room, Kaela's senses heightened. She felt it then. An uncanny sensation, as though someone, or something, was watching them. Her pulse quickened, and she glanced over her shoulder, half-expecting to see eyes peering from the shadows. But when she turned, there was nothing. The corridor ahead was still, eerily so. Her instincts screamed at her to keep moving, but the feeling of being watched clung to her, like a shadow she couldn't shake.

Ronan must have sensed it too. He stepped closer, his voice barely a whisper. "Keep your guard up. We're not alone here."

Kaela nodded, her hand tightening around the hilt of her blade. Every fiber of her being was on edge as they made their way through the labyrinthine hallways. She could feel the weight of the truth, of their connection to the Garden, bearing down on her. But there was something else. Something about the way the Technomancers were closing in on them, something more sinister than she had realized.

The door to the hallway slid open with a soft hiss, and they were back in the dimly lit corridors. The tension between them was palpable, especially between her and Ronan. His proximity, the unspoken bond between them, had her heart racing faster than it should. She felt the pull between them, the connection that neither of them could deny, even if they didn't fully understand it. But there was no time for words, for understanding. Not yet.

Ronan glanced at her, his expression unreadable. His voice was steady, but she could hear the edge in it. "Stay close. We can't afford any mistakes."

Kaela nodded, her heart thundering in her chest as the weight of their situation pressed down on her. Survival was their only option, and every instinct screamed at her to keep moving, to push forward. Yet, amidst the chaos and danger, a quiet realization settled over her—she wasn't facing this alone. For the first time in what felt like forever, she had people she could truly rely on, and that made all the difference.

Chapter 30

The air inside the facility felt heavier as they delved deeper. Every step echoed in the narrow corridors, the sound bouncing off cold, metallic walls. The tension between the group was palpable, each of them weighed down by the implications of what they had uncovered so far. Kaela could barely think, her mind racing with fragments of information. Her connection to the Garden, the Technomancers' relentless pursuit, and the haunting feeling that someone had been watching them since their arrival.

Milo's device beeped softly in his bag, the only indication it was still working as they navigated the labyrinthine halls. His face was tight with concentration as he studied the small holographic map projected from his wrist. "We're close to the main power chamber," he whispered. "If the Garden's tied to this place, we'll find proof there."

Kaela glanced at Ronan, who walked silently beside her, his

broad shoulders rigid, every step deliberate. His golden-green eyes flickered with an intensity that both reassured and unsettled her, like a beacon in the dark that could either guide or burn. His presence, as always, was a steady force, grounding her amid the chaos of their mission, yet there was an edge to him now that hadn't been there before, a tension coiled just beneath the surface. The way his jaw tightened, the faint furrow in his brow, the occasional glance toward the shadows, all spoke of a man bracing himself for a storm that hadn't yet broken. She wondered what weight he carried in his silence, what sacrifices he anticipated, and if, when the time came, he would share the burden or bear it alone as he so often seemed determined to do.

Melana brought up the rear, her sharp amber eyes scanning their surroundings with practiced precision. Every movement she made was fluid, the grace of someone who had faced countless dangers and lived to tell the tale. Kaela couldn't help but admire her composure, even as her own nerves frayed with each passing step. The quiet confidence Melana exuded was both reassuring and humbling in the face of their growing peril.

The hallway expanded suddenly, the narrow, confining walls giving way to a vast, open space that loomed ahead. At its center stood a massive steel door, its surface gleaming faintly, almost as if it were alive, rippling with a strange, iridescent energy that seemed to hum in the air. Intricate, glowing symbols were etched into the metal, pulsing faintly like a heartbeat, their patterns shifting and twisting as though reacting to the group's presence. Milo stepped forward, his brow furrowed in concentration as his fingers flew over his device, each keystroke echoing in the silence. With a soft, serpentine hiss, the door responded, sliding open to reveal a cavernous chamber beyond, awash in an unsettling, pulsating light that bathed the space in shifting hues of green and gold.

Kaela's breath caught in her throat as she stepped inside, her senses immediately overwhelmed by the sight before her. The walls of the chamber were lined with an intricate web of conduits and crystalline structures, their surfaces slick with an oily sheen. These glowing veins pulsed with an unnatural, sickly green light, sending eerie ripples through the air, as if the room itself was alive, breathing in time with the energy flowing through the walls. The conduits twisted and wound like serpents, veins of energy running through them like blood through arteries, crackling with a low, ominous hum that vibrated in her chest. In the center of the room, dominating the space, stood a colossal cylindrical core, its surface encased in translucent, almost ethereal panels. Inside, vibrant tendrils of energy swirled in chaotic patterns, their colors shifting from deep emerald to fiery orange, constantly shifting and undulating with a life of their own. The sight was both mesmerizing and horrifying, the raw power contained within the core palpable, yet twisted, like a force that should never have been harnessed. Kaela's skin prickled, her heart racing as she took in the magnitude of what stood before her, a force of unimaginable power, both beautiful and terrifying in its potential.

"What is this?" Kaela whispered, her voice barely audible over the low hum of the machinery.

Milo approached the core, his expression darkening as he examined the controls. "This . . . this is a siphoning system," he said, his voice trembling with anger. "They're draining energy from the Garden. This is how they're powering the domes."

Kaela's stomach churned. "What do you mean? The domes . . . the entire city . . . runs on this?"

Milo nodded grimly. "The domes were designed to be self-sustaining, but the Technomancers found a way to tap into the Garden's magic. This isn't just a power source. It's a lifeline. And they're bleeding it dry."

Melana let out a low whistle, her expression hardening. "So that's why the Garden is dying," she said. "It's not just neglect. They're killing it to keep the domes alive."

Kaela's knees weakened as the weight of the revelation hit her. The Garden, the place her father had dedicated his life to finding, the place that held her own mysterious connection, was being drained to fuel the very system that had kept them all trapped. The domes, which she had once believed to be a sanctuary, were revealed to be nothing more than a parasite. The realization twisted in her gut, a bitter truth she couldn't ignore.

Ronan's eyes narrowed as he studied the siphoning core, his voice laced with frustration. "This—this is what they've been working toward all along. They've been draining the Garden's power to build something bigger, something that will give them control over everything."

Kaela's hands clenched into fists, her anger flaring. "And we're just supposed to let them do it? Let them turn the Garden into a weapon?"

Ronan's expression hardened, his tone quiet but fierce. "We don't have a choice. If we don't stop them now, everything we've fought for will be destroyed. And we'll never get a second chance."

Kaela's mind spun, each new realization hitting her like a wave crashing against the shore. The truth was suffocating, its weight pressing heavily on her chest, threatening to crush her. She thought of her father, his tireless search for the Garden, the sacrifices he had made, and the pain he must have endured knowing the cost of his mission. The memory of Aelera's vision surfaced, the ethereal guardian urging her to embrace bold risks, to fight for something greater. Her thoughts then turned to the people in the domes, living in blissful ignorance, unaware of the immense cost that sustained their fragile existence. Each breath felt harder to take as the magnitude of it all settled into her bones.

"We have to stop this," she said, her voice firm despite the tremor in her hands. "We can't let them keep doing this."

Milo looked up from the console, his face pale but determined. "If I can overload the core, it'll disrupt the siphoning system. It won't destroy the domes outright, but it'll give the Garden a chance to recover."

"Do it," Kaela said without hesitation.

Melana stepped forward, her expression serious. "We need to be smart about this. If we trigger an overload, they'll know we're here. We'll have to fight our way out."

Ronan's gaze shifted to Kaela, a flicker of something unspoken passing between them. "We've come this far," he said quietly. "There's no turning back now."

Kaela nodded, her resolve hardening. She couldn't let fear hold her back. Not when so much was at stake. "Let's do it."

Milo began working on the console, his hands steady despite the tension in the air. The hum of the core grew louder, its light flickering as the system began to destabilize. Kaela felt the hair on the back of her neck stand on end, the energy in the room crackling like a storm about to break. Suddenly, Kaela felt it again. That eerie sensation of being watched. Her eyes darted around the room, but there was no one there. Yet the feeling persisted, a gnawing presence at the edge of her awareness.

"Kaela?" Ronan's voice broke through her thoughts, drawing her attention back to him. His expression was tense, his eyes searching hers. "What's wrong?"

She hesitated, unsure how to put the feeling into words. "I . . . I think someone's watching us."

Ronan's gaze sharpened, and he scanned the room with a predator's intensity. "We need to move. Now."

The shrill wail of alarms echoed through the chamber, drowning out all other sounds. Red lights flickered to life, casting an eerie glow across the room. Kaela's heart raced as she realized the Technomancers had detected the disruption. The sense of urgency in the air was palpable as the seconds ticked by.

"They're coming!" Melana shouted, drawing her weapon.

Milo grabbed his device, his voice urgent. "I've set the overload. We have ten minutes to get out of here."

The group moved as one, racing back through the corridors with the sound of boots and shouts echoing behind them. Kaela's heart pounded as she ran, the weight of the truth fueling her determination. The Garden's survival, and their own, depended on their escape. But as they rounded a corner, Kaela couldn't shake the feeling that whoever, or whatever, had been watching them wasn't finished yet.

The group's hurried footsteps reverberated through the winding corridors, the blaring alarms creating a haunting rhythm in the air. Kaela's heart pounded in her chest, her mind racing as an unsettling feeling washed over her. The sense of being watched intensified, like invisible eyes were tracking their every move. It wasn't just paranoia. Something, or someone, was lurking just beyond her awareness, waiting.

Ronan's sharp gaze swept their surroundings, his hand brushing the hilt of his blade. Melana moved with equal precision, her body tense as she covered their rear. "Whatever's out there," she muttered, "it's not just the Technomancers."

Kaela's breath hitched as they rounded another corner, coming to a sudden halt. In the dim glow of the flickering emergency lights stood a figure cloaked in shadow, their form impossibly still. The light behind them cast an eerie halo around their silhouette, obscuring their features but amplifying the menacing aura that surrounded them. Kaela's pulse quickened, a chill creeping down her spine as the figure seemed to be waiting, as though expecting them.

"Who's there?" Ronan barked, his voice sharp and commanding.

The figure stepped forward with deliberate slowness, the hood of their cloak sliding back to reveal a man whose presence seemed to consume the dim light. His piercing silver-gray eyes gleamed with an unsettling intensity, cutting through the shadows like a blade, as if he could see right through Kaela and the others. His dark hair, streaked with white at the temples, framed a face that was impossibly calm, almost unnervingly so, but there was an underlying sharpness in his features, a quiet menace lurking beneath his composed expression. His gaze lingered on them, as though he were studying each of them with an eerie familiarity, the tension in the air thickening with every passing second.

"Ronan," the man said, his voice smooth and deliberate. "So, the prodigal son returns."

Ronan stopped dead in his tracks, his body stiffening as if frozen in place. His hand fell from his blade, the tension in his posture betraying a sudden, deep unease. For a fleeting moment, Kaela caught a rare glimpse of raw emotion on his face. Recognition, anger, and something far more conflicted, like a storm brewing beneath his calm exterior. It was gone almost as quickly as it appeared, leaving Kaela to wonder what, or who, had caused it.

"Kaelith," Ronan said, his tone low and simmering with restrained fury. "What are you doing here?"

Kaela moved closer to Ronan, her gaze flicking between him and the stranger. The air between them crackled with unspoken tension. "Who is he?" she asked, her voice tight.

Kaelith's gaze shifted to her, his expression softening with a faint, almost condescending amusement. "Ah, Kaela. So, we finally meet. The Garden speaks of you often."

Kaela's stomach twisted. "What are you talking about? Who are you?"

"I am Kaelith," he replied, his tone maddeningly calm. "A Watcher, bound to the Garden. I safeguard its secrets and ensure its warnings are heeded. And you . . . " His gaze lingered on her, heavy and unnerving. "You are far more important to it than you realize."

Kaela took a step back, her heart pounding. "The Garden sent you?"

"Not quite," Kaelith said with a faint smile. "I've been watching from the periphery, ensuring those who would harm the Garden—" His sharp eyes flicked to Ronan. "—are kept in check."

Ronan stepped forward, his posture taut with tension. "You have no authority here, Kaelith. Not anymore."

Kaelith's serene expression didn't waver. "And you have no claim to authority at all, Ronan. Not after what you've done." He turned to Kaela, his silver gaze pinning her in place. "Tell me, Kaela, has he shared the truth with you? About the bargain he struck?"

Kaela frowned, confusion and unease churning in her chest. "Not completely. What does that have to do with anything?"

Kaelith's voice turned sharper, his calm cracking just enough to reveal the depth of his disdain. "He sacrificed his true love to the Garden. He thought it wouldn't matter. Thought it would never come to pass. But the Garden has a cruel sense of irony, doesn't it, Ronan?"

Kaela's breath hitched as her gaze snapped to Ronan. His golden-green eyes were wide, a rare vulnerability bleeding through his usual composure. "What does he mean?" she demanded, her voice shaking.

Ronan looked away, his jaw tight. "Kaela, it's not what you

think—"

"Then tell me what it is!" she snapped, stepping toward him.

Kaelith let out a soft, humorless laugh. "He gave up his true love, Kaela. The Garden demanded it in exchange for his survival, and he agreed. What he didn't know. What none of us knew. Was that you would be the one it claimed?"

Kaela felt as though the ground had dropped out from under her. "You . . . you bargained with the Garden?" Her voice was barely above a whisper.

"I didn't know," Ronan said, his voice raw. "I didn't know it would be you. I thought—I thought I was giving up something I couldn't have, something I'd never find."

Kaelith's smirk was cold and unyielding. "And yet here she is, the key to the Garden's salvation. The very person you betrayed before you even knew her."

The weight of Kaelith's words pressed down on Kaela, suffocating her thoughts like a crushing tide. She opened her mouth, ready to respond, but the sound of distant boots and shouted orders cut through the tension, jolting her back to the present. The Technomancers were closing in, their approach relentless and inevitable. Panic surged through her, but she forced herself to focus, knowing there was no time for hesitation.

"We don't have time for this," Melana said sharply, her weapon already drawn. "Kaelith, if you're here to help, then help. Otherwise, get out of the way."

Kaelith tilted his head, considering her for a moment before stepping aside with an exaggerated bow. "Very well. I'll lend my aid for now. But this conversation isn't over."

As they moved past him, Kaela felt his gaze burning into her back. Her mind raced, the weight of Ronan's secret pressing down on her chest. She wanted answers, needed them, but survival came first. The truth, as devastating as it might be, would have to wait. When they reached the next corridor, Kaela finally glanced at Ronan. His expression was strained, his usual confidence nowhere to be found. Despite everything, she felt an ache of sympathy for him, but the questions swirling in her mind wouldn't let her fully give in. For now, she turned her focus to the mission. The truth, painful and tangled as it was, would unravel soon enough.

Chapter 31

The tension from their encounter with Kaelith lingered in the air, thick and suffocating. Kaela's mind raced with questions about the Watcher and his cryptic warnings, but she pushed them aside, unwilling to let them distract her. The journey through the facility had raised more questions than it answered, and every moment felt like a step deeper into uncertainty. She couldn't afford to let her emotions take control, not now, when the stakes were higher than ever.

They had taken refuge in a hidden cavern just beyond the Technomancer facility, surrounded by thick woods that offered them a momentary shield from pursuit. The cavern, though temporary, provided some semblance of safety as the dense foliage concealed their presence. Melana kept watch, her sharp amber eyes cutting through the darkness, while Milo sat cross-legged by a flickering lantern, absorbed in the data drive he'd stolen from the facility. The quiet was oppressive, the tension hanging in the air as they waited for whatever came next.

"I think I've found something," Milo murmured, his voice tight with concentration.

Kaela and Ronan both looked up, their attention drawn to Milo as he worked. Ronan had been sharpening his blade in silence, the rhythmic scrape of metal against stone a calming but focused sound in the quiet cavern. Kaela's gaze shifted to Milo, her heart quickening at the sight of his furrowed brow as he examined the data drive. The tension in the air grew thicker, each of them aware that time was running out.

"What is it?" she asked, her voice barely above a whisper.

Milo didn't answer immediately. His fingers danced across the device, pulling up files and encryptions that glowed faintly in the dim light. Finally, he exhaled sharply, leaning back. "It's . . . my parents," he said, his voice cracking.

Kaela's stomach sank. "What do you mean?"

Milo turned the device toward her, revealing a series of documents that flickered on the screen, their contents illuminated by the soft glow of the lantern. The papers were aged, their edges pixelated from years of wear, yet the insignia of the Technomancers was unmistakable, stamped boldly across the top. As the documents came into focus, two names jumped out at Kaela immediately: Lyra and Doran Alaric. The names felt like a punch to her gut, stirring something deep within her. Memories, questions, and a gnawing sense of dread. She leaned in closer, her breath catching in her throat as she scanned the rest of the text.

"They knew," Milo said, his voice trembling. "They knew about the Garden, about what the Technomancers were doing to it. They tried to stop it."

Kaela's chest tightened as she scanned the documents, her fingers trembling slightly. The reports outlined covert attempts to sabotage the Technomancer network, encrypted messages warning of the Garden's decay, and plans to expose the truth to the domes. Each effort, however, was stamped with a chilling finality, marked as "neutralized" or "terminated." The realization sank in like a stone, the weight of her father's involvement in these failed attempts pressing down on her.

"They were silenced," Milo continued, his jaw tightening. "The Technomancers didn't just stop them; they erased everything. Every trace of what they tried to do."

Ronan leaned forward, his golden-green eyes dark with understanding. "That's probably why they've always been so careful," he said. "Why they never spoke about their past."

Kaela placed a hand on Milo's shoulder, her heart aching for him. "I'm so sorry, Milo," she said softly.

Milo shook his head, his lips pressed into a thin line. "They've been living with this, hiding it from me, from everyone. And for what? So the domes could keep running while the Garden dies?" His voice broke, and he turned away, his shoulders trembling.

Melana approached from the shadows, her footsteps soft but deliberate. "Your parents were brave," she said, her voice low and steady. "They tried to fight a system designed to crush dissent. That's no small thing."

Milo looked up at her, his expression a mix of grief and gratitude. "It wasn't enough," he said bitterly.

"It never is," Melana replied, crouching beside him. "But they planted seeds. Seeds that we're carrying forward now. What we do next is what matters."

Kaela glanced at Ronan, who had gone silent once more, his expression a mask of unreadable emotion. She wondered if he saw himself in Milo's pain, if the burden of his own past choices felt heavier now. His golden-green eyes were distant, and for a brief moment, she saw a flicker of something, regret, perhaps, or a quiet understanding. The silence between them deepened, thick with the weight of unspoken thoughts.

As the night deepened, the group fell into a tense silence, each lost in their thoughts. Kaela's mind churned with everything they had uncovered: Kaelith, Milo's parents, and the growing threat of the Convergence Engine. She turned to Ronan, who had set his blade aside and was staring into the dim glow of the lantern. His face was shadowed, his jaw tight, and his eyes distant.

"Ronan," Kaela's voice was soft but urgent as she took a step closer, her eyes searching his face.

He didn't respond right away, his eyes fixed on something far off, as if the sight of her was too much to bear. When he finally met her gaze, his golden-green eyes were heavy with an emotion she couldn't quite place. The intensity of his stare struck her like a physical blow, a sharp pang lodging in her chest. It was as though he was carrying a burden too great to share, and she felt the weight of it, helplessly.

"I need to understand," Kaela said, her words steady despite the tremor in her voice. "I know what the bargain cost you, but I need to know. What does it mean for us? What happens now?"

Ronan's expression faltered, and he exhaled slowly, running a hand through his dark hair. "I never wanted this for you," he murmured, almost to himself. "I never wanted you to bear this burden, Kaela. I tried so hard to stop myself."

Her heart twisted in confusion. "What do you mean? I am bearing it, Ronan. I'm already tied to you. I'm already here."

He turned away slightly, his body tense, and Kaela's frustration bubbled up. "Why didn't you tell me sooner? Why didn't you warn me about this? About us?"

Ronan's shoulders stiffened. "Because I thought it would be easier for you to hate me. I thought it would be safer for you to believe that everything I've done was for the Garden, for the mission. I thought . . . I thought you'd be better off not knowing what I'd given up."

Kaela's chest tightened, and she stepped forward again, her voice raw. "You gave up your true love, Ronan. You gave me up for your own safety. And now you're telling me that I should hate you for it?" Her eyes were wide, searching his face for any sign that he understood the weight of what he was saying. "You didn't just give up anyone, you gave up me."

Ronan closed his eyes, as if the words physically hurt him. "I never thought I'd find love. I didn't believe I could. So when I made the bargain, I didn't know . . . How could I have known that it would be you. I didn't even know you then."

The silence between them was thick, filled with the unsaid. Kaela's mind reeled with the enormity of it all. "But you're still here. You're still with me. You still chose to stay even after you knew what it would cost."

Ronan turned to face her fully, his expression tortured. "I didn't want to stay. I didn't want to fall in love with you, Kaela. But I did. And now I don't know how to undo what's been done." His voice cracked, and for the first time, Kaela saw the raw, unguarded emotion that lay beneath his tough exterior. "Every moment I'm with you, I feel like I'm breaking some promise I made to myself. But I can't stop. I can't stay away."

Kaela's breath hitched as his words washed over her. She felt the weight of everything. The bargain, the love, the sacrifice, pressing down on her, suffocating her with its intensity. She wanted to scream at him, to tell him it was unfair, that she couldn't carry the burden of his past mistakes. But in that moment, all she could do was close the distance between them, her heart pounding as she whispered, "Ronan, I'll find a way. I'll find a way to fix this. I won't let it keep us apart. I just want to be with you."

His hand reached for hers, trembling, and for the first time, she felt the full weight of his love and the fear that came with it. "I love you, Kaela. I've loved you from the moment I met you, but I couldn't let myself admit it. Not when I knew what it meant. Not when I knew what it would cost us."

Kaela's chest ached with the force of his words, her heart breaking for him and for herself. "I don't care about the cost," she whispered, tears finally slipping down her cheeks. "I just care about us."

Ronan pulled her into his arms then, as if he couldn't bear to be apart any longer. Kaela buried her face in his chest, her body trembling as she held onto him tightly. "I don't want to lose you," she whispered.

As they accepted the truth of their love, Kaela felt a strange tingling sensation sweep through her, a jolt of energy that lasted only a split second. It was unlike anything she had ever experienced, as if something in the universe was shifting. Before she could process it, Ronan's hand cupped her cheek, pulling her closer. In that moment, the world around them seemed to fall away.

"You won't," he promised, his voice thick with emotion. "Not now. Not ever."

Before she could respond, Milo's voice broke the tension. "I found something else," he called, his tone urgent.

Kaela turned, the moment slipping away as reality crashed back in. The intensity of what they had shared still lingered, but it couldn't distract her from the mission. Whatever was between her and Ronan would have to wait; more pressing matters called. They had a world to save and the clock was ticking.

Chapter 32

Kaela stood at the edge of the rebel camp, the cool dawn light casting long shadows across the dense forest before her. The air smelled of pine and damp earth, but a weight pressed down on her chest, a heaviness she couldn't shake. The revelations of the past few days swirled in her mind, how the Garden's magic was being used as a weapon, the Technomancers' ruthless control, and the dark truth behind the Convergence Engine. But it was Milo's discovery that hit hardest: his parents had tried to stop the madness, only to be silenced, their efforts buried. The pieces of the puzzle were falling into place, and the picture they formed was nothing short of terrifying. For most of her life, Kaela had felt powerless, a pawn in a game she didn't understand. But now, the stakes were clear, and she had a choice.

Her powers, once a source of confusion and fear, could now be the key to fighting back. If the Garden's magic could be twisted into a weapon, then surely it could also be wielded as a shield. She had to find a way to use it before it was too late. Her thoughts were interrupted by the sound of footsteps, and she turned to see Melana approaching, her amber eyes sharp with intent.

"You've been quiet this morning," Melana said, stopping beside her. "Something on your mind?"

Kaela let out a long breath. "I've been trying to figure out how to use what I have. What the Garden gave me. I need to know if I can make it work for us, not against us."

Melana studied her for a moment before nodding. "You've already done more than most would in your position. But I can see it in you. You're ready for the next step."

Kaela's gaze hardened with determination. "I have to be. If we don't stop the Technomancers, the Garden will die. And everything connected to it will fall with it."

Melana's hand landed firmly on her shoulder, grounding her. "Then let's make sure you're ready. We'll figure this out together."

With a renewed sense of resolve, Kaela turned toward the camp. She could see Milo hunched over the schematics of the Convergence Engine, his brow furrowed in concentration. Ronan stood nearby, arms crossed, listening intently as Milo explained something in hushed tones. When Kaela approached, Ronan's gaze immediately found hers, a silent connection passing between them. Her heart fluttered, a reminder of everything they had shared, and everything still left unsaid.

But just as she was about to speak, the unmistakable sound of heavy boots crunching on the forest floor interrupted her thoughts. She looked up to see two men striding toward her. Theo and Callen, brothers who had joined their fight days earlier. Both were taller than her, with weathered faces marked by the harsh realities of surviving outside the domes. Theo's strong, quiet presence was matched only by Callen's sharp, calculating eyes. They had lost their parents to not just any Technomancer offensive, one led by Ronan. Their mistrust of Ronan still lingered, but Kaela could see how much they had come to respect him.

Theo gave her a small, nodding greeting, his usual silence filled with unspoken weight. Callen, on the other hand, gave her a tight smile, though it didn't quite reach his eyes. They were more than allies now; they were part of the growing resistance, their survival skills invaluable in the fight ahead.

"Milo," Kaela said, her voice steady despite the whirlwind inside her. "I need to understand how my powers work. If I can channel them, maybe I can disrupt the Convergence Engine, or at least weaken it."

Milo glanced up, concern flickering in his eyes. "It's risky, Kaela. We don't know the full extent of what you're capable of yet."

"That's why we need to find out," she replied, meeting his gaze with unwavering resolve. "If I'm going to fight back, I need to know what I can do."

Ronan stepped closer, his presence a comforting weight beside her. "If you're going to do this, you're not doing it alone."

Kaela looked at him, her gaze hardening with the same resolve she saw in his eyes. "I know. But this is something I have to figure out for myself."

Theo and Callen stood silently behind them, the weight of their presence grounding the conversation. Both brothers knew the stakes as well as anyone, maybe even better. They had seen the Technomancers' destruction firsthand and had lost everything to their regime. Their loyalty to the cause was unshakeable, and their silent support was a reminder that they, too, were fighting for something bigger than themselves.

The camp settled into an uneasy quiet as night fell, the crackling fire the only sound breaking the stillness. Kaela sat alone, her thoughts spinning with the magic of the Garden and the enormity of what was to come. She could feel its power pulsing within her, a constant hum that had grown louder since their infiltration of the Technomancer facility. It was as though the Garden itself was urging her to act, to fight, to protect everything it had given her.

Kaela was lost in her thoughts, unaware of Ronan's approach until he was standing beside her. His dark curls were tousled by the wind, and his golden-green eyes were shadowed with worry. The intensity of his gaze made her heart skip a beat. She met his eyes, feeling a quiet weight settle between them.

"You've been distant," he said, his voice soft as he sat down beside her.

Kaela offered a small, tired smile. "Just thinking."

"About what?" His tone was gentle, coaxing her to share.

"About everything," she admitted, her voice tinged with exhaustion. "The Garden. My powers. What's at stake. I'm scared, Ronan. What if I'm not enough?"

Ronan's gaze softened, and without a word, he reached for her hand. His fingers brushed hers, a quiet, tender contact that sent a surge of warmth through her. It was a comfort she hadn't realized she desperately needed. In that instant, the world seemed to still, as if the chaos around them paused, leaving only the weight of their shared silence. His touch anchored her, grounding her in a way nothing else could.

"You are enough," he said, his voice low but firm. "You're stronger than you realize, Kaela. I've seen it."

Kaela turned to face him, her chest tightening at the raw sincerity in his golden-green eyes. There was vulnerability in his voice, trembling in the air between them. His emotions hung heavily in that silence, palpable and undeniable. Each glance he gave her, each word he spoke, felt like a fragile thread binding them closer. It stirred something deep within her, something beautiful, yet terrifying. Her heart ached as she held his gaze, feeling the truth of his feelings reverberating through her very bones. It was almost too much to bear, but she couldn't look away.

"Ronan . . ." she began, her voice faltering, but the words died in her throat as he leaned in closer.

The firelight danced across his face, casting shadows that deepened the intensity in his eyes. She could feel the heat of his presence, the magnetic pull between them, growing stronger with every passing moment. He closed the space between them, his lips brushing hers with a tenderness that stole her breath away.

"I can't stay away from you anymore," Ronan murmured, his voice thick with emotion. "I've tried, but I can't."

Kaela's heart raced, every beat loud in her ears as she kissed him back. Her fingers tangled in his dark curls, drawing him closer as the world around them blurred into a haze. The sounds of the camp faded, the crackling of the fire turning into nothingness. The only thing that mattered was the desperate need to be near him, the way his lips tasted of fire and longing. Time stretched, an eternity contained in that single moment. When they finally pulled apart, Kaela's breath came in shallow, uneven gasps. Her forehead rested against his, grounding herself in the warmth of his presence, her heart still pounding, her body humming from the aftershock of their kiss.

"We'll figure this out," she whispered, her voice barely audible, trembling in the quiet night.

Ronan nodded, his hands cradling her face, his touch reassuring. "Together."

In that moment, Kaela understood. No matter what the future held, they could face it together. The uncertainty of what lay ahead weighed heavily on her shoulders, but with Ronan by her side, she felt something stir within her. A quiet determination. The bond between them gave her a renewed sense of purpose, and in that bond, she found strength. Whatever came next, she would fight with everything in her, knowing they were stronger together, facing the unknown as one.

Chapter 33

As the group made their way back to the rebel camp, the weight of their shared resolve settled over them. The air was thick with tension, as if the very ground beneath their feet hummed with anticipation. When they entered the camp, all eyes turned to them. The firelight flickered across their faces, but it was Kaelith who drew the most attention. His presence, imposing yet enigmatic, stirred whispers among the rebels. Some regarded him with caution, others with curiosity, but all sensed the gravity of his arrival. Despite the bond they had formed, Kaela could feel the wariness in the air, a reminder that not everyone shared her trust in Kaelith's intentions.

The rebel camp was alive with a tense, crackling energy as word spread of Kaela's decision to fight back. Fires blazed high against the night sky, casting flickering shadows over determined faces. Kaela stood near the largest of the campfires, her copper hair catching the light like a beacon. Around her, the core group had gathered. Ronan, Milo, Melana, and now Kealith, whose unexpected arrival had sent ripples through the camp.

Ronan leaned against a nearby post, arms crossed, his golden-green eyes locked on Kaela. Though he appeared relaxed, there was an intensity in his gaze that spoke volumes. Kaela felt it like a physical pull, her chest tightening with the weight of what they were about to do. The night before still lingered between them. A newfound intimacy that neither had spoken of aloud but that colored every glance, every touch. She stole a look at him now, her pulse quickening at the memory of his hands on her skin, his whispered promises in the dark.

Milo, oblivious to the tension between them, was hunched over a map spread across a wooden table, his brow furrowed. "If we hit them here," he said, pointing to a weak spot in the Technomancers' outer defenses, "we can cut off their supply lines before they even know what's happening."

Melana leaned over his shoulder, her amber eyes sharp. "It's a good plan, but we'll need more people. The Technomancers won't just roll over and let us take this without a fight."

Kaela nodded, her jaw set. "That's why we're not just relying on the rebels. We'll need to reach out to other groups. The outlanders, the smugglers, anyone who's suffered under the Technomancers' rule."

Kealith, who had been quietly observing, stepped forward. "There are people in the southern domes who would fight if they knew the truth. I can reach out to them, but it won't be easy. They're wary of outsiders."

Kaela studied him, her mind racing. There was something about Kealith. His calm, unyielding presence, the way he seemed to take everything in with quiet calculation, that inspired trust. "Do it," she said. "We'll need every ally we can get."

The group fell into a tense silence, each lost in their own thoughts. Kaela glanced at Melana, who was sharpening her blade with slow, deliberate movements. "Melana," Kaela said softly, "how did you get involved with the rebels?"

Melana paused, her gaze flickering to Kaela. For a moment, Kaela thought she wouldn't answer, but then Melana sighed and set the blade down. "I grew up outside the domes," she said, her voice low. "My family . . . we tried to make a life out there, but the Technomancers came for us anyway. My parents were killed, and I was taken to one of their facilities. I escaped, but not before I saw what they were doing to people. I swore I'd never let anyone else suffer like that if I could help it."

Kaela felt a surge of admiration for the other woman. "You've been through so much," she said, her voice soft. "And yet, here you are, fighting for others."

Melana shrugged, a faint smile tugging at her lips. "We all have our scars. The question is what we do with them."

As the night stretched on, the camp hummed with activity, a flurry of movement and low conversations. Groups of rebels gathered around the fire, discussing plans and sharpening weapons in preparation for the fight ahead. Milo sat off to the side, focused intently on refining his device, his fingers moving with practiced speed. The air was thick with tension, but there was also a sense of determination in every action, a quiet promise that they would stand together.

Kaela felt an unspoken pull toward Ronan, who had retreated to the edge of the camp. He stood there, staring into the darkness, his features shadowed and unreadable. She paused for a heartbeat, uncertainty flickering through her, but then took a step toward him. Without a word, she settled beside him, the space between them filled with an unspoken understanding.

"Do you think we can do this?" Kaela asked quietly.

Ronan turned to her, his gaze softening. "If anyone can, it's you," he said. "You've already brought people together in a way I didn't think was possible."

Kaela felt her cheeks flush under his praise. "I couldn't do it without you," she admitted.

Ronan stepped closer, his voice dropping to a low murmur. "You're stronger than you realize, Kaela. And whatever happens, I'll be right beside you."

Their eyes locked, and for a brief, suspended moment, everything else faded into the background. Kaela's heart raced in her chest, her breath catching as Ronan's gaze softened, a silent understanding passing between them. He reached out slowly, his fingers grazing her cheek as he tucked a stray lock of copper hair behind her ear. The touch was gentle but charged with an intensity that left her skin tingling, a warmth spreading through her that lingered long after his hand had retreated.

Before either of them could speak, Milo called out, breaking the spell. "Kaela! We need you over here!"

Kaela stepped back, her cheeks burning. "I'll be right there," she said, her voice steady despite the storm raging inside her.

As Kaela turned to walk back to the fire, she couldn't resist glancing over her shoulder. Ronan stood where she had left him, his gaze fixed on her with an intensity that made her pulse quicken. His expression remained unreadable, but the depth of his stare spoke volumes, filled with something raw and unspoken. A flicker of warmth spread through her chest as she turned away, knowing he was still watching.

The rebel camp was alive with a frenetic energy, the air thick with the sounds of strategy and preparation. Figures moved quickly between the campfires, voices rising and falling as plans were solidified and weapons were sharpened. The crackle of the flames and the hum of determination filled the night, a sense of unity binding everyone together. Yet beneath the surface, Kaela could feel the underlying tension, a weight pressing on her chest. This wasn't just another mission or skirmish, it was the moment that would shape the future of the Garden, the domes, and every life intertwined with them, and the stakes had never felt higher.

Kaela stood beside Milo as he explained the latest adjustments to the device, now encased in reinforced metal. His voice was quick, full of excitement, as his hands moved in fluid gestures, outlining the new functions. She watched intently, her focus on the intricate details he was pointing out. Despite the urgency of their mission, there was a spark in Milo's eyes that made the moment feel almost normal, as if they weren't on the brink of a war.

"This should scramble any nearby Technomancer signals," Milo said, his voice tight with excitement and exhaustion. "Their machines, their comms, everything should short out for at least a few minutes. It's not much time, but it might be all we need."

Melana crossed her arms, her piercing amber eyes locked on the device. "And what happens if it doesn't work?"

Milo hesitated, his fingers twitching against the edge of the table. "Then we improvise," he admitted.

Melana's lips pressed into a thin line, but she nodded. "I've seen worse odds," she said. "But we'll need a backup plan. The Technomancers won't go down easy, especially if they realize what you're carrying."

Kealith, who had been silent for most of the discussion, finally spoke up. "If this works, it'll change everything," he said, his deep voice steady. "But we can't rely on it alone. We need to hit them hard and fast, no hesitation."

Kaela studied Kealith, noting the quiet authority with which he carried himself. There was a magnetic presence about him, an unshakable resolve that seemed to pull people toward him. She understood why others followed him, drawn to his strength and certainty. Yet, beneath the surface, she could sense the weight of the burden he bore, a heaviness that made his calm demeanor all the more striking.

"Agreed," Kaela said. "We'll split into teams. Melana and Kealith can lead the frontal assault. Milo, you'll stay close to me with the device. Ronan . . ."

Her voice faltered as she turned to him. Ronan stood at the edge of the group, his golden-green eyes locked on hers, filled with an intensity that made her heart skip a beat. The way he watched her, unwavering and full of unspoken emotions, left her momentarily speechless. Kaela could feel the pull between them, a silent connection that was impossible to ignore.

"I'll watch your back," Ronan said simply, his voice low but firm.

Kaela nodded, her heart pounding. "Then it's settled," she said.

As the night deepened, Kaela sat by the fire, her mind swirling with thoughts of what lay ahead. She watched the flames flicker, their warm light casting dancing shadows across the camp. The rebels had grown quieter, many gathered in small groups, exchanging hushed words or sharpening their weapons in preparation. The weight of the upcoming battle hung heavily in the air, adding to the tension that had settled over them all.

Melana sat down beside her, breaking the silence. "You've got a lot on your shoulders," she said, her voice soft but steady.

Kaela glanced at her, surprised by the sudden openness. "We all do," she said.

Melana smirked faintly. "True. But you're the one they're looking to. It's not an easy position to be in."

Kaela sighed, the weight of Melana's words settling over her. "Sometimes I feel like I'm in over my head," she admitted. "But I can't turn back now."

Melana's expression softened. "No one expects you to have all the answers, Kaela. Just keep moving forward. That's all any of us can do."

Kaela nodded, feeling a quiet sense of gratitude for Melana's support. Despite her sharp edges, Melana had a unique ability to ground those around her. She cut through the chaos with calm practicality, offering a steady presence when it was most needed. In that moment, Kaela found comfort in the other woman's unwavering resolve.

As Melana rose and walked away, Kaela's gaze wandered across the camp, settling on Ronan. He stood near the treeline, his silhouette sharp against the dark woods. There was a tension in the way he carried himself, a restlessness that seemed to pull her in. Without a second thought, she stood and moved toward him.

"Couldn't sleep?" she asked as she approached.

Ronan turned to her, a faint smile tugging at his lips. "Too much on my mind," he admitted.

Kaela stopped a few steps away, her arms wrapped around herself against the chill. "You've been quiet tonight," she said. "More than usual."

Ronan hesitated, his gaze flickering to the ground before meeting hers. "Just thinking about what's ahead," he said. "And about you."

Her breath hitched at his words, her heart thudding in her chest. "Me?"

"You've changed," he said, his voice low. "When I first met you, I saw someone who didn't know her own strength. Now . . . you're leading an army, rallying people to fight for something bigger than themselves. It's incredible to watch."

Kaela's cheeks flushed, her heart swelling at his praise. "I couldn't have done it without you," she said.

Ronan stepped closer, his golden-green eyes locking onto hers. "You give me too much credit," he murmured. "But I'll take it if it means I get to stand by your side."

The air between them crackled with tension, everything else fading into the background. Kaela's heart raced as Ronan took a step closer, his presence overwhelming. His hand reached out, fingers brushing gently against her cheek, sending a shiver down her spine. The moment stretched between them, heavy with unspoken words.

"Ronan," she whispered, her voice trembling.

He leaned in, his lips hovering inches from hers. "Kaela," he said softly, his voice filled with longing.

For a moment, the rest of the world ceased to exist. Everything around them, the tension, the uncertainty, faded into nothingness as they drew closer. But just as their lips met, a sharp whistle rang out from the camp, shattering the fragile bubble they'd created. Kaela pulled back, her heart pounding in her chest as the sounds of activity reached them. Shouts, hurried footsteps, the unmistakable sense of urgency. Ronan's expression darkened, his hand falling to his side, and the connection between them seemed to break, replaced by the harsh reality of the situation.

"Looks like we're out of time," he said, his voice tight.

Kaela nodded, forcing herself to focus. "Let's go," she said.

As they hurried back to the camp, Kaela felt the lingering heat of his touch. His eyes held an unspoken promise. She couldn't shake the feeling of it. Whatever lay ahead, she knew they would face it together.

Chapter 34

The journey back to the Garden was fraught with a mix of anticipation and dread, every step weighed down by the enormity of what lay ahead. The once-unified group of rebels, allies, and friends who had rallied to their cause remained behind at the camp, their preparations for the next phase of the mission a constant reminder of the stakes. Kaela's heart was heavy as she led the smaller team, Ronan, Milo, Melana, and Kealith, through the desolate terrain, their shared silence filled with unspoken fears. Each of them carried their own burdens: Ronan's protective vigilance, Milo's simmering determination, Melana's sharp focus, and Kealith's quiet but commanding presence. The Garden, once a place of vibrant life and mystery, now loomed ahead as a battleground, its sickness a reflection of the war they had yet to fight.

The trek through the dense forests and jagged ravines carried an oppressive weight, the uneasy silence broken only by the rustle of leaves and the haunting cries of unseen creatures. Shadows stretched long beneath the canopy, and the air felt heavier with each step, thick with the scent of damp earth and decay. Kaela's mind churned with worry, every familiar twist in the terrain now tinged with a sense of foreboding. The Garden's magic pulsed faintly in her veins, like a distant heartbeat barely clinging to life. What had once been a vibrant, undeniable force now felt fractured, its energy flickering like a dying flame.

"Do you feel that?" she asked, her voice barely above a whisper as she glanced back at Ronan.

He met her gaze, his jaw clenched. "It's weaker," he murmured, his golden-green eyes shadowed with unease. "Like it's slipping away."

Milo, walking just behind them, frowned. "I thought the Garden was supposed to be this eternal source of power," he said. "How can it just . . . die?"

"It's not dying," Kaela said firmly, though her voice wavered. "It's being drained. The Technomancers are leeching its magic to fuel the domes, and if we don't stop them soon . . ." She didn't finish the thought, but the grim expressions on her companions' faces said enough.

Melana stepped closer, her amber eyes scanning the forest around them. "Then we can't afford to waste any time," she said.

"Whatever's waiting for us, we face it head-on."

Kealith, who had been walking at the rear of the group, spoke up. "The Garden's magic might be tied to you and Ronan," he said, his voice calm but laced with curiosity. "But if that's true, there might be something only the two of you can do to stabilize it."

Kaela met Ronan's gaze, and for a moment, the world seemed to narrow to just the two of them. Unease flickered between them, unspoken but palpable, a silent acknowledgment of the weight they both carried. Their connection to the Garden loomed like an uncharted storm on the horizon, vast, mysterious, and overwhelming in its implications. It tied them to something ancient and powerful, something neither fully understood but couldn't ignore. Yet, in the midst of the uncertainty, there was a steady, unshakable bond between them, a tether that neither time nor circumstance could sever.

"Then we'll figure it out," Ronan said, his voice steady. "Together."

When they reached the edge of the Garden, Kaela came to an abrupt halt, her breath catching in her throat. The scene before her was nothing short of devastation. The once-thriving expanse of verdant life was now a graveyard of decay. Trees that had once stretched toward the sky in proud defiance of the domes now sagged under the weight of withered branches, their leaves curling and blackened. The air, once alive with the hum of magic and the sweet scent of blossoms, hung heavy and stagnant, as if mourning the life it had lost. Kaela's chest tightened as she took it all in, her fingers curling into fists. The Garden, the heart of everything they had fought for, was dying, and with it, the faint hope that it could ever be restored.

The vast expanse of greenery and blossoms had withered into a shadow of its former self. Trees that had once stretched proudly toward the sky now stood gnarled and twisted, their trunks hollowed and branches bare, reaching out like skeletal fingers grasping for something lost. The air, once rich with the sweet scent of flowers and the gentle hum of life, now felt thick and oppressive, weighed down by the stench of decay. Pools of crystal-clear water, once shimmering with life, had turned stagnant and murky, their surfaces coated with an iridescent film that glistened unnaturally in the dim light.

"This can't be happening," Kaela murmured, her voice barely audible, tinged with disbelief and sorrow.

Ronan stepped forward, his gaze sweeping over the desolation with a grim intensity. "It's worse than I thought," he said, his tone low and unsteady. For a moment, the sharp edge of his usual confidence dulled, replaced by a rare flicker of vulnerability as his golden-green eyes lingered on the ruins of the Garden.

Kaela's fists tightened at her sides, her nails digging into her palms as she stared at the devastation before her. The Garden, once a haven of beauty and life, now stood as a hollow shell of its former self. Twisted trees reached toward the sky like skeletal hands, and the air hung heavy with the stench of decay. Her chest tightened with the weight of its ruin, a stark reminder of what they stood to lose. This place had always been more than a mystery. It was a lifeline, a promise of something greater, and now it was slipping through her fingers.

"It's not too late," she said, her voice barely steady, but laced with fierce determination. "We can still save it."

Melana crouched by one of the stagnant pools, her sharp eyes narrowing as she studied the iridescent film spreading across the water's surface. "This isn't just decay," she said, her voice cutting through the heavy silence. "It's deliberate. Corruption. Whatever the Technomancers have unleashed, it's poisoning the Garden at its core."

Kealith moved beside her, his expression grim as he ran a hand over the cracked soil. "She's right," he said quietly. "If we don't act soon, there won't be anything left to save."

Kaela felt the Garden's magic stir faintly within her, like the dying embers of a once-roaring fire. The sensation was weak, a fragile thread barely holding on, and it sent a pang of desperation through her. Her hand trembled as she pressed it against the gnarled trunk of a nearby tree, its bark rough and cold beneath her fingers. A faint pulse of energy flickered in response, but it was faint. So faint it felt as though the tree itself was struggling to stay alive. The magic, once a vibrant force that had surged through her veins, now felt distant, fractured, as though it was slipping beyond her reach.

"It's still alive," she said softly, her voice catching. Relief warred with despair in her chest. "But it's barely holding on."

Ronan stepped beside her, his presence grounding her as her emotions threatened to spiral. "We'll fix this," he said, his voice steady and low, carrying the weight of a promise.

Kaela turned to him, her gaze fierce despite the ache in her heart. "We have to," she said firmly. "The Garden isn't just magic. It's life itself. If it dies, everything we're fighting for dies with it."

Milo, who had been unusually quiet, suddenly straightened, a spark of determination lighting his eyes.

"Wait," he said, his voice cutting through the heavy silence. "What if the device could do more than disrupt Technomancer tech? What if it could reverse the damage they've done to the Garden?"

Melana turned to him sharply, her amber eyes narrowing. "You think that's possible?"

"It's a long shot," Milo admitted, his tone laced with urgency. "But if we can amplify the Garden's magic through the device and channel it back into itself, it might be enough to jumpstart the healing process."

Kaela's heart leapt at the possibility, hope flickering to life. But doubt crept in just as quickly. "And if it doesn't work?" she asked, her voice barely above a whisper.

Milo hesitated, his jaw tightening as the weight of the situation pressed down on him. "Then we'll have to come up with another plan," he said, his voice steady despite the uncertainty. "But it's worth trying."

Kaela took a deep breath, feeling the burden of the Garden's survival settle on her shoulders. "Then let's do it," she said firmly, her resolve hardening. "We've come too far to stop now."

The group immediately began to strategize, their hushed voices blending with the crackle of the fire. But as the plans formed, Kaela found her focus slipping, her thoughts fractured by an unsettling sensation. It began as a faint tickle at the back of her neck, subtle and easy to dismiss. Yet it grew steadily into something sharper, more persistent, a creeping awareness that set her on edge.

Her gaze darted around the camp, scanning the shifting shadows for signs of movement, but everything appeared as it should. Still, the feeling wouldn't relent. A gnawing presence that seemed to wrap itself around her, unseen yet undeniable. The hairs on the back of her neck stood on end, her pulse quickening as unease settled deep in her chest. Something was out there. And it was watching.

"Does anyone else feel that?" she asked, her voice low.

Ronan stiffened next to her, his hand moving instinctively toward the hilt of his blade. "Someone's here," he murmured, his voice low and filled with warning.

The group fell into an uneasy silence, their eyes scanning the barren expanse of the Garden. The usual sounds of rustling leaves, distant bird calls, and the soft hum of life had all vanished, replaced by a heavy, suffocating stillness that hung in the air. The once-vibrant landscape now felt alien, as if the very soul of the Garden had been drained. Kaela's heart pounded in her chest as she peered into the shadows, her senses heightened and on alert, an overwhelming sense of being watched crawling up her spine. Every crack of a twig, every whisper of the wind, made her muscles tense, her instincts screaming that something or someone, was waiting just beyond the edges of the darkness.

"Stay close," Ronan said, his voice steady despite the tension in his posture.

Kaela nodded, her fingers tightening around the hilt of her blade, the cold metal grounding her in the face of uncertainty. There was no room for hesitation, not with the Garden's survival hanging in the balance. Whatever lurked in the shadows, whether an enemy, a force of the Garden itself, or something else entirely, they had no choice but to confront it. The weight of responsibility pressed heavily on her, but she refused to falter. The fate of the Garden, and all it represented, depended on their ability to push forward.

The silence around them was almost oppressive, thick with an unease that coiled in the pit of her stomach. Kaela's senses sharpened as her gaze swept over the twisted remnants of the once-thriving landscape. The shadows seemed alive, shifting with an almost deliberate slowness, as if teasing her nerves. The presence she felt was unnervingly calm, its patience like a predator waiting for the perfect moment to strike. It wasn't just watching. It was calculating, and Kaela could feel its awareness pressing down on them, testing their resolve.

Ronan moved closer to her, his blade glinting faintly in the muted light. "Stay behind me," he murmured, his voice low but commanding.

"I'm not hiding," Kaela whispered back, her fingers brushing the hilt of her dagger.

Before Ronan could respond, the underbrush shifted, the rustling of leaves breaking the tense silence. Slowly, a figure stepped into view, moving with careful deliberation, as though every movement was measured. The man was tall, his sharp features etched with the lines of age and hardship, his dark hair streaked with silver at the temples, giving him an air of wisdom and experience. His clothes, tattered and faded, hung loosely on his frame, yet his posture was straight and unyielding, exuding a quiet authority that suggested he was a part of the Garden itself, rooted in its depths, a guardian in his own right.

"Who are you?" Ronan demanded, his blade steady in his hand.

The man's piercing gaze swept over the group, lingering on Kaela. "You've returned," he said, his voice rough but laced with familiarity.

Kaela frowned, stepping forward despite Ronan's protective stance. "Do I know you?" she asked, her tone wary.

The man tilted his head, his expression unreadable. "Not yet," he said cryptically. "But I know you, Kaela. You're the one the Garden has been waiting for."

The words sent a chill through her, but before she could respond, Kealith stepped forward, his hand raised in caution. "Who are you, and what do you want?" he asked.

The man's gaze shifted to Kealith, then to Ronan. "I am Varik," he said. "A guardian of what remains. And I've been watching you, waiting to see if you're worthy of saving this place."

"Watching us?" Milo echoed, his tone incredulous. "Why not help instead of lurking in the shadows?"

Varik's expression hardened. "Because trust is not given lightly. Not here," he said. "And certainly not to someone like him." His gaze landed on Ronan, the disdain in his tone unmistakable.

Kaela felt a surge of anger. "Ronan has risked his life to protect us," she said firmly. "If you have a problem with him, you'll have to deal with me."

Varik's lips twitched into something that might have been a smile. "Fiery," he said. "The Garden chose well."

Ronan stepped forward, his stance tense, but his voice calm. "If you have something to say, say it," he said.

Varik studied him for a long moment before speaking. "You were a Technomancer once. You're marked by their corruption," he said. "The Garden knows this. But perhaps . . . perhaps you've begun to redeem yourself."

Kaela bristled, her fists clenching. "He doesn't need your approval," she snapped.

Varik inclined his head, his gaze softening slightly. "Perhaps not," he said. "But he will need the Garden's."

Before Kaela could respond, Varik turned and began walking deeper into the Garden. "Follow me," he said. "If you truly wish to save this place, there's something you need to see."

The group exchanged uncertain glances, but Kaela's instincts told her to follow. She stepped forward, and one by one, the others fell in line behind her. The path Varik led them down wound through the heart of the Garden, where the decay was most pronounced. The ground beneath their feet was brittle, and the air was thick with the scent of rot. Kaela's chest tightened as she took it all in, the once-vibrant beauty reduced to a haunting shadow of itself.

They came to a clearing, and Varik stopped, gesturing to the ground. "This is what's left of the Garden's core," he said.

Kaela stepped closer, her breath catching in her throat. At the center of the clearing was a jagged fissure, faintly glowing with an otherworldly light. The light pulsed weakly, like a dying heartbeat. Its fragile glow filled the air with a quiet, haunting energy.

"The core is what keeps the Garden alive," Varik explained. "But the Technomancers have been draining its power, using it to fuel their machines and maintain the domes. Every time they draw from it, the Garden suffers."

Kaela dropped to her knees beside the fissure, her breath catching as she pressed her hand over the soft, glowing light. A faint warmth pulsed beneath her palm, fragile and fleeting, like the heartbeat of something barely holding on. The once-vibrant magic of the Garden was reduced to this, a flicker in the darkness, fighting against inevitable decay. Her fingers trembled as she traced the edges of the fissure, the weight of its fragility pressing into her chest. If the Garden's magic faded completely, it wouldn't just be the Garden that was lost. It would be hope itself. And in that moment, as the faint glow dimmed beneath her touch, Kaela vowed she wouldn't let that happen.

Chapter 35

The night air felt colder than usual, biting through the layers of clothing Kaela had wrapped around herself as she stood beside Ronan, her eyes tracing the broken landscape. The once-vibrant Garden, now dimmed and fading, was a cruel reminder of what they were up against. It was as if the very land reflected the weight of the battle they were fighting, but it wasn't just the Garden that seemed to be withering. It was Ronan too. She could feel the pull of his past, a heavy weight that settled around them, tugging at his every step. The silence between them stretched long, and Kaela could feel the distance between them, but it wasn't the same as before. There was no coldness, no walls between them. They had grown closer, had shared things neither of them expected to, but there were still moments like this, when the weight of the past crept in uninvited.

Ronan had been quiet for hours, lost in thought, his usually sharp eyes distant and clouded. Kaela knew better than to push him, but the silence was heavy with unsaid words. He looked every bit the man who had once been a Technomancer, a man who had carried out orders that haunted him. The guilt seemed to bleed into the very air around them, a weight that he couldn't escape. She watched him from the corner of her eye, his broad shoulders hunched, his face shadowed with regret. She had seen him fight, seen him stand strong in the face of danger, but now, there was a vulnerability in him she hadn't expected to see.

"Ronan," she said softly, breaking the silence.

He didn't respond immediately, but when he did, it was as if he were dragging the words from deep inside. "I can't keep running from this," he whispered, his voice low and strained. "What I did . . . what I helped them do . . . it's unforgivable."

Kaela's heart twisted at the rawness of his pain. She knew pieces of his past, knew the role he had played in the Technomancers' rise, but hearing him speak of it. Hearing the guilt in his voice, that was different. It was as though he had never truly confronted the weight of his actions. "I didn't just follow orders, Kaela," he continued, his gaze meeting hers, heavy with a burden that seemed to sink him lower. "I believed in their cause. I thought we were saving the world. But all we did was destroy something beautiful. I helped them drain the Garden. I watched it die. And now . . ." His words faltered, and Kaela saw the self-loathing in his eyes, as if he wished he could disappear into the ground beneath him.

Kaela's chest tightened at the sight of him, so broken and vulnerable. She reached out, her hand brushing his arm, a gentle but firm gesture. "You can't change what happened," she said softly, her voice steady but full of understanding. "But you can change what happens now. You're fighting for the right reasons, Ronan. You're not that man anymore."

For a long moment, Ronan was silent, his eyes closed as he took a deep breath, as though trying to center himself. When he opened them again, there was something in his gaze. A flicker of the man she had come to know, the man who had risked everything for those he cared about. "I don't know if I can ever make up for what I've done," he whispered, his voice thick with emotion. "But I'll spend the rest of my life trying."

Kaela's heart softened at his words, a warmth spreading through her chest. She didn't know if anyone could truly undo the past, but she knew that Ronan was no longer the man who had made those choices. He was someone else now, someone who had found the strength to fight for something better. "You don't have to do it alone," she said quietly, stepping closer, her voice full of quiet conviction. "I'm here. We're all here. And we'll fix this together."

Ronan's eyes softened as he looked at her, and for the first time in a long while, he seemed to exhale a breath he hadn't realized he'd been holding. Without another word, he pulled her into his arms, the embrace tight and warm. There was no hesitation, no fear of what might come next. They had crossed that line already, had fought through too much to let anything stand in their way now. Kaela melted to his touch, her body pressing against his, feeling the heat of him against her.

Then, without warning, his lips were on hers, urgent and desperate. It wasn't the first kiss they had shared, but this one was different. The kiss wasn't about hesitation or doubt. It was a release, a surrender to everything they had been holding back. Kaela's breath caught in her throat as Ronan's hands slid to her waist, pulling her closer. The kiss deepened, both of them giving in to the need, the desire that had been building between them for so long.

Kaela's fingers tangled in his hair, tugging him closer as her body responded instinctively, her heart pounding in her chest, everything else. The mission, the stakes, the weight of the world they carried, had faded away, leaving only the intensity of the moment, the urgency of their connection. Ronan's lips moved to her neck, his breath hot against her skin, sending a shiver down her spine. She felt him, every inch of him, as if they were no longer two separate people, but one. She knew, in that moment, that she couldn't stop now.

Her hands slid down his chest, feeling the taut muscles beneath his shirt, the heat of his skin. He groaned low in his throat, pulling her even tighter against him. Kaela's heart raced, her body alive with the intensity of their kiss. She had been afraid of this. Afraid of the undeniable feelings she had for him, afraid of the connection that had grown between them. But in this moment, all of that fear melted away. There was only him, only the burning desire that pulsed between them.

When they finally pulled apart, both breathless and flushed, Kaela's mind spun with everything they had just shared. Her heart pounded, the weight of unspoken emotions settling between them. But beneath the whirlwind of sensations, there was a quiet certainty. Something had shifted, an undeniable change in the air between them.

"I'm not going to leave you, Ronan," Kaela whispered, her voice full of quiet conviction. "We'll fix this together. Whatever it takes, we'll do it."

Ronan cupped her cheek, his thumb brushing across her skin in a tender gesture, his voice thick with emotion. "I don't deserve you."

Kaela smiled softly, her fingers tracing the line of his sharp jaw. "Maybe I don't deserve you either," she teased, though her voice held the truth behind her words. "But I'm not going anywhere."

Ronan chuckled, the sound warm and affectionate. "Good," he said, his eyes softening. "Because I'm not letting you go."

Chapter 36

The dawn was muted, shrouded by thick, low-hanging clouds that stretched across the horizon, casting a dim gray light over the Garden. Kaela stood at the edge of their camp, her arms crossed against the chill as she watched the fractured land before her. The air felt heavy with unspoken tension, the kind that had been growing steadily over the past few days. But beneath that tension, Kaela sensed something else. A quiet hum that thrummed in her veins, faint but undeniable. It was the Garden, reaching out to her, its presence like a whisper at the back of her mind.

She drew in a deep breath, the scent of damp earth mingling with a faint, bittersweet trace of fading magic. It filled her lungs like a memory, haunting, raw, and alive. The connection she felt to the Garden was no longer a quiet hum in the back of her mind; it had grown louder, more insistent, with each passing day. It thrummed beneath her skin, a heartbeat that wasn't her own, tethering her to something vast and ancient. But with that bond came an ache she couldn't ignore. The Garden was in agony, its magic flickering like a dying flame. Its pain surged through her, sharp and desperate, and she knew with bone-deep certainty: if they didn't act soon, the Garden's magic and everything it touched would vanish, lost to the void forever.

Milo was a flurry of focused motion, his fingers working with an almost frantic precision as he pieced together his latest invention. Small gears clicked into place, wires sparked faintly, and the device in his hands began to take form. It was a blend of brilliance and risk, something only Milo could create under such pressure. His jaw was tight, his brow furrowed in concentration, but there was a flicker of uncertainty in his eyes. He didn't speak, didn't look up, as if pouring all his energy into his work was the only way to stave off the doubt creeping into his thoughts. This was how he fought, crafting something that could give them an edge, no matter how impossible the odds seemed.

Melana sat a few feet away, her blade in hand, moving a whetstone along its edge in steady, deliberate strokes. The rhythmic sound of metal scraping against stone filled the quiet, an almost soothing contrast to the tension that hung in the air. Her posture was rigid, her movements precise, but there was a subtle tightness in her shoulders that betrayed her unease. She rarely let emotion show, yet the sharpness of her gaze as she focused on the blade spoke volumes. For Melana, preparation was more than a ritual; it was her armor against the fear that lingered at the edges of her thoughts. She wouldn't allow herself to falter, not when so much was at stake.

Ronan stood apart from the others, his figure outlined against the distant horizon. His gaze was fixed on something beyond their immediate surroundings, his expression unreadable and distant. He hadn't spoken much since the night before, and the silence around him felt heavier than usual. Kaela could sense the weight he carried, a burden that seemed to press on him more with every passing moment. Yet, even with the distance he kept, she felt his presence keenly. The memory of his kiss lingered, a spark that refused to fade, leaving her with a mix of emotions she couldn't quite untangle. Whatever thoughts held him in their grip, Kaela knew they ran deeper than he was willing to admit.

Kaela stood in the center of it all, her gaze shifting between her companions. Each of them carried their own weight, their own way of coping with the uncertainty that lay ahead. Milo channeled his energy into creation, Melana into preparation, and Ronan into the silent battle within himself. Kaela felt the pressure of their unspoken expectations, the knowledge that they looked to her to guide them forward. Her connection to the Garden thrummed faintly, a reminder of the purpose that united them. Together, they were an unlikely but determined group, bound by a shared mission and the quiet understanding that whatever challenges lay ahead, they would face them as one.

"We can't wait any longer," she said, her words cutting through the quiet. "The Garden is dying, and if we don't act now, it'll be too late. We have to figure out how to stabilize its magic. And we have to do it together."

Milo looked up from his work, his brow furrowed. "I've been thinking about that," he said, his voice thoughtful. "The Garden's magic is . . . complicated. It's not just energy; it's alive, interconnected. If we're going to stabilize it, we need to understand how it works, and that means tapping into its core."

"The core?" Melana asked, her amber eyes narrowing. "You mean the Heart of the Garden?"

Kaela blinked, her gaze shifting to Melana. "The Heart of the Garden? What is that?"

Melana paused, her sharpening stone stilling against her blade. "It's a legend," she said slowly. "The Heart is said to be the source of the Garden's magic. The place where its power is strongest. Some say it's hidden deep within the Garden, protected by layers of enchantments and guardians. Others say it's just a myth."

"It's not a myth," Ronan said quietly, his voice carrying a weight that drew everyone's attention. He turned to face them, his golden-green eyes steady. "I've seen it. Or at least, I've seen what's left of it."

Kaela's breath caught. "You've been to the Heart?"

Ronan nodded, his jaw tightening. "Years ago, when I was still with the Technomancers. They sent me to locate the Heart and find a way to harness its power. But the closer we got, the more . . . unstable things became. The magic there is unlike anything I've ever felt. It's raw, overwhelming. We barely made it out alive."

A heavy silence settled over the group, each of them grappling with the gravity of Ronan's revelation. Kaela's mind raced, fragments of everything she had learned about the Garden and its ancient magic snapping into place like shards of glass forming a picture. The Heart wasn't just the source of the Garden's power; it was the keystone holding its fragile existence together. To reach it meant more than saving the Garden. It meant unlocking a force that could reshape their world. But Ronan's warning hung in the air, sharp and unyielding, and Kaela knew that whatever guarded the Heart would test them in ways they weren't prepared for.

"We have to go there," Kaela said firmly, her voice cutting through the silence. "If the Heart is the source of the Garden's magic, then it's the only place we can stabilize it. We don't have a choice."

Milo frowned, his hands tightening around the device he had been working on. "Kaela, if the Heart is as unstable as Ronan says, it could be dangerous. We don't even know what we're dealing with."

"That's why we need to go together," Kaela replied, her gaze sweeping over the group. "We've made it this far because we've worked as a team. And if we're going to save the Garden, we need to keep trusting each other. We can do this, but only if we do it together."

Melana's expression softened, a flicker of respect crossing her face as she studied Kaela. "You're right," she said, sliding her blade into its sheath. "If the Heart is our best chance, then we need to take it. But we'll need a plan."

Kaela nodded, a spark of determination igniting in her chest. "Then let's make one."

The group spent the next few hours strategizing, each person focused on their task with a determination that matched the gravity of what lay ahead. Ronan crouched near the fire, sketching a rough map of the Garden from memory. His fingers moved steadily across the parchment as he marked the path to the Heart, pausing now and then to clarify a detail or adjust his recollection. Though his expression remained calm, there was an edge to his movements, as if the weight of what they were attempting bore down on him more than he let on.

Milo, seated a few feet away, was engrossed in his work. The faint hum of his device punctuated the quiet, and he explained its mechanics in clipped sentences without looking up. "If we can get close enough to the Heart," he said, adjusting a delicate wire, "this should stabilize the magic and give us a chance to reverse the damage." His words were confident, but the tension in his voice betrayed his worry. Every piece he adjusted felt like a gamble, one that could either save the Garden or leave them empty-handed.

Melana, meanwhile, moved with quiet efficiency, organizing their supplies and double-checking their provisions. Her blade caught the light as she inspected its edge, her focus unwavering. She worked in silence, her intensity radiating an unspoken resolve. Kaela caught the occasional glance from Melana, as if she were assessing her, silently offering reassurance without the need for words. Despite her stoic exterior, Kaela could sense the tension humming beneath her calm, like a string pulled too tight.

Kaela herself moved among them, her steps deliberate as she took stock of their weapons and rations. As she worked, she felt a shift within her, a growing sense of purpose that she hadn't fully embraced until now. She wasn't merely part of the group, she was leading them, guiding their efforts toward the impossible. It was a role she hadn't anticipated but one that felt natural, as if she had been preparing for this moment her entire life without realizing it. With every decision she made, a piece of herself clicked into place, the weight of responsibility transforming into a steady, unyielding resolve.

By the time they were ready to set out, the sun hung high in the sky, its pale light breaking through a shroud of gray clouds. The beams cast a muted glow over the Garden, highlighting its fractured beauty. Once, this place had been a haven of vibrant life, its trees humming with energy, its streams sparkling like liquid crystal. Now, the landscape was marred by deep cracks spidering through the earth, as if the Garden itself were splintering apart. Shadows pooled in the hollows of the ground, giving the impression that the land was holding its breath, waiting for either salvation or collapse.

Kaela's gaze swept across the terrain, her chest tightening as she took it all in. Even in its weakened state, the Garden still held an undeniable beauty, a fragile, aching kind of loveliness. Flowers that had once stood tall now wilted, their colors fading but not yet gone. Trees that had once stretched toward the sky with unyielding strength now sagged, their branches heavy with decay. And yet, here and there, tiny signs of life persisted. A patch of moss clung stubbornly to a rock, a single bloom unfurled amidst the ruins, as if refusing to give in to the inevitable.

It was a painful reminder of what they were fighting to protect. This wasn't just about saving a magical place; it was about preserving the heart of something far greater. The Garden wasn't merely a piece of land, it was a symbol of hope, a source of life that pulsed through everything connected to it. To lose it would be to lose a part of the world itself, a loss so profound that Kaela could hardly bring herself to imagine it.

Her fingers tightened around the hilt of her blade as she steeled herself for what lay ahead. They weren't just walking into danger;

they were walking into the unknown, into a battle that might demand more from them than any of them were prepared to give. But as Kaela looked at the Garden, at its fading beauty and the life that still clung to its edges, she knew they couldn't turn back. They had to fight, not just for the Garden, but for everything it represented.

Kaela led the way, her blade at her side and her senses on high alert. The others followed close behind, their footsteps careful and deliberate as they navigated the treacherous terrain. The path to the Heart was long and winding, taking them through parts of the Garden that none of them had ever seen before. The air grew thicker the deeper they went, heavy with magic that buzzed against Kaela's skin.

As they walked, Kaela found herself drawn to the subtle shifts in the Garden's energy. She could feel it pulsing beneath her feet, a rhythm that matched the beat of her heart. It was as if the Garden was alive, its magic flowing through her veins and guiding her steps. She didn't fully understand it, but she trusted it, letting it lead her toward their destination.

"Kaela," Ronan said quietly, his voice breaking the silence. "You feel it, don't you? The Garden's magic."

Kaela glanced at him, her eyes meeting his. "I do," she admitted. "It's like . . . it's calling to me."

Ronan nodded, his expression thoughtful. "The Garden chose

you," he said. "You're connected to it in a way that none of us are. That's why you can feel its magic. That's why you can lead us."

Kaela's heart swelled at Ronan's words, a mix of pride and responsibility settling over her. She had always felt deeply connected to the Garden, but hearing him acknowledge it gave her a sense of validation she hadn't realized she craved. That trust, that belief in her, steadied her as they prepared to press on. She glanced at her companions. Milo tinkering with his inventions, Melana checking their supplies, and Ronan standing with that unreadable expression he often wore. Together, they were stepping into the unknown, and Kaela could feel the weight of every decision resting squarely on her shoulders.

The journey to the Heart began as a cautious trek but quickly turned perilous. The once-vibrant paths were unrecognizable. Twisted roots sprawled like traps across the ground, and deep fissures marred the terrain. The air grew heavier the deeper they ventured, humming with magic that pressed against their skin. Shadows danced in the corners of their vision, moving unnaturally, as though alive.

"The Garden is watching us," Ronan said, his voice low. "It remembers what happened the last time I was here . . . and it's not happy."

"Great," Milo muttered, gripping his pack tighter. "Because we didn't have enough to worry about already."

Kaela slowed her pace, her grip tightening on her blade. "If it thinks we're a threat, we need to prove we're not," she said firmly. "We're here to save it, not destroy it."

Before anyone could respond, the ground rumbled violently beneath them. A deafening crack split the air as a jagged chasm tore through their path. Kaela's breath caught as she stumbled back, her heart pounding. Dust and debris swirled around them, the earth trembling with a raw, untamed force.

"Move!" Ronan shouted, grabbing her arm and pulling her to safety as the edge crumbled beneath their feet.

Melana darted forward, her movements swift and precise, hauling Milo out of the way just as another section gave way. "This place is falling apart," Milo gasped, his face pale.

"No," Ronan said, scanning the shifting landscape with a grim expression. "It's defending itself."

Kaela straightened, determination flaring in her chest. "Then we show it we're not the enemy," she said, her voice steady despite the chaos around them.

They pressed on, but the challenges only grew. A dense, unnatural mist rolled in, wrapping around them like a living thing. It muffled their voices and obscured their vision, and with it came the whispers, faint, insistent voices that tugged at Kaela's thoughts.

"Do you hear that?" Milo asked, his voice barely above a whisper.

"Ignore it," Melana said sharply, her blade at the ready. "It's trying to get into your head."

"It's more than that," Ronan murmured, his golden-green eyes narrowing as he glanced around. "It's testing us."

As if in response, the mist slowly parted, unveiling a massive, gnarled tree in their path. Its twisted branches reached outward like skeletal arms, casting eerie shadows in the dim light. The roots shifted and writhed, pulsing with an unnatural energy. The air around it felt heavy, thick with an ancient presence.

"What now?" Milo asked, his voice edged with unease.

"It's a Sentinel," Ronan said, his tone heavy. "A guardian of the Garden. It won't let us pass unless we prove ourselves."

Kaela stepped forward, her pulse quickening. "Then we prove it," she said, her voice steady.

The Sentinel reacted instantly, its roots lashing out like whips. Kaela ducked, narrowly avoiding one as it snapped past her head. "Stay together!" she shouted, raising her blade.

The group moved as one, each playing their part in the battle. Milo used one of his devices to emit bursts of energy that temporarily immobilized the roots, giving Kaela and Melana the opening they needed to strike. Ronan stood back, his hands glowing faintly as he sent waves of energy rippling through the Sentinel, weakening it.

The fight was fierce, and the Sentinel's strength was formidable.

But the group's unity carried them through. When the massive tree finally collapsed, its form dissolving into glowing embers, the air around them shifted. The oppressive energy that had weighed them down lightened, and the whispers fell silent.

Kaela glanced at Ronan, who was staring at the remnants of the Sentinel with a look of quiet understanding. "It's recognizing us," he said softly. "The Garden knows we're not here to destroy it."

The change was almost immediate. The shadows stopped shifting menacingly, and the air, though still charged with magic, felt less oppressive. Even the ground beneath their feet seemed steadier, as though the Garden itself had begun to trust them.

Finally, they reached the chamber that held the Heart. Kaela's breath caught as she stepped inside, her eyes widening at the sight before her. The chamber was vast, its walls pulsing with a soft, golden light that seemed to emanate from the center. The air was thick with magic, humming with a resonance that made her chest ache and her pulse quicken.

At the center of the chamber stood the Heart of the Garden. A massive, glowing tree with roots that twisted and curled like veins of pure magic, spreading out across the chamber floor and disappearing into the walls. The light it emitted was warm and golden, but it flickered weakly, a sign of its fragility.

"This is it," Ronan said quietly, his voice reverent. "The Heart of the Garden."

Kaela stepped forward, her gaze fixed on the Heart of the Garden. The tree pulsed with an energy so ancient, so pure, that it almost seemed to hum in the air around them. She could feel its power, its raw, unbridled energy, reaching out to her like a long-lost part of herself calling to be reunited. This was it, the source of the Garden's magic, the key to everything they had fought for. And now, standing before it, she realized just how much was at stake.

The Heart was not just the life force of the Garden; it was also the heartbeat of the world they knew. Without it, the Garden, and everything connected to it, would wither and die, its magic slipping away like sand through an open hand. She felt its desperate pull, the weight of its agony as it teetered on the edge of destruction. Kaela could sense the deep well of magic it contained, but also its fragility. It was bleeding, slowly and painfully, and if they didn't act soon, it would be lost forever.

As the group gathered around her, the air seemed to grow heavier, charged with the weight of their task. She could see the tension in their eyes. Milo, usually so calm and composed, now seemed on edge, his brow furrowed as he scanned the area around them. Melana's jaw was set, her hand never straying far from the hilt of her blade. Ronan stood closest to her, his gaze fixed on the Heart with an unreadable expression, though she could feel the turbulence inside him. This was personal for him.

Kaela took a deep breath, grounding herself in the moment. Her hands were trembling, but she clenched them into fists, pushing away the doubt and fear that tried to creep in. She had to do this. She was the one the Garden had chosen. The magic in her blood was linked to it, and she could feel the connection growing stronger by the second. She wasn't just standing here as a leader. She was standing here as the key to saving everything.

"Milo," she said, her voice steady despite the chaos swirling inside her. "Can you figure out how to harness the Garden's energy? We need to save it before the Technomancers find us."

Milo didn't answer right away. He was already working, his mind sharp as ever. He approached the glowing tree cautiously, running his fingers along the glowing veins that spread out like roots beneath the floor. The magic thrummed beneath his touch, and Kaela saw a spark of understanding light up in his eyes.

"I think I can," Milo muttered, more to himself than anyone else. "If I can tap into the energy from the Heart and stabilize it, I might be able to amplify its magic long enough to restore it. But we'll need to adjust the resonance, otherwise, the magic will just collapse in on itself."

Kaela's heart pounded in her chest. "How do we do that?"

Milo turned to her, his face a mixture of concentration and excitement. "It's like tuning an instrument. The Heart's energy has a frequency, but it's unstable right now. If we can match the frequency with the right device, I can amplify it. It won't fix everything, but it'll buy us time. Long enough to push the Technomancers back and hopefully, restore the Garden."

Kaela's mind raced as she processed what he was saying. This was their chance. She could feel the magic swirling around her, wrapping her in a protective embrace, but it was clear they didn't have much time. The longer they waited, the more fragile the Heart became.

She turned to Ronan, who was watching her with a strange intensity. "What do you think?" she asked, her voice low.

Ronan's gaze never left the Heart. His jaw tightened as he looked at the tree's fading light, his expression darkening. "We don't have much time. The Garden is dying, and the Technomancers are coming for it. We can't afford to fail."

Kaela nodded, his words sinking deep into her chest like a solemn vow. There was no need to ask if he would fight for the Garden. The answer was already written in his eyes, unwavering and sure. She simply took a breath, accepting what they both knew to be true.

As Milo began to work, his hands flying over his device, Kaela's mind wandered. She watched the glowing roots pulse in time with her own heartbeat, the magic humming beneath her skin. There was a bond here. A connection that went beyond just the Garden. This was part of her, and she was part of it. The magic, the energy, it wasn't something she could control, but something she could guide.

She could feel it now, rising within her, filling the space around her like an unseen force.

"Milo," she said again, her voice firmer now. "How long?"

He didn't look up from his work, but his voice was steady. "Not long. I just need a few more minutes."

Minutes. That was all they had. Kaela turned to face the others. Melana was keeping watch, her sharp eyes scanning the shadows, ever-vigilant. Ronan stood at her side, his arms crossed, the weight of his own connection to the Garden heavy on him.

"We'll be ready," Melana said, her voice low but resolute.

Kaela nodded. She could feel the storm brewing inside her. This wasn't just about saving the Garden anymore. It was about something much larger. The Garden was the source of all magic in the world, and if the Technomancers destroyed it, they would undo everything. Every ounce of progress, every hope they had.

Ronan stepped closer to Kaela, his hand brushing hers. "Whatever happens," he said, his voice rough with emotion, "we fight for this."

She met his gaze, her heart swelling with something she couldn't quite name. There was no room for doubt, no room for fear. They had a chance to make this right, to restore balance, to protect everything they loved. And they would do it together.

Milo's device beeped, drawing Kaela's attention back to him. He looked up from his work, his eyes wide with excitement. "It's working. The energy's stabilizing. But we need to get it to the core of the Garden. I'll need to set up a conduit."

Kaela nodded, taking a deep breath. This was it. This was their moment. They couldn't afford to waste it.

"We move fast," she said, her voice commanding. "We get to the heart of the Garden, we channel the energy, and we make sure the Technomancers don't stand a chance." The others nodded in agreement, their resolve matching hers.

As they moved into position, the magic around them swelled, the energy of the Garden pulsing in time with their hearts. Kaela felt the weight of the moment, but also the incredible sense of purpose that had settled within her. This was the path they had chosen. And with Milo's ingenuity, Melana's strength, Ronan's power, and her own connection to the Garden, they would restore the balance before the Technomancers could destroy it all. With the Heart before them, and the fate of the world in their hands, they were ready to face whatever came next.

Chapter 37

The forest surrounding the Heart of the Garden was unnervingly silent, as though the very air held its breath. The once-vibrant foliage had withered, and the trees loomed like twisted sentinels, their skeletal branches clawing at the sky. Every step the group took seemed to reverberate in the stillness, the faint crack of brittle leaves underfoot cutting through the unnatural quiet. The weight of the silence pressed in on Kaela, the air thick with a tension that made her skin prickle, as if something unseen was watching them.

Her senses were on high alert, every rustle of wind sending a shiver down her spine. Shadows flickered at the edge of her vision, making her heart pound. It felt as if the Garden itself was holding its breath, tense and expectant. Whether it waited for their mistake or something far worse, she couldn't be sure.

Kaela stole a glance over her shoulder, her gaze meeting Milo's.

He was adjusting the straps of his pack, his brow furrowed in concentration, but there was a weight in his eyes that she hadn't seen before. The usual banter that flowed so easily from him was gone, replaced by a quiet, steely determination. He wasn't the boy she'd grown up with anymore, he was someone who had seen the stakes of their journey and understood the cost.

The solemnity in his expression mirrored her own. They had crossed the point of no return, and there was no turning back. The pressure of what they were about to face, the danger, the uncertainty. It all seemed to hang in the air like a storm, waiting to break. And yet, despite the dread that clawed at her insides, Kaela couldn't ignore the pulse of magic that thrummed in the depths of the forest. It was alive, dying, and desperate to be saved.

Without a word, Milo met her gaze again, his eyes telling her everything she needed to know. There was no more time for fear. There was only the mission. They had to succeed. The weight of it all settled over her once more, but Kaela stood taller, feeling the pull of the Garden's magic, and the growing fire in her chest. The Heart was close. And no matter the cost, they would reach it.

The plan was simple in theory, but in reality, it was anything but. Their first priority was to reach the Technomancer headquarters, an imposing fortress built on the outskirts of the Garden, surrounded by miles of desolate wasteland that had once been teeming with life. The headquarters itself was a labyrinth of metal and stone, a place where the heart of the Technomancers' power beat strongest. It was there that they held control over the stolen magic of the Garden, a force they had twisted and weaponized for their own gain.

Milo's device was their only hope. Designed to amplify and stabilize the Garden's energy, it was the key to breaking the Technomancers' stranglehold on the Garden's magic. The device, a mix of intricate gears, glowing crystals, and delicate wires, had been fine-tuned over days of sleepless nights. It wasn't just a tool, it was their lifeline. If they could get close enough to the Heart, close enough to the Garden's true magic, Milo's invention would disrupt the Technomancers' control, severing the connection between the Garden and the machines they had enslaved it with. The hope was that once the device activated, the magic would flow freely again, restoring balance to the Garden and weakening the Technomancers' grip on the land.

But nothing about the journey ahead was certain. Kaela knew this all too well. The Technomancers had eyes everywhere, and their forces were ruthless. There was no question that they would try to stop them at any cost. The further they got from the safety of the hidden paths, the more dangerous it would become. Every mile they traveled would bring them closer to the Technomancer's reach. They had no illusions about what they were walking into. They would be outnumbered, outgunned, and facing an enemy who had mastered the art of control.

The plan was to move swiftly and carefully, avoiding detection whenever possible. They couldn't afford to draw attention before they reached their destination. The closer they got to the Technomancer headquarters, the more the landscape itself would be twisted by their influence. The once lush surroundings would give way to barren, lifeless stretches of land, the air thick with the remnants of magic twisted and poisoned by the Technomancers.

To get there, they would have to cross the Outer Reaches, a stretch of land where the Garden's magic was weakest and the Technomancers' surveillance was strongest. The Outer Reaches were a desolate wasteland, a place where even the bravest had perished. It was littered with remnants of past skirmishes, ruined villages, crumbled walls, and abandoned tech towers, silent witnesses to the Technomancers' reign of terror.

Milo had devised a way to temporarily mask their presence, using the device's subtle energy fluctuations as a cloak. It wasn't foolproof, but it was their best chance. They would travel under the cover of night, avoiding major Technomancer patrols. Sticking to the shadows was their only option.

Once they reached the Technomancer headquarters, things would get more complicated. They had no idea how the building was laid out, but they knew the heart of their operation would be deep within. Kaela, Milo, and Ronan would have to fight their way through the compound, using their skills, their magic, and their wits to survive. The device would need to be deployed in the central chamber, a place where the Technomancers kept the most critical elements of their control over the Garden's magic.

The plan wasn't perfect. In fact, it was far from it. They didn't have the numbers, the weapons, or the resources to take on the Technomancers head-on. But what they had was the knowledge of the Garden's power and a resolve that burned brighter than anything the Technomancers could throw at them. They had each other, and they had the knowledge that the fate of the Garden, and perhaps the world itself, rested in their hands.

Kaela felt the weight of that responsibility settling over her like a mantle. She wasn't just leading them to a battle; she was leading them to the edge of a war. This wasn't about winning or losing. It was about survival, about reclaiming the Garden's magic and setting things right. The stakes had never been higher. But there was no turning back. Not now.

She looked around at her team. Milo, whose hands shook slightly as he adjusted the straps of his pack, his eyes narrowed in determination; Ronan, whose gaze was distant, his expression unreadable, but Kaela knew him well enough to see the fierce resolve in his posture; and Melana, who was silently preparing her weapons, her focus unwavering. They were all in this together.

"We move at first light," Kaela said, her voice steady despite the uncertainty gnawing at her. "Stay sharp. And remember. This is about more than just us. We're fighting for the Garden. For everything it represents." There was no hesitation in her voice, no doubt in her words. They had a mission, and they would see it through. Together.

Ahead of her, Ronan moved with a quiet grace, each step calculated and nearly silent. He was the first to scout the path, his dark figure blending seamlessly into the shadows. Kaela watched him closely, noticing how his every movement was precise, almost instinctive. His senses seemed sharpened, as if he could feel the weight of their mission pressing against the air itself. There was something almost otherworldly about the way he moved, a man both haunted and driven.

Melana followed closely behind, her grip firm on the hilt of her blade, her amber eyes sharp and constantly scanning the treeline. Her posture was rigid, every muscle coiled in readiness, a quiet reflection of the unease that seemed to cling to them all. The tension was palpable, a silent understanding between them that danger was never far, but the path ahead was one they had to take together.

The group had been walking for hours, the dense forest around them slowly shifting into something far more ominous. The canopy above thickened, casting deep shadows that seemed to swallow the fading light, and the air grew heavy, thick with an unnatural stillness. The deeper they went, the more the forest seemed to close in on them, the trees leaning in as if watching, listening. The magic that lingered in the air was different here. Darker, tainted, like a sickness had settled into the very roots of the land. Kaela could feel it with every breath, a subtle, pulsating hum that crawled beneath her skin, setting her nerves on edge. It wasn't the kind of magic that resonated with her, the kind that called to her soul. It was twisted, wrong.

She exchanged a brief glance with Ronan, who walked beside her, his eyes narrowed as he scanned their surroundings. His face was set in a hard, grim line, the usual glint of playful confidence replaced with something more dangerous, more wary. Without a word, he gave her a slight nod, acknowledging the tension in the air. The silence between them spoke volumes. This place was not just dangerous. It was something worse. They were venturing deeper into the heart of the Garden's decay, and whatever lay ahead, they weren't prepared for it. Not fully.

"We're close," he said, his voice low but carrying enough weight to make everyone pause. "This is where their patrols start."

Kaela nodded, gripping the hilt of her blade. "Stay alert," she said, her voice steady. "We stick together. No one falls behind."

The group moved as one, their steps careful and deliberate. Kaela's senses were on high alert, her connection to the Garden pulsing faintly in the back of her mind. She could feel the magic shifting, like ripples in a pond. Something was coming. And then, all at once, the forest exploded into chaos.

The first sign of the ambush came in the form of a high-pitched whine, a sharp, shrieking sound that sliced through the still air like a predator's warning. Kaela barely had time to process the noise before the world around her erupted into chaos. With a violent snap, a projectile slammed into the tree beside her, the impact reverberating through the ground as the bark splintered and shattered, sending jagged pieces of wood flying in all directions. The deafening crack of the explosion filled her ears, and she instinctively ducked, her heart hammering in her chest. The air around her seemed to hum with the aftershock, and she knew, without a doubt, that they had walked straight into a trap.

"Scatter!" Ronan shouted, his voice cutting through the din.

Kaela's instincts kicked in the moment the first soldier emerged from the shadows. With a sharp breath, she dove to the side, her body rolling across the uneven ground, her muscles already springing into action as she came to her feet in a fluid motion. The world around her blurred, her focus narrowing to the looming threat. The Technomancer soldiers, their faces hidden behind dark, emotionless helmets, moved in perfect synchrony, their every step calculated, their weapons crackling with stolen magic. The air seemed to vibrate with the hum of their energy, a menacing reminder of the power they wielded.

Milo was already at work, his fingers flying over the device's controls with the precision of a seasoned inventor, seeking a way to tip the scales in their favor. He ducked behind a fallen log, the rapid clicks of his adjustments drowned out by the chaos unfolding. Melana was a blur of motion herself, her battle cry ringing out like a war drum as her blade gleamed under the muted light, meeting the nearest soldier head-on with a fierce, practiced strike. Ronan, as always, was an unstoppable force. He was everywhere at once, his movements graceful and deadly as he dispatched one opponent after another with fluid, almost effortless precision. His eyes never left Kaela, a silent promise that he'd keep her safe as long as he could.

Kaela's heart hammered in her chest, a drumbeat of adrenaline that fueled her every move. She drew her blade, the weight of it grounding her in the chaos. She was ready. The first soldier came at her with a brutal swing, but she was faster, her blade a streak of silver as it sliced through the air, meeting his in a resounding clash. The force of the impact vibrated through her arm, but she didn't hesitate. Her body moved of its own accord, each strike, each parry a dance of survival, the rhythm driven by instinct and the fierce, burning fire that coursed through her veins. She pressed forward, her blade cutting through the air with a vengeance, each motion powered by the weight of everything they were fighting for.

The battle raged around her like a storm, the sounds of clashing metal and magical energy filling the air, the battlefield alive with the heat of battle. The Technomancers pressed in from all sides, their relentless advance like a tide that refused to break. For every soldier they felled, two more seemed to rise in their place, their numbers seemingly endless. Kaela's breath came in sharp gasps as she fought, her muscles screaming in protest, but she didn't stop. She couldn't stop. She had to hold the line. The clash of steel, the crackle of magic, the grunts of effort. All of it melded into a single, chaotic symphony as Kaela fought to protect the Garden, her friends, and everything they had risked to get here.

"We're outnumbered!" Milo shouted, his voice strained as he fired off a burst of energy from his device.

Kaela's mind raced, thoughts colliding in a chaotic whirl as she searched for a way out. The enemy was closing in fast, and the odds were stacking against them. She knew they couldn't hold this position much longer. If they didn't act now, they'd be overrun. Every instinct screamed for action, but she needed a plan, and she needed it fast.

"Fall back!" she called, her voice cutting through the chaos. "Regroup by the ridge!"

The group moved as one, their retreat a calculated maneuver as they fought toward higher ground. Kaela's breath came in short bursts, muscles burning with exertion as she struggled to keep pace. Suddenly, her eyes locked onto a soldier closing in on Milo, his weapon raised and aimed at her friend's back. Fear surged through her as she realized they were running out of time.

"No!" Kaela screamed, her legs moving before her mind could catch up. She threw herself between Milo and the soldier, her blade deflecting the strike just in time. The impact sent a shockwave up her arm, but she held her ground, her body acting on pure adrenaline.

Milo turned, his eyes wide with shock. "Kaela!"

"I'm fine!" she snapped, pushing the soldier back with a fierce strike. "Keep moving!"

They reached the ridge just as the enemy began to regroup, their movements chillingly coordinated and methodical, like a predator closing in on its prey. The air around Kaela seemed to thicken, the weight of their pursuit settling on her shoulders, suffocating in its intensity. She could feel the oppressive presence of their stolen magic, an invisible force that pressed down on her with a suffocating heaviness, making every breath feel labored. The landscape before them seemed to warp, as though the very earth itself was buckling under the weight of the enemy's dark power.

"We can't stay here," Melana said, her voice sharp as she scanned their surroundings. "They'll flank us."

Kaela's mind raced, her connection to the Garden sparking faintly as she searched for a solution, her thoughts a blur of urgency. She could feel the pressure of time closing in on her, but then, beneath her feet, she felt it. A pulse of energy, faint but steady, thrummed through the ground, sending a ripple of warmth up her legs. It was subtle at first, but it grew stronger, and Kaela's heart quickened as she realized the Garden was reaching out to her.

"This way!" she said, leading the group toward a narrow path that wound through the trees.

The magic guided her every step, a gentle pulse beneath her skin that grew stronger with each breath she took. The hum of it resonated in her veins, thrumming with the rhythm of the Garden itself, urging her forward. With each stride, the forest seemed to open before her, the path winding deeper into its heart. Though the Technomancers were close behind, their presence like a shadow stalking them, Kaela felt no fear. The connection to the Garden was clear, its power anchoring her, and she refused to falter now.

After what felt like an eternity, they finally reached a clearing. The air shimmered around them, alive with faint traces of magic that seemed to ripple in the atmosphere, bending the light in strange ways. Kaela paused for a moment, closing her eyes and letting the energy wash over her. She could feel it, fragile yet undeniable. Woven into the very fabric of the Garden. It was a quiet force, a pulse that gave her hope in the face of their impending battle. This was their last chance, and the Garden was still with them.

"We make our stand here," she said, her voice firm as she turned to face the group.

Milo nodded, his hands tightening around his device. "I can set up a perimeter," he said. "It won't hold them for long, but it'll buy us time."

"Do it," Kaela said, her gaze shifting to Melana and Ronan. "The rest of us hold the line."

The next few minutes exploded in a chaos of motion and sound. The air vibrated with the hum of magic, crackling and pulsing as the group readied themselves. Kaela's pulse hammered in her ears as she took her position, her fingers tightening around the hilt of her blade. Every sense was heightened, every muscle coiled with anticipation. The Technomancers were coming. She could feel their presence creeping through the forest, like a storm about to break. This was it.

When they emerged from the shadows, their dark armor gleaming under the faint light, weapons crackling with stolen magic, Kaela's heart surged with determination. The air seemed to thicken with the weight of their approach, but she refused to flinch. This was their fight, the moment they had been preparing for. The Garden had chosen her, and she would not let it fall. With a battle cry, Kaela lunged into the fray, her blade singing through the air as she cut down one Technomancer after another, her connection to the Garden fueling every strike.

But the cost was unbearable. Melana took a brutal blow to the shoulder, her sharp gasp echoing in Kaela's ears as she stumbled back, blood staining her tunic. Milo's device sputtered, sparks flying as it struggled to stay alive in his hands, the strain of the battle wearing it thin. The battlefield swirled around Kaela, but then she saw him.

Ronan. The name tore from her lips, a desperate whisper, the world spinning around her as her hands hovered over his unmoving form. She could feel the ache in her chest, the overwhelming weight of fear and sorrow threatening to consume her. She couldn't breathe. She couldn't think. Not like this.

In the chaos of the battlefield, in the depths of her anguish, something inside Kaela snapped. Without even thinking, without conscious thought, her connection to the Garden flared to life, a torrent of magic surging through her veins. It was as if her grief had unlocked the very power that had lain dormant within her. Her hands began to glow, a soft, radiant light that spread like fire, warming the air around them. Her pulse quickened, and her magic poured into him, filling the space between them with a crackling energy that seemed to fight against the darkness threatening to take him.

Kaela's breath hitched, the surge of power almost too much to control, but she couldn't stop. She wouldn't stop. She poured every ounce of her pain, her fear, her love into the healing light. The energy hummed in her chest, her connection to the Garden pulling her forward, pushing her to heal him, to save him.

And then, slowly, his eyelids fluttered. Kaela held her breath as his golden-green eyes opened, blinking against the pain and exhaustion. "I'm . . . fine," Ronan whispered, his voice a fragile rasp, but steady, like a soft whisper of reassurance in the storm.

But Kaela wasn't convinced. Not yet. She had to be sure. She had to feel him back. She leaned over him, her heart racing, hands still trembling from the power coursing through her, as if she had given him a piece of herself. Relief flooded through her, but there was no time to rest. The battle wasn't over, and they couldn't afford to lose.

"Get up," she said, her voice firm as she helped him to his feet. "We're not done yet."

Kaela could feel the weight of Ronan's struggle as they rejoined the fight. His body was battered, his breath shallow and labored, but his determination burned brighter than ever. The moment they stood side by side, Kaela could sense how hard he was pushing himself. His movements were fluid but sluggish, each strike a little slower, a little weaker than before. But still, he fought. The fire in his eyes hadn't gone out, and Kaela would be damned if she let him fall again.

They worked together seamlessly, their attacks synchronized as they cut through the enemy ranks. Kaela's blade moved with precision, each strike fueled by a need to protect, to keep Ronan standing. Her heart pounded in her chest, but she didn't let up. She couldn't afford to. The Technomancers were relentless, but so were they. With every swing, every parry, they carved their way through the battlefield, their connection a force that seemed to defy the chaos around them.

But Kaela could feel Ronan's weariness, see the way his shoulders trembled with each movement, how his grip on his weapon faltered for just a moment. She caught his gaze for a split second, just enough to see the pain, the strain behind his eyes, and knew that he was fighting against more than just the enemy. He was fighting against his own limits, his own body threatening to give in.

"Stay with me," she whispered under her breath, even as they pushed forward. Her own resolve hardened as she watched him, refusing to let him break, refusing to let him fall. He wasn't alone in this. Not now. Not ever.

They fought back-to-back, a dance of power and desperation, pushing against the tide of enemies that seemed to grow with each passing second. Despite his exhaustion, despite the blood staining his clothes, Ronan was there. His presence was a constant, steadying force beside her. And Kaela would do whatever it took to keep him standing, to keep them both fighting, until the battle was won.

When the last Technomancer fell, the clearing fell silent, save for the ragged breaths of the group. Their bodies were battered, covered in cuts and bruises, but they had made it through the battle. The air was thick with the smell of blood and magic, the ground littered with the remnants of their fight. Kaela looked at her friends. Melana, bruised but standing strong, Milo, his hands shaking as he checked his device, and Ronan, still on his feet though clearly struggling to keep himself upright.

A surge of pride filled her chest, but it was quickly replaced by the weight of what was still to come. They had made it this far, but the Technomancers weren't done yet. And the Heart . . . the Heart was still out of reach. As Kaela opened her mouth to speak, to rally them for the next leg of their journey, a low rumble echoed through the air. The ground beneath them trembled, and the trees around them seemed to shift, as though the Garden itself was reacting to something. And then, from the shadows, something moved. A figure stepped into the clearing, its presence dark and imposing. The air around them grew colder, and Kaela's heart skipped a beat. They weren't alone anymore.

Chapter 38

The figure materialized from the shadows, moving with an eerie, deliberate grace, as if it had always been there, waiting. Shrouded in a flowing cloak, its face remained obscured within the depths of its hood, revealing nothing but darkness. The air grew thick, charged with an unspoken tension that pressed against Kaela's skin, making every breath feel heavier. Yet, beneath the rising unease, a strange pull coiled in her chest, something about the figure was achingly familiar, like a half-forgotten dream slipping just out of reach.

"Who's there?" Kaela demanded, her voice sharp, though her heart hammered in her chest.

The figure didn't answer immediately. Instead, it took a step forward, revealing the face hidden beneath the cloak. Kaela's breath caught in her throat as recognition hit her like a blow. Her father.

But this wasn't the man she had once known. The warm, loving father who had disappeared without a trace. This man, standing before her now, was different. His face was gaunt, his eyes gleaming with an unsettling intensity. His expression was cold, unreadable, but there was something about him that still carried the weight of a long-lost familiarity.

"Dad?" Kaela whispered, her voice trembling with disbelief. She stepped forward, reaching out as though she might touch him and prove he was real.

Her father's eyes softened, but there was a hardness to him that hadn't been there before. "Kaela," he said, his voice low, steady. "You've come. Just as I knew you would."

Kaela's heart raced, a maelstrom of emotions churning inside her. She took another step, her hand shaking at her side. "What are you doing here? Why are you with the Technomancers? Are you one of them?"

Her father's gaze flickered briefly to the others, Milo, Ronan, and Melana, before returning to her. "No," he said firmly. "I'm not one of them. I'm . . . undercover."

Kaela's mind reeled, the words crashing over her like a tidal wave, each one heavier than the last. Undercover. Was that even possible? Her father, the man she had spent years mourning, was here, in the very heart of Technomancer territory. Not just surviving, but working against them, hidden in the shadows of their stronghold.

She shook her head in disbelief. "Undercover? You've been with them all this time? How could you—how could you hide this from me?"

"I didn't want you to know, Kaela," he said quietly, his voice tinged with regret. "I couldn't risk it. I knew you'd come looking for me eventually, and when you did, I'd have to make a choice. But this . . . the Garden, the Heart. It's all connected. And I've been working with the resistance from the inside, gathering intel, trying to sabotage their operations."

Her heart pounded as the weight of his words settled over her like a crushing force. Her father, the man she had grieved for so long, had never been lost at all. He had been alive, hidden in plain sight, moving like a ghost within the enemy's ranks. All this time, he had been fighting against the very forces that had stolen everything from them.

"I never wanted you to get caught up in this," he continued, his voice softening. "But the Garden is in danger, Kaela. And you . . . you're the key to saving it."

The shock of his revelation hit her like a physical blow. Her mind struggled to process it. Her father had known all along, had planned this out from the beginning, waiting for the day she would come to him. He had been watching her, waiting for her to grow into the person who could help him stop the Technomancers.

"You knew I'd find you?" she whispered, her voice a mix of awe and disbelief.

He nodded, his expression resolute. "I knew you would. You've always had the power, Kaela. The Garden's magic runs through you, and I've been watching, waiting for you to realize it."

Her thoughts spun, a whirlwind of confusion and betrayal tightening in her chest. Before she could speak, a low rumble vibrated through the air, shaking the ground beneath them. The clearing darkened, the trees groaning as though the very Garden was reacting to the new presence. A sense of impending danger hung thick in the air, adding weight to the already tense moment.

Her father's gaze flickered toward the horizon, his eyes narrowing. "We need to move. The Technomancers will be looking for us."

Kaela swallowed hard, the weight of his words settling over her like a heavy cloak. "What do we do?"

He looked to the others, his expression unreadable. "We have a chance to take them down, to destroy their power source. I've set up a way to disable their central core, but we have to move quickly. The longer we stay here, the more likely they'll find us."

Milo adjusted the strap on his satchel, glancing at Kaela. "Then let's move. We've got one shot at this."

Kaela nodded, her mind racing with the weight of the revelation. Her father, the man she had thought lost forever, was here, fighting against the Technomancers. He had secretly been a part of the resistance all along, working from the shadows. Now, they were all united in a desperate struggle to save the Garden.

The group began to move, the shadows of the trees stretching long as they hurried through the underbrush. The path ahead was uncertain, fraught with danger, but Kaela's heart was steady for the first time in days. She had found her father, but the true battle was only just beginning. As they reached the Technomancer headquarters, a dark shape emerged from the shadows, blocking their path. The Technomancer leader.

Kaela's breath caught in her throat as he stepped forward, his cold eyes locking onto hers. She recognized him instantly, the man who had always lurked in the background, orchestrating everything from the shadows. The threat he posed was undeniable, and now, standing before her, he was more dangerous than ever. Every instinct screamed that this was the moment everything changed.

Her father's hand tightened on her shoulder, his voice low and urgent. "This is it. No turning back now."

The fight for the Garden had reached its final stage, and Kaela knew that no matter the cost, she had to win. For the Garden. For her father. And for everything they had lost. Kaela's pulse hammered in her chest as she stood tall, her father by her side, Ronan staggering weakly behind her. She had seen the fire in his eyes earlier, but now, weakened from the earlier attack, it flickered, fragile, almost extinguished. Still, his presence grounded her. They were here for a reason. The Garden's power surged within her, but the weight of it was now unbearable. The Technomancers would stop at nothing to claim the Heart, and if they did, all was lost.

The Technomancer leader's eyes glinted coldly as he took in the scene before him. "So, you think you can defeat us?" His voice was thick with contempt, each word a threat. "The Heart belongs to us. Your blood, your struggles. It all means nothing."

Kaela's father's jaw tightened, and he stepped closer to Kaela. "Don't listen to him," he murmured, his voice rough with emotion. "You've come this far. It's your fight now."

Kaela turned her head slightly, her gaze meeting her father's. "You've always known I'd come. That's why you left. Why you stayed behind?"

His eyes softened for a fleeting moment, a sadness she couldn't quite understand passing between them. But there was no time to question it now. They had a battle to fight, and she would do whatever it took to protect them all. Before anyone could move, Ronan's energy surged. He was slower than usual, but his resolve was as strong as ever. With a roar, he thrust his hand forward, sending a burst of golden-green energy toward the oncoming soldiers. The blast cut through the air like a blade, but it wasn't enough. The Technomancers had adapted. They were prepared for him. Kaela's heart clenched. She couldn't let him fight alone. Not like this.

"Ronan!" she cried, pushing herself forward, the magic of the Garden responding to her will. She thrust her hands outward, the ground beneath them shuddering as roots spiraled up, wrapping around the enemy soldiers, pinning them in place. But the energy was heavier here, pressing against her like a suffocating weight. It was as if the Technomancers had tainted everything, and she felt it deep in her bones.

Ronan stumbled, his breath ragged, his hand still extended. "Kaela, don't—" he started, but she wasn't listening. She couldn't stop now.

She turned to Milo, who was furiously working on his device. "Milo, how long?" she shouted, her voice tight with urgency.

"Just a few more seconds!" he yelled back, his face drawn with exhaustion. "I'm trying to destabilize the core, but the magic's interfering. It's like fighting against a storm!"

She couldn't wait any longer. Her heart pounded in her chest as she felt the stolen magic surging through the building, pulsing like a sickening heartbeat. "We don't have a few seconds!" she shouted. "We need to move, now!"

Before Milo could respond, the Technomancer leader stepped forward, his eyes gleaming with malevolent satisfaction. "You think you can stop this? You think you can take down everything we've built?"

Kaela didn't hesitate. With a scream, she channeled the power of the Garden through her, the earth beneath her feet cracking open, tendrils of energy reaching for the Technomancer leader. But he was ready. With a swipe of his hand, he sent a shockwave of energy toward her, knocking her off her feet and sending her sprawling to the ground. The air was knocked from her lungs as she gasped for breath, pain flaring through her chest.

"Kaela!" Ronan's voice rang out, full of panic. He stumbled forward, but his movements were sluggish, his body clearly failing him.

She could see it in his eyes. He would do anything to protect her. Even now, in his weakened state, he was ready to sacrifice himself. The thought nearly shattered her. She couldn't lose him, not like this. With every ounce of strength she had left, Kaela rose to her feet, her body trembling. The world around her felt like it was falling apart, but she couldn't afford to falter. Not when so many lives were on the line.

"Ronan, no!" she cried, reaching for him. "Stay back!"

But he was already pushing forward, his hand raised, golden-green energy flickering around his fingers like a spark of life itself. His gaze met hers, intense and unwavering, and in that moment, something unspoken passed between them. She knew, deep in her bones, that if it came to it, he would sacrifice everything for her. The realization hit her like a wave, she couldn't let that happen.

The Technomancer leader smirked, sensing the shift in the air.

"Foolish," he muttered. "You're too late. The Heart is already ours."

With a snarl, Kaela forced the magic within her to surge. She felt the Garden's agony, its despair, and harnessed it into a final, desperate explosion of power. The ground shook beneath her feet as the Technomancer leader's smirk faltered, a wave of raw magic hurtling toward him. The air crackled with energy, and Kaela's heart raced as she fought to hold the magic in check.

But just as the energy surged forward, a sharp cry pierced the air. Milo's voice, raw and choked with agony. Her heart lurched, the magic in her hands faltering for a split second. Panic surged through her veins as she turned toward him, her focus split between the fight and the sound of his pain. Time seemed to freeze, and Kaela's world narrowed to his voice, desperate and full of fear.

"Milo!" she screamed, her heart dropping into her stomach.

She turned just in time to see him collapse, his body writhing as sparks of electricity erupted from his device, overloading. The machine he had been working on exploded in a blinding flash, the shockwave sending him flying backward. Her breath caught as he hit the ground hard, his body unmoving for a terrifying moment. Panic surged through her, but she rushed toward him, heart pounding in her chest.

"No!" Kaela rushed to his side, kneeling beside him, her hands shaking as she checked for any sign of life. Blood was seeping from a wound on his forehead, his eyes fluttering open only briefly before closing again.

"Kaela . . ." His voice was weak, barely a whisper, but it was enough to tear at her heart. "I'm sorry . . . I didn't—" He coughed, wincing from the pain. "I couldn't . . . finish it . . ."

Tears burned her eyes, but she didn't let them fall. Not yet. She couldn't lose him. Not now.

"Don't you dare say that," she hissed, gripping his hand tightly. "You've done more than enough. Stay with me, Milo. Please. We can still do this. We're not done."

His lips parted in a strained smile, though it was clear how much it hurt him. "I'm . . . sorry, Kaela . . . I wanted to be there . . . with you. To finish this." His hand weakly squeezed hers. "You'll . . . save the Garden. You'll save us all."

"No, don't talk like that," Kaela begged, shaking her head, though her voice cracked with emotion. "You're not going anywhere. We're not done yet, Milo. Not while I still have breath in my body."

Even as she spoke, Kaela could feel the Garden's magic tightening around them, its power swelling with an intensity that left her breathless. The Technomancer leader, unfazed, remained standing, his smirk never wavering as he watched their every move. She knew he was waiting, testing their limits, savoring the tension. The air crackled with the promise of an impending confrontation, and Kaela's resolve hardened.

Kaela wasn't sure how much longer they could hold on, but in that moment, she made a vow to herself. No matter the cost, no matter the pain she had to endure, she would make sure they finished this together. She would save Milo, protect Ronan, and fight until the very end to save the Garden. The weight of that promise fueled her, igniting a fierce determination deep within her soul.

With all the strength she could muster, Kaela turned toward the Technomancer leader, her vision blurred by tears and fury. The world around her seemed to slow, the battle fading into the background as her magic surged wildly. The air around her crackled with raw energy, vibrating with the force of the Garden's power. She could feel the energy building within her, ready to explode in a final, desperate act.

The leader stood at the center of the crumbling chamber, his dark robes billowing as he siphoned the last remnants of corrupted magic from the Heart. His face was calm, cold, and utterly devoid of remorse, a mask of unshakable control. He didn't flinch as Kaela approached, her copper hair streaming behind her like a banner of war. The air between them crackled, the weight of their confrontation heavy with unspoken tension.

"You've taken enough," Kaela growled, her voice trembling with fury. Her fists clenched, and the ground beneath her feet cracked, vines forcing their way through the metallic floor. The Heart pulsed behind her, its light growing stronger with each passing second, as though lending her its strength.

The leader sneered, his eyes gleaming with disdain. "You think your power will save you? You're a child playing with forces you can't possibly understand. This magic belongs to us now. To me."

"No," Kaela spat, stepping closer, the raw magic swirling around her. "It belongs to the Garden. And I'll tear you apart before I let you take it."

The leader raised his hands, dark energy swirling between them in a roiling sphere of pure malice. With a sneer, he hurled it toward Kaela, the force of the attack ripping through the air with a deafening roar. The sphere surged forward, a pulse of overwhelming power that seemed to distort the very fabric of reality. Kaela's heart raced as she prepared to meet the oncoming storm, her magic rising to meet it. Kaela didn't flinch as the dark energy hurtled toward her. With a fierce determination, she thrust her hands forward, her magic colliding with his in a violent burst. The chamber exploded in a blinding light, the impact rattling the walls and sending shards of metal cascading through the air. Despite the suffocating weight of his power pressing against her, Kaela stood firm, refusing to yield.

She thought of Milo, unconscious and bleeding, his inventions abandoned around him. She thought of Ronan, battered yet still standing, protecting her from the looming threat. She thought of the Garden, its quiet plea echoing in her mind, urging her to fight. In that moment, she found the strength to push forward, fueled by love, loyalty, and the desperate need to protect all they had left.

Kaela roared, the sound tearing from her chest as her magic surged with a blistering heat. The vines around her writhed and twisted, reaching for the leader like sentient creatures hungry for their prey. They coiled around his legs, his arms, and his throat, squeezing with unrelenting force as he fought against their grip. His struggle only fueled her determination, and with each desperate movement, she tightened the hold, unwilling to let him escape.

"You've destroyed enough lives," Kaela said, her voice steady now, though her body trembled with the effort. "You've taken enough from me. From all of us. This ends now."

The leader's eyes widened in shock as the vines constricted tighter, their razor-sharp thorns biting deep into his flesh. His dark magic sputtered and weakened, unable to fight against the purity of the Garden's force. Desperation flashed across his face as the corruption inside him began to unravel. The power that had once made him invincible was crumbling, replaced by the raw, untamed magic of the Garden. Kaela stepped forward, her gaze never leaving his, and she saw the fear creeping into his eyes, shattering his arrogance. The confidence that had once radiated from him now faltered, replaced by the growing realization of his defeat. With a steady hand, she raised it, and the vines obeyed, lifting him off the ground, their grip tightening as her magic flowed into him. The once untouchable leader now hung helplessly, trapped by the raw power of the Garden.

"You wanted the Garden's power?" she said, her voice low and cold. "Then take it."

With a final surge of energy, Kaela unleashed everything she had, channeling the Garden's magic directly into the leader. The light was blinding, consuming him in a torrent of pure energy. He screamed, the sound high and inhuman, before the light overtook him completely. When it faded, the leader was gone. Only a faint shimmer of ash remained, scattering into the air. Kaela fell to her knees, her strength spent, the weight of her magic settling into a quiet hum within her. The chamber was silent now, save for the steady pulse of the restored Heart.

Ronan limped toward her, his golden-green eyes wide with awe and concern. "Kaela," he said, his voice soft as he knelt beside her. "Are you—"

"I'm fine," she interrupted, though her voice was hoarse. She looked past him to where Milo lay, her heart tightening. "But we need to get out of here. Now."

Ronan nodded, helping her to her feet. Her father was already lifting Milo, his face grim but determined. As they made their way out of the crumbling chamber, Kaela glanced back one last time. The Heart glowed brightly now, its magic no longer tainted, its light a beacon of hope. They had won. But the cost of victory lingered in her chest, a heavy reminder that the fight was far from over.

Chapter 39

The smoke still lingered in the air, a bitter reminder of the destruction that had followed them. The chamber was vast and pulsing with a sinister energy, the stolen magic thrumming in discordant waves that made Kaela's skin crawl. At the center of the room, surrounded by jagged conduits and towering machines, was the Heart of the Garden—a glowing core of energy suspended within a lattice of twisted metal. It was beautiful and terrible all at once, a fractured echo of the Garden's true magic.

Kaela knelt beside Milo, her hands trembling as she pressed fabric to the gash on his forehead. His breathing was shallow, and his face was pale. Yet, his eyes remained open, full of determination. He was still fighting to stay with her.

"Milo, just hold on," she whispered, her voice cracking. "We're almost there. I promise."

Ronan staggered to her side, leaning heavily against the wall for support. His golden-green eyes, dulled by exhaustion, were fixed on her. "Kaela . . . we don't have time," he rasped. "The longer we wait, the more power they draw from the Heart. If we don't stop it now . . ."

Kaela looked at him, her heart clenching with emotion. Strain was etched into every line of his face, his body sagging under the weight of his injuries. He had already given so much, yet he stood ready to fight. Despite everything, he would still sacrifice whatever remained of himself for her and the Garden.

Her father's voice broke through the haze of her thoughts, steady and resolute. "He's right," he said, stepping forward, his expression grim and his gaze fixed firmly on the Heart. There was a weight to his words, a depth of understanding that came from years of knowledge and sacrifice. "This place is a siphon," he continued, his voice low but charged with urgency. "They've twisted the Heart's energy, corrupted its purpose, but it's still connected to the Garden. If we can sever their control, the magic will return to where it belongs, restoring the balance." His tone carried both a warning and a sliver of hope, urging Kaela to act before it was too late.

Kaela turned to him, desperation lacing her voice. "How? How do we stop it?"

He hesitated, his jaw tightening. "The machines are feeding off the Heart's energy, amplifying it and redirecting it to their forces. If we disable the conduits, it will destabilize the system. But . . ."

"But what?" she demanded, her voice rising.

Her father's gaze softened, and for the first time, she saw the pain in his eyes. "The Heart's been corrupted. Severing their control will unleash that corrupted energy. It could destroy the Heart entirely—or whoever is closest to it when it happens."

Kaela's breath caught in her throat, a sharp ache spreading through her chest. Her father's words hung heavy in the air, each one pressing down on her like a crushing weight. She turned her gaze to the Heart, its glow faltering like a dying ember, fragile and broken. It was right there, so close she could almost feel its power calling to her, yet the cost of freeing it loomed like a shadow, vast and unthinkable. A knot of fear and determination twisted inside her, and for a moment, she wasn't sure she could bear it.

Ronan pushed himself off the wall, his steps unsteady as he approached her. "I'll do it," he said, his voice low but steady.

"No!" Kaela snapped, her head whipping toward him. "You can barely stand, Ronan. I won't let you."

"And I won't let you risk your life!" he shot back, his voice rising despite his obvious weakness. His eyes locked with hers, and for a moment, the world seemed to fade away. "Kaela, you mean too much to the Garden, to all of us. To me."

Her heart clenched at the pain in his voice, but she couldn't let him carry this weight. He had already given so much, pushed himself past every limit to protect her and the Garden. Letting him take this risk now would break something inside her. She had to be the one to see it through, no matter the cost.

Milo stirred beside her, his voice weak but insistent. "Stop . . . arguing," he mumbled, his eyes fluttering open. "This . . . isn't about . . . who deserves to live. It's about . . . who can finish the fight."

Kaela's throat tightened as she looked down at Milo, his face pale and streaked with blood. Even in his weakened state, barely clinging to consciousness, he was still fighting for them, still trying to guide them forward. His whispered words were a reminder of the purpose that had brought them this far, a plea not to lose sight of what they were fighting for. The sight of him like this, so vulnerable yet unyielding, sent a fresh wave of determination surging through her.

Her father stepped closer, his voice quiet but firm. "Kaela, you have the Garden's magic in you. You're the only one right now who can restore the Heart, the only one strong enough to withstand the backlash."

She looked at him, her mind racing. "But if I fail—"

"You won't," he said, his voice breaking slightly. "You're stronger than you know. And I . . . I believe in you."

The words hit her like a physical blow. Her father, who had been gone for so long, who she had thought she would never see again, was here now, asking her to trust herself. Kaela's hands clenched into fists as she rose to her feet, the magic of the Garden humming faintly in her veins. She could feel its pain, its desperation, but also its strength. It was waiting for her, calling to her.

"I'll do it," she said, her voice steady despite the storm raging inside her. "I'll restore the Heart."

Ronan reached for her, his hand brushing against hers. "Kaela—"

She turned to him, her eyes blazing with determination. "I need you to trust me, Ronan. Just this once. Please."

He hesitated, his hand tightening around hers, but finally, he nodded. "I trust you. Always."

Her father moved to Milo's side, his face pale but resolute. "We'll keep them off your back," he said. "Do what you need to do."

Kaela nodded, her pulse thundering in her ears as she stepped toward the Heart. Each step felt like wading into a storm, the corrupted energy clawing at her skin, cold and malevolent, as if it recognized her intent. The air around her crackled with power, thick and suffocating, but she forced herself forward. She could feel Ronan's gaze burning into her, his silent plea screaming louder than words. This was it. The moment she had fought for, bled for.

Her fingers trembled as she reached out, brushing against the swirling energy of the Heart. It burned like fire and froze like ice, a clash of opposites that seared her nerves and stole her breath. The Garden's magic inside her surged, colliding with the Heart's fractured power in a chaotic torrent that felt like it might tear her apart. Pain ripped through her body, sharp and unrelenting, but she didn't let go. She couldn't.

Kaela's cry shattered the heavy silence as she poured everything she had into the Heart. The magic roared through her, a tidal wave of light and sound, ripping through the room like a hurricane. Energy lashed out in jagged streaks, shattering walls and sending shards of metal and stone raining down. The force slammed into her chest, driving her to her knees, but she locked her grip on the twisted lattice encasing the core. The Heart pulsed violently, fighting her, its corrupted energy clawing at her mind and body, but Kaela screamed against the pain. She wasn't just fighting for herself—she was fighting for Ronan, for Milo, for her father, for the Garden itself. And she would not lose. Not now. With a final, guttural roar, Kaela unleashed everything, the magic within her erupting like a star, engulfing the Heart in pure, radiant light. The chamber exploded with brilliance, blinding and all-consuming, as the battle reached its crescendo.

The Garden's magic surged through Kaela, clashing violently with the toxic energy festering within the Heart. It was chaos incarnate. Pain and light, fire and ice, each vying for control in a relentless storm that threatened to tear her apart. Every nerve in her body screamed in agony, but Kaela gritted her teeth, her determination burning brighter than the torment. She couldn't falter, not now, not when everything was at stake.

Behind her, the chamber descended into chaos. The Technomancers, drawn by the overwhelming surge of power, poured into the room like a flood. Ronan was the first to face them, his body trembling under the weight of his earlier injuries. His hands glowed faintly with the last remnants of his magic, and with a desperate cry, he unleashed a burst of energy, sending two soldiers crashing back. The effort nearly cost him, his knees buckling as he struggled to stay upright, but his resolve never wavered.

"Ronan, fall back!" her father shouted, stepping in with a weapon he had wrestled from one of the fallen guards. He fired precise shots, his movements efficient and cold, but the sheer number of Technomancers made it clear they were outmatched.

"I'm fine!" Ronan snarled, though his face was pale, and his breathing was labored. "Keep them off Kaela!"

Milo, barely upright, worked feverishly at the pried-open control panel. His trembling fingers fumbled with the tools, each slip costing precious seconds. Sweat dripped down his face as he fought to override the systems corrupting the Heart. Every motion was a battle against his failing strength, but he refused to stop.

"Almost . . . got it . . ." he muttered through gritted teeth, his face slick with sweat.

Kaela barely noticed the chaos erupting around her, her focus consumed by the storm of the Heart. The magic surged within her, threatening to tear her apart, but she held on. Her connection to the

Garden was her only anchor, a lifeline in the tempest. She could feel its strength and its determination to heal, and she clung to it with every ounce of her will.

"I won't let you win," she whispered through the pain, her voice barely audible over the roar of the energy.

A sharp cry cut through the chaos, snapping Kaela's focus back to the room. Her heart froze as she turned to see Ronan collapse to his knees, a blade glinting cruelly by his side. Blood seeped through his shirt, staining the floor beneath him as he struggled to stay upright. The sight of him brought a surge of panic that threatened to drown her.

"Ronan!" she screamed, her voice raw with desperation. She tried to move, to rise, but the heart's power anchored her in place, holding her in an unrelenting grip. His golden green eyes locked on hers, filled with both searing pain and unshakable resolve. It was a silent message, a plea, and a promise that she could barely bring herself to understand.

"Don't stop," he rasped, blood dripping from his lips. "Finish it, Kaela. Don't you dare stop."

Her heart twisted, every instinct screaming at her to run to him, to pull him away from the fight. But she couldn't, not when the Heart's power was slipping through her fingers. The Garden needed her, and she couldn't afford to fail. Ronan's pain had to wait.

A loud crack filled the air, and Milo's voice broke through the chaos. "I've severed the main conduits!" he shouted, his voice hoarse but triumphant. "It's all on you now, Kaela!"

The room trembled violently as the machines surrounding the Heart began to overload, their shrieks of protest echoing through the chamber. Sparks exploded from the walls, the acrid scent of burning circuits thick in the air, stinging Kaela's senses. The Technomancers staggered back, their once-confident stances faltering as the unstable energy surged unpredictably, striking at random. Kaela felt the shift, the weight of the corrupted magic starting to pull away, but it wasn't enough—she needed more. She couldn't stop now.

With her heart pounding in her chest, Kaela drew in a shaky breath and reached deeper into the Heart, her mind pushing through the chaos to seek out the Garden's essence. Help me, she pleaded, the words silent but desperate. For a long moment, there was nothing but cold emptiness. But then—warmth, like a long-lost embrace, flooded her senses. The Garden's magic responded, fierce and unrelenting, its pure energy surging through her veins, pushing back against the corruption that had tainted it for so long.

Kaela's body trembled under the strain, but she held firm, pouring everything she had into the Heart. With a final, raw cry, she unleashed the full force of the Garden's magic. The lattice around the Heart shattered with an explosive crack, the corrupted energy vaporizing in a blinding flash of light. When the light receded, the room fell eerily silent. The Heart hovered before her, its glow steady and pure once again, no longer tainted by the Technomancers' grasp. The battle was over. Kaela collapsed to the floor, her body trembling from the immense effort it had taken to restore the Heart. The Garden's magic still pulsed within her, but it was no longer the chaotic storm it had been—it was a gentle, calming current, settling into her with a peaceful rhythm. Her breath came in ragged gasps as she tried to steady herself, her limbs heavy with exhaustion. Every fiber of her being felt both drained and full, as though she had just crossed a threshold she couldn't quite comprehend.

She lifted her head, her eyes frantically searching for Ronan in the haze of smoke and fading light. He was slumped against the wall, his face pale, but the steady rise and fall of his chest brought her a brief moment of relief. The sight of him alive was a balm to her frayed nerves, but that relief was fleeting—she could see the blood on his side, the damage still far from healed. She pushed herself to her feet, determination burning through her exhaustion. Milo. Her heart skipped a beat as she turned toward where he had been working. Her stomach sank when she saw him lying on the ground, motionless, with tools scattered around him. Panic surged through her as she rushed to his side, hoping, praying, that he was still alive.

"No," she whispered, scrambling to her feet. Her legs buckled, but she forced herself forward, collapsing beside him.

"Milo," she said, her hands shaking as she turned him over. His face was ashen, his eyes closed, and blood seeped from a wound in his side. "Milo, please. Wake up."

Her father knelt beside her, his expression grim as he pressed his fingers to Milo's neck. "He's alive," he said quietly. "But barely."

Kaela let out a choked sob, her hands clutching at Milo's shirt. "We need to get him out of here," she said, her voice breaking. "He can't die. He can't."

Ronan staggered to their side, his face drawn with pain. "We will," he said, his voice hoarse. "We'll get him out. But we have to move. Now."

Kaela nodded, tears streaming down her face as she helped lift Milo, her hands shaking with fear and exhaustion. Her father took most of the weight, his movements steady despite the chaos around them. The sounds of crumbling metal and distant explosions filled the air, but Kaela barely heard them, her focus solely on Milo. His shallow breathing was the only thing grounding her in the moment, and she couldn't stop the surge of dread that clutched her chest.

As they fled the crumbling chamber, Kaela glanced back at the Heart. Its light was strong now, pulsing with the Garden's true magic, and for the first time in what felt like forever, she felt hope stir within her. They had done it. They had restored the Heart. But as she looked at Milo, his life hanging by a thread, she knew their fight was far from over. The Garden was alive again, but the cost of saving it was only beginning to reveal itself.

Chapter 40

The weight of the Garden's restored magic pressed down on Kaela's chest, its warmth a stark contrast to the cold terror coiling in her gut. She glanced at her father, his strong hands holding Milo steady as they moved through the crumbling halls of the Technomancer's stronghold. The air was thick with smoke and the scent of burning circuits, the walls around them shaking with the aftershocks of their victory. They were barely escaping, but Kaela couldn't shake the feeling that the worst was yet to come.

"Stay close," her father murmured, his voice tight with the strain of carrying Milo's unconscious form. "We're almost there."

Kaela nodded, though the tightness in her chest made it hard to breathe. The ground trembled beneath their feet as if the very structure of the Technomancer's base was unraveling, and yet, through it all, her focus never wavered from Milo. His pulse was weak, but steady, a fragile thread of life hanging between them.

Every step they took felt like a countdown to something terrible, and she couldn't shake the feeling that they were being hunted.

Behind them, a shrill cry echoed through the crumbling chamber, sharp and jagged, slicing through the chaos. Kaela's heart skipped a beat, her blood freezing in her veins as she turned to face the source of the sound. A group of Technomancer soldiers emerged from the darkness, their movements swift and calculated, eyes glowing with an unnatural, eerie light that seemed to hunger for violence. The metallic sheen of their armor reflected the flickering lights of the ruined facility, their weapons raised and crackling with energy, the air thick with the promise of destruction. Kaela's breath caught in her throat as she saw the intent in their eyes—this was no mere skirmish. They were here to end everything.

The fear that gripped her was cold and suffocating, but in the midst of it, her father's voice broke through the haze of panic, steady and commanding. "Stay behind me," he ordered, his tone unwavering despite the urgency in the air. The familiar strength in his voice anchored her, reminding her that she wasn't alone in this fight. Even as the Technomancers closed in, their malicious presence pressing on all sides, Kaela's hands clenched into fists at her sides, her resolve hardening.

"No!" Kaela's voice cracked, her hands reaching for him, but her father was already moving into position. His body was a shield between her and the oncoming threat, his eyes hard with the same determination that had driven him through every battle of his life. He wasn't going to let anything happen to her.

The first wave of Technomancer soldiers surged forward like a tidal wave, their weapons crackling with lethal energy. The air hummed with the tension of the impending battle, the crackling of electricity and the thrum of power mingling in a deadly symphony. Kaela's father met them head-on, moving with the practiced precision of a warrior who had fought countless battles. His hands glowed with the faintest remnants of the magic that had once been his greatest strength. Magic that had been drained over the years, but not entirely gone. His movements were still fluid, still powerful, as he took down two soldiers in quick succession, but Kaela could see it, the strain in his every step, the way his shoulders sagged slightly, the exhaustion that had taken root in his body.

Her heart hammered in her chest, a sickening weight pressing down on her as she watched her father fight, knowing that every move he made drained him more. Her powers flared instinctively, the magic that had once felt like a distant dream now thrumming beneath her skin, urging her to act. Her hand shot out, reaching for him, but before she could close the distance, the Technomancer soldiers charged forward again. One of them, faster than the rest, lunged with a blade gleaming in the dim light. Kaela's heart skipped a beat as she watched him aim the blade directly for her father's side. Her breath caught in her throat as her father, already weakened, tried to dodge, but the soldier was too quick. The blade drove deep into his ribs with a sickening crack, and her father staggered back, his face contorted in pain, his body unable to withstand the blow.

"No!" Kaela's scream tore through the chaos, raw and broken as she rushed forward, magic lashing out uncontrollably. The air around her crackled with power, but it wasn't enough to stop what had already been set in motion.

Her father's knees buckled, and he collapsed, blood spreading beneath him like a dark stain. He planted a trembling hand on the ground, struggling to stay upright. His breaths came in shallow gasps, each one weaker than the last. But when his eyes met hers, she saw the truth. He wasn't going to make it.

"Kaela . . ." His voice was barely a whisper, breath shallow, filled with pain and love. "You have to finish this. You can't let it end like this."

A sob caught in her throat as she dropped to his side, pressing her hands to the wound, desperately willing her magic to heal him. But the power wouldn't obey, slipping through her fingers like sand. The Garden's presence loomed around her, heavy and suffocating, and in that moment, she understood. The bargain had been made and her father was the price.

The tingling she had felt when she and Ronan had finally given in to their feelings, the shift she had ignored, had been the Garden rewriting fate. Ronan's bargain had changed in that moment, silently, irrevocably. The Garden had claimed a different price, taking not his love, but hers. Her father had been the cost.

The words struck her like a physical blow, and she collapsed to her knees beside him, her hands shaking as they hovered over the wound. Tears blurred her vision, her heart aching with the helplessness that gripped her. She searched desperately for any way to heal him, to undo the damage that had already been done. But the weight of reality crushed her. There was nothing she could do.

"No, please . . . you can't leave me . . . I just got you back . . ." Her voice cracked, the words raw with desperation.

Her father's eyes softened, a flicker of that familiar warmth still there despite the agony that wracked his body. "I'm sorry," he whispered, his voice faint but full of love. "I've always loved you. And I'm proud of you."

His hand reached up, brushing a stray lock of hair from her face with what little strength he had left. In that moment, everything seemed to stand still. Her heart, her world, the very breath in her lungs. She could feel his love surrounding her, but it wasn't enough to stop the devastation from crashing through her like a tidal wave. She wanted to scream, to beg him to stay, but the words wouldn't come. Instead, she could only hold his hand, her heart shattering as she whispered, "I love you, too. Please don't leave me."

Her father's eyes fluttered closed, and in that moment, she felt his body go limp in her arms. The warmth that had once filled him was gone, leaving only the cold emptiness of loss. His final breath, so faint, seemed to whisper goodbye, and she could feel the last remnants of his strength slipping away. He had been her everything. The man who had guided her, protected her, and filled her world with love and now, she was left with nothing but the hollow ache of his absence.

With those final words, he closed his eyes, his body going limp in her arms. Kaela's scream tore through the air, raw and agonized, as the weight of his loss crashed down on her. The room around her seemed to spin, the world narrowing to a single point. The broken, lifeless body of the man who had given everything for her, for the Garden, for the fight they'd been waging for so long.

Behind her, the Technomancers were closing in, but Kaela couldn't move. Her body felt like stone, her heart a hollow void as she cradled her father's lifeless form. She had just gotten him back after so long, only to lose him again, this time for good. The grief hit her like a tidal wave, drowning her in its overwhelming force, and she could do nothing but hold onto him, her chest heaving with sobs that felt too heavy to bear. She could hear Ronan's voice, frantic and distant, calling her name, but it was like it came from another world. She was lost, consumed by the devastation that had ripped through her soul, her world shattering once more.

But then, a soft, familiar warmth blossomed in her chest, as though a part of her father's love and strength had ignited deep within her. The magic of the Garden surged, not just around her, but through her, wrapping her in its protective embrace like a shield forged from the very earth itself. It wasn't only the magic of the Heart that pulsed within her now, it was something more profound, a bond forged in her father's final moments. His love, his courage, and his unspoken belief in her had been passed down in that fleeting instant, infusing her with a strength she had never known she possessed. The warmth spread through her limbs, filling her with a fierce, unyielding determination to honor his sacrifice, to protect everything he had fought for.

Through her tears, Kaela's eyes locked onto the Technomancers, their smug expressions faltering as they realized what was happening. Her body trembled, not from fear, but from the surge of raw emotion and power coursing through her. She rose to her feet, the energy around her crackling and spiraling, a brilliant storm of magic fueled by grief and fury. "You will not take anything else from me," she vowed, her voice trembling with the weight of her pain, but steady and deadly as she faced them. The loss of her father had broken her, but it had also ignited something within her, something fierce, something unstoppable.

With a raw, anguished cry, Kaela unleashed the full force of the Garden's magic, a violent torrent of energy that ripped through the room, sending the Technomancers crashing back in a storm of light and destruction. The air crackled with power, and the ground trembled beneath her feet as the energy surged forward, wild and uncontrollable. Each wave of magic seemed to tear at the very fabric of the chamber, the force of her grief and fury amplifying the power of the Garden itself. Kaela's heart pounded in her chest, her breath ragged, but she didn't hesitate. This was her moment to reclaim everything that had been taken from her.

The battle raged on, but this time, Kaela was no longer the victim of the Technomancers' manipulation. With every strike, every burst of magic, she was carving out her vengeance, her soul burning with the memory of her father's sacrifice. Her mind was a haze of pain and purpose, but the clarity of her mission cut through it all, she would not stop until they were all destroyed. Her father had given everything to protect the Garden, to protect her, and she would make sure that his sacrifice meant something. With each blow, the Technomancers faltered, and Kaela knew this was the beginning of the end for them.

Chapter 41

The chaos around her faded into a distant hum, swallowed by the roar of the magic surging within her. Kaela stood, trembling but resolute, her father's lifeless body still clutched in her arms. His absence was a gaping void, an abyss that threatened to consume her whole. The weight of it crashed down on her, suffocating, an unbearable truth she could neither change nor escape.

The tingling she had felt when she and Ronan had accepted their feelings, the shift she had ignored, had been the Garden rewriting fate. Ronan's bargain had changed, and the Garden had taken its due. Not him. Not his love. Someone else. Someone she loved just as deeply. Her father had been the cost.

A sob shuddered through her, but amidst the pain, a fire ignited, burning away the numbness. This wasn't just grief; it was fury, raw and consuming, a force stronger than anything she had ever known.

The Garden's magic, once a whisper in her mind, was now a roar, flowing through her like molten fire. She could feel it, its desperation, its hunger for vengeance, its will entwined with hers.

The connection to the Heart, to everything her father had fought to protect, blazed inside her. It was no longer a distant dream or an impossible hope. It was hers now. The burden of the Garden's survival, the weight of its magic, rested on her shoulders alone. As her power surged outward, she could feel the domes. The dark, oppressive barriers that had severed the Garden's connection to the world, beginning to weaken. Their hold loosened with every pulse of her magic, and she knew, with unshakable certainty, that she would tear them down. She would finish this for her father.

Kaela lifted her arms, her fingers outstretched toward the Heart, her chest heaving with each breath. Her father's voice echoed in her mind, urging her to finish what they had started. "You have to finish this." She had no choice. She had to honor his sacrifice, not just with her words, but with her actions. She closed her eyes, focusing all her energy on the Heart, on the magic that flowed through her like lifeblood.

With a single, powerful cry, she channeled everything she had left into the Heart. The energy of the Garden, pure and unyielding, surged forward, its light blinding, overwhelming her senses. The domes that had bound the Garden's magic to the Technomancers' control shattered, their grip splintering under the force of her will.

Kaela's body trembled with the strain, her skin burning as if the very energy of the Garden was consuming her from the inside out. She could feel the magic of the Garden healing, shifting, realigning itself with the world. But it came at a price. Her strength was waning, the power she had unleashed pulling from the deepest, most fragile parts of her.

Her father's death had given her the strength to do what had to be done, but now, as the magic flowed through her, Kaela realized the cost. She could feel herself unraveling, her life force tethered to the magic she had unleashed. Each breath she took felt heavier, more labored. The Garden was healing, but at the cost of her own vitality. She gritted her teeth, refusing to stop, refusing to let the magic slip away. She would give everything, everything her father had given to ensure the Garden's survival.

The world around her blurred, the light from the Heart shining brighter than ever, but Kaela could feel herself slipping, her connection to the magic beginning to fray. She knew that if she didn't finish this, the Garden would die. The Technomancers would win. And her father's death would be for nothing. So she pushed harder, deeper, her heart pounding in time with the rhythm of the magic, until the last of the domes shattered, the final link severed. The room fell silent, the hum of the Garden's magic quieting, and Kaela collapsed to her knees, her vision fading to black.

The silence that followed the storm of magic was deafening.

Kaela's chest rose and fell in shallow gasps, her vision blurred and flickering. She could feel the Garden's pulse slowing, the magic now restored, the Heart's light soft and steady. But it was as if the very air around her had thickened, pressing down on her, making it hard to breathe. She collapsed to the ground, her limbs weak, her head spinning. The last remnants of the energy that had surged through her now felt like a distant echo, a fading tide she couldn't reach. The weight of what she had just done. What she had given, threatened to crush her.

"Kaela!" Ronan's voice pierced the haze in her mind, a lifeline in the dark. His strong arms were suddenly around her, pulling her up, steadying her. His warmth was the only thing she could focus on as he wrapped her in his embrace, his breath ragged, his hands shaking. She could feel the frantic beat of his heart, his desperation to keep her from slipping away. "Kaela, look at me. Stay with me. Please."

Her eyes met his, and in them, she saw the depth of his fear, his anguish. He had always been a man of control, of strength, but in that moment, she saw him for what he truly was. Vulnerable, torn apart by the thought of losing her. His fingers brushed her face, his touch gentle despite the urgency in his voice. "You did it. You saved the Garden. You—" His words faltered as his gaze dropped to her trembling hands, the faint glow of the magic still lingering around her fingertips. "But you've given so much. Too much."

Kaela's lips parted, but she couldn't find the strength to speak.

The weight of everything, the battle, the loss of her father, the magic that had drained her dry was too much to bear. She wanted to apologize, to tell him she was sorry for pulling him into this, for the pain she had caused, but all that came out was a broken whisper. "I—I don't know how much longer I can hold on."

Ronan's jaw tightened, and for a long moment, he said nothing. His gaze, fierce with worry and unspoken pain, locked onto hers. Without another word, he pulled her closer, pressing his forehead gently against hers. The intensity of his grip, the warmth of his body, and the depth of his emotions flowed between them in silence. "I'm not going to let you go," he whispered, his voice thick with raw emotion. "Not after everything. We've come this far. We've lost so much. But I'm here. I'm not going anywhere."

The air around them pulsed with the remnants of the Garden's magic, a soft, swirling energy that had become a familiar presence. It hummed through the room like a gentle breeze, its power healing, soothing, yet Kaela felt herself slipping. Her vision blurred, her strength fading, as the connection to the magic, to everything she had fought for, began to slip through her fingers. She closed her eyes, leaning into Ronan's warmth, finding solace in his touch, the only anchor that kept her from being swallowed by the darkness creeping in at the edges of her mind.

Ronan's hands were warm on her skin, trembling just slightly from his own exhaustion and injury, but he focused, pushing his own pain aside for her. His breath came in ragged gasps as he drew on the last of his strength, his power reaching into her, flowing like a fragile thread between them. He wasn't capable of fully healing her, not like he had in the past, not when his own body was so weakened, but he did what he could. A faint pulse of energy coursed through her, just enough to steady her, to keep her from fading into the abyss that threatened to take her.

Her chest still ached, her limbs heavy and weak, but the darkness receded, just enough for her to feel the world around her. She leaned into him, unable to speak, but the silent gratitude in her eyes was all he needed. Ronan's voice was barely a whisper as he held her close, his own breathing labored. "Stay with me, Kaela. Just a little longer." The words were desperate, a plea he couldn't hide, but in that moment, it was all he could give. He was here. He wouldn't let her go. Not now. Not ever.

Behind them, Kaela's eyes fluttered open at the faint sound of movement. She turned her head and saw Aelera, her father's old friend, carefully lifting his lifeless body from where he had fallen. Her chest tightened at the sight, a fresh wave of grief threatening to overwhelm her, but her focus shifted as her gaze landed on Milo. He was pale and weak, his movements sluggish as he struggled to stay upright, but his eyes met hers. In their depths, she saw an unspoken question and a flicker of concern, a silent connection that reminded her they were both still here, still fighting to hold on despite the weight of their losses.

"You're alive," Milo said, his voice hoarse, filled with awe and disbelief. He limped over to her, his movements stiff but determined. His gaze shifted between Kaela and Ronan, and though he said nothing, his eyes were full of gratitude and unspoken emotion. "We did it. The Garden's alive again." His voice cracked, the weight of the words settling in, but his eyes never left Kaela.

"I couldn't have done it without you," Kaela whispered, her voice barely audible. She reached out for Milo, her hand trembling as she touched his arm, feeling the strength of their bond, the years of friendship, and now, this shared journey. "You—Milo—you're still here. We're still here."

Milo gave her a weak smile, though it didn't reach his eyes. "You're stronger than you think," he said, though his words were full of a sadness that she couldn't quite place. "But we've all paid a price for this."

Kaela nodded, the weight of his words sinking into her chest. Saving the Garden had come at an unimaginable cost, her father's life, Ronan's sacrifices, and the toll on her own body and soul. Yet, despite the pain, they had triumphed. The Garden was alive again, a victory no one could ever take from them.

As Kaela looked at Ronan, Milo, and Aelera, Melana and the weight of what lay ahead settled over her like a heavy cloak. The battle for the Garden had been won, but it wasn't truly over. They had fought for survival, for hope, and for everything they had lost along the way, but the scars of their struggle ran deep. Now, they faced the daunting task of rebuilding, not just the Garden's magic, but the fragile pieces of their own hearts and lives. Healing would take time, and the road forward would be as challenging as the one behind them, but Kaela knew they would face it together.

Ronan's hand found hers, his grip firm, steady. "We're not done yet, Kaela. But we'll face whatever comes next together."

Kaela squeezed his hand, her heart swelling with something fierce and beautiful. "Together," she whispered, the word carrying more weight than it ever had before. She wasn't alone. She would never be alone again.

And as the room began to settle, the light of the Garden still glowing softly around them, Kaela knew that their journey was far from over. The road ahead would be long, but with Ronan, Milo, and Aelera by her side, she would face whatever challenges lay ahead. The Garden had been saved. Now, it was time to rebuild, to honor the sacrifices made, and to find the strength to continue, together.

The Garden's magic still hummed in the air, but Kaela felt the weight of exhaustion pulling at her, each breath more difficult than the last. She leaned heavily against Ronan, her body trembling from the aftershocks of the magic she had channeled. The pain in her chest, the emptiness left by her father's death, was overwhelming, but the presence of her friends, of the people who had fought by her side, was the only thing keeping her tethered to reality.

Milo, though pale and unsteady, moved to Kaela's side, his steps deliberate and weighted by grief. The lightness that usually defined him was absent, replaced by a somber determination. He looked at her, his voice quiet but resolute. "We did it, Kaela. The Garden's safe, but . . ." He paused, his throat tightening. "It's not just the Garden that needs rebuilding."

Kaela swallowed hard, her gaze dropping to the ground before shifting to Ronan. His face was pale, his posture rigid with the strain of everything they had endured, yet his eyes burned with a quiet resolve. The cost of their victory pressed heavily on her. The loss of her father, the scars etched into each of them, but in Ronan's presence, she felt a fragile thread of strength. "I couldn't have done this without you," she murmured, her voice raw. "You kept me from falling apart when it felt like the whole world was breaking."

Ronan stepped closer, his hand brushing against her cheek, the warmth of his touch steadying her. "Kaela," he said, his voice firm yet gentle, "you were always strong enough. I didn't carry you, I just stood beside you. And I'll keep standing beside you, as long as it takes." He glanced toward Milo and Aelera, who lingered nearby, their silence heavy with shared understanding. "We'll rebuild," he continued. "We'll honor the ones we've lost, and we'll fight for the ones still with us. Together."

Milo nodded, his jaw set as he spoke. "The fight's not over. The

Technomancers are still out there, and they'll come for us again. But this time, we're ready. We have each other, and we're stronger than they'll ever be."

Kaela felt a deep ache in her chest, a bittersweet mixture of loss and hope. They had won a battle, but the road ahead was still uncertain, filled with challenges and wounds that would take time to heal. Yet for the first time in what felt like forever, she didn't feel alone. She had Ronan, who had become her anchor in the storm. She had Milo, her steadfast friend, and Aelera, a guide who believed in their mission as deeply as they did.

"I don't know what's waiting for us," Kaela said, her voice thick with emotion. "But we'll face it together. For my father. For everyone we've lost. And for the future, we're fighting to build."

Ronan's hand slipped into hers, his grip firm, a quiet promise in his touch. "We're not just surviving anymore," he said softly. "We're fighting for something better. And we won't stop until we've won."

As the words settled into the space between them, the tension that had been building for hours began to ease. The room was quiet now, save for the faint hum of the Garden's magic, which still flowed gently through the air, its energy stabilizing with each passing moment. It was as if the Garden itself was breathing a sigh of relief, finally free from the corruption that had threatened to destroy it.

Kaela felt her strength returning, slowly but surely. The pain of losing her father, of everything they had sacrificed, was still there, lingering like a shadow in her heart. But she had a purpose now, a new determination that burned brighter than the grief. She couldn't bring her father back, but she could honor his legacy. She could rebuild what had been broken.

With Ronan's arm around her waist, she turned toward the door, where Aelera was waiting, her expression unreadable. "We need to make sure the Garden stays protected," Aelera said, her voice steady and calm. "The Technomancers will regroup. They won't stop until they've destroyed what we've fought so hard to protect."

"We'll stop them," Kaela said, her voice stronger now, the rawness of grief tempered by the fire of determination. "We'll stop them together."

As they stepped out of the chamber and into the quiet, uncertain world beyond, Kaela felt a shift deep within her. The battle was over, but the war loomed ahead, a shadow that would not be ignored. The Garden had been saved, but its survival was only the beginning. They would face the Technomancers again, they would confront every threat the future held, and they would do so together. The weight of what they had lost pressed heavily on her heart, but it was tempered by the resolve to honor those sacrifices by protecting the Garden and building something stronger.

With Ronan, Milo, Aelera and Melana at her side, Kaela felt a flicker of hope, fragile but growing. They had been tested, broken, and scarred, yet they had endured. Whatever challenges awaited, they would meet them head-on, bound by their shared losses and unshakable determination. For the first time in what felt like forever, Kaela believed in their strength. Together, they were no longer just survivors. They were a force, ready to reshape their world.

Chapter 42

The Garden began to breathe again. It's magic, once a mere whisper trapped beneath the Technomancers' domes, now pulsed like a heartbeat, steady and growing stronger with each passing moment. Light cascaded from the Heart, bathing the room in hues of gold and emerald, its energy radiating outward. Beyond the chamber, the devastation of battle lingered, but the Garden's energy crept through the cracks, bringing life where there had been ruin. The air smelled fresher, tinged with the scent of blooming flowers and damp earth, though the faint tang of smoke and ash reminded them of the cost of their victory.

Kaela stood at the edge of the Heart's platform, her gaze fixed on the faint light stretching toward the horizon. The domes, once opaque and unyielding, had begun to crack and crumble, their oppressive presence lifting like a storm finally breaking. She could see glimpses of the world beyond. The sky was a pale blue streaked with the fiery orange of dawn. But the world outside wasn't as it had been before. Fields lay scorched, buildings reduced to rubble, and humanity was no longer shielded from the raw, untamed power of the Garden. It was beautiful and terrifying all at once.

Kaela's legs trembled beneath her, exhaustion wrapping around her like a heavy cloak after the storm of magic she had unleashed. Every muscle ached, her breaths shallow as the adrenaline began to fade, leaving her drained. Ronan's hand lingered at her back, a steady anchor amidst the swirling fatigue, though his own weariness was impossible to miss. The tightness of his jaw and the faint pallor of his usually vibrant skin betrayed the toll the battle had taken on him. Yet, even in his fatigue, his golden-green eyes softened as they met hers, a quiet strength and unwavering resolve radiating from his presence.

"We've torn the chains away," he murmured, his voice low. "But the world isn't ready for this. Not yet."

Kaela nodded, her fingers brushing the edge of the Heart's dais. The warmth of its magic buzzed beneath her fingertips, alive and eager, as if urging her to keep moving forward. "It'll take time," she said softly. "Time to rebuild. Time to heal. But the Garden's free now. That's all that matters."

Kaela's legs buckled beneath her, the weight of the battle crashing down like a tidal wave as the adrenaline drained from her veins. Her breath came in ragged gasps, the searing ache of magic still flickering in her fingertips, a painful reminder of the power she had unleashed. Ronan's hand remained firm at her back, his touch grounding her even as his own body trembled with fatigue, sweat glistening on his brow. His golden-green eyes met hers, weary but unyielding, and in their depths was a flicker of pride, a silent acknowledgment of the hell they had survived together. The scent of smoke and scorched earth lingered in the air, a bitter reminder of the chaos that had raged only hours before, but in that moment, their shared silence felt like the first fragile step toward hope.

Milo stepped forward, his movements slow but deliberate. He gave Kaela a lopsided smile, though his voice was tinged with fatigue. "The Garden's already spreading. The fields outside are starting to grow again. It's . . . amazing." He hesitated, his gaze flickering to the Heart, then back to Kaela. "You did it."

"We all did," Kaela replied, her voice firm despite the ache in her chest. She reached out, resting a hand on Milo's arm. "None of this would've been possible without you, Milo. You brought us here. You never gave up."

Milo ducked his head, a faint flush creeping into his cheeks. "Yeah, well, you've got a knack for inspiring reckless loyalty," he joked, though his voice softened as he added, "I'm just glad we're still standing."

The journey back to Kaela's home village was slow and somber, the weight of what they had endured pressing down on the group like an unseen burden. The landscape stretched before them, scarred and battered from the aftermath of the battle. Where Dome 5 once loomed as a symbol of oppression, only fragments of its metallic shell remained, scattered across the plains like the broken exoskeleton of a long-dead creature. Twisted beams jutted skyward, half-buried in the scorched earth, while patches of wildflowers had already begun to reclaim the soil, their stubborn blooms a defiant sign of renewal.

As they walked, the group fell into a reflective silence, each step stirring the dust and ash that had settled over the ground. Milo glanced toward the horizon, where smoke from distant fires still lingered in the air, its acrid scent mingling with the faint sweetness of rain-soaked grass. "It's strange," he murmured, his voice barely audible over the rustling wind. "It feels like the world is holding its breath, waiting to see what happens next."

Melana nodded, her amber eyes scanning the remnants of makeshift barricades and shattered weapons littering the path. "The battle may be over," she said quietly, "but the fight to rebuild is only beginning." Her tone carried a gravity that Kaela knew all too well.

The closer they drew to the village, the more evident the aftermath of the war became. Houses bore scorch marks and jagged holes where stray blasts had struck. Families worked tirelessly to clear debris, their faces a mixture of exhaustion and quiet resolve. Children played nearby, their laughter tinged with a resilience that belied their youth, as though even they understood the importance of finding joy amid the ruins.

When the group finally reached Kaela's cottage, the familiar sight of its ivy-covered walls brought a flicker of relief to her chest, a fragile anchor in a world that had been upended. The once-vivid flowers in the small front garden lay crushed and broken, their vibrant petals scattered across the soil like forgotten remnants of peace. The wooden gate hung slightly ajar, its hinges creaking faintly in the breeze, as though mourning the intrusion of chaos. Yet, despite the signs of upheaval, the cottage itself stood resolute, a quiet testament to resilience, and Kaela felt a glimmer of hope stir within her.

The sound of shuffling footsteps drew their attention to the doorway, where Eila emerged, leaning heavily on a carved wooden staff that dwarfed her slight, frail frame. The staff, intricately adorned with swirling patterns, looked almost ceremonial, a stark contrast to the weary woman who clutched it for support. Her face was pale, her olive-toned skin drawn thin over her cheekbones, and the deepened lines of her features bore the weight of weeks spent fighting her illness. Yet, her eyes, sharp and unwavering, cut through the space like twin beacons, brimming with both worry and unyielding determination. She paused in the threshold, her gaze sweeping over Kaela, Milo, Ronan, and Melana, lingering on their battle-worn faces, the faint scars and bruises a testament to the trials they had endured. Her lips parted slightly as if to speak, but for a moment, she simply stood there, her expression a mix of relief and concern, silently absorbing the toll the war had taken on them.

"You've come back to me," she said softly, her voice a blend of relief and reprimand, as though she couldn't decide whether to scold them for their recklessness or simply hold them close.

"Aunt Eila," Kaela breathed, rushing to her side.

Eila raised a hand to stop her. "I'm fine," she said, though her voice wavered. Her gaze swept over Kaela, taking in the exhaustion etched into her niece's face. "But you . . . you look like you've been through the depths of the storm and back."

Kaela swallowed hard, her throat tightening as she met her aunt's eyes. "It's over," she said, her voice barely above a whisper. "The Garden's free. But . . . we lost so much."

Eila reached out, her frail hand brushing Kaela's cheek. "You've done more than I ever could have imagined, child," she said, her voice trembling with emotion. "Your father would be so proud of you. I am so proud of you."

Tears welled in Kaela's eyes, and she leaned into her aunt's touch, the weight of everything she had carried finally beginning to ease. "I just hope it's enough," she murmured.

"It's more than enough," Eila said firmly. "The world will rebuild, just as the Garden will. And you'll lead them, Kaela. I know you will."

As Kaela embraced her aunt, Milo stepped away, his shoulders tense and his gaze distant as he looked out toward the horizon, where the sun dipped low, casting fiery streaks across the sky. His thoughts seemed miles away, tangled in the weight of everything they had lost and the uncertainty of what lay ahead. He didn't notice Melana watching him, her amber eyes studying his profile with a quiet understanding. She stepped closer, her movements deliberate yet unhurried, the soft crunch of her boots against the dirt drawing his attention at last.

"You've been quiet," she said, her voice low.

Milo glanced at her, a faint smile tugging at his lips. "Just thinking. There's so much to do. So much we've lost."

"And so much we've gained," Melana countered, her amber eyes searching his. "You've done something incredible, Milo. You should let yourself feel that."

He let out a soft laugh, rubbing the back of his neck. "Guess I'm not great at stopping to appreciate the moment."

Melana stepped closer, her hand brushing his. "Then let me help you."

The touch was light, but it sent a jolt through Milo, his heart skipping a beat as if he'd been struck by a bolt of electricity. He looked at her, really looked at her for the first time, noticing the quiet strength in her posture and the warmth in her amber eyes. There was no hesitation now, only a deep understanding between them, something unspoken but undeniable. He reached for her hand, his fingers brushing hers before intertwining, as if they had always been meant to be connected.

"Thanks, Melana," he said softly.

"For what?" she asked.

"For being here," he replied. "For staying."

Melana smiled, a quiet, tender curve of her lips that seemed to speak volumes without a single word. In that moment, the weight of the battle, the loss, the struggle, the chaos, seemed to melt away, leaving only the warmth of their shared connection. It was a fleeting but profound moment of peace, a breath between storms. Milo felt it too, the unspoken bond between them solidifying in the silence they shared.

The group left Kaela's cottage at dawn, their footsteps light but determined as they made their way to the Garden. The air was crisp, carrying with it the faint hum of magic that had grown stronger since the battle. The path, though familiar, seemed transformed. Verdant vines crept along the ground, and flowers bloomed where once there was only barren earth. It was as if the Garden itself was guiding them, pulling them closer to its heart.

The Garden's light pulsed around them, a promise of renewal and hope. And as Kaela, Ronan, Milo, and Melana stood together, they knew their journey was far from over. But they also knew they would face it together, their bonds unbreakable, their purpose clear. The world was broken, but the Garden was alive, and with it, the promise of a brighter future.

The sun hung low in the sky, casting long shadows over the landscape as the group made their way to the outer edge of the Garden. Here, the damage from the Technomancers' rule was starkest. Fields scorched to ash, rivers diverted or dried, and villages once bustling with life now eerily quiet. Yet even amid the desolation, there were signs of hope. The Garden's energy had already begun to work its way outward, coaxing stubborn green shoots from the cracked soil and filling the air with the faint scent of blooming wildflowers.

Kaela walked beside Milo, their footsteps crunching over the remnants of what had once been a cobblestone path, now cracked and worn from the aftermath of the battle. The air was heavy with the scent of damp earth and the lingering echoes of destruction, but there was a strange stillness that hung over the land, as if the world itself was waiting. Ahead of them, Melana and Ronan led the way, their voices low as they discussed plans for securing the Garden's borders, their words filled with quiet determination. Kaela's thoughts were distant, her mind spinning with the enormity of the task ahead, the weight of responsibility pressing down on her shoulders as she tried to make sense of the uncertain future that awaited them.

"Hey," Milo said softly, nudging her with his elbow. "You're awfully quiet."

Kaela glanced at him, a faint smile tugging at her lips. "Just thinking. About everything we've lost . . . and everything we still have to do."

Milo nodded, his expression serious. "It's overwhelming, isn't it? But we're not alone in this. And we don't have to do it all at once."

Before Kaela could respond, the sound of voices carried on the breeze, faint at first but steadily growing louder. She stopped, her heart quickening as she recognized the unmistakable sound of laughter and conversation, the familiar cadence of voices she hadn't heard in far too long. It was a sound she hadn't realized she'd been missing until that moment, a reminder of life beyond the chaos. Her gaze shifted toward the source, her pulse quickening with a mix of relief and anticipation.

The group crested a small hill, and Kaela's breath caught. Below them, a crowd of villagers had gathered, their faces a mix of curiosity and determination. They were the same people Kaela and her companions had allied with weeks ago, during their first desperate attempts to undermine the Technomancers' hold on the region. Farmers, traders, blacksmiths, and weavers, all of them stood together, their makeshift tools and weapons glinting in the fading sunlight.

At the front of the crowd stood a tall man with Brown hair and a weathered face. His name was Theo, a leader among the resistance, one of the many who had fought to liberate their people from the Technomancers' grasp. He raised a hand in greeting, his voice strong as he called out, "Kaela! Milo! Ronan! Melana! It's good to see you all alive." Relief and recognition flashed across his face, the weight of their shared struggles evident in his gaze.

The group descended the hill, Kaela's heart swelling with gratitude and relief as the familiar sight of the village below came into view. The sounds of life, laughter, chatter, and the rhythmic thump of hammers filled the air, a stark contrast to the silence that had followed the battle. As they reached the crowd, Theo stepped forward, his gaze sweeping over each of them in turn, a mixture of respect and recognition in his eyes. The tension in the air seemed to lift as he met Kaela's gaze, offering a silent but profound acknowledgment of all they had endured.

"We heard the domes had fallen," he said. "And we saw the signs of the Garden's magic spreading across the land. We knew it had to be your doing."

"It wasn't just us," Kaela replied, her voice steady. "It was all of us. Your resistance, your strength. It gave us the chance to fight back."

Theo's expression softened, and he placed a hand on Kaela's shoulder. "You gave us hope when we had none. Now it's our turn to help. Whatever you need, we're here to rebuild."

Kaela looked around at the faces of the villagers, her chest tightening with emotion. These were people who had lost so much.

Families, homes, livelihoods, yet they stood ready to face an uncertain future with courage and unity. The weight of responsibility pressed against her, but she knew she wasn't carrying it alone. They had each other, and that was enough to begin again.

"We can't do this without you," Kaela said, her voice firm. "The Garden is alive, but it needs time to grow, to heal. And the world outside the domes . . ." She trailed off, her gaze flicking to the horizon. "It's going to take all of us to make it whole again."

Theo nodded. "Then let's get to work."

The villagers began to disperse, their voices rising in animated conversation as they discussed plans for rebuilding. Some spoke of replanting crops, others of repairing the shattered remains of their homes, while a few shared stories of lost loved ones and the toll the war had taken. Despite the pain, there was a tangible sense of resilience in the air, a shared understanding that life, in whatever form it might take, would continue. Kaela watched them, her heart swelling with admiration, a sense of purpose settling over her like a warm cloak.

As the crowd thinned, Milo lingered at the edge of the group, his eyes scanning the faces of the villagers with a quiet intensity. The warmth of the scene around him seemed to fade as his gaze fixed on two figures standing near the fire, their postures stiff but their eyes unmistakably familiar. His breath caught in his throat as he recognized them. His parents. The last time he had seen them, they had been swept up in the chaos of the war, leaving him with only fleeting memories and unanswered questions.

"Milo!" his mother called, her voice trembling with emotion.

Milo turned, his heart pounding as his parents hurried toward him, their faces etched with relief and exhaustion. Before he could speak, his mother's arms enveloped him, holding him close as if she feared he might vanish. His father's hand clapped firmly on his shoulder, the touch strong and reassuring, grounding him in the moment. Words failed them, but the bond between them was clear, a silent promise that no matter what had happened, they were together again.

As the villagers worked together, the sun dipped lower, casting the world in shades of gold and crimson, painting the scene with a quiet beauty. Melana approached Milo, her steps slow and deliberate, her expression softening as she took in the sight of him standing with his parents. She could see the rawness of his emotions, the tenderness in his gaze as he stood surrounded by those he loved. Without a word, she stood beside him, her presence a silent support, offering him a space to process the moment without the weight of expectation.

The world was still in the aftermath of war, but there was a sense of unity in the air, a shared purpose that drove them all forward. Fires crackled in the distance, casting flickering shadows that danced across makeshift workstations, where tools were sharpened, maps were redrawn, and strategies debated. The remnants of the Technomancers' destruction were still visible in the broken structures and scorched earth, yet there was an undeniable sense of hope in the air. It was as though, even after everything they had lost, something new was being born in the ruins.

Kaela stood on the ridge, the fading firelight casting a warm glow on her copper hair, which seemed to catch the light and shimmer like molten metal. Her gaze swept over the scene below, where villagers and resistance members worked side by side, their faces etched with exhaustion but also an unshakable resolve. The soft crunch of footsteps behind her drew her attention, and Kaela turned to find Ronan approaching. His golden-green eyes caught the light of the nearby flames, their intensity revealing a quiet strength beneath his usual playful demeanor.

"Taking it all in?" he asked, stopping beside her.

Kaela nodded. "It's hard to believe we're standing here. After everything . . ." Her voice trailed off, heavy with the weight of the past months.

Ronan tilted his head, studying her. "You should be proud. None of this would have been possible without you."

Kaela shook her head. "It wasn't just me. It was all of us. You, Milo, Melana, the villagers . . . even the Garden itself." She looked up at him, her eyes searching his. "Do you think we can really do this? Rebuild the world?"

A faint smile curved Ronan's lips. "If there's one thing I've learned, it's that people are resilient. And with the Garden's power behind us, we have a fighting chance."

Kaela let out a breath she hadn't realized she was holding. "A fighting chance," she echoed, the words both daunting and comforting. As the last light of day slipped away, the stars emerged, scattering the heavens with their faint glow. The night settled over the Garden, wrapping everything in a quiet blanket of calm. And for the first time in a long while, Kaela allowed herself to believe in the future.

Chapter 43

Near the heart of the camp, Milo worked alongside a group of villagers to construct a new irrigation system, his hands steady as he dug into the earth. The rhythmic sound of shovels striking dirt and the low murmur of conversation around him offered a sense of normalcy he hadn't realized he needed. Sweat beaded on his brow, and he wiped it away with the back of his hand, the physical labor a welcome distraction from the emotional turmoil that still lingered in his chest. With each shovel of dirt he moved, Milo felt a quiet satisfaction, knowing that, step by step, they were rebuilding not just the land, but their lives.

"Careful with that beam!" he called, gesturing to a young man struggling to steady a heavy wooden plank.

The villagers responded quickly, their movements fluid and purposeful as they worked together in synchronized effort. Some carried heavy stones, their muscles straining with the weight, while others bent low to measure and cut timber, their tools clicking with practiced precision. The air was filled with the scent of fresh earth and the rhythmic sounds of hammers and axes, punctuated by the occasional command or word of encouragement. Milo stepped back, his gaze following the steady progress as the structure began to take shape, its frame rising from the ground like a promise of stability. The team's energy was infectious, and he couldn't help but feel a sense of awe at the speed and determination with which they were transforming the landscape.

"You've got quite the knack for this," Melana's voice came from behind him.

Milo turned, his lips twitching into a smile. "Engineering runs in the family," he said, brushing dirt from his hands.

Melana crossed her arms, a teasing glint in her amber eyes. "I thought you were more into inventing gadgets than rebuilding villages."

"I'm versatile," he replied with a shrug, his tone playful.

She laughed softly, the sound low and warm, a sound that seemed to carry with it the weight of everything they had endured. It was a sound of relief, of a momentary break from the chaos that had dominated their lives for so long. For a moment, they stood together in comfortable silence, the bustling noise of the camp. Voices shouting, tools clanging, and fires crackling, fading into the background as they simply existed in each other's presence. The air between them was calm, filled with an unspoken understanding, a shared sense of peace that felt rare in the aftermath of everything they had faced.

"You've done good work here, Milo," Melana said, her voice softening. "These people look up to you. They trust you."

He glanced at her, his expression unreadable. "I didn't do it for that. I just . . . I couldn't stand by and do nothing."

"I know," she said, stepping closer. "That's what makes you different. You care, even when it's hard. Even when it hurts."

Milo met her gaze, and in that fleeting moment, something unspoken passed between them, a quiet understanding that neither of them could fully name. Slowly, almost hesitantly, he reached for her hand, his fingers trembling slightly with the weight of the gesture. When she didn't pull away, a small spark of relief flickered within him, and he laced his fingers through hers, his grip firm and steady. The warmth of her touch grounded him, and for the first time in what felt like forever, he felt a sense of peace.

"Melana," he began, his voice barely above a whisper. "I—"

Before Milo could finish his sentence, a villager's voice called his name from across the camp, breaking the moment. He hesitated, a sense of frustration rising in his chest as he turned toward the voice. Sighing, he let his shoulders slump slightly, the weight of the responsibility pressing on him once again. The fleeting sense of peace he had felt with Melana was quickly overshadowed by the demands of rebuilding and the chaos that still loomed over them.

"Duty calls," he said with a faint smile.

Melana squeezed his hand before letting go. "We'll finish this conversation later," she promised, her eyes lingering on his.

As Melana walked away, Milo stood there for a moment, watching her blend into the crowd. The sound of hammers and voices filled the air, but there was a strange calm in him, like a quiet center amidst the storm. He felt the weight of everything. Rebuilding, the battles, the loss, but it didn't seem as overwhelming now. For the first time in a long while, he realized that, despite the chaos surrounding them, he was exactly where he was meant to be.

By the time the moon hung high in the sky, casting a pale glow over the camp, the air had cooled, and the camp's earlier buzz of activity had settled into a soft murmur. Fires flickered low, their orange glow casting long shadows across the faces of those still awake. Most of the villagers had retired to their makeshift tents or gathered shelters, their exhausted bodies seeking rest after the day's work. The quiet felt like a fragile breath between battles, the weight of the past weeks pressing down on them all. Kaela, Ronan, Milo, and Melana had gathered around a small fire near the Garden's edge, the warmth of the flames the only comfort in the still night.

Kaela broke the silence, her voice quiet but firm. "We've made it this far," she said, her eyes scanning the faces of her companions. "But this is just the beginning." The flickering flames reflected in her eyes, showing the strength and determination that had carried them through the darkest moments.

Milo shifted, his expression resolute as he leaned forward, his voice steady despite the weariness that tugged at him. "We know," he said, meeting her gaze. "And we're ready." His words were simple, but there was a depth to them, a promise that the journey ahead would not be faced alone.

Ronan, who had been watching the fire with a contemplative look, finally spoke. His usual smirk was gone, replaced by something more earnest. "The world's been broken before," he said, his voice low but confident. "It can be rebuilt. And this time, we'll make it stronger." He paused, looking each of them in the eye. "We're not just rebuilding structures. We're rebuilding hope."

Melana, her face illuminated by the firelight, nodded thoughtfully. Her eyes remained fixed on the flames, as though drawing strength from them. "We have the Garden. We have the people. Now, we just need to hold on to what we've built," she said, her voice steady and grounded.

Kaela glanced at each of them, her chest swelling with gratitude and a deep, unwavering resolve. The fire crackled between them, its warmth a reminder of the bond they shared, of the battles they had fought and the victories they had claimed. Whatever lay ahead, whatever new challenges the world might throw at them, they would face it together, as they always had. For the first time in a long while, Kaela allowed herself to believe in their success, to trust that they could build something lasting, something better.

The Garden hummed with quiet energy, its rejuvenation spreading out like ripples in a pond. Beneath its canopy, the air felt alive, buzzing with an almost imperceptible vibrancy. New shoots pushed through the soil, reclaiming land that had once been scorched and barren. Streams that had run dry now bubbled with crystal-clear water, their courses winding outward to nourish the land.

Kaela stood at the heart of the Garden, her fingers lightly tracing the rough, weathered bark of the ancient tree. The wood felt alive beneath her hand, warm and strong, as though it held the very pulse of the earth within it. With each breath she took, she could feel a rhythmic thrum deep within the tree's core, a steady beat that seemed to resonate through her bones, as though the Garden itself was alive, breathing in time with her. The air around her was thick with the scent of earth and wildflowers, the soft rustle of leaves above adding to the sensation of quiet reverence that enveloped her. In that moment, it was as though the Garden was reaching out to her, its gratitude and strength flowing into her through the connection of her touch. It's ancient energy whispering in a language beyond words, a language only her soul could comprehend.

Behind her, the others waited in a loose circle, their presence a steady reminder of the unity they had forged. Milo leaned against a low boulder, his hands tucked into his pockets, his eyes scanning the surroundings with a focused intensity as he observed the Garden's restoration. Melana stood beside him, arms crossed over her chest, her lips curling into a faint, approving smile as she watched a group of children eagerly planting saplings in the freshly turned soil. Ronan lingered in the shadows of the towering foliage, his golden-green eyes fixed on Kaela with an unwavering intensity, his gaze carrying a weight that made her heart skip a beat.

Kaela turned to face them, drawing in a deep breath. "It's happening faster than I thought," she said, her voice carrying over the gentle rustle of leaves. "The Garden is healing."

"It's more than that," Ronan said, stepping forward. His golden-green eyes glinted in the dappled light. "It's spreading. Look at the horizon."

Kaela followed his gaze, her eyes narrowing as she focused on the horizon where the Garden's vibrant greenery met the wider world. In the distance, the sky shimmered with a soft, ethereal glow, as if the very air itself was charged with the Garden's magic. It was a subtle, almost imperceptible ripple, but to Kaela, it was unmistakable. Like a pulse of life spreading outward, reaching beyond the Garden's borders. The land seemed to respond, as though the Garden was slowly, deliberately reclaiming what had been lost, one inch at a time.

Milo pushed off the boulder, his expression a mix of awe and apprehension. "That's incredible, but it also means people will notice. The Technomancers may be gone, but their followers aren't. Not all of them, anyway."

Melana nodded, her voice calm but firm. "He's right. There will be those who see this as a threat. And others who will try to exploit it."

Kaela looked at them, her heart heavy with the weight of their words, a deep sense of responsibility settling over her. She knew they were right. Every step forward was a step into uncharted territory, fraught with danger. The Garden's resurgence was a beacon, a symbol of hope for some, but to others, it was a target, a source of power to be exploited. She felt the weight of the future pressing down on her, knowing that the path ahead would be anything but easy.

"We'll protect it," she said, her voice steady despite the knot in her chest. "Whatever it takes, we'll keep it safe."

Ronan stepped closer, his presence a steadying force. "You don't have to do it alone, Kaela. None of us do."

Kaela met his gaze, her heart softening at the unspoken bond they shared. The weight of their journey, the battles they had fought, and the sacrifices they had made all seemed to hang in the air between them. She glanced at Milo and Melana, their expressions steady and unwavering, a silent promise that no matter the trials ahead, they would face them together. They had come so far, and the strength of their unity was all that kept them moving forward.

As the sun began to rise, casting a golden light over the landscape, the world seemed to breathe with them, the first light of dawn breaking over the horizon in a burst of pink and orange. The villagers and resistance members gathered near the Garden's edge, their faces filled with a quiet determination as they prepared for the next steps in rebuilding. Among them, Eila stood, her frailty a sharp contrast to the fire burning in her eyes, a woman who had seen so much but remained resolute in the face of it all. She raised a hand, her gaze locking with Kaela's, a silent invitation to come closer, and Kaela felt a lump form in her throat as she stepped toward the woman who had been her anchor, her guide through the storm of uncertainty.

"You've done something extraordinary," Eila said, her voice trembling but strong. "Your father would be proud."

Kaela swallowed hard, emotion welling up in her chest. "I couldn't have done it without all of you."

Eila reached out, taking Kaela's hand in hers. "You have a gift, Kaela. The Garden chose you for a reason. But it's not just about protecting it, it's about what you'll build with it."

Kaela nodded, her aunt's words sinking in with a quiet weight, grounding her in the reality of the task ahead. The connection she felt with the Garden, with everything they had fought for, deepened with every passing moment, and her aunt's wisdom echoed in her mind. As she turned back to the group, her gaze found Milo, standing just a few paces away. He was close to Melana now, their bodies aligned as they spoke softly, the comfort of their proximity clear in the way their shoulders brushed together. Melana's hand rested gently on Milo's arm, a simple yet undeniable gesture of affection, one that spoke volumes in the silence between them. Kaela's chest swelled with a quiet sense of gratitude, her heart warmed by the sight of them, knowing that despite the chaos and uncertainty that had defined their lives, they had found something real, something good, in each other.

Ronan appeared at her side, his voice low. "You're thinking about what comes next."

Kaela glanced at him, a faint smile tugging at her lips. "Aren't you?"

"Always," he replied, his tone light but his eyes serious.

She looked out over the Garden, its magic pulsing in rhythm with her heartbeat. "This is just the beginning, isn't it?"

Ronan nodded. "The world's changed. And it'll keep changing. But that's the beauty of it, Kaela. We're not just rebuilding what was. We're creating something new."

As the first rays of sunlight bathed the Garden, casting a golden glow over the rejuvenated landscape, Kaela stood at its heart, a quiet thrill stirring within her. The air was crisp, the soft rustle of leaves and the distant hum of life filling the space around her. For the first time in what felt like an eternity, the weight of their struggle seemed to lift, replaced by the glimmer of something brighter. The journey ahead would be long, uncertain, and fraught with danger, but it was theirs to take. There was no more running, no more hiding. They had found their place in this new world, and together, they would forge a path forward.

Behind her, the sounds of the camp coming to life echoed softly in the background. Milo, Melana, and Ronan moved among the villagers, offering their help, their guidance. The Garden's magic hummed, a quiet reminder of how far they had come and how much further they still had to go. The people who had once been broken now stood tall, their eyes filled with determination and hope. But Kaela knew the road would not be easy. There were still threats on the horizon, forces that would seek to undo everything they had worked for. But in that moment, standing alongside the people she had come to call family, Kaela felt something she hadn't in years: a sense of belonging. They were ready.

And yet, as the sun rose higher, painting the sky in shades of pink and lavender, a strange stirring tugged at her chest. Something beyond the Garden, beyond the rebuilding, called to her. A whisper in the wind, a flicker of magic just out of reach. The world was vast, full of untold stories and mysteries yet to be uncovered. She could feel the pull of it, the promise of new adventures just beyond the horizon. Whatever lay ahead, Kaela knew she wasn't alone. She had her friends, her family, and a world of possibilities waiting for them.

Together, they had faced the impossible, and together, they would face whatever came next. The future was unknown, yes, but it was full of promise, and for the first time in a long while, Kaela wasn't afraid, she was ready. The Garden was reborn, and so, too, was she.

www.ingramcontent.com/pod-product-compliance
Lightning Source LLC
Chambersburg PA
CBHW070538030726
47505CB00001B/80